Holloway House Originals
By Iceberg Slim (Robert Beck)

THE NAKED SOUL OF ICEBERG SLIM

MAMA BLACK WIDOW

TRICK BABY

PIMP: THE STORY OF MY LIFE

DEATH WISH

AIRTIGHT WILLIE & ME

LONG WHITE CON

The con game from A to Z as it
was lived by White Folks—
a white Negro—in the deadly
jungle of southside Chicago—
all the thrills, the danger,
the triumphs (and failures)
of men who made their livings in
one of the most treacherous
professions—and the mistake
that sent them running
for their lives . . .

TRICK BABY

ICEBERG SLIM

HOLLOWAY HOUSE PUBLISHING CO.
LOS ANGELES, CALIFORNIA

TRICK BABY

An Original Holloway House Edition

This edition reprinted 2004

Printed in the United States of America.
Published by Holloway House Publishing Company,
8060 Melrose Avenue,
Los Angeles, California.

0-87067-933-3

www.hollowayhousebooks.com
or
www.hhbookstore.com

PREFACE

In the middle of October in Nineteen Sixty, I was nervously pacing cell A-4 in Chicago's House of Correction. I was having a bitch of a quarrel with a stupid jerk inside me.

Over and over I hollered at him, "You're Iceberg Slim, the pimp. You can't cash out like a square."

I was trying to convince the screwy bastard that he shouldn't go crazy and hang himself from the steel-barred cell door.

I had been arrested on an old fugitive warrant for a spectacular escape, thirteen years before from the joint.

I heard a screw's key grate in my cell door lock. I spun around. The screw pushed a tall white con into the cell.

He could have been Errol Flynn's twin. I wondered why the hell I was getting a cellmate. Were they planting a fink to bleed my secret of how I had made the escape long ago?

He didn't speak. He nodded. I nodded back. He stood for a moment sweeping his sky-blue eyes over the crummy cell. He sighed and jumped to the top bunk.

I went to the crapper and sat on the stool waiting for him to rap something to tip me that he was a fink.

He was stretched out on his bunk staring through the cell door bars at the blank cellhouse wall. I stared at him. But I just couldn't place him.

I said, "I'm Iceberg. You look slightly familiar. It worries me, because the only white studs I know are rollers and bastard undercover rats. Who are you, buddy?"

He turned quickly on his side and looked down at me with a hurt look on his handsome face.

He laughed like a nut and said, "Relax, Iceberg. I'm not white. I'm a Nigger hustler. My friends call me White Folks. My enemies call me Trick Baby. Blue Howard and I were pals, and played con together for twenty years. Can you place me now?"

I said, "I goddamn sure do. You and Blue got on the syndicate wipe-out list a while ago. The wire had it that you got knocked off with him. What the hell are you doing back in Chicago?"

He said, "It's a long story. I don't want to talk about it. Christ, if I had known the bastards would shove me in this pigsty, I wouldn't have refused to sling a mop for my lousy ten-day bit. In here, it will be like a ten-year bit."

I lay there that night on the bottom bunk remembering what I'd heard about him in the street. He was one of the slickest con men in Chicago.

One thing puzzled me. How did a fast grifter like him wind up serving a chump's ten-day bit? One thing for sure, he knew the con game backward.

So, since I was getting rather elderly for the pimp game, I figured I'd pick his brain and play con when I got out. After all, I'd picked Sweet Jones for the secrets of the pimp game.

That first night, White Folks gave me a bitch of a time. He kept waking up and hollering from nightmares all night long. I didn't sleep two hours. I had a screw that I was tight with. I scored for sleeping pills from him. I laid them on Folks. He was so happy, you'd have thought I gave him a million dollars.

Within a couple of days, White Folks and I were like brothers. A prison cell has the strange power to quickly create friendships and trusts that would never happen in the free world. I guess it's the loneliness and misery that draws two cellmates close enough to confide their secrets. And plus, in Folks's case, the sleeping pills.

Five days before his release, after the lights had gone out, White Folks started to tell me his life story. He started at the point when he and his pal, Blue Howard, got their toughest break.

I lay there in the gloom forgetting my own troubles in the fascination of his story.

CHAPTER ONE

A Shakedown Squeeze by Dot the Cop

Blue Leon Howard and I sat in the front booth of the Brass Rail Bar on Forty-seventh Street, Southside Chicago. I felt that thrilling complacency that a con man has after a clean fat score. I couldn't know a messenger of death would join us within minutes.

The Westside mark had been sweet as honeysuckle. He had blown ten grand on our slick version of the rocks.

I looked out the panoramic front window as we waited for our steaks. I felt sorry for the passing parade of hunched chumps buffeted by the December barrage of freezing winds screaming off Lake Michigan.

A gaunt car prowler paused and peered into my sparkling new fifty-nine Fleetwood at the curb. A squad load of Eleventh Street detectives cruised through the twilight. The prowler faded into the parade. I thought about Aunt Lula's crazy cathouse in Indiana Harbor. I'd slip up there later tonight.

I figured it was cheaper and smarter to simply rent a dame's machinery for a few hours. My fountain of romantic love was dust dry. The Goddess had cured me permanently. Old Blue was of a different opinion. He had to have a marriage lock on his dame. I turned toward him. His ebony face was almost invisible in the dimness. His processed white hair gleamed like burnished silver.

I said, "Blue, that score this morning just put us under the wire. Christmas is only a week off. I bet you make Cleo the happiest fluff in town. I bet you go down to Rothschild's and plank down your five-G end on a sable coat for her."

"A guy has to keep his wife happy, you know. The

young fancy ones get itchy feet in a hurry."

His eyes flashed white lightning. His eyebrows zoomed up his brow like frosted boomerangs. Blue couldn't stand the needle into his love life. Believe me, if I had known this was to be our last time in the Rail together I wouldn't have ribbed him about the nineteen-year-old Cleo.

I had pricked him to the tender quick, because he blew air through the gap in his front uppers. His thick lips opened and closed over the dazzle of his chalky teeth like banging shutters in a windstorm.

In that whispery rich voice of his, he said, "White Folks, please don't worry about what happens to my end of that score. If I stepped out on that street and played chump Santa Claus to my last deemer, that would be Blue's happiness, not yours.

"And, White Folks, please, for Christ's sake, don't forget that twenty years ago I had my foot on the gaff in my flat joint when I turned you out on the grift as a belly-stick. You blow your end your way. I'll blow mine my way."

He was an old man really hooked by a pretty tramp. I had seen Cleo sneaking around with several young punks. She'd even wiggled her fabulous rear end in my direction. I couldn't tell Blue. I couldn't tear him to pieces.

The waitress with our steaks stamped out the blaze. I noticed when she leaned over to place our plates, her orange hair was loaded with glitter dust. I remembered Roxie at that cathouse in Indiana. I had found several of the glamour dots sparkling in my navel the morning after.

I had sliced off an aromatic piece of the filet with my fork. I started to chew the succulent hunk. I was enjoying the delicious juices flooding my taste buds when a fearful silence crushed down on the crowded room.

I swung my eyes to the bar. The hustlers were like mute crows still-lifed on a mahogany fence. Blue was staring toward the door. He was hissing air through that gap like a berserk steam boiler. Then I saw him! He was standing in the gloom near the door. Blue turned his head away and dug into his salad.

He just stood there like a polka-dotted mummy. Only his crafty, hazel eyes moved. It was Dot Murray, and those frigid eyes were locked on us.

I was mesmerized. Blue stomped on my instep. I came out of the trance and glued my eyes to my plate. The steak tasted like the charcoal that had cooked it. The savory well went dry.

Blue whispered, "Play the chill for him. Remember, son, he's not bunco, he's only robbery detail. Just play the chill for him."

My right leg twitched and bumped Blue's thigh. Blue groaned in disgust. I was thinking about how, years ago, Murray had clubbed the Memphis Kid into a slobbery vegetable with the butt of his thirty-eight special. The Kid's partner said Murray grinned like a hyena all the while.

The Kid and his partner, St. Louis Shorty, had made a smack score near the bus station at Sixty-third and Stony Island Avenue. They were blowing off the mark when Murray showed. He wasn't bunco then, but he had a fine eye for the grift in play. He had gone mad dog. In his frenzy he accidentally smashed the mark's nose. He had a big hate for grifters all right.

The raucous crows resumed their cawing. I wondered why. Had he gone? To cover my gander, I trembled my water glass off the booth top. I raised it high and pointed it toward the aisle.

Murray was standing at the edge of our booth grinning down at us. Through the watery screen his jagged teeth made his mouth look like the open jaws of a famished shark.

In the velvet tones of a psychiatrist soothing a manic-depressive, Blue said, "Ah, Mr. Murray. Please, won't you sit down and join us? Have a drink, or perhaps a steak."

Dot bent his knees and slithered over the leather seat facing us. He sat there silently with that sneering grin on his face. His spotted hands were splayed out on the table top. Puddles of dirty yellow had started to wash out the brown pigment. It was hard to believe they had once been dark brown.

Our waitress came toward him to take his order. He waved her away. Finally in a fruity, soprano voice, he said, "Blue, you knew I was going to join your party, didn't you? You really didn't have to give me an invitation, now did you?"

Before Dot's mouth could remold that awful grin, Blue said, "Now, Mr. Murray, how could Blue know you had a social interest or any other kind in him. You never have in the thirty years I've known you. So, since I'm a courteous gentleman, I couldn't just let you stand there in the aisle, now could I?"

Dot whipped his mottled hands off the table and spanked his palms together. His narrow grin closed shop. His hands were out of sight in his lap. I wondered if he had eased his rod from a waist holster.

Then his grin reopened as a wide corporation. He said, "Now, Blue, it's true we've never been friends, but it's the Christmas season. Maybe in my old age I'm getting sentimental. Suppose I told you it would be a wise practical gesture for us to exchange Christmas gifts this year."

I took a huge drink of water. Perhaps I could cool those hot spasms in my gullet.

Blue leaned toward him and said, "Mr. Murray, I appreciate your sentiments. Unfortunately, I don't share them. Christmas is just another day to me. Besides, wouldn't it be at least slightly out of line for a robbery detective and a mere carny spindle-man to exchange gifts?

"In my opinion, such a gesture would not be wise, but stupid to the extreme. After all, I'm not a heavy gee. Cheer up, Mr. Murray, you have almost a week to find a heister or safecracker to share your Christmas sentiments."

Blue glanced at his wristwatch, turned to me, and said, "Son, we better hurry. I'm afraid we'll be late for our appointment."

Blue took a sawbuck from his raise and put it on top of our eight-dollar check. He started to rise. I rose with him.

We made it to the aisle. I stood behind Blue. He reached for our hats and coats on the chrome rack at the top of the booth.

He looked down at Dot and said, "Well, Mr. Murray, the chances are I won't see you again before Christmas, so best wishes to you for the holidays."

Dot still sat there grinning. He looked straight ahead as we struggled into our coats. Then, without turning his head, he casually said, "Blue, I can't miss seeing you again soon. I'll duck into the homicide bureau and enjoy your morgue shots, maybe as soon as tomorrow. I'll count the ice-pick holes in your black lard ass. You and your trick baby partner could be walking corpses."

I cut in. I was hot as hell. I said, "Goddamnit, Mr. Murray, I was no trick baby. My mother was no whore. She married a white man. Do I have to pin her marriage license on my chest? And Blue and I haven't done anything to wind up dead."

He said, "I'll believe a license when I see it. I'm bullshit proof. Get wise and sit down. You high-powered grifters could save your lives. You two greedy bastards took off dangerous dough today.

"Like I said before, old sentimental Murray just wants to exchange early Christmas presents. Now you're interested as hell, I betcha."

Before the blast Blue was handing me my hat. Now, he was crushing it lopsided. He turned and looked up at me. His face had turned gray. His big nose was dewy. For an instant I didn't get it.

Then I thought, *Icepick stabs! We took off dangerous dough! Mary, Mother of Jesus! It just couldn't be! It couldn't be true! The cop was kidding us. Yes, that was it. The outfit, the syndicate wanted us dead? It had to be hokum. We weren't idiots. We would never cross them.*

Blue stood silently looking down at the top of Dot's head. His eyes were almost closed like a condemned man in prayer. I wondered why his magic tongue was taking such a long vacation. I fell into the booth. Dot's eyes stared into space over my head.

I said, "Mr. Murray, somebody's sold you a phony steer. Neither Blue nor I are in outfit trouble. It's impossible. Only a rank sucker would gamble against that kind of fate. We're smarter than that. We like steaks, clothes, dames and breathing too much to commit suicide."

He didn't say anything. The waitress came to clear our plates away. She gave Blue a warm two-dollar smile as she brushed by him in the aisle.

Blue sighed and floated his right hand before my face. He rippled his fingers through the air like a kid making waves in a creek.

The seat of my pants was damp. My wet palms oared across the cool leather. Blue dropped heavy anchor beside me. We waited for Dot's lead.

He said, "Boys, I had to be the luckiest sonuvabitch in the department today. There I was cruising down Roosevelt Road. I felt lousy as hell. I had a hangover and six dollars in my pocket a week before Christmas.

"I stopped for the red at Kedsie, near Roosevelt Road. Who should go roaring across the intersection but old man Frascati. You know, the old dago fence who owns the secondhand clothing shop. Guess who his passenger was?"

Dot paused and chortled. I was paralyzed. Blue was rigid beside me. Frascati was the mark we had played for the ten grand. Dot had seen Blue lugging the old man to me for the kill.

He continued his fun, "It didn't register until I passed the old man's shop on Madison. It was closed. Frascati had to be awfully excited to do that in midday.

"It was too late to pick up the trail so I staked out the shop. I figured the old man would come back on the send for his money. I knew he hated banks. He kept a bundle stashed inside his shop somewhere.

"All the Westside heisters knew about the stash. But the old man's loot was safe. Ten years ago two foolish heisters from out of town raided his cash register. Two days later they were found in an alley. They were ice-picked from

head to toe. Their butts had been sliced off to the bone.
The Westside heisters knew what you dough-crazy grifters
were too stupid to find out before you played for Frascati.
Do you know who the old man's sister happens to be? The
mother of Nino Parelli, that's who! Nino loved the old
man. He set him up in the clothing shop."

He gaped his mouth open and bucked his eyes wide in
mock terror. He just sat there with that creepy look frozen
on his face. I didn't need his grim clowning to chill my
blood.

Blue looked at me. I looked at Blue. There wasn't a
hustler on the Southside who hadn't heard of Nino Parelli.

He was a fast rising talent of terror and murder in the
outfit. His dominion was the lush policy wheels and dope
operations on the southside. His spine-tingling reputation
kept the black figureheads in a state of trembling honesty.

Blue's usually silky voice was ragged. He said, "Mr.
Murray, on the face of it I admit things do look dark for
me. Believe me, White Folks was not involved in the
Frascati affair. In fact, I was a mere dupe myself.

"But I've got connections. My position is reversible. I'll
make a phone call tonight, and walk in the sun again. Give
me a solid reason why I should hold still for your shakedown?"

Joy lighted Dot's face. He said, "Blue, I thought you'd
never ask. The greatest connection on earth couldn't get
you a stay of execution once I fingered you. Listen
carefully and I'll give you rock-hard reason.

"When the old man got back to his shop he rushed to
the phone in the front window. I could tell he was happy
and excited as he talked. He hung up. Then he did an odd
thing. He scrambled into that heap of his and drove
toward the Loop. I tailed him to hockshop row at Van
Buren and State.

"He was beginning to really puzzle me now. The old
man never fenced anything but whiskey from hijackers
and clothes from smash-and-grab store burglars. He had
been a former tailor in Rome. He was smart to traffic in

items he knew.

"He parked his jalopy three feet from the curb in a red zone on State. I parked maybe fifty feet in front of the jalopy on State. I kept watch in my rear-view mirror.

"He hustled into Jerry Profacci's joint. I knew that Jerry was Chicago's top hot-ice dealer. Blue, at that instant I got the thought that you had stepped into the heavy rackets."

Dot paused and stuck his index finger into his ear. He rapidly jiggled it like an itchy mutt scratching at fleas. He rolled his eyes in the ecstasy of it all like a dame in orgasm. With that squeaky, high voice of his and all, a fellow would have to wonder about him. Even so I could pity the fruit hustler who tried to put the strong-arm on him.

Blue shifted his bulk and glanced nervously at his watch.

I looked over Dot's head at the frostbitten chumps passing the window. I envied them now. They would go on living and at least die a natural death.

Dot was sharp for a juice head. He sensed out tenseness. He said, "Now, Blue, don't get jumpy. Nino's not wise, yet, that you are the dirty bird who fouled up the old man.

"Anyway, after ten minutes or so, I got restless and walked by Jerry's to the corner. There was only a clerk at the counter. I knew the old man was in the rear transacting business with Jerry.

"On my way back to my car, the old man staggered out to the sidewalk. He was in a bad way. He was in a shocked daze. He looked right into my face. His eyes were blank. It was spooky because he had known me fifteen years. I walked by him. I went back to my car to take up the tail when he pulled out.

"The gears screeched when his heap careened into traffic. A southbound streetcar skidded a shower of sparks. I knew it couldn't stop in time. The streetcar crushed in the driver's side of the jalopy. The old man flew through the window like he had been shot from a cannon.

"His head busted wide open against the street. It

sounded like an ax splitting a two-by-four. I sat there helpless. I knew he was dead.

"I was sitting there long after they took him away. Blue, I knew that in some way you were responsible. At first I couldn't tie you in. Then when it hit me, it was easy. The old man had gotten bad news at Profacci's.

"He had been in high spirits when he left you. What was the news that put him into that fatal daze? Profacci bought hot rocks. I knew then it was rocks, phony rocks that he thought were real!

"I was sure you had swindled him on some twist of the rocks con. Profacci had broken the bad news to Frascati. Boys, I believe that score was no less than fifteen gees. I want five gees no matter what it was.

"A million dollars couldn't cool Nino if I tipped him. But you're lucky at that. I'm the only one who can put a finger on you. Give me the five gees now and walk out that door. Don't give it to me and I rush my finger to Nino."

CHAPTER TWO

Copper Dot's Sucker Ear

I had to admire the way Dot had spun the steel web. Dot gazed at us. His body had the floppy looseness of a card hustler who had dealt himself a mortal cinch.

I started to take a cold steam bath inside my overcoat when Blue said, "Mr. Murray, your eyes told your brain a lie. It's true you saw me with Frascati. But I didn't get a nickel for myself. Too bad he isn't alive to support the truth.

"You must understand, Mr. Murray, that I was just a good Samaritan when you saw us together. This whole unfortunate affair revolves around a certain white gentleman of now stainless reputation who was a former inside man on the big con. He's been a true friend through the years. His name would flabbergast you if I were not pledged to secrecy. I am sure even Nino would be impressed to hear his name.

"As a matter of fact so powerful is he that on occasion he has influenced police department policy. In a manner of speaking it could be said that you, Mr. Murray, under certain circumstances, might be affected by this influence, for better or for worse.

"This gentleman had been doing soft-goods business with Mr. Frascati and a score of others here in the city. Like you, Mr. Murray, I have not been free of sinful interest in a fast buck."

Blue paused and looked over the booth top toward the waitress. He waved. She came and waited for the order. Blue ordered cognac. Dot, Cutty Sark, triple shot, straight. Cutty Sark had been my favorite drink long ago. Now I didn't dare touch a single drop of alcohol. I ordered Seven

Up.

The glamour dust in her hair reminded me of how locks of silicon jeweled the granite markers in a cemetery on a sunny day.

She brought the drinks. Blue lit a cigar and slowly sipped his cognac. He looked at Dot and winked at me.

Dot's eyes were locked shut. He poked out his angry bottom lip between gulps of the straight Scotch. He was crawling his fingers over his glass like vipers at the rim of a pit.

I wondered if, under the strain of everything, Blue was off his rocker. Didn't he realize Dot plus the Scotch could be almost as dangerous as Nino? I didn't know Blue's full angle yet. But at this point I was ready to tear my pocket off in haste to pay off.

Blue continued, "Now, Mr. Murray, to make a short story shorter, first I must make you understand that I too was a victim of the white gentleman's disregard of principle. It was inhuman of him not to mention that Nino was Frascati's nephew.

"I didn't know that Mr. Frascati existed until I received a call from my white friend. He had discovered a distressing number of sub-par garments among a delivery made to him by an agent of Mr. Frascati the day before.

"Unfortunately he had been generous and advanced Mr. Frascati a sizeable sum of money a week ago. The gentleman explained to me that whether Frascati had willfully cheated him or not was not really important. He had to give the old man a lesson.

"He wanted the old man to use careful respect in future dealings with him. He told me he really liked the old man. But he couldn't let even the small timers cheat him with impunity. It made sense to me.

"You're a robbery detective and you read the papers. They said a cat burglar made a hundred-and-fifty-gee score from the room of a jewelry salesman in a downtown hotel several days ago.

"The gentleman located a Southside whiskey hijacker

who had done business with the old man. The hijacker must have electrified the old man with the story that the hotel score had been made by an amateur.

"The amateur was a maid at the hotel with sticky mitts. She had taken it on impulse. Now she wanted to get rid of it fast. She would take fifteen gees. The hijacker was her agent. Right away the old man called my gentleman for advice. I was there when the call came through.

"The gentleman said it was a great deal if the merchandise was really the Loop loot. But a body had to be careful when dealing in rocks. There was phony stuff around an inexpert eye couldn't detect from the genuine.

"The gentleman told him he would send an expert ex-con jewel thief to go with him to look at the stuff. I played the role of that expert. Mr. Murray, I was indebted to the gentleman. How could I refuse him?

"Before the old man hung up he got the gentleman's promise that if the ice tested out he would lend him eight gees to go with the seven he had in hand. He swore the old man to secrecy. I took a cab to the clothing shop."

Blue leaned back and puffed his cigar end into a fiery eye. I was beginning to feel better. Maybe Blue's tale would get us off the shakedown hook.

Those feet sledging against the floor had stopped. There is something about solid con that wraps the mind in a pleasant cocoon-world of unreality that replaces the world of reality. I almost believed Blue's tale myself.

Dot's eyes were wide open. He was more wary, now, than disbelieving. But one flaw in the fabric of Blue's con and we'd really be in a bad cross.

Blue leaned toward Dot. He gently pressed his palms against Dot's elbows. I could barely hear Blue as he continued the airtight lie.

He whispered, "Mr. Murray, I lugged the old man to a hotel room at Thirtieth and Indiana Avenue. The hijacker and a stranger were waiting. The stranger was the gentleman's watchdog.

"He was going to take the fifteen gees from the hijacker

after the old man had been trimmed. I guess the gentleman figured that since the hijacker was a heavy gee he
might get tempted and not be satisfied with his half grand
payoff for the play. A grand was my end. God knows I
owed the gentleman a favor, so I turned it down.

"The flash was in a black velvet pouch. The hijacker
dumped that slum to the top of the dresser under a bright
lamp. It was like the display at Tiffany's. The two dozen
blue-tinted gem-cut Zircons blazed blue-white greed inside
the old man. He was shaking beside me.

"Mr. Murray, let me tell you the whole truth. That old
man elbowed me out the way. He fondled those phony
rocks as if they were the trillion-dollar collection at
Buckingham Palace.

"Finally I was able to examine each with my prop
jeweler's glass. I declared they were all gem quality stones
and worth perhaps more than a hundred and fifty gees.

"Hell, the gentleman hadn't really needed me to back
up the slum. The old man kept a sharp eye on the pile of
glass as he called the gentleman. He was making certain
no one of the three of us filched from the treasure that was
soon to be his. He was panting to close the deal.

"Within fifteen minutes a runner showed with the eight
gees from the white gentleman. The old man trembled his
seven-gee bundle from his coat lining. He gave fifteen gees
to the hijacker. He scooped up the flash and fled the scene
like the thief he thought he was. I left behind him and
went home.

"Mr. Murray, as the saints in heaven are my witnesses I
have told you the snow-white truth. I have one regret, Mr.
Murray. I wish when you saw me with the old man you
had collared me and held me on some beef no matter
what. The awful tragedy of the old man's accident will
plague me to my deathbed."

Blue had sold the tale! Dot sagged in the booth like a
crippled fox, clubbed and poisoned. He blinked his eyelids
across his bloodshot eyes. Blue's con had stomped his
strong upper hand into confused gristle.

Blue's eyes were glowing in the dimness. Many times in the past I had noticed how the con charged him up.

Dot's lips pouted to a smooching stance. Tiny springs of sweat welled inside the sudden tattoo of wrinkles on his chin. He opened his mouth to speak. He didn't make it.

Blue said, "Now, Mr. Murray, it isn't the end of the world. I am a realist and a generous one at that. The mistaken impression that you had before you heard the truth does give you a temporarily dangerous nuisance value.

"It would be stupid of me not to reward you for your complete silence. I need time to filter the truth to Nino. I have a plan to make him understand I was a mere dupe myself in this whole unfortunate affair.

"I realize how horrible it would be for me were you to relate to Nino the untrue version that you first believed. I have one big worry, Mr. Murray. Everybody knows about your hard-on for grifters. Say I gave you fifteen hundred or a couple of grand right now? What insurance would I have that you wouldn't break your finger pointing me out to Nino? You could do it a minute after you got your payoff. Then I wouldn't have the time I need.

"Incidentally, just why do you have your big hate for grifters?"

Dot jerked erect. The veins in his hands corded as he squeezed his glass. Frothy droplets of spit showered my overcoat sleeve.

He shouted, "Hate 'em? Goddamnit! How I hate them! You treacherous bastards heist with a smile. You'll play con for a paralyzed blind man. You destroy with your cunning lies. All of you cold-hearted mother-fuckers should be handcuffed together and burned to cinders.

"You said I had two grand coming? Give it to me and blow. I could jug you both on an open charge that would keep you on ice for the night.

"Then maybe overnight I could find out whether the old man had confided in detail with Profacci, the fence. Maybe your story was all con. If it was, Profacci will tell

Nino the truth. All Nino will need is your name from me.

"So, it's not what I do that earns the two grand. It's what I don't do. So, give me the two grand before I change my mind."

Blue shoved his palms through the air toward Dot. He said, "Now, Mr. Murray, you're going to get the two grand. But I've got to know you won't welsh on our deal.

"My bladder is going to burst if I don't get to the john. Can you wait a moment for the dough? When I get back we'll find a solution to the problem.

"You know with a gut like mine, I'd never get between the bars in the john window. Besides, the john door is right in your plain view. I couldn't go through the rear kitchen door if I wanted to. You know I wouldn't leave White Folks in a jam like this."

Blue got to his feet. He looked wistfully down at me. He said, "White Folks, when we came in here tonight I never dreamed two grand in cold green would go through a chimney in smoke."

He turned and walked toward the john. Dot slid to the aisle end of the booth. He kept his eyes in the direction of the john. I was glad Dot's eyes were busy elsewhere.

He couldn't see my hands trembling. I didn't want to believe Blue's last words. He didn't intend to give Dot the two grand! He had told me in code he was going to lay the flue for Dot.

My legs were quivering. They wanted to sprint me into that john and plead with Blue not to risk it. I shut my eyes. Dot might glance my way and see something there to tip him that the weather was getting foul.

CHAPTER THREE

The Dummy Payoff

I closed my eyes and imagined what Blue was doing in the john. He was slitting an opening in the crease at the bottom of one of those envelopes he always carried. After that he would peel off, from his end of the Frascati score, four of those five-hundred-dollar bills.

He'd take enough toilet tissue to equal the weight and bulk of the money. He'd fold the tissue lengthwise down the middle and put it inside the envelope. Then he would put the loaded envelope among the several other empty ones in his coat pocket.

Ordinarily we used the flue as a short con game on barkeeps and small businessmen in the small towns surrounding the city.

The gimmick was to put tne dummy envelope in trust to the sucker. Then borrow against the money that had been removed through the slit in the bottom of the sealed envelope. It made for easy frequent touches.

It was our interim game between larger scores on the longer rocks, drag and smack con games we played.

Believe me, the flue had not been devised to bilk a dangerous roller out of his shakedown. The most disturbing question was, what if he were wise to the flue?

When Blue went to the john I was only partially in the heat of the dangerous affair. That is from Dot's point of view. Blue's velvet tale off the top of his head had eased me away from the core of the flame. Now, when Blue came back he'd need me to set up the crossfire to make it logical to Dot that the flue and the mail-away were necessary and fair arrangements for us all.

The mail-away was most important. It would be damn

unfunny for Dot to rip open to toilet paper befo e v e
copped a heel. Blue came back and slid into t' : boot
beside me.

I turned and looked at him. He thumb-stroke.: the lot o
of his right ear. It was our secret crossfire signal. He was
ready to play. I heaved a sigh and leaped into the center
of the fire.

I said, "Blue, for Chrissake give Mr. Murray the two
grand. Let's get the hell out of here now! You need every
precious minute for the Nino square-up."

Blue gave me a pained look like a father catching his
sweetheart laying his son. He thrust his hand into his coat
pocket. He took out four five-hundred notes. He slammed
them to the tabletop.

He fanned them apart with the heel of his palm. Dot's
eyes rocketed down for a fast count. His right hand did a
spastic jerk.

Blue scooped up the bills and said, "White Folks, don't
get panicky. Mr. Murray will get the two grand as surely
as God is in His heaven. I'm not stalling. I'm just puzzled
and worried.

"If we were not grifters we could trust him all the way, I
believe. Mr. Murray is a fine gentleman and his word is
like a gold bond under normal circumstances. But you
heard him say how much he hated con players."

Dot coughed Blue to a halt. He said, "What the hell?
There's no problem. Give me the two grand and we can
stay together until you make your contacts. How about it?"

Blue said, "No, thanks. Even you can't be sure that you
wouldn't cross me immediately that you got your payoff.
But I'll give you the two grand and you stick to us li:e
flypaper until I square Nino, right? What do you think,
White Folks?"

It was my cue to introduce the flue.

I said, "Blue, it's almost a perfect idea. It has one flaw
that makes it impossible. You can't reveal the identity of
the powerful white gentleman that tricked you into this
bind. It seems to me you are forced to make a personal call

on him in your efforts to get straight with Nino. You can't afford to let Mr. Murray or anyone else know who he is.

"You could pay him a visit while I stayed with Mr. Murray. But that's out. I'd have a stroke if left alone with him. I just can't think of—oh! Wait a minute. Say, I've got it! Real estate escrow! That's how to do it!"

Blue cut in. "White Folks, where the hell have your brains been since Mr. Murray joined us? This isn't even close to a real estate deal. I don't follow you."

I quavered my voice in excitement. I said, "I understand it isn't that kind of deal. But, don't you see? You can fit the escrow plan to this deal like a glove.

"We can imagine Mr. Murray has an acre of silence to sell. You're the buyer, cautious and sensible. You can't risk the two-grand purchase price until you're sure you have clear and absolute title to Mr. Murray's property for the stipulated time.

"Your contact would be disastrously null and void if Nino had a prior lien on that real estate in Mr. Murray's mind. You simply place the two grand in an envelope. Seal it before Mr. Murray's alert eyes. Have Mr. Murray address it to himself. Together you drop it in the mailbox on the corner before your watchful eyes. That way nobody worries. It's perfect."

Dot's mouth smugged at the corners. He saw the escape hatch in my plan for his double cross of Blue.

Blue barred the hole with rolled steel. He said, "White Folks, it's going to murder your ego, but I'm going to say your escrow idea is pure stupidity. I may as well give Mr. Murray the two grand now and pray a rosary that he won't cross me.

"Mr. Murray is a clever man, my disrespectful friend. He'd figure in seconds that he couldn't lose the payoff once it went into that mailbox. He could tip Nino with glee and meet the mailman at his door in the morning. He knows Uncle Sam's mail is inviolate. Your plan is worse than Mr. Murray's. Want to try again, genius?"

I screwed my face into a wounded mask of distress. I

closed my eyes and swayed from side to side like a cobra in rapport with a fakir. Then I popped my eyes wide and hammered my fists to the tabletop. Dot flinched away from the thudding. I mimicked Blue.

I said, "Want to try again, genius? I sure do. Mr. Murray won't cross you. I've thought of ironclad insurance. It's simple and Mr. Murray can't object if he's on the square with you.

"Mr. Murray has been a central headquarters detective for years. Instead of sending the two grand to his home, address it to the headquarters instead. Everybody knows him down there. It wouldn't be a bit odd for a star robbery detective to receive mail.

"It could be a letter from one of his informers tipping him to a robbery caper. Insert a note with the two grand. Let it indicate that the money is Mr. Murray's end of the Frascati score. There's one change. Blue, you address it in your handwriting.

"Say Mr. Murray tips Nino before the mail delivery in the morning before you can square Nino. Maybe you fail and you need time to run. Our friend Felix the Fixer would know within an hour from his Rush Street source.

"Say, right after that letter is dropped in the box, Mr. Murray takes us in on a phony rap and then tipped Nino. When we got downtown to the lockup we'd start bellowing for the commissioner.

"Maybe we can't get him, but it's a cinch we'll get brass down there to listen. We'll put them on the alert for the payoff letter. He'd have a terrible time explaining.

"But his greatest danger in crossing us would be Nino. Nino certainly has ears and eyes in the department. Within an hour he'd know the contents of the letter. Then Mr. Murray would be as hot as you.

"Nino would figure Mr. Murray's tip was a desperate play to cover his own hand in the matter. That letter would still be a ticking bomb for Mr. Murray if he didn't arrest us after the letter dropped. First thing you'd call Felix. He'd call the commissioner personally before mail delivery to put the cross on the double-crossing Mr. Murray. That is if Felix got a flash that the finger was on you.

"Blue, there's one thing you're long on, and that's imagination. You'd find it easy to build an iron frame to support that payoff letter. I'm sure you could get Mr. Murray indicted for something on top of his Nino trouble.

"No, Blue, my plan guarantees Mr. Murray's integrity. All he has to do is play fair and pluck his two grand out of the mail basket at headquarters in the morning. Now, be careful and don't crack my spine when you pat me on the back."

Blue said, "Folks, congratulations! A mouthpiece would envy your plan. It's fair and airtight."

I saw Dot's eyes congeal. Blue had flung the pack of stamped envelopes on the tabletop between them. Dot folded his arms across his chest and leaned back.

He was pounding his feet against the floor again. Blue reached into the pack and pulled out the glued envelope. He casually placed it to the side. He tore a section from one of the others. I handed him my ball point.

He started to scribble the incriminating note. He finished it and pushed it across the table to Dot. Dot, without unfastening his arms, leaned forward and peered intently at it. He grunted agreement to its text. Blue fanned the two grand again and folded it lengthwise down the middle. He placed his glass over the bills.

Blue addressed the trick envelope. Then slipped the note inside it. He picked it up. Held it in his left hand with the addressed side square in Dot's view. His thumb and index finger grasped it at bottom center. The slit in its bottom crease was an inch or so above the fleshy web between Blue's thumb and index finger.

Blue pulled the folded money from beneath the glass with his right hand and held it under Dot's eyes for a moment. The money magnetized Dot's head. He was half out of his seat as Blue started to thrust the bills into the envelope.

Dot's eyes were no more than six inches from the front of it. Blue's hands were steady as he threaded the bills past the wad of paper down the flue. Only the cavorting vein at the side of his hand leading to that web betrayed his terrible tension.

I thanked the saints I wasn't laying that flue for Dot. I saw the money peep through the slit. Then ride down to the cup of the web. I dropped my right hand to my lap. I had to retrieve the money from Blue.

Blue tightened the web around it. The envelope almost touched Dot's face, blocking his view. Blue's left hand, web and money, blurred to his lap. He casually licked the flap of the envelope now in his right hand. His empty left hand had streaked back to the table top. The blur and streak had been one.

With both hands he tightly pressed the moistened flap against the envelope lying on top of the others. I had reached to the side of Blue's thigh when Dot screamed. My hand was paralyzed holding the bills beneath the table.

"Hold it now, you slick bastard! Don't move your hands!"

He wasn't screaming at me. He had vised his hands around Blue's wrists. Now he turned to me. I was really nervous now. Maybe he was wise to the flue. He still held Blue's wrists.

He said, "Now you, Trick Baby, riffle those envelopes apart. If there's a twin to the one with my payoff in that pile you slick sonsuvbitches will never play the switch again."

I was ecstatic! Dot had suspected that we'd pulled the ancient switch-game on him. He hadn't been wise to the flue.

My right hand left the two grand temporarily. I speared the pile of envelopes apart with my index finger. They were all blank and clean. Dot freed Blue's wrists. They both grabbed at the dummy envelope at the same time. Each had a firm grip on each end of it. They both stood holding it between them. Blue put his hat on.

He said, "Do we have to go to the mailbox in this ridiculous manner, Mr. Murray?"

Dot tightened his grip on the fake payoff.

He said, "Blue, I'll die and go to the bottomless pits of hell before I let you flimflam me out of my two grand. We'll drop it in the box together."

I palmed the two grand off the seat. I stood up and released it into my overcoat pocket. I took a sawbuck from my trouser pocket and dropped it on the table. I picked up my battered hat from the floor, straightened the crown and put it on.

Blue and Dot were side to side as they went down the aisle toward the door. I followed them. I looked back. The waitress and bartender were radiant with relief to see us go.

I stepped out to the street. Electric needles pricked inside my stiffened legs. A jolting blast of wind teared my eyes. Overhead, a Jackson Park el punched screeching rivets of sound into my temples as it grated to a stop. The icy sidewalk was a black mirror reflecting the morose starless sky. A pang of guilty pity shot through me for old man Frascati.

We walked toward the mailbox at Forty-seventh and Calumet. A rotten meaty stench poisoned the fresh, wintry air. My nostrils quivered in panic as a pair of decaying junkies ghosted past me like animated dead.

I couldn't help smiling as Blue and Dot in front of me tiptoed across the ice clutching the worthless paper oblong between them. They looked like grotesque children playing a strange game. I looked at my watch. It was a minute to nine P.M. We had been under Dot's pressure for three hours. How our lives had changed in that brief span of hours.

Blue and Dot stood at the mailbox. Their heads were bowed down toward the envelope. They were spotlighted for an instant by the headlights of a turning car. They were like corrupt worshippers penitent before an altar.

Then together they pushed the envelope through the slot.

Blue grinned at me as Dot walked away toward South
Parkway. He had a funny, mincing, forward-stumble style.
It was like each step was a contrived mistake. It was a
relief all right to blow him off. But what about Nino?

CHAPTER FOUR

Flight to Jewtown

We walked back to my Fleetwood parked in front of the bar. We got in. Blue's Cadillac was in for transmission adjustment. I gave Blue his prop two grand back. We sat there silently as I warmed up the engine. I pulled away and turned right on Calumet. We were in the heart of the area known as Dopeville, U. S. A.

Bryson and Sims, probably the most feared and efficient narcotics detectives in Chicago, were frisking a suspect in front of the poolroom on Calumet.

I saw Midge, Blue's daughter, in one of the doorways talking to Mose, a dope peddler. She waved. I nodded. She looked a hundred. The sad sight of her tore at my insides. I was glad Blue hadn't seen her.

I continued South on Calumet toward Garfield Boulevard. Junkie whores on both sides of Calumet clung to the fetid doorways and rotted stoops like painted lice to a filthy crotch. I was certain our destination had to be Felix the Fixer.

Blue gave me a puzzled look. "Son, if you're headed for the Fixer's, forget it for now. A fin will get a C-note that we're blazing hot already. Since noon Nino has had the chance to cinch make us. After all, our mark had to bleat our descriptions to Profacci when he found out the rocks were phony. Nino might even remember us from the flat joint days.

"Search your mind. There isn't another con team like us in Chicago. How easy could it be for Nino to pressure our names from his spies all over the Southside. They get paid, it's true, for watching the policy game operators. But what the hell, it wouldn't make them bawl in sorrow to pick up an extra two bills for fingering us.

"Face the bitter truth, son. I'm the only big, black grifter with white hair teamed with a six-four blond white boot who is a dead ringer for Errol Flynn.

"I knew Dot really had nothing to sell us. That's why I risked laying the flue for him. Son, we have to get off the Southside fast, and off the street, period! Do you have any ideas?"

I turned right at Forty-eighth Street. Whirly bits of confused thought stormed my mind. I had planned out of some dangerous situations before. But now my slick, instant machine was crippled. I turned down Michigan Avenue, heading north to the Loop.

Finally I said, "How about Gary, Indiana? Nobody knows us there. We could get a furnished room in an upright neighborhood for a couple of days. It would be enough time to plan out of this thing."

Blue jumped like he had been scalded. He said, "My God, no! Have you forgotten how Hutch, the policy banker, was shotgunned to ribbons there on a busy street in broad daylight? The killers loaded ball bearings in the shells.

"The outfit has a full nelson on the town. Besides, it's too small. Son, you've got to realize we've hit the bad-luck jackpot. The F.B.I. and Pinkertons, by comparison, are kindly amateurs.

"The torturers of the outfit have almost a one hundred percent find-and-murder average. White Folks, the damn sad thing is that I am responsible for all of this happening to you."

I said, "Now, Blue, you know better than that. Sure the play for the old man was your idea. But I know damn well you didn't know he was tied to Nino. We both know it's never a good idea to play for a home guard. It was a worse mistake not to research him.

"I wasn't tricked or pressured into playing for Frascati, you know. I don't understand how and why you can take the blame for a blunder we made together. Blue, we can't afford to confuse each other.

"Blue, I owe you my life. I can't forget how you stood by me when the Goddess put me into that crazy drunken tailspin. Nothing can change that or the sincere affection I feel for you. We're not going to die. Like always we'll come up with the perfect con to escape the trap."

It was pure bravado. Blue didn't answer. I had desolate death-tinged thoughts as we passed the gleaming row of Michigan Avenue's luxury shops.

Finally Blue broke the morbid spell. He said, "Folks, turn left at Lake. We'll go to Jewtown. I've got an idea."

I turned and drove westward. I was puzzled. I wondered why Blue wanted to go to Jewtown. It was a tragic Westside slum inhabited by poverty-mauled blacks.

Jewish merchants operated the countless shops and bazaars by day. At nightfall the thronging bargain hunters from all over the city deserted it. Few, if any, of the Jewish merchants lived there.

I just couldn't figure Blue's angle. Blue had ignored my question of his lone guilt for our desperate plight. I was at the point of reopening the matter when Blue coupled onto my train of thought. He almost whispered.

He said, "John Patrick O'Brien, you will be thirty-six years old January fifteenth. That means that for the last twenty years my grifting way of life in this cold world has been yours. Inside you feel and think black like me. Outside you're lily white. It's a damn sad combination.

"The black Southside taught you that bitter lesson for all of your life. You're a whiz at the grift. Don't say it, I'll say it. Yes, I taught you all the con you know. It was easy, because you had a natural feel for the con. You feel close to me, indebted to me.

"Some blacks have hated you because they believed you were really white. Some have despised you even though they knew you were Phala's child. As a white child born of a brown mother they *had* to hate you. For them you are the symbol of your white father's sexual violation of a black woman.

"Son, in your mind I have been some kind of sympathet-is unselfish stepfather. I've been a constant buffer for you against the black haters. And, yes, it's true, I possibly saved your life when that nigger-hating white broad almost cracked you up. But that life I saved was one I had selfishly molded to danger.

"Son, I'm old and weary now, and I care about you too much to con you. Folks, the time has come to give you the complete, from-the-heart truth.

"Sure I took you in off those brutal streets. I took the risk and sheltered you from the juvenile authorities who wanted to make you a ward of the court, after those filthy black dogs drove Phala to madness.

"You probably thought at the time that I had a pure golden heart as big as Chicago. Well, son, you conned yourself. I used you across the board.

"I saw Midge turning into a goddamned lesbian. A father should spend some time with his child. It was my fault. The grift kept me on the go. After her mother died, Midge had only the freakish street tramps for company. Midge was all I had left. It was the worst kind of setup for a precocious fifteen-year-old girl.

"Son, then you came along, tall and spectacularly hand-some. I couldn't see how any dame could say no to you. I figured I would throw you two together. It was a cold-blooded stud bitch idea. I hoped you'd knocked her up and slow her down. I was that desperate.

"Perhaps she'd fall for you and you would rod that hellish yen for girls out of her. My plan was too late to save her.

"Instead, you two loved each other like real sister and brother. You started getting to me, too. But still I had to use you. I had long-range plans. I'd start you out as a belly-stick for my flat joint. Later, I'd develop you into my full-fledged grifting partner.

"To a black grifter you were a rare gift from heaven. I'd be able to give a fine convincing play to fat, white suckers with a partner who looked white. I knew ten years ago you had the grifting sense to play with a big-time white con mob.

"But I was too selfish, perhaps even afraid the student would outshine his teacher. I know that I loved you as a son in my twisted grifter's way. But I envied your white skin.

"You've heard me brag that I had once been with the big con. I lied to you, son. I never roped or played the inside. I was never even a shill. I was with it, all right. I was a mere stagehand, a flunky who set up the props and then tore them down after a sucker had been played in a big store.

"Just a clean-up man, that's all. I can't blame the Vicksburg Kid for that lowly spot. In fact I owe him everything for taking me out of the South. It wasn't his fault that a black grifter couldn't play rich white suckers in a big store.

"Oh sure, I got wise to all the principles of big con. I was a smart black lackey who eyeballed and stayed on the earie. You met the Vicksburg Kid when he came through Chicago that summer.

"He cracked to me then I should let you come to Montreal to his big store. He said you were smooth. He felt a talented white boy like you was wasted on the smack and drag. I never told him you were really black.

"He said you were smooth with great personality and mark appeal. He gave me his personal telephone number and address in Montreal. The way you impressed him, it was a cinch he'd have let you start as a shill for his store. With your natural flair for the con, in months he'd have honed you to razor sharpness as a roper.

"Now, son, can you understand why I said I am responsible for all of this latest trouble happening to you? I'm just a narrow-minded, dumb bastard. I couldn't let you leave me. I couldn't stand to see you get cut in to that long green. I knew up there you'd learn the truth about me.

"So old flunky Blue, your fake friend, held on and never tipped you that the big con was wide open to you. So, son, go on and hate me. I can't blame you. But at least I've come clean with you at last. Pull up to that phone booth. I'll check with Fixer."

We were on Halsted Street. I pulled to the curb. The booth was next to a filling station. Blue's eyes avoided me as he got out. He walked slowly to the phone. His eyes flashed sadly at me as he dialed. Poor Blue really thought he was a dirty double-crosser who had barred me from the big-time con and the white world. He wasn't so dumb either. Neither of us had done any time.

At no time during our twenty years together had I given serious thought to sneaking over the racial fence to pass for white. I wouldn't have moved from our pink frame house on Langley Avenue to a castle on the Riviera, unless of course Blue came along.

He hung up the phone and dialed another number. He was probably calling Cloe. He put up the receiver after a few seconds. His shoulders were slumped as he walked toward the car. He got in and sighed. I pulled out and drove south on Halsted.

I said, "Has Fixer heard anything?"

He stared straight ahead. He said, "Son, it's worse than bad for us. We were lucky to get off the Southside. Felix told me Nino and two of his killers are already on the Southside looking for us. He is also posting his spies to look out for us.

"Nino's chief spy, that stupid ass-kissing sonuvabitch, Butcher Knife Brown, is on the prowl for us. That crazy black sucker would croak us for free. He'd suck Nino's ass with a straw.

"I told you we were hot! I told you! Felix said we would be better off if we were grand jury witnesses against the syndicate. He can't help us, son. Nino is crazy with grief. Oh! Why did I have to play for old man Frascati?

"Son, it's all my fault. The whole stupid mess. Folks, you don't know how glad I am that I made those pre-need arrangements with Metropolitan Funeral Home. You told me Phala wanted to be cremated and her ashes thrown to the winds. I carried out her wishes. But I want every nigger hustler in Chicago to turn green with envy. I want everybody to know old Blue was put away like a white aristocrat. I want to lie there in my luxury casket for all to see."

I felt guilt shoot through me. Phala had been dead for weeks before I knew. I had been out of town in a drunken tailspin. The Goddess sure had been my poison.

I said, "Goddamnit! Blue, stop it! You make me want to vomit! You're talking like a lop-eared mark. We're going to come through this thing alive. I suffered through your lousy confession. But damn if I can stand any more of the same bullshit.

"Blue, I have some news for you. Even a fetus in its mother's belly is starting to die before its birth. What the hell, you want to live forever? Every hustler in Chicago is going to know you were a sucker to toss ten grand to the worms.

"Besides, you're not going to die in an alley with your shoes on. You'll die a buck-naked sucker between Cleo's legs. Your lovesick heart is going to burst like a pricked balloon.

"Sure I hate you for chaining me and holding me prisoner in a nigger world. You put a pistol on me and forced me to make the Frascati play. That's why I copped a heel when you went to the phone. It would have been easy to have driven away and left you alone out there.

"I'll say it for the last time, Blue, we're friends. Nino or even the end of the world couldn't change that. Now, Blue, let's be sensible. Why go to Jewtown? As hot as we are, shouldn't I just head out of town away from the furnace? Chicago is a deathtrap for us.

"I could drive to New York in less than a day. You could send for Cleo later. How about it, pal? Blue, I'm sorry I made that personal remark about you and Cleo. Forgive me?"

His eyes were downcast. He cracked his knuckles in his lap. Finally he said, "Son, I've forgotten and forgiven your crack about Cleo. Folks, Cleo is like a baby. I just couldn't leave her in Chicago alone. Besides, Nino might see an angle in her to even the score.

"The sweet little doll would go out of her mind without me. She's like Midge was long ago. I destroyed Midge with neglect. I can't destroy Cleo. Wherever I go she has to go with me.

"Folks, we can't risk renting a room anywhere in town. Some hustler renting a room for the night with a dame could spot us. Don't worry, the bird we're going to owes me a million favors. Furthermore, he's a boyhood chum of mine. We're from the same town in Mississippi. He was Joe Coleman. But now he calls himself Reverend Josephus.

"Who could imagine that Blue and White Folks were hiding out in the house of an ex-wino turned religious fanatic? Twenty years ago he hung out and flunkied in the joints around Thirty-ninth and Cottage Grove. He was never underworld. He was just a Deep South chump driven to the grape by the confusion and disappointment of a big city.

"He knew your mother well. He's married to a country girl from down home. He and Bertha Mae had a house in Jewtown when I ran into him several years ago preaching in the street. He's a nut all right. But he's our only hope for a safe hideout. He's in my debt. But he'll put the chill on us if he thinks our troubles are crooked ones.

"Son, I give you my sacred promise. I'll have Cleo with us before the night is over. Monday morning I'll get to my safe deposit box in the Loop. While I'm down there I'll give my mouthpiece power of attorney to sell the house, car and furniture. We'll be out of Chicago no later than Monday noon. Fair enough, Folks?"

I didn't answer. I thought, "Should I tell him how damn unfair it is? Should I blurt out, 'Blue, she's a cheap chippie. Don't you understand she isn't worth a hair on your head?

"'She's not interested in you. She knows how close we are, but I could have laid her a hundred times. She only cares for the jewelry and furs and money you shower on her. Blue, she's going to rip your heart out of you one day. You're just an old black chump to her.

" 'Dump her now for your own good. We'll drive to New York right now. There are thousands of young dames in New York you can screw. You can always come back later and handle your business affairs. Blue, you risk your life for her. Don't risk mine.' "

He startled me from my silent tirade.

He said, "Folks, maybe I'm being selfish again. Here I am asking you to stay in Chicago until I straighten out my affairs. After all, Cleo is my wife, not yours. If you've got the slightest thought that you should blow tonight, then drop me off. We can use Fixer as a contact."

I said, "Blue, you're making me sick at my stomach again. That silly thought never crossed my mind. Say, we're at Roosevelt and Halsted. Which way now?"

He said, "We're in Jewtown all right. Just go down Halsted to the corner of Maxwell. This is Saturday night. Our holy host should be on the corner giving the sinners hell."

I parked at the curb on Halsted facing the northwest corner of Maxwell, less than fifteen feet away. I let my window down. I left the motor and heater on. Three porcine gourmets stood in front of a Kosher hot dog joint gobbling Jewtown's famous delicacy.

There he was hopping about on the corner in a threadbare forest-green greatcoat. He looked like a monstrous happy frog bathing in the red pool of light shimmering from a battered steel-drum stove on the sidewalk. His huge maroon eyes were popping globes focused on the night sky. They seemed ready to explode from their black-rimmed sockets.

A dozen amen-ing shadows semicircled Josephus, transfixed in the bitter cold, watching him commune with the fearsome Son of God. He hurled his skeletal hands clutching a Bible toward heaven. His withered, yellow throat trembled as he hoarsely croaked his divine incantations.

His bald skull glistened in the flickering blaze.

"Oh, Sweet Jesus, I owe you so much, Sweet Jesus. Have mercy, Jesus, on all sinful disbelievers. Don't strike 'em dead, Jesus, before I get 'em ready for they heavenly home.

"Kind Jesus, you called me to heal the sick and afflicted. Wonderful Jesus, you drove the wine demon out of me. I ain't got no more desire.

"I got running water, Jesus. I don't worry when it rains no more. My roof don't leak. Sweet Jesus, you showed me how to make my livin' off what the white people throws away.

"Thank you, Jesus, I don't go outside no more to no privy. No more corn cobs, Lord; I got toilet paper. I don't ride no onery mule no more. I got a truck, Lord

"I know what you done for me, Lord. Thank you, Jesus. No more fat-back and beans seven days a—"

A gang of ragged black teenagers had come around the corner of Maxwell. They had stopped and stood staring at him. Then they descended on him like a Biblical plague and strangled his eulogy.

The biggest one kicked over the fiery drum. Glowing jewels of fire skittered across the ice-pocked sidewalk like enormous rubies flung from the mischievous hand of a colossus.

As they moved past the stricken preacher, the kicker screamed, "You shit-colored, square-ass poor mother-fucking junkman. Stop bullshitting the people. Ain't no God for Niggers. Fuck you and your peckerwood God in the ass, and fuck the Virgin Mary, too."

The preacher received an instant, foolish charge of divine courage. He shouted at the retreating backs of the mob, "You black crazy devils will burn in eternal hell. The Lord punishes evil blasphemers."

They turned as one and started back to him. Blue opened the door on his side.

He said, "Folks, you got that button? Those Mau Mau are going to maim our damn-fool host."

I reached under the seat and got the fake detective badge. Blue took out his wallet and pinned the shield to the inner leather. He got out fast and lumbered toward the preacher. I followed him. I left the Caddie's motor running.

The gang had almost reached Josephus cowering alone against a store window. The superstitious shadows had vanished into the bleak catacombs of Jewtown. The gang froze and then back-pedaled down the sidewalk.

Blue didn't need to flash the button. They were certain we were a detective team. Little doubt that I looked white to them. Blue weighed forty pounds more than my two hundred. He was only two inches shorter than my six feet four. The Mau Mau pounded out of sight.

At first even Josephus thought we were heat. His frog eyes leaped for the top of his head looking up at Blue. He nervously dabbed a dirty rag at twin ropes of snot dangling from his wide nostrils

He was startled by Blue's bull bulk looming up before him. In his alarm he performed a clumsy matador's veronica as his hips spun sideways. The rag fluttered in his hand like a tiny cape as he leaned away.

Then recognition gurgled in his throat. He threw himself forward and embraced Blue. Blue winked at me and hugged our hideout angel tightly.

Blue said, "How are you and Bertha Mae?"

Josephus stepped out of the clinch, looked heavenward and said, "Blue, we doing fine, thank you. We still in love. Don't the Lord work in mysterious ways his wonders to perform? It's been over five years since I seen you right on this corner. He sent you to drive Satan's imps away. I'm going to pray and give thanks to Jesus. Let's bow our heads."

Blue said, "Reverend Joe, I have no objections to prayer. But suppose we go to your place now. We'd like to stay at your place for a day or so. I've got an urgent matter to take up with you. We're in trouble. Reverend, this is Johnny O'Brien, Phala's boy."

He said, "Pleased to make your acquaintance, son."

I said, "Reverend, it's a pleasure."

Then he gave me a long look and said, "I think I remember you as a lad around Thirty-ninth Street. Many nights I used to see you standing outside the cabaret waiting for your mama. But I knew your mother well. Have faith and pray. Only Jesus can help her. Believe in His power, and He will cast out the demons in her poor head."

I said, "Reverend, it's much too late for that. She died in Forty-five."

Blue took him urgently by the arm and steered him toward the car. I followed them. Three dapper white men passed slowly by in a dark sedan. They turned swarthy cruel faces and glared at us.

Blue's steps faltered. Wild currents revved up my heartbeat. Blue looked over his shoulder at me. His awful terror of the outfit shone in the phosphorescent whites of his eyes.

We got into the Fleetwood. The preacher sat between us. His eyes were closed. My foot trembled on the gas pedal. I cut the wheels sharply to the left. I was going to smash down on the pedal and bullet away in a U-turn if the sedan came back. Blue and I stared through the windshield until the sedan's taillights became harmless red pinpoints in the distance. I inflated my cheeks with air and blew out in relief.

Blue said, "Reverend Joe, do you live in the same house?"

Joe said, "Yes, indeedy. Just turn right on Fourteenth Place and go to Newberry, then turn left. It's the two story white house in the middle of the block. It ain't no mansion, but thank Jesus it's mine and Bertha Mae's.

"I got a big shed in the backyard. A big fine car like this wouldn't last long on these streets. These slick Jewtown thieves could pick it clean as a chitlin' in half an hour. They ain't going to bother with my old truck."

I pulled around the corner and drove to the middle of

the block. No one would possibly imagine that Joe's house could be the hideout for two fast grifters. It was a nineteenth-century cadaver, hacked hideous by weather and time. The ancient white paint on the brownstone had rotted away in scabby slabs. The scarred relic was leaning crookedly toward us as I turned into the alley beside it. I drove to the back of it and started to turn into the backyard.

The Reverend said, "Son, let me out and pull up the alley a piece. I'll put my old truck on the street. Wait for me at the back door."

Blue let him out and got back in. I cut into the backyard and backed twenty feet up the alley. My headlights beamed on the Reverend just as he went into the black maw of the shed.

We heard the asthmatic wheezing of the elderly engine when the Reverend tried to start it.

Blue said. "I sure hope Jesus starts that wreck for him. This Fleetwood has a bitch of a need for cover. Now listen, Folks, when we get inside, I'll handle the tale of our troubles. A ding-a-ling like him might spook out on us if the tale isn't, as you always say, a glove-fit. Chumps prefer a beautiful lie to an ugly truth."

The truck finally stuttered to a clanking roar. The Reverend backed it out and went down the alley to the street. I pulled the Fleetwood into the shed and cut the lights and engine. Blue and I got out and walked to the tunnel blackness at the back door.

The hot, sexy voice of Billy Daniels torched faintly through the chilling air. He was singing *Old Black Magic*. I looked up into a second-floor bedroom window across the alley. The shade was up. I nudged Blue.

A naked yellow dame was standing beside a dresser near the window. In the light from the lamp on the dresser we saw her grinning and talking to someone out of our sight. She took a drink from a tall glass. She backed up to the dresser. She put her palms on it. Then she leaped up to a sitting position on the dresser top.

She jackknifed her curvy legs. She held her wide-apart thighs against her fat breasts with her hands. She scooted her massive rear-end to the edge of the dresser and leaned her back against the mirror.

Blue said, "That filthy slut is posing for dirty pictures. I wonder what the hell is keeping Joe. I'm freezing to death."

A milk-white barrel-chested giant hulked into view. His great biceps rippled as he adjusted his long blond wig. Huge shiny earrings dangled to his rouged cheeks. He reached and got a chair and sat down in front of the dame.

He leaned forward and put his elbows on his thighs. He supported his big ugly head in his cupped hands. He just sat there, gazing into the wondrous valley of womanhood that was, alas, painfully absent in him.

I said, "Blue, that bird ain't no photographer."

Blue said, "Folks, a freakish jack-off like that should be stroked with a barbed-wire club, then tarred and feathered."

I said, "Now, Blue, what the hell is so horrible about that pitiful jerk aching to be a fluff? Dames have the best of it, you know."

CHAPTER FIVE

The Voice of Satan Cons the Preacher

There was a fumbling rattle at the back door. We turned away from the scene across the alley. A pale river of yellow light suddenly flooded the darkness. Reverend Josephus stood in the doorway pressing an index finger against his lips. We went by him into a soot-stained kitchen reeking of stale collard greens.

He shut the door and whispered, "Bertha Mae is been feeling mighty cranky of late. Ain't no sense to have her up running her mouth and asking about our goings on. 'Course, I'm the boss of this house. You just follow me. We'll go to the back bedroom upstairs to talk."

He pulled a long piece of greasy string hanging from a bald light bulb in the cracked ceiling. The yellow light winked out. He stepped through an arch and started up a rickety stairway.

We followed in the dim glow from a wall light at the top of the musty stairs. We passed a half-opened toilet door as we went down the upstairs hallway on our way to the rear bedroom. In the distance behind me I heard Bertha Mae snoring in guttural growls.

The Reverend went in and pulled another string. An amber light came on. Blue and I stepped inside. We stood looking around the curtainless room. Ragged shades hung at two windows facing the backyard. A lopsided bunk-bed sat near the windows on a mildewed gray carpet.

I saw my funhouse image in a shattered dresser mirror, spiderwebbed beneath a faded picture of a savage Christ, cat-o'-nining the terrified grifters down the temple steps. The peeling purple wallpaper was smallpoxed by gray grime. It was going to be a helluva long pleasant weekend.

Blue and I took off our hats and coats and threw them across the top bunk-bed. Reverend stood in the middle of the room with that big question in his eyes.

He said, "What trouble you in, Blue? You ain't still robbing honest people on the carnival wheel, is you? Bertha Mae and me can't shelter no crooks. The Lord would strike us dead."

Blue said, "You haven't heard? Johnny and I are in the restaurant business. I've repented my evil ways. Say, Reverend Joe, I have a call to make. Do you have a phone?"

Reverend said, "I got the same phone and number I had five years ago. I give it to you on my preaching corner. But you ain't never called like you promised. It's on a table down that hall from the kitchen. You ain't making no long-distance call is you, Blue?"

Blue said, "No, it's just to the Southside."

Blue walked toward the doorway. He looked over his shoulder and said, "Reverend Joe, I wouldn't dare double-cross the Lord."

I heard Blue's fourteens slugging the stairs. The Reverend stood looking up at me in a strange way.

He said, "Johnny, excepting for your mouth, you don't look much like Phala. She sure had a beautiful angel-face. She were that teasing color of them half-chink gals that got white pappies. I were the bar porter in that cabaret where she danced until I got fired for nipping from the bar bottles. She used to talk about your paw. To the end, she thought he were coming back to her. She were my friend.

"She used to slip me coins for my wine when I couldn't ketch up to Blue. All them no-account nigger hustlers and winos around Thirty-Ninth and Cottage was just aching to fool around with Phala. But she'd put her pretty nose in the air and pass 'em like the dirt they was.

"They know'd she'd married a white man and they hated her proudness. Oh, son, I could have saved her from those sinful imps. But I were stinking drunk in the lobby of the flea-bag where they abused her."

He stopped talking to wipe at his tears with his sleeve. I had never found out how Phala had been tricked and mass raped. Blue had heard what had happened that early morning, but I could never get him to go into detail.

I said, "Reverend, tell me just what happened. Don't worry, I'm numb after twenty years. I won't be hurt to hear about it."

He said, "It's a awful story. Everybody on them streets know'd what happened to your mama that morning. One of them slick hustlers eased up beside her at the bar just before closing time.

"Phala was drinking and tired. She didn't see the pill go in her glass. Two of them dirty niggers carried her out to the back door of the flea-bag across the street. They had rented a back room on the alley for the night. They say that cold-hearted nigger what owned the cabaret just grinned when she were carried out. He were glad because she'd never let him have her.

"When them devils finished they rotten fun, they went in them streets for blocks around. They told all the tramps and winos about your beautiful mama laid helpless and naked in that room.

"They say them dogs went in and out of there until daybreak. 1 were sobering up in a chair near the lobby window. I heard the pitiful screams of a woman. Then your mama came running by.

"She were naked as the day she were born. Her belly and thighs was caked white with jism. She were cutting herself bloody with her fingernails. I guess she were trying to scrape them niggers' filth off her. She had woke up and know'd by the stink what had happened.

"I ain't never going to forget her face. Johnny, her eyes was twice bigger and she tored hunks of hair from out her head. I stumbled to my feet to ketch her. But she were running too quick.

"The last I seen, she were going down Cottage Grove, screaming her heart out. The Lord is surely just, though. The sneaking nigger who put that pill in her glass got his throat cut the week after. Forgive me, son, for not being in shape to save her."

I put my hand on his shoulder. I said, "Reverend, don't feel guilty. I can't blame you. Thanks for telling me the whole story. I don't have to wonder now."

My legs were shaky. I sat down on the couch. I wiped the sweat off my palms with my handkerchief. I wondered for the ten-thousandth time since that night when it happened if the awful guilt were mine.

If I just had gone home when I got off from the theatre, I would have been there outside the cabaret to walk Phala home as always. Then for the ten-thousandth time I told myself it had had to happen to her.

It wasn't really my fault. It would have happened at some other time and place. I heard Blue coming slowly up the stairs. His face was tense when he came through the doorway. I guessed that Cleo still wasn't home.

Blue stood and looked down at Reverend Joe. He said, "Reverend Joe, when is the last time you and Bertha got any news from down home in Vicksburg?"

Reverend's thumb and index finger seized and shimmied the tip of his bulby nose. He closed his eyes in deep thought. He raked his forty-dollar uppers against his bottom lip and sat down on the bottom bunk cross-legged.

He said, "My goodness gracious. We ain't writ or got a scratch from down there for mighty near ten years. All Bertha Mae's kin is long dead. My grandpaw, Isaac, passed away in Forty-eight. I got baptised with the Holy Ghost and the Fire. I ain't heard from them good-time niggers I grow'd up with in twenty years, near 'bout. Why you ask, Blue?"

Blue got to his feet and took the stage. He was in action to cinch our hideout until Monday noon. He stood before the Reverend with bowed head and narrowed eyes. His fists were clenched at his sides. He swung his head from side to side in anguish. He crashed his fists against his thighs and sobbed.

"Reverend Joe, I'm the biggest fool there ever was. I've

let my sympathy for one of our old hometown niggers get the Klan and the Mississippi police at my throat.

"I thought sure you and Bertha had heard about the Bigelow Brothers. You remember Sporty? His brother Bob got that hunk of watermelon out of your throat. You had almost choked to death. He blew air into your mouth and saved your life.

"It was just before I left home with the carnival. You, Bob and Sporty Richard were always great pals. My troubles started when I ran into Sporty on the Southside about three weeks ago.

"He had just hoboed to Chicago from down home. He was a sad sight and acted like a crazy man. I took him home with me to a bath and a hot meal.

"Sporty told me he and Bob were walking down the road. They were high as Georgia pines, heading home to their shack in the country. They saw a new Mercedes-Benz stalled on the roadside.

"They saw a beautiful young white girl sitting inside it. She was grinding the starter. Reverend Joe, they had to be two crazy, drunk, unlucky Niggers. They walked up to a white woman on a lonely road at two A. M. in the morning in Mississippi to offer help. Even half-wit Niggers would have run like hell from her even if she had been dying.

"She was big-shot Doctor Landry's daughter. He's a wheel in the Klan. Old Sporty and Bob stuck their heads through the car windows. Now you know neither of them would run second to King Kong in a beauty contest. Marva, that's her name, took one look at them, screamed and leaped from the car door on the other side.

"The idiots tried to hold her, to reason with her. She was quick and agile. She fought free of them, leaving Sporty holding her torn coat and dress in his stupid hands. They got cold sober when she raced down the highway shouting 'help' and 'rape.'

"Reverend, they found a hiding place that will bring back many memories to you. You can't have forgotten that cave we boys dug in thick woods on the old Buchanan

Plantation. Your grandpaw, Isaac, beat us almost senseless in that cave. He caught us nipping on the potato hooch we'd made. Remember, dear old friend?"

The Reverend had been straining forward, gnawing at his dirty fingernails. Tears were oozing from the corners of his sad maroon eyes.

He moaned, "Oh Lord have mercy! 'Course I remember. Oh, Blue! Did the Klan ketch Bob in the cave?"

Blue leaned down and placed his hands tenderly on the Reverend's shoulders for an instant. Then Blue said, "No, thank God, the Klan didn't find him. Sporty and Bob hid in that fearful darkness until almost daybreak. They didn't know where to turn. Finally Sporty decided their only hope was to swing onto a fast freight going North.

"Bob was paralyzed with fear. Sporty begged him to leave. Bob wouldn't budge. Sporty left him whimpering, huddled into a ball like an unborn baby in that black cave.

"Reverend Joe, to make a short story shorter, Sporty made it to the railroad line. He swung onto a northbound train and made it to Chicago.

"I got Bob's childhood sweetheart's address from Sporty. You know, Jessie, with the clubfoot and hazy mind? Jessie could get Bob's friends to go out there and get him to safety. I had the phone in my hands to have Western Union send the telegram. I was going to have Jessie call me right away, collect.

"Reverend Joe, someone or something snatched that phone from my hands. An unearthly voice started talking to me. It kept saying over and over, 'Blue, you don't want the Klan to get Bob. You know you can't trust any of those poor frightened black people to get Bob to freedom. Jessie can't be trusted with Bob's life. Blue, only you can save him. Go to him and rescue him. No harm will come to you.'

"I don't know who or what snatched that phone and talked to me. But, Reverend Joe, please believe me, it really hap—"

The Reverend cut off the tale. He leaped to his feet. He

threw his arms around Blue. The embrace locked Blue's arms to his sides. The Reverend was dancing an ecstatic little jig as he nested his face in Blue's chest.

Blue grinned and winked at me. I shook my head and smiled.

The Reverend raised his head from the nest. He looked up at Blue. His yellow face was radiant. His craggy features were softened, almost saintly.

He chirped joyously, "Blue, you big black fool! Ain't you got enough sense to know that were the Lord Hisself? Oh, praise His holy name! Thank You, precious Lamb! You touched a sinner with Your immortal spirit. Hallelujah, Jesus! Hallelujah!"

Blue took the Reverend gently by his shoulders and guided him backwards to his seat on the bunk. Blue had a smug look on his face as he stepped back.

He was approaching that stage in his tale that black grifters call the hook. White grifters call it the convincer. vincer.

When con is played for money alone, it's that point at which the sucker is hooked or convinced by actual or paper profits that he can reap a bonanza. Once on the hook, a sucker usually can't get off. But the buyer must believe the final decision to buy is his alone.

The Reverend had to believe at the end of the tale that the decision to hide us out was his. The Reverend's conscience had to be allowed to take over and buy Blue's tale.

Blue said, softly, "Reverend Joe, you have made me see the light. Johnny and I were on a divine mission when we went down South and brought Bob to Chicago. We borrowed an old but roadworthy Dodge from a friend. We got down there around dusk, two days after I tried to call Western Union. We went right to the cave.

"I put my flashlight on him. Bob covered his eyes and screamed. He thought we were the white mob come to lynch him. We carried him through the woods and fields to the Dodge. We got back to Chicago three days ago around eight P. M. I was proud and happy I had saved him. We were all safe, I thought.

"Johnny and I got up early the next morning and went to open our restaurant. That evening when we got home Sporty told me Bob had written Jessie to tell her where he was and how Johnny and I had driven down and rescued him. If Cleo, my wife, had not been with her sick mother, she would have stopped him.

"I was angry and worried. If they hadn't been half sick, with no place to go, I would have turned the stupid twins out then and there.

"Early Friday morning, Johnny and I were dressing to go to the restaurant. The doorbell rang. It was a telegram for Bob from Jessie. I tore it open.

"In crude code it said, 'Bad Landry rigmarole. Said you the ones. I'm praying for you both. Love, Jessie.'

"She was warning Bob that the white people were looking for him and Sporty for raping Marva Landry. Lying or not, Marva's charge could get them lynched.

"That white clerk at the Western Union office in Vicksburg had to be awfully drunk or careless. It was a miracle that the telegram had ever been sent from Vicksburg.

"Jessie, by now, was most likely in jail. The Mississippi police would have Bob's letter proving our part in his flight.

"Reverend Joe, no more than ten minutes after that telegram came all of us were out of the house. It wasn't too soon. In his rear-view mirror, Johnny saw two squad cars stop at our house.

"We drove to a friend's home who has big political connections. We needed advice and to get off the street. Our friend stayed on the phone for most of Friday and today. Finally, he told us he could clear us if we told him where the twins were hiding.

"Reverend Joe, I told my disgusted friend I just couldn't see them taken back to Mississippi. He was very angry. Tonight around ten, he ordered us from his house. We didn't know where to go until I remembered you. And here we are."

Suddenly, Blue clapped his palms against his ears. He twisted and pounded them against the side of his head in a savage ritual of mental agony. He pointed his chin at the ceiling.

I heard a creaky pop as he wobbled his head around like a punchy pug loosening up before the phantom clang of an inner gong. The hook, the convincer was in play. By whatever name, its purpose was the same. The Reverend's mouth was an awed chasm.

Then, in tinny tones of an amateur ventriloquist's dummy, Blue said, "Think of yourself, Blue. You're sixty-seven years old. Why stick your neck out? Call the police and turn in those no-good niggers. They're not worth the money you plan to spend Monday to get them out of the country.

"I know Bob Bigelow worries you. You can't forget his one noble deed. You feel you're in his debt. You don't owe him anything. He didn't save your life. Turn them in and enjoy what's left of your life."

Then in his true voice, Blue said, "Thank you, Lord, for guiding me again."

Like a sleepwalker Blue went to the bed. He got our coats and hats. He walked over to me. I took my hat and coat. I rose from the couch and put them on. I helped Blue put on his.

The Reverend sat there staring at us. We weren't worried. Reverend was like a bloody barroom brawler, too excited in the fray to feel the pain right away of the knife in his back. We walked toward the doorway.

The delayed pain of Blue's hook struck and wrenched a cry of anguish from Reverend Joe. He propelled himself from the bunk. He charged past me and grabbed Blue's arm and spun him around. His eyes were wild.

He shouted, "Satan's trying to trick you. That ain't the Lord's voice you heard. Satan's trying to fool you into hell. You got sense enough to know that were Satan lying when he told you I ain't caring for my friend that saved my life.

"He knows the Lord ain't never going to allow you in heaven if you betray our friends in need. I ain't going to let you do it. You ain't going nowhere. The Lord will forgive the vilest sinner and take him to his bosom.

"I ain't going to let you leave here until Monday. Blue, the Lord ain't going to let no harm befall you here. He knows, just like Satan, that you planning to get them boys away. You'll be blessed when you do."

Blue shrugged him off.

He said, "Reverend Joe, I'm afraid to stay. That voice I heard was the same voice I heard when that phone was snatched from my hands. I can't afford to disobey the Lord. Johnny, what do you think?"

I said, "Blue, I just don't know. I know the devil is pretty clever. He bamboozled Adam and Eve into the original sin. Reverend Joe's word can be trusted. Let's stay here in the safe hands of Reverend Josephus and Jesus."

Blue said, "Johnny, maybe you're right. I love Reverend Josephus and trust his judgement."

Reverend said, "Praise the Lord. Good night, friends."

He walked from the room.

I took off my suit-coat and shoes. I couldn't get Phala off my mind. I kept thinking about the filth and her screaming and all. I put my coat on the couch. I loosened my tie and sprang to the top bunk. I didn't turn the blanket back. If bedbugs were there I didn't want to see them.

For a long moment I stared through the doorless entrance to the bedroom. The tiny wall light gave the hallway the murky dimness of a mortuary slumber-room.

Blue's bulk shook the bed when he lay down. I didn't want to talk. We lay there in the shadows. I listened to Blue's heavy breathing for a long time.

Finally he said, "I wonder why the hell Cleo isn't home yet? God! I hope those torturers haven't got her!

"Son, life is like a crazy crap game. I'm like a sucker who gets a long run of good luck. Then the dice turn against him. The silly creep had conned himself. He had thought his good luck run was all due to his big brain.

"The bubble bursts and the chump finds himself broke and in a gutter. I'm not broke. But think of it—I had to con that square bastard until I got hoarse, just to stay in this pigsty for a weekend.

"At this moment I'm wishing my ass off that I had stayed down South. What the hell good did it do me to leave there and try to improve myself?

"Goddamnit! I taught myself to read and write, and speak fair English. I had a horror of winding up like the ignorant niggers I grew up with. Tonight I had to kiss the black ass of one of those same niggers I've held in contempt. I've come a full, funky circle, Folks."

I said, "Blue, you've really had it tough, haven't you? Even though your mother and father died in your teens, at least, Blue, you had a taste of happy home life.

"I barely remember my father. The weak white sonuvabitch fled back to his white world after his hot yen for a nigger body went cold.

"Your mother's heart died. My mother's brain withered. She died a drooling mental cripple. The first time I went to see her she tried to snatch my balls off.

"So, Blue, I could get a license to bellyache. You're lucky to be jet black. What if you had been a racial freak like me?

"It isn't exactly a happy limbo to be a white Nigger in a black world driven paranoid by a white world to hate white skin. But, pal, I'm thankful you came North. I would have been a lost ball in high weeds without you. Say, shouldn't you call home again?"

Blue said, "I think I will."

The bed creaked and he stood up. He was a blank silhouette in the near darkness.

He said, "Folks, you're right about my limited advantage in having black visibility. I know you've shown raw heart for all your life in this black world.

"But now you can turn that white skin into an advantage I've been denied. You're still young; I'm old. You don't need me. When we get out of Chicago, go across that invisible steel fence and pass as one of the privileged.

"Folks, you'll have lots of company. I wouldn't be shocked to learn that several millions of white Niggers just like you are in that sweet garden of opportunity on that other side.

"It's really kind of comical when you think about it. I can almost see those Niggers squirming and suffering at their interracial breakfast tables. Even in the executive suites of some of America's most honored corporations, those white fakes get hot flashes at that word nigger. Of course, some of the fakes don't quake. They revel in secret glee at the epithet.

"Their lives are booby trapped with the constant terror of exposure. But a fin will get a C-note that for them the reward outweighs the tensions.

"Don't be a sucker, son. All the milk and honey is on the other side of this hell."

He glided through the bedroom doorway. I lay there hoping Cleo was home. I wondered how I could phrase the truth about her to Blue. Then I thought about his determination to take her with us. No, he'd be immune no matter how I phrased it.

I heard Bertha's growls lengthen in sequence. I hoped she wouldn't awaken. I couldn't stand a repeat of Blue's cave tale. I couldn't understand how Reverend could get a wink of sleep so close to the guttural muzzle of Bertha's snoring.

I heard muffled thudding, perhaps like a runt elephant stomping on a bale of cotton. It was Blue stocking-footing it up the stairway. He came in and fell into the bunk.

He said, "I didn't get an answer. I let it ring a dozen times. I don't understand it. I tried to call Felix. He's probably at a poker game.

"It's after midnight. I called the Sutherland Hotel Lounge. Ray Charles is there, I think. She'd go a hundred miles to hear him. I got her paged. No dice.

"There's a big dance in Robbins. She could be there. Anyway, I'm going to make one more call at three. I'm going to that Southside if she's not home then. I have to know what's wrong. Like I told you, I can't leave without her."

I started to point out the obvious danger for him. But then I thought about the flaming passion I had felt for the Goddess.

Perhaps if I were in Blue's spot, and it were the Goddess over there, I'd be chump enough to risk my own life. I decided to soothe him. The odds were long against it, but maybe I could still get an angle later to persuade him to leave town and send for her.

I said, "There's nothing to worry about. I'm sure she'll be there at three. If she's not, you could slip to the Southside in Reverend's truck. Or you could let Fixer find her for you. Wait until three like you said. No point in getting upset about the unknown. Only suckers do that."

He said, "I'm not the worrying kind. I just want to get her off the Southside before daybreak. I want to keep my promise to you, that we leave Chicago on schedule."

We lay there, two slick grifters at bay. We had a load of spending money. But it couldn't buy us a clean bed.

CHAPTER SIX

Tears for a Lost Drum

Bertha had stopped snoring. The tomb silence was broken by the rapid throbbing of a car engine. I could hear tires gnashing their rubber teeth against the gritty alley floor. The car screeched to a halt. The engine idled.

Then I heard the faint thumping of a jazz drummer from the car's radio playing counterpoint to the presto racing of my heart beat. Was it Nino out there in the alley? Had he found some way to trace us?

I sat up. I had started to swing my leg over the bunk rim. I was going to the window to look out on the alley. Then I sank back to the bunk in relief. The car throbbed away down the alley.

For some strange reason, I couldn't forget the sound of that drum. I wondered why. I tried to turn my mind from it. It was no use. Then I closed my eyes and let my mind grope back through the past. Perhaps it could make some kind of connection there.

Then the painful reason why the sound of that drum was so insistent came in a blinding burst of chrome! The connnection lay, not in a sound, but in pictures! On the screen behind my closed eyes, I saw once again that glittery, elusive drum. . . .

I saw the featureless image of the blond giant striding through the hazy doorway. I felt again the transient, joyful fear in the pit of my stomach when the shadow hurled me into the air. He'd catch me and squeeze his cheek against mine.

At his feet would be the drum. I heard Phala's cries of happiness as she rushed into the visitor's arms.

I heard her soft sobbing moans behind her bedroom

door. I saw me so lonely, amusing myself making faces in the gleaming trim of the drum.

I felt an aching boulder of tension roll and tumble inside my chest when I saw me waking up the next morning. I rushed frantically through the apartment.

I couldn't find it anywhere! The drum! That mute, shiny drum was gone again.

Phala tried to blink back her tears. I got in her lap and we bawled together, because the drum was gone. One day the drum did come and never came again.

The pictures were becoming more vivid. Spinning on the reel of memory, back to Kansas City, Missouri. It was perhaps like the total recall that a dying man might experience.

Shortly after the drum left for the last time, Phala's loneliness and heartbreak became real to me.

There were blond white men, many of them, in drunken succession. But no drum. They brought bottles, and far into the night I'd lie awake listening to Phala's wild sad laughter.

I was a little past three years of age My terrible crying seizures started. I'd cry until I threw up. Sometimes Phala would hear me above the clamor of the drunken revelry.

She'd come to me in the darkness. I'd be holding my testicles. She'd turn on the light and look. My testicles would be swollen to big sore lumps from my bitter crying.

It's a strange thing, I don't ever remember calling my mother anything except P.G. to her face. The G was for Grisby, her maiden name. She hadn't liked it. She'd begged me to call her mama. She'd threatened, and even tried to bribe me. Finally she gave up.

In Nineteen Twenty-six she became a waitress-hostess. She was eighteen years old. She had a magnificent body and an Eurasian appearance. Silky clouds of jet hair floated to her twenty-inch waist. She'd found it easy to get work in the wooly Roaring-Twenties nightspot in Kansas City, Missouri.

Later, in my teens, she told me how she had run away

from her home in the country outside of New Orleans. She'd left her father and mother, one sister and four brothers.

She got work as a waitress in a Rampart Street gumbo house. My father and several other white musicians came there one early morning from Bourbon Street. My father was half drunk. He was stricken foolish at the wondrous sight of Phala. He was stone drunk that same week when he actually married my ravishing fourteen-year-old mother. He was twenty-five.

When his gig on Bourbon Street played out, he and Phala went to Kansas City. Phala said he was a good drummer when sober. His trouble was he couldn't stay sober for long.

A second-rate band took him on in Kansas City. The band toured the country, doing one-night stands. Phala got pregnant with me shortly after. John Patrick O'Brien, Jr. was born January fifteenth, Nineteen Twenty-three.

My father had drummed for three bands by the time I was three. Somehow, despite his drinking, he managed to keep food in our mouths and a roof over our heads. He came to see us only when his band was playing near Kansas City.

When he came, it was usually for only overnight. Then he didn't come at all. Phala told me later he had fallen in love with a wealthy white girl and was living common law with her in the East.

Phala loved him too much to get a divorce. She always hoped he'd come back to us. Maybe I'm better off that he never came back. He might have made a drummer out of me. At least as a con man I could give my brain a play.

Yes, Phala really needed her waitress-hostess job. But there was one awful drawback. Phala would leave me in the care of a young couple when she left in the evenings for work.

They lived in a decrepit frame house next door to our apartment building. Many times they left me alone. I would go to a front window and watch for Phala. I'd leap with joy when finally she came home in the early morning.

One night I had been deserted by the fun-loving black couple. I was keeping a terrified vigil at the window. I fingered an old-fashioned window spring. It was attached to a sharp hook screwed into the window sill.

The hook slashed into the fleshy tip of my thumb and went to the bone. I remember how I tried, in vain, to twist the thumb free from the fish hook sharpness. I remember pounding on the window with my free hand.

None of the dusky passersby heard it. They were perhaps too enchanted by the magnetic pull of the bright festival of cabaret neon at Kansas City's famous Eighteenth and Vine Streets, a block away.

Finally I was exhausted by my thrashing agony. I fell asleep on my knees at the window. That hook gouged a scar that I'll take to my grave.

It was about six months after my musician father and his drum had gone for the last time that a wonderful thing happened. Phala brought Grandma Annie home with her. She was a four-foot-tall, eighty-pound bundle of pure love and kindness.

Her face had the look of a cheerful prune, topped with kinky whipped cream. She was an ex-slave from Georgia. She admitted to ninety-five years of life. Allowing for the certain female shrinkage in this painful area, she was possibly well past the century mark.

In any case, except for cataracted vision and a hobbled pair of feet brutally bunioned by sheer mileage, she was a marvel of physical preservation and mental clarity.

During slavery, as a girl, she had been taught to read and write by a mulatto house Nigger. After slavery, she had gone to Ohio and married. She and her husband built a rough cabin in the wilderness.

It was there that she over the years had taught hundreds of poor, ignorant freed slaves her magic secrets of reading and writing. The tuition? Hogs, poultry, grain and other currency of the soil.

Phala had brought her home when lame Grandma

Annie was fired from one of the cabaret kitchens on Vine Street. She slept in my bedroom. I slept on the sofa.

Less than a month after she came, she had started me to read. She prepared a large chart upon which she'd printed a legend in tall letters. It read, "My name is Johnny O'Brien. I am not a baby. I am a boy. Babies cry. I will try not to cry when Mommy goes to work."

I clung desperately to the sweet miracle of Grandma Annie. My crying stopped. My loneliness vanished into the fairyland of Mother Goose, Pinocchio, and all the other adventures related nightly to me by Annie.

I followed constantly in the crisp, whispery wake of her starched, old-fashioned, bustled skirts, hemlined below her ankles. Annie was also a good influence for Phala. No more loud-mouth white men with bottles came to call.

It was Nineteen Twenty-nine, the year of the great stock-market crash and I was six years old. That year my brief shelter of contentment collapsed.

Grandma Annie had been helping me with my school lessons. I fell asleep. She had been sitting in an easy chair beside the sofa. I woke up hours later to go to the bathroom. There was Annie, still sitting stiffly erect in the chair with her eyes open.

I'll never forget my panic when I called her name. She didn't move. She just sat there like a black zombie, silently staring through me.

I touched her knee. It was cold and hard through her skirt. I jumped up screaming her name. I shook her. She tumbled to the carpet. Her frail body lay there, open eyed, in the same frozen sitting position it had had in the chair. Her soft kindly chimpanzee face was harsh in death.

I cried myself dry of tears. She was still stiff dead there on the floor when Phala got home at eight that morning. I was asleep beside my Grandma Annie, the kindest friend I've ever known. Phala couldn't afford to bury her. The city disposed of the body.

CHAPTER SEVEN

The Big Cruel Windy

The time until we moved to Chicago is a dismal, tearful blur. We moved into a furnished ten-unit slum apartment building. It was at Thirty-ninth Street and Cottage Grove Avenue on the Southside. I was eight years old. Our apartment had running rats and water.

It had a bedroom and a bathroom. The kitchen we shared with legions of cockroaches. At that we were blessed. Hundreds in Chicago had no place to live.

Every Saturday night some guy in the building would beat his woman. The screams were awful. Many times on the morning after, I'd notice dried blood in the hallways and on the stairs.

Phala scrubbed every inch of our apartment with a solution of raw lye. Still a rank odor clung to it. I don't think anything can kill the singular stink of an old slum apartment. It's everlasting fixatives perhaps are in the decayed urine in the kitchen-sink pipes.

Perhaps the very pores of the walls have held the sharp stenches of cancer pus and tubercular phlegm from the rotted lungs of perpetual paupers who have perished there, unnoticed, unmourned.

A tidal wave of poverty had flooded the country. Phala took a job as a domestic in River Forest, Illinois, a plush white suburb of Chicago.

There were at least ten to twelve youngsters my age who lived in our building. I was to enroll in school that fall. I was lonesome. I tried several times to join little groups of my neighbors playing on the front stoop and in the hallways. Each time they would break up and move away from me.

One day I saw a band of them playing blackjack for matches. I approached them. They looked up at me wide-eyed. They started to move away.

I said, "My name is Johnny O'Brien. I'd like to play cards with you. I live in apartment seven. Is it okay if I play?"

The lanky black leader of the clique scooped up the deck from the hall floor. The others snatched their matches and stuffed the wooden stakes into their pockets. He gave me an evil slit-eyed look.

He said, "You is a trick baby. My paw whup my ass, I play wid you."

The young gamblers scrambled up and raced for the sidewalk. They chanted over their shoulders, "You is a nasty trick baby. You is a nasty trick baby."

I burst into tears. I didn't know what a trick baby was supposed to be. I cried at their rejection. I couldn't wait for Phala to come home that night. I went down to the streetcar stop and waited for her. She had scarcely stepped off the streetcar when I tugged at her sleeve.

I said, "What is a trick baby, P.G.?"

She was startled like I had cursed at her. She stopped on the sidewalk. Her mouth was a thin, tight line. She held me by the shoulders and looked down at me for a long moment.

Then she said, "Who said that word? Where did you hear it, Johnny?"

I was really bewildered then. I had hoped all day that it had been just nonsense.

I said, "A bunch of kids in the building called me a nasty trick baby today. What does it mean, P.G.?"

She didn't answer. Her eyes glistened as she squeezed me close. We walked home silently through the steamy July night. I sensed my question had no easy answer. I didn't press it.

Two of the blackjack players were on the front stoop. They tittered as we passed them on the way to the third floor. We sat in our smelly combination bedroom-living room on a battered couch.

Phala sighed deeply. She leaned forward and cupped my face in her palms. Her breath was heavy with whiskey odor. I looked down at her open purse at the side of the couch. The shiny neck of a whiskey bottle flashed inside it. She moved her head from one side to the other like a puzzled robin. She always did that under emotional stress.

She said, "Honey, don't let what they called you upset you. Because it's a lie, Johnny. It means a very bad thing. If it was true, then I would be a dirty woman who goes to bed with men for money. You wouldn't really know who your father was. Do you understand, Johnny?"

I said, "P.G., I understand what you said. But why did they say it when it's a lie?"

She said, "Even they didn't know why they said it. They heard the ugly name from their mamas and papas. Johnny, it's so hard for Mother to explain the way I should. It all has to do with your white skin and blue eyes.

"You see, honey, this world is really two worlds. The white world and the black world we're in now. If mother had married a black man, you wouldn't look white. Then those boys would love you as one of them.

"If we lived in the white world and you had a black face, then the white kids would hate and tease you with hateful words. It's not the kids, black or white, to blame. It's their mamas and papas poisoning their young minds with ugly hate for skin colors.

"Johnny, you have to be strong and proud. Don't let hate and ugliness tear you down. Mother's going to send you to college, if it's the last thing I do on this earth. You'll be grown and educated with the brains to do your part to change things.

"Don't hate your father. His parents disowned him when he married me. Their hate ruined him and made him weak. He really loved us, Johnny. The ugly outside pressure was just too much for him to bear.

"Johnny, I have an older sister right here in Chicago. She owns a big white stone apartment building near the

corner of Garfield Boulevard and Calumet. She made a lot
of money selling bootleg whiskey.

"Guess why we never visited her? She's hated me all her
life. She has color poisoning. She's dark brown skin like my
mother. She hates me because I'm light skinned like papa.
When we were girls, she always felt I thought I was better
than her. It wasn't true, Johnny. I tried so hard to make
her love me.

"Anyway, who knows, maybe your father will come
back one day for us and take us into his world? With him
to back me up, I could pass easy over there.

"I borrowed you real T-bone steak and mushrooms from
Mrs. Goldstein's icebox. Let's eat supper and go to bed.
Mother's got to get up at five-thirty tomorrow morning."

I lay sleepless until almost daybreak on my couch-bed.
All of what she'd said was too darkly deep for an eight-
year-old brain to fathom. I fell into nightmare sleep. The
small boys became mammoth black monsters. They
screamed down at me in a thunderous chorus.

"Nasty trick baby! Nasty trick baby!"

Their teeth were white fangs bared in their angry faces.
I was frightened and ashamed.

I shouted, "I'm not! I'm not! I know who my father is!"

I was about to burst inside with the tensions of my
frustration. My tormentors couldn't hear my pleas of
innocence. My voice was drowned out in the fury of their
condemnation. Then in the dream, I felt a sudden glad
relief.

My hands turned black. Just as suddenly the huge
creatures smiled. They cheered for me and lifted me high
into the air. They carried me aloft on their shoulders like I
was a hero football star who had scored a crucial touch-
down. I cried with joy.

The friendly sea of black faces turned white and hostile.
Rough hands threw me down, down ... I lay on my back,
looking up at the circle of terrible faces. I shrieked in
terror. The white giants towered above me. They raised
their spiked feet high above my face.

They shouted, "Black nigger! Black nigger!" Before the avalanche of spikes could pulp my face I woke up in sweaty, near delirium.

Phala didn't hear my cries of distress. She had gone to work. A square of white paper was pinned to the couch above my eyes.

It read, "Honey, there's a quarter on the table. Get some neckbones and put the navy beans on for lunch. Get some pop with what's left. Please don't worry, Johnny, darling. Mama loves you very much."

I enrolled in school that fall in the third grade. My social luck changed. Right there in my own class I found a pal my age. He was Lester Gray.

Years later, he'd enjoy brief fame as Livin' Swell, con man, dope peddler.

He looked like a huge eight-ball with steel pipestems for legs and arms. His voice was gruff like a man's. His jolly face was welded to his roly-poly body by an amazingly short, thick neck.

His long coarse eyelashes shadowed the deeply set very light brown eyes, lurking in their black deep sockets. When he was excited or angry, the eyes would blaze eerily like tawny brutes raging in their cages.

He lived on Thirty-seventh Street in Chicago, with foster parents. When he was six, his father had shot his mother through the heart in a jealous frenzy. He saw the whole thing. The only time I ever saw him cry was when he told me about it. His old man got life in Joliet Prison. The second day at school our friendship was sealed.

I walked out the school door to go home several blocks away. A gang of boys blocked the sidewalk. They started cursing me and punching me around. I wrapped my arms around my head to block the blows.

Then I heard screams of pain from my attackers. I peeped out through the barricade. Lester was flailing hell out of them with an old bicycle chain. Lucky for me he had a soft spot for underdogs.

We were bosom buddies from that day. He was a slick

thief at his tender age. We stole goodies from groceries
and delicatessens. At twelve we branched out.

We would ride the elevated trains on nights Phala gave
me permission to stay overnight at his house. I watched
him pick the pockets of tired, sleeping commuters. It
wasn't long before I had mastered the art.

We were so talented, or lucky, that we never had a beef
or an arrest. I'd buy clothes and tell Phala Lester let me
wear them. She thought his father was a clothing salesman.

Phala had quit domestic work. She was doing an exotic
dance at a dingy cabaret on Cottage Grove near Drexel
Boulevard. She was drinking heavily, both on the job and
at home. There were piles of empty Old Crow whiskey
bottles throughout the apartment and on the back porch.
Phala never felt like cleaning the house anymore. I did the
best I could at cleaning. It stayed awfully dirty.

Phala's neat waistline had thickened. Her once low,
creamy voice was louder and coarsened by whiskey. She
was still unusually attractive. She was a fixture at the
cabaret.

She'd spend a long time at the mirror preparing her face
for work. It took a thick mask of makeup to hide the
ravages of time and whiskey on her face.

We hadn't moved from our apartment. I can't forget
that summer in Nineteen Thirty-seven. I was fourteen and
six feet tall. I had a girl friend named Minnie Franklin.
We met on an el.

We had been going steady for about six months. She
was a beautiful yellow-skinned girl. We went on double
dates with Lester and his girlfriend.

We went to amusement parks and movies. Then we'd all
go to my couch-bed when Phala was away. Minnie wore
honeysuckle perfume. My bed would be fragrant with it
long after she'd gone.

She lived in a middle class neighborhood near Sixty-
second Street and Woodlawn Avenue on Chicago's Southside. I never met her parents. She was afraid to introduce

me. She said her mother was okay. But her father hated white people. She was certain her father would have a stroke if he ever saw my white face. So we took our torrid young love affair underground.

In midsummer Lester and I let the operator of a shine stand on Thirty-ninth Street con us into making an honest dollar.

Right away I figured an angle. The boss would come in the evening to check us out. He was cagey and suspicious. He would use small wine bottle tops as polish containers. The contents of each would shine one pair of shoes, no more. When he came, first thing he'd count the empty bottle tops. Then he'd check the register.

We bought four cans of polish. Two black, two tan. We gathered a collection of our own bottle tops and filled them each day. We hid them behind the stand. If our boss had sent a spy in during the day, everything was always above board. The two hard-working boys would be shining from bottle tops.

It was that summer of Thirty-seven that cabaret life and whiskey really started getting to Phala. I got off from the shine stand around seven P.M. Phala would get to the mirror about that time. I had begged her to stop the drinking and the dancing job. It was no use.

During every summer vacation from school, I'd go at two A.M. and wait for her outside the cabaret where she danced, to take her home.

One night I had delivered several pairs of shoes to a gambler who lived on Drexel Boulevard. I was passing the dull red front of the cabaret where Phala danced.

I stopped and looked at the glamour stills of her. They were inside a cracked-glass case screwed into the concrete front. I stood staring at her paper image in the gaudy rhinestone G-string.

She seemed to be smiling sadly at me. Her lustrous black eyes were slumberous in professional sexiness. She looked so pitiful. It was like she was imprisoned there.

I had half turned to walk away toward home. Then I

saw it! A filthy legend and gigantic penis drawn in yellow chalk beneath the glass case.

"This is fucking good, eating pussy."

I went rigid. Anger, sorrow, and pity whirlpooled inside me. I spit on my palms and whimpered as I scrubbed the dirty legend into a yellow blur.

I cursed the unknown artist. "Black nigger bastard! Black sonuvabitching low-life mother-fucker!"

A small crowd gathered around me, awed. I smashed the heels of my palms into the glass. I freed the photographs. I ripped them to pieces with my bleeding hands. I threw the pieces to the sidewalk. Phala's decapitated head smiled innocently up at me from the littered sidewalk.

Blindly, I made it to the front of our building. There were exactly twenty-six steps to our door. I stood there for a long time gazing at the first of those tragic twenty-six.

I knew she'd be up there at the mirror. Her greeting would tear at my insides. I'd hear the whiskey slur in her voice. The thickness of that slur was always the measure of the emptiness of the always-present fifth of Old Crow whiskey.

I went slowly up the stairs to the front of our door. I was more sorrowful now than angry. I twisted my key in the lock and walked into the apartment. Her eyes were more tragic than ever in the mirror. Her greeting was thick and flat with Old Crow. She said, "Hi, babee. How is Mama's tall, pretty sweetheart?"

The sight of her and my love and pity kept my bitter, angry thoughts from my voice. I held my gashed palms away from her. I was afraid to let her suspect what violent emotion had exploded inside me down there on the street. I didn't want her to drink any more than she had. I walked to her and kissed her on the crown of her head.

I said, "I'm okay, P.G. How are you doing?"

I moved past her into the bathroom. I cleaned out the slivers of glass from the punctures of my palms. My wounded palms tingled as I sat on the couch and watched her put on her dancer's face.

She turned her head toward the bottle of Old Crow on the dresser top. She was facing me. She bent her head down toward the bottle. Her eyes were filmy. She was staring at the dapper crow on the paper label.

She said, "Now listen old black nigger crow. Ain't no use to roll your wicked eyes at me. I ain't young and tender any more. But you still ain't got a chance. You too black. If you white, you right. If you light, stick around. But if you black, get back, way back."

I got up from the couch. I eased the door open. I went out carefully and pushed it shut. I cried all the way to Lester's house.

I can't forget the summer of Thirty-seven for many reasons, all of them bad. In the middle of August, Minnie's parents sent her to Tampa, Florida, to stay with relatives.

They had gotten worried about her. We had over-sported our after-midnight sessions on the couch. The last of August Lester did a solo hustle after work in an el car. His intended mark was a transit cop.

Stouthearted Lester wouldn't hold still for the pinch. He weighed nearly a hundred and eighty pounds at fourteen. He was powerful enough to hospitalize the cop. A half dozen city police finally subdued him. He got an indeterminate sentence to Saint Charles Reform School.

CHAPTER EIGHT

White Lamb in the Black Jungle

I went back to school that fall. Life was very dull without Lester and the sweet, pulsatinng roundness of Minnie. I found a way to lick loneliness. I started to draw. Several of my school teachers praised my drawings. I got excited and bought a painting kit.

In the summer, when Phala felt like it, we would go to the beach and to Washington Park. She'd relax while I sketched her. Then many times, in the park, I'd put my head on her bosom. She'd stroke my head and croon me to sleep. Later at home I'd paint her. I was careful to paint her as she once was.

One sunny day she looked up at me from the grassy carpet. She said, "Johnny, promise me that when I die, you'll have me cremated. I dan't want to be lying old and ugly in a casket and have people seeing me like that."

I said, "Why talk about that now? You'll live to get a hundred and you'll always be beautiful."

By the spring of Nineteen Thirty-nine we had both changed a great deal since the old days. Phala was carrying one hundred and sixty pounds on her five-feet-four-inch frame.

Her once clear velvet skin was muddy and bumpy from her drinking excesses. They still whistled and gaped when she walked down the street. She was buxom with big hips and curvy legs. But all her freshness had vanished. At a distance she was still pretty. Close up, she looked old and haggard.

But then, perhaps, they hadn't known her when, as I had. I was in my last semester of high school. I was in the top ten of my class. Phala hadn't mentioned college for me in years. Her drinking hadn't let us save a dime.

I was lugging one hundred and seventy-five pounds on my six-feet-two-inch frame. I had been a reserve center on the Wendell Phillip High School basketball team. I played exactly one hundred and thirty minutes all of my senior year.

In the hundred yard dash I ran next to last in the city track meet. For some reason I wasn't much of an athlete—that's the guaranteed truth.

I had several acquaintances, but I had no real pal like Lester Gray. In June I graduated. I took an usher's job at the Regal Theatre near Forty-seventh Street and South Parkway. I was paid twelve dollars a week.

On July Sixth the flimsy bottom of my life dropped out. I was at work that afternoon. I was scorching for a tiny doll-faced girl. She had come to see a stage show that matinee. I had persuaded her to stay in the theatre until I got off.

I took the pocket-size creature posthaste to the Manor House Hotel down the street from the theatre. She proved more interesting than even my fevered imagination. I could have been arrested for possession of the pictures I drew of her.

It was four A. M. before I got home. Phala wasn't there. At first I was worried. Then I remembered the young white cab driver. He had been sniffing after Phala for a couple of weeks.

Several times at two A. M. I'd left alone from in front of the cabaret. Phala and the young cabby would come out arm and arm on their way to some after-hours-spot. She liked him even though he was only twenty-two or so. He was tall and blond. With Phala, he had a lot going for him.

I figured she had gone somewhere with him when the cabaret closed. I drank a glass of milk and went to sleep.

I was awakened by a loud pounding on the door. The clock showed eight o'clock. I glanced into Phala's bedroom. She wasn't home. I knew it wasn't the landlord. Maybe it was Phala. She had lost her key.

I had taken my pay the week before and paid our

weekly rent. I got up and opened the door. It was the old whore who lived across the hall. I could see she was excited and slightly drunk. She stepped inside. She didn't say anything right away. She just stood and held both hands over her chest and drew deep breaths.

I said, "What's wrong?"

She stammered, "Joh— Johnny, something bad has happened to Phala."

I said, "What? Where?"

She said, "She was brutalized by street niggers. The law took her off the streets hollering and stark naked."

I snatched my trousers on over my pajamas. In bare feet, I dashed past her and ran a block to the Du Sable Hotel's public phone on Oakwood Boulevard.

A half hour later after a half dozen calls, I located Phala. She was in Cook County Hospital's Psychiatric Division. She couldn't receive visitors. She was too disturbed. The guy said that in cases like Phala's, it could be weeks, even months, before they could release them.

I stood there at the phone. I didn't know what my next move should be. I didn't have a friend in the world. I thought about my grandparents down in Louisiana. What could they do?

Then I remembered my Aunt Pearl, Phala's older sister out at Garfield and Calumet. Perhaps she was in the phone book under her maiden name. Surely in a serious situation like this she'd be eager to help her only baby sister.

She'd probably be thrilled to meet and to advise her nephew she'd never seen. Her girlhood hang-up on the color thing was most likely now a dim, humorous memory. After all, she was now at least in her late forties. She shouldn't have any color regrets. With her dark brown skin, she had done better in life than my near-white mother.

It took a while to scan through all the listed Grigsby's. There was no Pearl Grigsby in the book. I'd have to pay her a personal call. I went back to the apartment and dressed. On my way out, the whore across the hall stuck her head through her open door.

She whispered, "Come in here, Johnny, quick."

I went in. She shut the door. She was wearing a pair of transparent lavender panties. Her withered udders were deformed by a navy-blue network of cable veins. A ragged mound of frizzly gray hair jutted against the crotch lavender. I wondered how she made a living. Perhaps all her tricks were blind men.

I stood fidgeting, looking down into her yellow gargoyle face. She patted her palms against my chest. She said, "Johnny, the district cops was here looking for you. I guess they got questions about your mother. Johnny, those bastards ain't no good. After they grill you, they could take you in to the juvenile people. You're a minor with no support or family in Chicago.

"Johnny, Phala ain't coming back for a long time, if at all. I got an idea for you. I could look out for you. I'd hide you here. How about it, honey-long-legs?"

I backed away toward the door and opened it. I said, "Sure, beautiful, it's a fine idea. I'll be right back after I go out to see Phala."

I went across the hall and got my painting kit. I took my pajamas off and put on a tan slack suit. I went out the back door. I walked to South Park and Oakwood Boulevard. I took a jitney cab for a dime to Garfield Boulevard. I walked west to Calumet. I went into the foyer of Pearl's building.

I pushed the manager's bell on a lettered panel. A release buzzer for the inner front door sounded. I twisted the doorknob and stepped through it into the ground-floor hallway. I heard a hinge squeak to my right. I looked.

A mountainous bulk filled the doorway. It was a dark brown-skinned woman in a peach-colored housecoat. Well, at least partly in it. The front of her nightgowned belly poked through the front gap in it like a midget blimp, half-hangared.

I said, "Good morning. I'm trying to get in touch with Miss Pearl Grigsby. Could you help me?"

The Saint Bernard jowls quivered. The pea-sized eyes flickered malevolently. A bizarre doll hand stroked across the scraggly mop of dyed-red hair. The tiny mouth opened and finked on a decayed jumble of uneven teeth.

She said, "I'm Pearl. Who the hell are you?"

She had the sweetest softest voice I'd ever heard. It was hard to believe it came out of her.

She said, "Oh yeah, I heard about you. Come in."

She dredged herself aside. I stepped into her apartment. She had a severe sanitation problem. I held my breath when I passed her. She smelled like a bitch-dog's afterbirth. I could sympathize with her. She probably found it impossible to reach her disaster areas.

Her apartment was cluttered with gaudy fixtures and furniture. I sat in a shocking-pink chair in the living room, near a window looking out on the street. She sat on a matching sofa next to me.

She said, "Damn if you don't look like a peckerwood. How is Phala? Did she send you?"

I said, "She's in terrible trouble. She's out of her mind at County Hospital. I was able to find you because she mentioned your building here a long time ago."

She shrugged and said, "No wonder, them freakish peckerwoods would drive anybody crazy."

I said, "No, it isn't like that. I think she was raped by a bunch of niggers last night. I don't know what to do. What would you do?"

She said, "You're full of shitty baloney. Who the hell would have to rape Phala? She'd gap her legs open for any bum. All he'd need to do was bullshit her that she was beautiful. She thinks she's the prettiest woman walking the earth.

"And listen, don't use the word nigger in my house. It's like I'm letting a peckerwood get away with it. I would do what I've been doing, and that's forgetting she was ever born."

She was hurting me badly, and she was doing it in that same soft, syrupy voice. I fought for control.

I said, "Aunt Pearl, you're all wrong about her. And from what I know you've always been wrong. Don't you feel any thing for your only sister?"

She said, "I knew that dizzy bitch before you were born. You ain't got the nerve, I hope, to sit in my house and preach to me.

"She ain't never had nothing. She's been poor as Lazarus all her life. That color-struck fool could have had herself a black doctor ar even a lawyer. But no, she had to fuck that tramp peckerwood father of yours.

"Hell no, I don't feel a goddamn thing. She's found out now that light skin and white folks' hair ain't all of it. I'm black, fat and ugly, but I amount to something."

I checked a murderous impulse to split her skull with a heavy lamp on a table beside me.

She stopped to catch her breath. I got up and walked to the door. I knew I was going to cry. I had to get out of there fast. I couldn't let her see my tears.

I said, over my shoulder, "Pearl, you are a big funky liar."

I heard her grunting up from her sofa as I went into the hall and slammed her door. I went through the foyer to the street. I walked to Garfield. I heard a sliding sound behind me.

I glanced over my shoulder. Pearl's black hog body was thrust across the windowsill of the open window.

She screamed, "Don't you ever put a foot on my property again, you white nigger sonuvabitch."

I had stopped crying when I noticed the elevated train station on Garfield. I paid a fare and walked up the stairway to the train platform.

I got on a Howard Street train going to the Loop. All the rest of the day, I rode from South to North. I'd get off at one end of the line, then cross over to the opposite platform going in the other direction.

I couldn't go home. The old whore was probably right about those juvenile authorities. At nine P. M. I got off at Forty-third Street on the Southside. I went into a chili joint for a bowl of chili.

I sat at the counter near the front window. Five black teenagers were at a table in the rear. The old Mexican behind the counter kept stealing frightened glances at them.

I was eating my chili when a young brown-skinned girl in shorts came in. She stood next to my stool and ordered chili to go. She reached down to the paper-napkin holder beside me. She said. "Excuse me, will you push that bowl of pepper to me?"

I said, "Yes."

I pushed the red dried pepper across the counter to her. She dumped a load of it into a napkin and put it into her purse.

Then she said, "Say, don't you live around Thirty-ninth and Cottage?"

I said, "I did until a short time ago. Why?"

She said, "Oh, nothing. I just remembered seeing you around there."

I felt a tap on my shoulder. I half-turned on the stool and looked up. One of the loud-mouth teenagers was standing behind me, glaring down at me.

He said, "Man, why you fucking with this girl? You got pussies in you own neighborhood."

The girl cut in. She said. "He didn't hit on me."

He said, "You dumb bitch, get on the dummy."

I said, "Hell, buddy, what's the matter? You high or something? This is a free country. I got a right to—"

The punk sucker-punched me hard in my right cheek bone.

The room reeled. I fell to the floor next to the counter. I held my hand against my cheek and looked up at him.

He reached into his pocket. I heard a metallic click and saw the wicked gleam of the switchblade in his hand. His eyes were spinning in his head. He bent over toward me.

I rolled away toward the door and threw my feet up to keep him from gutting me. The door opened and a pair of khakied legs stepped across me. It was a young soldier. He was between me and the shiv man.

The soldier looked down curiously at me. I scooted backward through the closing door to the sidewalk. I got to my feet and raced down Forty-third Street.

I heard pounding feet behind me. I looked back. The whole pack was running toward me.

I hollered as loud as I could, "I'm a Nigger! I'm a Nigger! I'm a Nigger!"

I turned into the el station. I threw a handful of coins across the fare collector's counter. I raced up the stairs to the train platform. A Jackson Park El was closing its doors. I slipped through the closing slit. I fell into a cushion and looked down on Forty-third Street.

The pack was down there looking up at me. Three of them waved knives that glinted under a street lamp. I settled back in the seat, closed my eyes and started to figure my next move.

The train had stopped at Fifty-first Street. I realized that I didn't have the leatherette case filled with my paintings and art materials. I had left it on the floor beneath the stool in the chili joint. I wouldn't have gone back for it if it had been stuffed with Rembrandts.

A pair of hippy-dippys came into the car. They had two fancy brown-skinned broads with them. They sat down in the two seats directly in front of me.

The train pulled out toward Garfield Boulevard. The young broad with the hippy just in front of me turned her head back toward me. She smiled hotly at me. My eyes scrambled to the coach ceiling. I felt the throbbing lump on my cheekbone. I escaped down the aisle to another seat.

An elderly black woman was nodding next to the window. Her purse was on the seat between us. I eased my right hand across my thigh to the side of the purse. My fingers touched the heavy brass clasp on the top of it.

I looked at the wrinkled side of her face as I slowly worked her purse open. My fingers were suddenly frozen numb. I jerked my hand away to my lap. I couldn't rob her.

The old lady's coarse kindly face had reminded me of sweet Grandma Annie.

The train stopped at Garfield Boulevard. In the distance I saw Aunt Pearl's building. I wondered if she had felt any regret after she had driven me away. I had an urge to go back to see if she had had a change of heart. Then I remembered that sweetly poisonous voice. I just couldn't understand. How could she have been so cruel? Phala and I needed her so much.

I rode to the Sixty-third Street stop. I got off and went to the opposite platform. I took a Howard Street train going toward the Loop.

I tried to think of someone who could advise me about Phala. There was no one. I felt lost, lonely and desperate.

I decided to get off at Forty-seventh Street. I wasn't due to report for work at the theatre until three o'clock. I wasn't excited about going to work in that darkness, the way I was feeling and all.

I walked east down Forty-seventh Street. I didn't know what to do about Phala or anything else. I was friendless and homeless in the cold heart of Chicago's Southside.

I got to Calumet Avenue. I walked around the corner to a poolroom. A silent crowd stood watching a straight pool game at the front table.

I stood next to a glass cigar case near the door. For almost an hour I watched a slender black man run one rack of balls after another. He controlled the cue ball like he had it on an invisible string.

I turned to an old man standing beside me. He had clucked his praise of the thin wizard's skill. I whispered, "I wish I could shoot pool like that guy. I could sure get rich in a hurry."

He whispered, "White boy, if wishes were cars, damn fools would ride. He is one of the best big-buck pool players in the country. I wish he'd play me. But he won't. Since you just wishing, wish for his feet. Them slick dogs of his done made him more dollars than Carter is got pills.

That's Bill Bojangles Robinson in the livin' meat."

The wizard telescoped his stick. He slipped it into a leather case. The crowd moved away.

I said, "Listen, Mister, I'm not a white boy. I'm colored like you. Honest, I'm really colored. My mother is about your color."

A very black zoot-suited kid strutted and stood in front of us on his way out the door. He ignored me.

He said to the old man beside me. "One Pocket, ain't life a mother-fucker? My old lady must of fucked hundreds of peckerwoods for three bucks a hump.

"Didn't one of them silky-haired, straight-nosed bastards knock her up. Hell no, the blackest, kinkiest-haired, ugliest trick on Thirty-first Street rammed me up her ass.

"Now, Pocket, I ain't hip to a white trick baby so square he's passing for a Nigger. I just ain't never heard of it, Pocket. Shit, a dumb bastard like that oughta' have his ass kicked to the top of his stupid head. And by me."

I slugged my fist into the side of his jaw. I heard a flat crack like a bat against a baseball. I felt the shuddery shock of it to my elbow. He fell backwards and bounced hard. He lay flat on his back moaning. A snake of mustard vomit wiggled across his cheek.

Through a red haze of fury I went to the wall rack for a cue stick. He had driven me out of my mind with his wise crack about Phala.

I stood over him and raised the lead-loaded butt of the cue stick high over my head. I was going to crush his ugly face into a blob of black jelly. I drew a deep breath for the downward slam.

Then something locked my upraised arms to the sides of my head. I felt myself pulled away from the terrified eyes on the floor.

There wasn't a sound in the crowded poolroom. I half-twisted my head around. It was One Pocket holding me. That Irish in me was raging. I was screaming, "Let me go! I'm going to murder that signifying sonuvabitch."

One Pocket had one hell of a time holding me until after

the wise apple had struggled to his feet and fled to safety.

I walked through the door and stood on the sidewalk. One Pocket came out and stood beside me. I kept my eyes on the sidewalk. He was sweating and panting like a thirsty pooch. I was ashamed that I had lost my temper.

He said, "Goddamn, it took a lotta' muscle to stop you from playing the murder game. I got a sucker's tender ticker. I couldn't stand to see even that rat croaked.

"What the hell, you didn't need to waste him to convince him your old lady wasn't no whore. Besides, you're lucky those scufflers in there didn't stomp you to death. I guess they hate that rat stool pigeon worse than your white skin."

I said, "I'm sorry. Your'e right. I'm glad I didn't kill him. I don't know what happened to me in there. I've never been that mad in my life. Thanks for stopping me. One Pocket."

CHAPTER NINE

Flat-Joint Flimflam

A tomato-red Cadillac glided to the curb in front of us.
A tall heavyset guy in a white shimmery tropical suit got
out. I'd seen him a hundred times going into the Du Sable
Hotel on Oakwood near Thirty-ninth Street.

His processed black hair glittered like a satin skullcap
in the sun. A monstrous rock on his ebony right hand
flashed like a hunk of rainbow.

I said, "Who is the rich guy?"

Pocket said, "He's Blue Howard."

He came across the sidewalk towards us. One Pocket
took a step to meet him and said, "Well, Blue, what's in
the barnyard for a hawk?"

The giant grinned down at One Pocket. In a very soft
voice, he said, "I'm flat-jointing with an outfit operation on
Lake Street. I fired all of my thieving boost last night.
Pocket, I could use you on the outside to feed the
belly-sticks and to heckle the marks for the usual ten
percent of the box. Don't worry, you'll make a buck. Do I
have to tell you that the dagos don't play in bad locations?
Well?"

One Pocket threw his hands into the air palms up. He
said, "Blue, I ain't played nothing but funny pool in a
week. My rep has all the hustlers scared shitless. I gotta
wait for chumps who ain't heard of me to get a game. I'll
rib marks and handle the sticks for you. How many sticks
you using?"

Blue looked over Pocket's head and said, "I need three.
How about your young white friend? Maybe he'd like to
pick up a sawbuck or so. He'd give the joint inviting flavor
for any white marks over there."

Pocket said, "Blue, the kid ain't white. He's a boot. But its the same difference ain't it? Blue, I like him. You should have seen him punch the puke outta Double-crossing Sammy."

Then he glanced over his shoulder at me. He said, "Kid, you want a job?"

I said, "Sure, but I don't know anything about it."

Blue said, "You're the whitest spade I've ever seen. Kid, there isn't a helluva lot a belly-stick has to know. All you do is keep your belly against the joint counter and let me make you lucky on the wheel. Pocket will give you a rundown on the scratch and the feed. You get paid every night."

I said, "I learn fast. I'll be the best stick you ever saw."

Pocket turned and went to the poolroom doorway. He shouted, "First and last call for two sober belly-sticks in clean clothes. It's a Westside spot, there and back in a brand new Cadillac."

A half dozen prospects galloped to the sidewalk. They stood in slouched attention like a squad of bedraggled soldiers waiting for a pass from no man's land.

Pocket eyed them from head to toe. Finally he said, "I want Precious Jimmy and Old Man Mule. The rest of you ain't in the shape like you could have the measly scratch to blow on a wheel."

Precious was a tall handsome light brown-skinned fellow about twenty-two years old. Mule was old, black and ugly, with the longest ears I'd ever seen except on a mule.

The turndowns dragged back into the poolroom. We all got into the Cadillac. Pocket sat in the front seat with Blue. The Caddie leaped from the curb like a red jackrabbit.

I closed my eyes and leaned back in the plush seat between precious and Mule. It was like floating on air. It felt a little like the train ride Phala and I took from Kansas City to Chicago, long ago. This ride was smoother and I didn't feel so tiny and afraid like on the train.

Blue said, "What's your name, kid?"

I opened my eyes. They met his in the rear-view mirror. I said, "Johnny O'Brien."

He said, "That's no name at all for a young hustler. You've got to have a street monicker that's jazzy and proper. How about 'White Folks?' It's a natural for you, just like 'Blue' for me because I'm so black."

I said, "I don't like that one. I don't want people hating me because they think I'm bragging I'm white. If I'm going to have a monicker it ought to brag that I'm a Nigger."

Blue said, "I'm glad you said that. That's just what that monicker does for you. It's got a solid Nigger sound. There never was, and there never will be a genuine white hustler with that tag. It shouts that you're really a Nigger with white skin. Convinced, White Folks?"

I said, "The way you explain it makes sense. I just hope it makes everybody sure that I'm a Nigger."

We had reached the Westside when Pocket turned his long head back toward me and said, "White Folks, don't never speak to me when we're playing a mark in the joint. You run out of dough to make your plays on the wheel, you hold your mitts palms up so on your last play Blue can see you're tapped. He'll toss you a light cop on your number.

"Say a mark is right beside you in the joint, Blue is gonna gaff that wheel on your number and heave you a heavy cop to excite the mark. Now I'm telling the three of you belly-sticks the time to go off to piss ain't that time when you got that big scratch in your duke.

"Put that heavy cop in your mitt flat against your thigh furtherest from the mark. I'm gonna be right there patting your mitt to take off that scratch. Just slap that scratch easy-like into my palm.

"Then like a real happy winner get the hell away from the joint. Come back after them marks in the joint have been played.

"You get five percent of the box. The joint takes in two bills, you get a sawbuck. It takes in a half a grand, you got twenty-five slats coming.

"There ain't no roller problems. The mob's got that captain in the district in their ass pocket. Any questions?"

I said, "What is a gaff?"

Precious and Mule snickered.

Pocket said, "It's a gimmick that stops that wheel wherever Blue wants. He can stop that paper arrow on the middle of a pinhead.

"There's the spot. We'll get out first. Then split up and walk around the lot until Blue gets ready for us. Ain't no use to let early suckers see us together. Keep your eyes on me. I'm gonna scratch my chin to pull you into the joint."

Blue pulled to the side of a huge lot at Hoyne Avenue and Lake Street. We scrambled out and walked into the dusty lot.

There were several Puerto Rican men and women with just a few black women and children on the lot. About a dozen canvas tents in a rough circle squatted in the gray dust like tattered buzzards.

In the center were the ferris wheel, a midget car ride and food stands. A candy-striped merry-go-round spun in the champagne sun like a mammoth musical top. It was calliope-ing *Stairway to the Stairs* I felt a quick quake of sorrow. It was Phala's favorite tune.

I noticed that Blue was the only black operator on the lot. He was counting stacks of coins glinting on the joint's long counter.

I saw Pocket casually walk to the front of Blue's joint. I saw Pocket's index finger scratching the point of his chin. Mule and Precious drifted into the joint seconds after I got there.

Pocket gave each of us three dollars in quarters to play the numbers on a long oilcloth strip stretched the length of the pine-board counter. Those numbers matched the numbers on the wheel in the center of the counter.

When the wheel was spun, a slender paper indicator fitted to a center arm of the wheel would stop at a number. Each number was bracketed by nails that circled the outer edge of the wheel.

Within a couple of hours the lot was crowded with blacks, whites and Puerto Ricans. Only a few marks came into our joint. None had dropped more than several dollars.

I was sweaty, bored and hungry. I had started to wonder whether belly-sticking was better than ushering at the theater.

Then some excitement started. An elderly white man stopped and started playing the wheel. His wallet bulged with tens and twenties. Blue leaned across the counter to case the contents.

He stood next to Mule. Blue started building him for the kill. Each time the wheel was spun Blue would cover a number on the wheel with a red disc.

Then Blue would chant, "Your number wins and you win if it stops on any red. Ten dollars still gets a hundred."

Pocket stood behind Mule and the mark. He fed Mule paper money against the thigh.

He kept telling Mule in loud whispers before each bet, "Jesus Christ, man! What the hell you hesitatin' for. Are you blind? Can't you see? You can't lose now. The wheel is almost all red."

The old man had dropped close to two hundred dollars. The wheel had only four black spaces.

Blue chanted, "A hundred gets a thousand."

Pocket fed Mule a wad of bills and said to him, "By gravy, you've got him by the balls now. Goddammit, put the hundred on your number."

The white mark was still fumbling inside his wallet when Mule put down the hundred and spun the wheel. Blue stopped the wheel on red. Blue threw a bundle of bills to Mule.

Blue said, "Count it fair and you'll find it's there."

Mule scooped it off the counter. He turned sideways and fanned through it. He dropped his right hand to his side holding the bills. Pocket took it off. Mule walked away.

Blue covered a black space with a red disc. Only the mark's number and two other black spaces were left on the wheel. Blue chanted again, "I haven't been hurt. That thousand was chicken feed. Any lucky number or any red gets two thousand for two hundred."

The mark trembled a thin sheaf of bills from his wallet.

The mark turned to Pocket and said, "I have only a hundred and eighty-three dollars left."

Blue turned his head and coughed.

Pocket winked at the mark and placed a twenty dollar bill in his hand. The mark wavered and rubbed his nose.

Pocket punched the old man hard in the side with his elbow and shouted, "Are you crazy? You can't lose now. Ain't you got as much faith in yourself as I got in you? Put that two hundred on your number and make that big nigger cry."

The mark just stood there in a trance. Pocket snatched the bills from his hand and threw them on his number. Blue spun the wheel. The mark's head revolved with the wheel. It stopped in a black losing space.

Blue picked up the money and shoved the three dollar bills back toward the mark. Pocket picked them up and stuck them into the mark's shirt pocket. The mark walked away muttering.

Blue threw a fifty-cent piece to each stick. He said, "You can go one at a time for a sandwich and a cold drink."

I went last.

Blue counted all the silver and paper money in the joint. Then he stuck the bills the old mark had lost into the slot of a padlocked steel box.

Then he said to Pocket, "You're a good man on the outside of a joint. But don't tear off white marks like that. It would foul up the fix for the whole carnival if we got an important white beef. The spades and spics we can rough-house. But I'm telling you, go easy and smooth on white marks in this district."

After I'd eaten, I felt better about my new job. I felt

sorry for the old mark. But I remembered that I had more than twenty dollars coming from that box. When I got off I'd rent a room in a hotel until Phala got out of the hospital. I'd have to go back to our apartment soon to get our things out before the rent was due again.

At twilight the carnival lights blazed on. The crowd was bigger and noiser. By ten o'clock, our joint had taken in close to six hundred dollars, according to my secret tally. I was thinking about how that twenty had grown to thirty dollars I had made.

I was feeling very good. Then I saw the old white mark and two uniformed white cops coming toward the joint. Pocket melted into the crowd. Blue grinned at them when they got to the front of the joint.

The taller cop said, "This gentleman charges that he lost close to four hundred dollars to you in a gambling game. What about it?"

Blue looked shocked and said, "Now officer, the dumbest fool in town knows it's against the law to gamble in Chicago. The only money anybody can lose here is quarters. Everybody is welcome to his chance to win one of those gorgeous stuffed animals, hanging back there.

"I don't know why this fine gentleman is lying. But maybe he doesn't know that if I'm arrested for gambling, you'd have to arrest him, too. I sure as hell can't gamble by myself, now can I, officers?"

The old man turned flour white and whispered something to the short cop. The cop whispered back and waved the mark away. He scurried away into the crowd. There was a flash of green in Blue's palm when he shook hands with the tall cop. Both cops smiled happily and walked away.

Pocket popped back on the scene.

Blue said, "Pocket, I squared that squeal with a lousy double saw. If that mark had a brain in his head, he would have by-passed the district police with his beef.

"All he had to do was go downtown to the commissioner and the old bastard probably could have gotten every nickel of his loss kicked back.

"You sticks turn in your silver. I'm breaking the joint down. The outfit boys have started to check the other joints anyway. You sticks walk around the lot until after the box is checked. Pocket will pull you back for the payoff."

The three of us walked away and stood against a cotton candy stand. The crowd was thinning fast.

Precious said, "I hope we don't get burned for our fair share of that box."

Mule said, "Blue ain't going to burn us. I just hope those slick dago bastards don't ram a bad count into Blue."

I said, "How much does Blue get of that box?"

Mule said, "He gets fifty percent of what's left after the sticks and the outside man are paid, minus maybe a half a hundred a night for the district rollers.

"Blue should clear for himself something like a bill, twenty-five for the night's work. It ain't bad scratch. But the outfit gets the real gravy.

"They ain't doing nothing but collecting and they get fifty percent of every flat-joint box on this lot."

We saw two sharply dressed white men go behind Blue's counter. They unlocked the box and started counting money.

Mule said, "That skinny, baby-faced dago is Nino Parelli. He's only twenty-two. His old man is a powerful wheel in the syndicate.

"Nino is learning the ABC's of the rackets. Don't let that baby face fool you. He's cold as a grave. His old man beat a murder rap for him in his teens. He blew his best pal's brains out in a dime card game."

Blue had dismantled the wheel and taken the flash dolls and stuffed animals off the back wall when the dapper hoodlums finished their counting. They handed Blue a roll of money and went to a flat-joint at the corner of the lot.

Pocket finally scratched his chin. We went to the joint. Blue slapped thin rolls of bills into our palms.

He said, "The box was six and a half bills. You got

thirty-three slats each, a half a buck overpay. It's almost midnight. You sticks take the car keys, grab that wheel and that box of flash. Put them in the trunk of the car. We're getting the hell out of here."

Blue and Pocket came moments later. It really felt fine to sit down on the Cadillac's soft seat after bellying up to the joint for almost twelve hours.

We were crossing Cermak Road going south on Michigan Avenue when Blue said, "Pocket, that punk Nino lopped that double saw I gave the heat from our end of the take. I should have held out a C note or so from that box."

Pocket snorted like a dog with pepper up his muzzle.

He said, "Bullshit, Blue, even if you had guts like that, you'd rather put the heist on Fort Knox. You ain't stupid. You ain't never gonna fuck with one mill of syndicate scratch.

"If Nino ever heard you crack it, the odds are he'd dump you in a sewer with a mouth full of your balls. He'd figure you'd burned him all along. In fact, Nino could shove his bare ass in your face and you'd kiss his dago ass cherry red."

Blue chuckled and said, "You're right, Pocket. But I can dream, can't I?

"Mule, you repaired stills for the Genna brothers back in the Twenties. You've seen a lot of tough young hoods come and go. How do you rate Nino?"

Mule said, "He ain't nothing but a baby. If he don't get croaked, ain't no doubt that down the road he'll make a lot of mob bigshots shit bloody turds. He ain't the type to be happy with crumbs."

Blue turned into Forty-seventh Street. He turned again at Calumet Ave. and stopped in front of the poolroom.

He said, "Tomorrow is Sunday. Anybody that wants to work, be here at noon."

We all got out. Pocket and the two sticks went into the poolroom. I stood on the sidewalk thinking about where I could rent a room by the week. I watched Blue pull out.

He went about thirty feet up Calumet. He braked hard and blew his horn. I walked over to the driver's side.

He said, "White Folks, are you showing for work tomorrow?"

I said, "I sure am. That was the easiest thirty-three dollars I ever made. Thanks a lot for the chance."

He said, "I've never seen you around here. Where do you live?"

I said, "On Thirty-ninth Street."

He said, "Well, get in. I'll drop you off down there."

I said, "I can't stay there anymore. I'm dodging some people."

Blue said, "If you're in trouble maybe I can help you. Get in and tell me about it."

I got in. He parked on Calumet. I told him all about Phala and Pearl. And about how I was afraid the juvenile officers would lock me up.

When I finished, he said, "I would never have guessed you were only sixteen years old. You're tall and big enough to be twenty at least. You've got problems all right.

"White Folks, I like you. You've got lots of heart and class. Tell you what. You can stay at my place until you get things straightened out. Midge, my daughter, is your age. You'll like her.

"You'll get work in the flat-joint for the rest of the summer. I'll find out the score on your mother in the morning. You haven't any reason to worry when Blue's your friend. Okay?"

I said, "Mr. Blue, I appreciate everything. But I was going to pay rent some place anyway. I've got to pay you if I stay in your house. Would seven bucks a week be all right with you?"

He frowned and said, "White Folks, I don't run a rooming house. Anybody who stays at my house is a guest. Keep your scratch and try to build a bankroll. No hustler is worth a bottle of shit without one.

"And for Chrissake, don't put a sucker handle on my name. Just call me plain Blue."

It was one A.M. on the Caddie's dashboard clock when Blue pulled into the driveway of his house. It was on the far Southside, in the middle of the block on Langley Avenue between Sixty-second and Sixty-third Streets.

We got out. Blue locked the car. I stood there in the driveway for a long moment and gazed at the house. I swear to heaven that the very thought that I was going to live in the pink frame dream wobbled my knees.

We walked across the lawn that was like scented sable beneath my airy feet. We went down the walk toward the front door. The lush spice of honeysuckle floated about me.

I thought about Minnie. She had worn the scent beneath her golden pyramids, honey-dipped. And she had worn it between her yellow satin thighs. Tiny spasms jerked at the very root of my plunger when I remembered inhaling pungent little zephyrs of raw female and honeysuckle at each thrust when our bellies smashed together.

I followed Blue up four white steps to the latticed porch. Moonlight rippled indigo stripes across his white suit. Blue unlocked the door.

We walked through a deep red-carpeted hallway to the living room. He flicked a wall switch near the doorway. A crystal chandelier glittered like a cache of diamonds in the lavender ceiling.

Blue said, "White Folks, make yourself comfortable. It's getting late. I want to make sure Midge is home."

He walked away to the hallway. I walked across the tawny oriental carpet to a long, red silk sofa. I eased down onto it. A huge fireplace yawned across the room. There was a wide mirror above it. I wondered who played the white grand piano squatting starkly against the midnight-blue backdrop of floor-to-ceiling drapes.

I was dazzled. It was like in the movies and pictures I had seen in the magazines that Phala had brought home from River Forest.

I looked at a wedding picture on a table at the end of the sofa. A slender black giant towered above a sweet-faced mulatto girl in a lace wedding dress. A shadow fell across the picture. I looked up. Blue was standing before me with a wry look on his face. He sighed and said, "I was a happy sucker the day that shot was taken. She was a fine wife and mother.

"For a helluva long time I thought Pauline and I would never take the marriage leap. Her old man was one of those highfalutin Nigger doctors. He lectured her goofy from the moment he met me. He wanted her to be a concert pianist. In his eyes I was just a black tramp with only the gutter to offer his pet.

"I had to take her away from him, kid. That yellow chump bawled more at the wedding than he did at her funeral a year ago."

I said, "Is your daughter home?"

He bit his bottom lip and sat down beside me. He spun a red porcelain ashtray on the blue glass top of the coffee table in front of us.

He said softly, "No, she's still out. She hangs out in Cocktails For Two on Forty-seventh Street, under the el. She's gone wild since Pauline passed. It's a goddamn crime that I take this torture after those long hours in the flat-joint. She does it every Friday and Saturday."

I said, "Blue, you could have stopped on our way to let us out at the poolroom. You could have brought her home then."

He grunted and said, "I tried that not long ago. I went into that funky nest of pansies and freaks. When she saw me come in the door, she giggled and ran behind the bar.

"I chased her around the joint for ten minutes. Those bastard faggots and lesbians had a screaming cheering ball. I never did catch her. I felt like a goddamn circus clown who had done his bit in the center ring."

I said, "Why does she hang around people like that?"

He said, "She claims they're more sincere and understand life and her better than other kinds of people, including me, her own father. Too bad she isn't sweet and obedient like Pauline was. Come on, I'll show you your room."

I followed him down the red-carpeted hallway. He paused at a doorway on the left. I looked through it at the biggest, shiniest bedroom I'd ever seen.

The massive mahogany dresser and bed had a rich red glow. A large gold-framed print of Botticelli's "Allegory Of Spring" hung on the pearl wall over the carved headboard of the bed. The midnight-blue rug matched the floor-to-ceiling drapes. A fat candle burned inside a crystal jar sitting on a nightstand. The nymphs in the picture seemed alive with movement in the flickering light.

He said, "This is my bedroom." I was wondering about the candle when he said, "That seven-day candle is the only religion I have. I burn them for good luck. It never fails to keep suckers coming my way."

We walked down the hallway. We passed another doorway. I got a glimpse of soft pink and white.

Blue said, "That's Midge's room."

At the end of the hallway, we went into my bedroom. He flipped a wall switch. If I had been a dame I would have kissed him in joy. I stood on the cushiony beige carpet and gazed at the white furniture flecked with antique gold. Gold satin drapes at the windows matched the spread on the wide bed.

Blue opened a door to a gleaming green-tiled bathroom. He said, "My room has a private bath. You and Midge will have to share this one. Well, Folks, how do you like the setup?"

I said, "Blue, I'm in a dream. Don't worry, I'll keep the whole place clean."

He said, "White Folks, hustlers don't do housework. Besides I have an old dame who comes in to clean and wash and iron. I have a gardener that comes once a week to do the yard. How about a snack?"

I said, "I'm not a bit hungry. I think I'll take a bath and go to bed."

He said, "You'll find towels in the cabinet. I'll bring you a pair of pajamas. Christ! I wish Midge would come in."

He went down the hall. I stripped and hung my slack suit in the closet. I went to the bathroom and drew a tub full of steamy water. I lay there in the giant tub, soaking the tiredness and carnival grime from my body.

It was wonderful. I'd never enjoyed a bath so much. And that's the guaranteed truth. I got out of the tub and toweled off.

I washed my socks, shorts and tee shirt in the bathtub and hung them on a towel rack. I scrubbed the tub clean and went into the bedroom.

I slipped into a pair of blue silk pajamas lying across the bed. The sight of the frosty glass of milk and ham sandwich made me suddenly hungry, I sat in a beige leather chair and wolfed down the sandwich. Blue was sure a thoughtful guy.

I remembered my toothbrush in my trouser pocket. I went to the bathroom and brushed my teeth. I opened the door to Midge's room. Her furniture was like mine.

I went back to my room and put the light out. Moonlight flooded the room when I pulled the drape cord. I looked out the window into the backyard. Clusters of tulips and roses swayed in the pale blueness.

I pulled back the covers and got into bed. I closed my eyes. I heard the gleeful chirping of crickets. And far away the bubbly song of a night bird echoed through the whispery rustle of trees and flowers.

It was the first time in my life I'd heard the music of a summer night. I fell asleep on the fresh white pillowcase.

CHAPTER TEN

A Doll with a Lust for Dames

I awoke and felt the pajama silk plastered to my sweaty chest. I thought I'd heard an angry female voice.

Dawn's gray drab brush had blotted out the moon's soft-blue tapestry on the ceiling. For a pounding moment I thought I was back in the concrete swamp on Thirty-ninth Street.

Then I heard Blue's voice, loud and angry. He said, "Goddamnit, Midge, I'm no sucker. If you must lie to me about where you've been all night, make up a good one. You know, one that at least a moron would believe. Midge, I'm warning you. You're going to get that fast little ass of yours in a sling."

She said, contemptuously, "Blue, everybody knows you aren't a sucker. Oh, no! You're a thief, a robber who never gives a poor sucker an even break. You're sick, Blue, like your con pal, Dirty Red. You wouldn't know the truth, if it walked up and blew your brains out. You lie for a living. Shit, I bet you're the biggest liar in Chicago."

Blue shouted, "What the hell do you know? You dumb little broad, you'd starve to death in the gutter if you didn't have me to love you and take care of you. Now shut up and go to bed before I lose my temper."

She laughed wildly and said, "I heard you say that word. But I can't believe you really said it! Love! You never loved Mama or me or anything, except Blue and money.

"If I don't shut up, what will you do, Blue? Slap hell out of me and make me stand with my face in a corner like you did Mama.

"I'm not Mama, Blue. You wouldn't put your black paws

on me but one time. You'd have to go to sleep sometime. I take an oath on Mama's grave that I wouldn't let you wake up."

There was a long silence.

Then Blue said, "Midge, you don't realize what you're saying to your father. Those slimy freaks you hang out with are poisoning your mind against me. aren't they, baby?

"You're a good-looking girl. Why not sweetheart around with some nice boy? Stay away from those stinking lesbians and funky sissies. You'll see how much better off you'll be.

"We can be happy then. I'm worried about you, little baby. Be sweet and stay at home like you did when Pauline was alive. It's a crime, baby, to treat me like you do."

Midge said, "Blue, don't try to con me into deserting my friends. Sure, I stayed at home with Mama. You seldom did. She loved and needed me. We were all each other had.

"It was a crime that Mama married you and had me. It was a double crime that Mama and my baby sister had to die at her birth. No man will ever mistreat me like you did Mama. So save your breath, Blue. I love girls and girls are mad about me."

I got up and went into the bathroom. Her connecting door to the bathroom was ajar. I gently pushed it shut.

I heard Blue say softly, "I forgot we have a guest in our happy home. If he heard you—I know you're proud. All right, Midge, it's your funeral.

"Those freaks are treacherous and crazy jealous. I hope you don't wind up in the morgue with your throat cut. Just don't ever bring those sewer rats into this house."

I flushed the toilet and went to the beige leather chair at the window. I sat there thinking about what I'd heard. None of it was too clear to me.

Midge had to be out of her mind not to realize how lucky she was to live in a house like this. So Blue made

Pauline stand in a corner like a child. That was more comical than brutal. Maybe he had good reasons. It was sure nicer punishment than the bloody beatings some of the guys in the apartment building on Thirty-ninth Street gave their women every weekend.

So Blue conned suckers. It sure as hell was smarter and better than beating a drum for chump change like my old man. It was the guaranteed truth it was better than walking a thousand miles up and down the aisles of a theatre for twelve bucks a week. It was even better than picking pockets and dodging rollers with Lester Gray on the el trains.

I knew why I liked girls and I had the tool to enjoy the fun. But how could Midge, a girl, get down into the deep hot heart of the fun?

That Dirty Red crack puzzled me, too. I wished my old man had been slick like Blue and had stuck around to put Phala and me in a fine house. It was a crying shame Midge didn't appreciate Blue. In my book Blue was the best thing that could happen to me, Midge or anybody else.

I heard water splashing into the bathtub. Midge was humming in the bathroom to faint radio music. Finally I heard the tub draining.

I went into the bathroom and brushed my teeth and sponged off. I brushed my hair with a clean brush I found in a cabinet drawer. I had taken my laundry off the towel rack when curiosity stuck my eye into Midge's keyhole. She was naked, sitting in the middle of her bed facing the keyhole.

Her back was arched and her head was down too low to get a glimpse of her face. She was painting her toenails. The sight of her voluptuous body and pouted gold-lipped pussy parched my throat. My hot slippery palms skied on the tile when she raised her wickedly cute face.

In a cat-like spin of her fanny she swung her honey-colored legs to the carpet. A shiny cloud of blue-black hair swirled at her dimpled shoulder blades.

She stood at the dresser mirror and flogged the jet mane

with a silver brush. Fingers of morning sun stroked across her heavenly butt and sparkled its twin champagne balloons. I trembled off my knees and sponged off again.

The cunning little devil started to sing. I heard her low sugary voice moaning a hit song. "I want to be loved with inspiration. I want to be loved until I tingle. I want to be kissed—"

I dressed and went down the hall to the back room. I unlatched it and stepped into the backyard. I sat down on a lawn chair and felt the morning breeze cool away my fever. I closed my eyes and wondered how soon I could make her like boys. A happy robin warbled me into a half doze. I heard the back door squeak open.

I half-opened my eyes. Midge was coming toward me wearing tight white toreador pants and a red bandana halter across the peaked jut of her breasts. I closed my eyes and pretended to be asleep.

I felt her hand gently shake my shoulder. I looked up into almond-shaped eyes, black and dreamy behind the silky veil of long curly eyelashes.

We both said, "Good morning" at the same time.

There was a fleeting dazzle of perfect pearl when she smiled and said, "You must be the guest Blue told me about. I'm Midge. Who are you, Mr. Fine, Errol Flynn's twin brother?"

I said, "No. I'm Johnny—I mean they call me White Folks. It's a pleasure to meet you, Miss Luscious."

She sat on the grass beside the chair and looked up into my eyes. She said. "Gee, your eyes make me feel funny. They're so blue, like pieces of sky. How long have you known my dad?"

I said, "Since yesterday. I'm helping him at the carnival."

She said, "Do you think I'm pretty?"

I said, "No, not really. I go for boys."

She said, "You're jiving me. You heard that argument this morning, didn't you?"

I said, "Yes, I couldn't help but hear it. I still say I go

for boys. They've got what girls wish they had. You should try some good boy-loving before you get to be an ugly old lady.

She giggled and said, "That's a crock of crap. I had some for the first time when I was fourteen right over there by those roses. It was just bloody and painful and no kicks at all.

"Then last year a college boy named Tommy rented a room in that big white house at the end of the block. He was as pretty as a girl.

"One night, he slipped me into his room. I was really crazy about him. And I wanted him to have me. We were doing it when I did a terrible thing. I was so ashamed of myself. Tommy wouldn't even speak to me after that night."

I said, "What happened? What did you do?"

She looked away at the sky and said, "I won't tell you. It's too awful. Say, listen, I didn't mean half of that stuff I said to Blue this morning. I was awfully mad at him.

"I don't hate him really. I wouldn't kill him. But I have to talk to him like that to scare him. He's a big bully and he'd keep my ass on fire if I didn't bluff him."

I said, "Were you joking about loving girls? You sure don't look like that kind of freak to me."

She wrinkled her cute pug nose and raised her thick black eyebrows. She toyed with a leather thong on her red sandals.

I said, "Are you sweet on girls? Yes or no?"

She said, "Why the hell do I have to tell you how I get my kicks. It's none of your business." She got up. She put her hands on her hips and stood wide legged in front of me. The lustrous mound of jet hair I'd seen at the keyhole lumped the crotch of her pants.

I said, "Forgive me. I guess it's a hurting thing for a girl to know she hasn't got enough on the ball to hook a guy. Too bad about you, Midge. But as they say, that's life."

The dreamy eyes blazed angrily. She was trembling. She shouted, "You paddy square. You should see me walk

down South Parkway. I shake the guys up and make t'..m
drool like hungry dogs.

"I go for guys. I go for Errol Flynn, Robert Tayl r nd
Charles Boyer. I like beautiful, classy guys. There are n..e
like that on the Southside

"So until I find what I want, it's girls for me. You're a
freak yourself. You said you went for boys."

I said, "Midge, you need straightening out on a few
things. My father was a paddy. But I'm not. I'm from
Thirty-ninth Street. There are no squares down there. ː ᵥ
old lady was a boot.

"Like you said at first, Midge, I was jiving about going
for boys. I go for girls like you with nice round twisters
and big tits. Maybe some night I'll sleepwalk through the
bathroom and prove to you how much I like girls."

She said, "You better stop talking to your boss' daughter
like that. You ever put a foot inside my room, I'll split your
head open with a high heel. Your blue eyes and yellow
hair don't excite me, flunky."

I watched the awesome twin balloons twist away from
me. She met Blue coming out the back door. He stooped
and kissed her on the cheek as she swept by him. He came
toward me. I stood up. He was dressed in a gray seer-
sucker suit. I wondered if my jazzy crack to Midge would
get me thrown out of Blue's house.

Blue's eyes were bloodshot. He said, "Well, Folks, I see
you and Midge have met. How do you like her?"

I said, "I like her, but I don't think she likes me. I made
a horny crack about her shape. I think I insulted her. I'm
sorry, Blue."

He threw his head back and laughed. He said, "You
work fast, Folks. Forget it. She likes you. She was smiling
when she walked away from you.

"Say, kid, I called about your mother. I've got bad news
for you. She still doesn't know who she is or anything.
We've got to get her into a private sanitarium before they
commit her to the state joint.

"She'll never come to herself in that madhouse. Don't

worry, Folks, I'll pull all the strings this week coming."

The bad news shook me. My chest felt like it was stuffed with hot lead. I mumbled, "Thanks for everything, Blue."

He said, "It's ten o'clock. Midge isn't in the mood to make breakfast for us. We'll go to Power's Restaurant on Forty-seventh Street."

Forty-seventh Street was quiet when Blue pulled into the curb in front of the cafeteria. We got out of the car and went inside.

We ordered ham and eggs with coffee and toast. Blue gave me an argument but I paid for our orders. We took our trays and sat down at a long table facing the front window.

I hadn't eaten a meal in a long time. But I wasn't hungry. I couldn't get Phala off my mind. I had forced down most of the breakfast when Blue lit a cigar.

He gazed out at the sunny street and said, "It sure is a beautiful day. It just isn't right that a man forty-seven years old with my grifting talent and experience has to sweat it out with cheap suckers in a flat-joint and give up fifty percent."

I said, "I wish I had my own flat-joint and could make half of the money you make."

He said, "Kid, I can understand why you feel like that. But if you had your own flat-joint, do you know where you'd be on the con ladder? You'd be on the bottom.

"Just a short con bum who plays his heart out for a C-note now and then. I'm just a slim cut above a belly-stick. The biggest sucker mistake I ever made was to cut out from the Vicksburg Kid and the long con."

I said, "Blue, what is the difference between short and long con?"

He looked at his wristwatch and said, "Folks, we play short con in the flat-joint. It's short con because the play for the sucker is short and we can only trim the sucker for the goddamn scratch in his pocket. He could have a million in the jug. But the flat-joint short con is too weak to touch a deemer of that long green.

"In other words, the mark can't be put on the send for his scratch in the bank. I didn't know the difference myself until I met the Vicksburg Kid. He was a white flat-joint operator. When I left Mississippi with him as a belly-stick, I was about your age."

"When I was twenty, he had become one of the best long con players in the country. He taught me long con and how to rope suckers for a wire store he set up in Denver, Colorado.

"In long con the sucker is given a powerful play to convince him that whatever scratch he has is only a drop in the bucket compared to what he can take off from the long con proposition. In long con the sucker is eager to race away on the send for his money."

I said, "Gosh! What is a wire store? And what are the things you tell a guy to make him get all his money and bring it back to you?"

He laughed and pushed his huge palms toward me. He said, "Easy now, Folks. You stick with Blue long enough and I'll teach you all the con you can handle. I like you. But I'm not fattening frogs for snakes."

We went to the Caddie. My head was in an excited whirl. I had to find out the magic words that would make suckers drop bales of dough into my pockets. I was aching to learn con. And that's the guaranteed truth.

We played the Hoyne Avenue and Lake Street spot for another week. Our next spot was on Loomis Street near Roosevelt Road on the Westside.

Pocket and the belly-sticks were friendly and treated me like I was coal black. Believe me, that was wonderful for me. Blue treated me like a son. And that was even more wonderful. The flat-joint pay was good, too. I had over a C-note under the rug in my room.

Blue sure kept his promises. He took me to pick up Phala's and my things on Thirty-ninth Street. He got Phala into a small private sanitarium run by a Baptist organization.

It was located outside Robbins, Illinois, a short distance from Chicago. I asked Blue about the cost. He said it was a free setup. I found out later that he was footing the hundred and fifty dollar a month bill.

In the first part of September Blue drove me up to see Phala. He waited for me in the parking lot.

A husky female nurse led me across a small fenced park. She stopped beneath the black shadow of a giant weeping willow tree. I saw Phala sitting on a bench in the sunshine ahead. I heard the willow sigh mournfully under the lash of the strong summer breeze.

The nurse said in a low voice, "Speak softly to her and don't press her for recognition. She's very disturbed."

We walked across the manicured jade toward Phala. She was wearing a faded blue smock. She had her head down. There was a new blossom of white hair in the crown of her head.

She was so thin her shinbones were shiny in the sun. We stood in front of her. She didn't raise her head. She was growling deep inside her throat and rapidly bumping together the tips of her skeletal fingers in her lap.

The nurse said softly, "Phala, honey, you have company. It's your son, Johnny. Look at the beautiful roses he brought you."

The nurse nodded her head toward a huddle of patients across the lawn. She whispered in my ear, "I'll be over there if you want me."

Phala slowly raised her head and looked up at me. The once radiant brown eyes were gigantic dull blanks in her razor-thin face. I put the bouquet of roses on the bench beside her. For the first time in my life I called her mama.

I said, "Hi, Mama. It's Johnny. Gee, I've missed you."

She drew away. Her fingers were a blur in her lap as she pounded together her fingertips even more furiously. They made a staccato pulpy sound.

I stooped down and leaned close to her. I thought maybe I could coax at least a shadow of remembrance into the cold vacant eyes. I gazed into them for a long time.

But I saw only the ghostly image of the sighing willow tree, swaying behind me. I stood up. I couldn't stand any more of it.

I felt a tight, aching ball of pity inflate inside my chest. I had to leave her before I broke down. I leaned over and kissed her gently on the mouth.

She giggled, rolled her belly and thrashed her thighs together. I leaped back from her hand streaking for my crotch. Tears rolled down her cheeks.

In a whiny voice she pleaded, "Lemme feel it, huh? Lemme snatch it off, huh? Lemme see it bleed, huh? Lemme mash it, huh? Lemme, huh? Lemme, huh?"

I turned and walked away to the administration building. I looked back. The husky nurse was massaging Phala's shoulders. Phala's bony hand was still clawing at the air.

I broke down on the way back to Chicago. I cried longer and harder than I did when Phala fussed at the crow on that bottle of Old Crow whiskey.

Blue patted my shouder and said, "How is she doing? Did she look bad?"

I said, "She looked terrible and old. It's a funny thing. I used to laugh when she'd tell me that she wanted to be cremated if she were old and ugly when she died. I thought she'd always be beautiful."

By the last of September the weather got awful chilly. Fewer and fewer suckers came to the carnival locations to get trimmed in the flat-joints. In October the season closed.

I had close to three bills under the rug. I hadn't yet walked through the bathroom to Midge's bedroom. I had lots of opportunity. Blue was out of town three or four days a week playing the smack with Memphis Shorty.

Blue promised me he'd teach me the smack and the next winter I would be his partner. Blue kept the big white kitchen well stocked with food.

I had learned to cook when I was a kid and Phala worked in River Forest. Midge and I took turns fixing our meals. Twice a week a woman came in to clean the house and do the laundry.

We had lots of fun playing cards on the dining room table. Whenever there was a Robert Taylor or Charles Boyer picture on, I'd take Midge to the Tivoli Theater at Sixty-third Street and Cottage Grove Avenue. She'd fidget in her seat, hot as hell. But she wouldn't let me kiss her.

We had a lot of good clean fun together. I figured I'd play it cool. And after I got her to really like me, I'd make a fast move into her pants. She was still knocking around with the queer broads at Cocktails For Two on most weekends. Except for that it would have been a breeze for a guy with my gift of gab to lay her down.

I was living the best life I'd ever lived. But I couldn't forget Phala's face and that creepy giggle that day at the sanitarium. Sometimes I'd dream about it. I'd wake up soaked with sweat.

Blue also kept a well-stocked liquor closet. I started downing a glass of rum and coke before I went to bed. Instead of nightmares about Phala, I had wild wet, half-nightmares about Midge. Jesus! They were weird.

At first Midge and I would be kissing and fooling around. Then I'd be taking a sweet ride. A burly broad would pop up. She had a loud coarse laugh. The ugly big-tit broad would stand there buck naked with a jock three times the size of my own.

She'd flop the damn thing from side to side with both her hands. I'd keep pushing Midge's head away so she'd stop staring at it. I'd leap up and hurl my foot with all my might against the broad's deformed pecker.

The broad would screech and vanish. Then the ride would get sweeter than ever. The final explosion would blast me awake. I'd lie there panting and hating my burly tormentor.

I'd get a headache trying to figure out what those slick queer broads did with a fluff in bed. It had to be mysterious, powerful loving. I knew that.

On Christmas Eve Blue drove me to see Phala. I took her a big basket of fruit and candy. She was even thinner.

We just sat in the visiting lounge and stared at each other for a half hour. I didn't kiss her goodbye. I was afraid she might get horny and break me down again.

I stopped on my way back home. I sent my old pal, Lester Gray, a sawbuck money order up in Saint Charles Reformatory.

On Christmas day Midge cooked the best dinner I'd ever eaten, for Blue and me. There were piles of gifts under the beautiful Christmas tree for Blue, Midge and me. A cheerful blaze roared in the fireplace.

That night a gang of con men friends of Blue came and drank until daybreak. It was the best Christmas I ever had.

Of all my gifts I liked best the Philco table radio from Blue. I listened to sweet music from the Aragon Ballroom until the wee hours and thought about Midge. Midge must have spent a considerable part of her Christmas allowance for the Bulova wristwatch she gave me.

I spent almost a hundred dollars on gifts for Midge and Blue. It seemed that I'd known them for a lifetime. I was sure happy and crazy about them, and that's the guaranteed truth.

Blue had a birthday party for me at home on January fifteenth, Nineteen Forty. Precious Jimmy, Mule and Pocket were there to see me blow out the seventeen candles on my big pink birthday cake.

Midge had promised me she'd be home to celebrate with me. At two A.M. the party broke up. She still wasn't home. I was lying in bed listening for her to come in. I was wondering if she was hollering in joy on some broad's bed, when Blue came in and sat down on the side of the bed.

I said, "Blue, I hope you're not worried about Midge. She'll come in pretty soon, safe as always."

He said, "Folks, I'm not worried about her. I couldn't sleep for another reason. Kid, we're not going back to the flat-joint this spring. I'm going to teach you con.

"You're only seventeen. But with your build and poise

you come off like twenty-five. I'm going to dump that whiskey head, Memphis Kid and build you into my full-time partner."

I said, "That's good news. Tell me all about the wire store and what I have to tell a sucker to put him on the send for all his money."

The shadow of his big head waggled on the wall.

He said, "Wire stores shouldn't concern you, now. Anyway, they're almost out of style. It's the rag and payoff stores that most white con mobs have set up to play for rich suckers that ropers lug in for trimming.

"It's all long con. But hell, kid, first you have to be taught the basics of the short con."

I said, "Are there any Nigger long con mobs?"

He said, "No, Niggers don't have the feel for the organization and the big dough to finance and operate a long con store. Besides, a store has to buy its fix from powerful white politicians. Niggers don't have connections like that.

"An all-Nigger store would have to play for Nigger marks. There just aren't enough fat, Nigger suckers to support a black store.

"The best black con men are drag men. The newspapers call it the pigeon drop. The drag is long con because the mark is put on the send for his money."

I said, "Are we going to play the drag together, Blue?"

He said, "Maybe. But a Nigger drag man sometimes has to prowl the streets for weeks looking for a mark. Along with its other bad features, it's a felony.

"No, Folks, I'm not going to do a ten spot in the joint for playing a slow game like drag. Fast frequent short con touches are best for us as a start. But maybe later, now I said maybe, if you are as bright as I think you are, I'll see Felix the Fixer and find out if he can handle the fix for drag.

"Since you look white, our drag scores would come off bigger and faster. You could catch white marks that a black grifter couldn't stop. We'll wait and see how apt you are for con."

I said, "But Blue, you still haven't told me how the stores and the drag work. Do you really know?"

He laughed and said, "You're a natural for the con all right. Here you are ribbing the teacher so he has to give you the dope you want.

"All right, I'll convince you I know everything about con, short and long. I'm going to give you a fast rundown on the stores and the drag. You don't really need it. But I'm going to make the student respect his teacher.

"Folks, a wire store is a fake telegraph office that a con mob sets up to look just like a real one. A roper brings the sucker to be trimmed to the boss of this store who is the inside con man just like I'm the boss inside the flat-joint.

"To the mark he pretends to be a dissatisfied employee of the vast Western Union Company. The inside man and the roper cut the mark in on a plot to beat horse-racing books.

"An idiot would know it's a cinch to make a fortune when you can pick a winner in a horse race that's already been run.

"The inside man cons the mark he will make it possible by delaying the teletyped race results to the books until after the roper and the mark have laid their bets.

"To test the system for the mark and to give him a powerful convincer, this inside man gives them a winner. The roper takes the mark to a phony bookie joint and they both win a small bet.

"The mark's head is swimming with greed. He's seen the shills lose and win stacks of long green. Now he believes it's a mortal cinch to cheat the book out of a fortune.

"The larceny in his heart makes it easy for the roper and the inside man to put him on the send for a bundle of his dough. Just like the sucker playing against the flat-joint, he's got no chance to win because the roper fouls up the inside man's dope on the crucial race.

"The sucker is stricken and fleeced by the roper's stupid mistake. The inside man and the mark curse and abuse the hell out of the roper.

"The inside man puts the mark on a train. He promises the mark he'll contact him and next time, with a new bankroll and no stupid guy like the roper around to foul things up, they'll win back their losses and make that big fortune to boot.

"Flunkies strip the fake stores of the convincing props until time to play for another mark. Now the—"

I was so excited I cut him off, "I look white. Let's get a bunch of real white guys together and open a store. You could train me for the inside. Nobody would get wise that it was really a nigger store."

He exploded, "Goddamnit, Folks! Stay cool and stop letting your mind leapfrog like a screwy sucker. Hell, even I couldn't do it.

"The marks are smart, high-class businessmen, doctors, even lawyers. The inside man is the guts of a store. He makes one mistake and he's lost the mark and the score.

"The Vicksburg Kid was playing inside at twenty-eight. But he's a genius. Control yourself. You get confused, I won't be able to teach you the lousy short con.

"As I was trying to say, the rag store play is almost like that of the wire store. It is rigged up as a brokerage office. The mark is trimmed with fake shares of stock and phony stock market information.

"The payoff store can be a wire store or a rag store setup. The inside man, instead of delaying race results and letting the mark bet his own money on a winner to convince him, gives the mark money to bet on a fixed race.

"The same powerful payoff gimmick is used for the rag store. No Western Union setup is used in the payoff on the nags.

"The first sure-shot tip on the fixed race is the reward the inside man gives the roper and the mark when they return his lost wallet stuffed with important and valuable papers.

"The sucker's greed is fired up and he's trimmed in a lavish bookie setup just like in the wire play. The same gimmicks are used in the rag store. It's the bogus shares of stock and fake inside market information that trim the sucker in that case.

"Now the drag is a crude distant relative of the stores."

I cut him off again. I said, "Blue, please don't blow up again, but I want you to tell me some of the real words that con men say to suckers."

He said, "All right, kid, all right! Now the drag is really a desperate try of poor Nigger con men to imitate the big front and play of the white long con.

"Before Dirty Red got con goofy we played the drag together. A working day started when the banks and post offices opened. We were open on both ends. We both could catch and cap. Which means that either of us was capable of cutting into a sucker, holding him and finding out if he had scratch to play for.

"Both of us could cap on or build up a sucker who had been caught. We caught and played for our marks in the streets. Say I saw an elderly man who looked like a prospect. I'd block his way and rip my hat off my head.

"I'd say, 'Excuse me, sir. I know it's bad manners to stop a stranger on the street without a proper introduction. But I'm black like you and I'm in desperate need of information. You look like a kind, intelligent gentleman. Please help me.'

"Then I'd tell him about how I had just came to town from Alabama. I was carrying a large sum of money. I was afraid because a white man on the train coming north warned me about flimflammers and unfair white banks.

"I wondered if it was true that the banks up North gave five percent interest to white depositors and only three percent to Nigger depositors. What were flimflammers, and did his experience with the banks make the white man on the train tell me a lie or the truth?

"If he'd never heard of flimflammers and he had money, I'd signal Red across the street that the mark was qualified. I'd nudge the mark and point to Red picking up a fat wallet in the gutter.

"I'd say, 'Now ain't that a shame, Mr. Smith? A rich white man just pulled away in a new Cadillac. He must have dropped that wallet. Look at the Nigger trembling and shaking. Don't he know that you ain't a thief when you find something? Besides, a white man lost it and poor Niggers ain't got nothing nohow. I think we ought to call him and put his mind at ease.'

"I'd wave Red over to us. He'd come over scared and excited as hell.

"He'd roll his eyes and say, 'You all ain't going to give me away, are you?'

"I'd say, 'No, since we're all Niggers we thought we'd call you and give you some good advice. The white man dropped that wallet. You're not a thief. Now get yourself together. The Lord has made this your lucky day, ain't that right, Mr. Smith?'

"Red would look around suspiciously.

"Then he'd say, 'I'm sure glad two kind, wise Niggers saw me, instead of two mean, foolish white folks. I was raised in a Christian home and my mama always told me good advice is precious and should be rewarded. Tell you what I'm gonna do. If there's three dollars in this wallet, I'm gonna give my black friends a dollar apiece. If there's three thousand, I'm gonna give you a thousand dollars apiece.'

"Red would give me and the mark a flash of green inside the bulging wallet.

"I'd say, 'My stars, man, you've struck it rich! But let's get off this street. That white man is sure to come back looking for that wallet.'

"We'd walk the excited mark to a side street. In a gangway or the foyer of a building, Red would start to open the wallet. His hands would tremble so much he'd drop it. I'd pick it up and turn away from the mark to look inside it. I'd whistle in amazement and hand it to Red.

"I'd say, 'It's crammed with thousand dollar bills. That white man might be a big-time crook.'

"Red would say, 'Good God! Then these bills could be

from a big robbery. They might even be counterfeit. What are we gonna do?'

"I'd say, 'They're not counterfeit. They may be registered. We need the advice of some bigshot Nigger or white man. I'm a stranger in town. How about you, Mr. Smith? Can you think of some smart bigshot we can trust?'

"Before the mark could answer Red would snap his fingers and say, 'I've got it! Mr. Silverstein, my boss, will help us. Ain't nobody smarter than a Jew. Ain't that right, Mr. Smith? We can trust Mr. Silverstein. He loves me because I saved his only son from the deep cold waters of Lake Michigan two years ago. The kid was swimming and got cramps. He was going down for the third time when I reached him and pulled him to shore. There ain't nothing Mr. Silverstein wouldn't do for this Nigger.

"He's got a big fine office no more than two blocks from here. Lord have mercy, I just remembered I was on an errand for my boss when I had this good luck. Friends, you wait right here until I get back. I'm sure Mr. Silverstein will change these big bills so we can split fair and safe.'

"When he left, I'd say to the mark, 'Mr. Smith, we've got nothing to lose if he doesn't come back. If he does, then we've found an honest man and a small fortune.'

"The mark would almost shed tears of joy when Red got back. Red would shake our hands and say, 'Friends, I told you we could count on my boss. That wallet belonged to an old business rival of his. He'll give us smaller bills for the big ones.

" 'But he wants to meet my two relatives who are sharing in my good fortune. He wants to be sure they're sensible people and won't go wild and get him in trouble for helping.

" 'Now he knows, that I've got only two relatives in the world, my cousin Louis and my Aunt Susie. It's a good thing he's never seen them.'

"Red would hand me a business card and say, 'Here's where the office is.'

"I'd take the mark by the arm and start to walk away.

"Red would shout, 'Hey, what you Niggers gonna do? You gonna make a liar out of me to my boss? I told you he knows I ain't got nobody in the world but cousin Louis and Aunt Susie. Mr. Smith ain't no woman.'

"I'd turn to the mark and say, 'Don't you worry about a thing, friend. The same arrangements I make for myself, I'll make for you.'

"While I was gone, Red would give the mark a detailed description of the mythical office and Mr. Silverstein. When I got back, I would breathlessly describe the elegant office and the wonderful Mr. Silverstein.

"I'd say to Red, 'Yes, Mr. Silverstein is sure a fine man. He told me about how you saved his son. I've never seen a white man that loved a Nigger like he does you.

" 'He likes me too and he was pleased when I was able to put up forty-five hundred dollars as proof of my worth and integrity to share a third of that fifteen thousand dollars in the wallet.

" 'He told me that he'd trust you with his life and that he takes care of business on the inside and you can take care of us on the outside.'

"Red would leave to bring back both my share and the mark's. At least the mark thought his was coming back with Red. When Red got back, he'd give me a paper sack fat with greenbacks.

"I'd say, 'Where is Mr. Smith's share?'

"Red would say, 'The boss said every tub must sit on its own bottom and every tongue must confess of its own soul. You put up a bond of good faith. Aunt Susie, I mean Mr. Smith, ain't showed his good faith in the right way.'

"I'd shove the bag back to Red.

"I'd say angrily, 'We're all Niggers in this together. Since Mr. Smith's share ain't here, take it all back. I don't want my share if he can't get his.'

"Red would say, 'Good gravy. I didn't say Mr. Smith couldn't get his share. 'Course he can if he pleases the boss like you did and puts up a reasonable bond to prove he's a solid person and won't get the boss in trouble.

" 'The boss just wants to be sure that everybody is used to money and won't go on a stupid spending spree and get police attention when he gets his five thousand dollars. The white man that lost the wallet would be glad to see my boss's fine reputation destroyed.'

"Most likely the mark would blurt out his ability to qualify before I could ask him.

"I'd go with the mark to raise his bond. When we came back, Red would take it back to the office. The mark and I would wait anxiously for Red to come back with our shares.

"Finally I'd point to Red coming toward us a block away. Red would stop and wave. I'd point to myself. Red would wag his head no. I'd point to the mark. Red would wag his head yes.

"The mark would start the long walk. When he was midway between us, we'd both fade and disappear.

"Folks, black con men call this the final. White grifters call it the blowoff. Well, kid, are you satisfied? That's most of the real words, as you say, of a con game in action."

I said, "Blue, it sure is slick. Please let's play that game together. I know I can memorize all the words."

He said, "Folks, that's ass backward. You can't learn con by memorizing words. Every mark and every play of any con game is different. You have to memorize the *elements* of con.

"When you've done that, you've got the secret key to all con games, from the biggest to the smallest. Now I want you to tear apart the drag that you heard. Tell me the elements of con that you could grasp."

I said, "Number one, Red and you had to catch Mr. Smith. Number two, you had to sound him out to find out if he had dough. It's obvious you wouldn't want to play for a broke sucker. And you found out that Mr. Smith knew nothing of flimflam or con.

"Under the number two step, you also had to rapidly

gain his confidence with your tale of distress and your need for his wise and kind help. Number three step was showing Red to the mark and bringing Red in for the play.

"Number four step was Red's offer to share his good luck. This excited the dishonesty in the mark. If the mark had been honest, he would have advised returning the white man's wallet. A mark has to be a thief himself.

"Number five step was Red coming back with your five gee share. This was the convincer for the mark. He knew he could get five gees.

"The convincer was tightened when you refused your share until the mark got his. The fifth step set the mark up for the sixth step, the send for his money so he could qualify for his share. The seventh step was the final or blowoff. How did I do, Blue?"

He said, "Hell, you're not bright, you're brilliant. I'll have you ready by spring for the smack at least. Then later the drag. Folks, it's almost four A.M. You go to sleep on what you've learned. I'm not waiting up for Midge. I need rest. Memphis and I are going out of town today."

Blue stood up.

I said, "Blue, what did you mean about Dirty Red going con goofy?"

He said, "Conning is lying. Red lied for forty years. Finally his brain was so twisted and poisoned by lies that he couldn't tell the difference between a lie and the truth.

"I was his partner. But he reached a point when I couldn't hold a conversation with him. Everything I'd say to him, no matter how innocent and commonplace, he'd blow up and stay mad for days.

"He thought I was lying to him, that I was making a fool out of him for kicks. I had to cut him loose. At the end he was dangerous. I was afraid of him. Nobody will play with him now.

"He tapes his right arm to his side and begs for a living. He bums around Fifty-first Street. Folks, what happened to Red can happen to anybody who lies for a living.

"Good night, Folks. You look out for Midge and the

house as always while I'm out of town."

I said, "Thanks, Blue, for the con lessons. I'll take care of everything. Good night."

I lay there listening to the shrill, frigid banshee of January winds. My heart jackhammered with the excitement of the con.

I heard footsteps in the hall. I turned my head. Blue's shadow was back in the room.

He said, "I forgot something important that you must remember until you go six feet under. Folks, there are only two kinds of people in the whole wide world, grifters and suckers.

"You're going to be a grifter, I'm certain of that. The secrets of con are priceless. Every grifter is surrounded by suckers that he for many reasons can't play for. There are charming, likeable suckers that you'll meet socially. But Folks, a grifter true to the con code never likes a sucker enough or lets the sucker come close enough to get the secrets of con.

"Let their stupid brains stay asleep in their chump world. Keep your own brain honed to razor sharpness in the secret world of con. Folks, you know I think a great deal of you. But if you ever violate the con code, I'll hate your guts. I swear it!"

He faded away into the hall blackness before I could answer. I felt like I had gulped down a handful of benny pills. I lay there in the gloom a long time and engraved on my brain every word that Blue had spoken.

I heard a rapping on the window. I thought it was the wind. Then it came louder and faster, I got up and pulled the drapes aside. It was Midge, wide eyed. She was huddled inside a man's heavy black overcoat. I raised the window and looked down at her.

She whispered, "I don't have my key. Let me in the back door."

I tiptoed down the hall to the back door. I let her in. She squeezed herself against me for an instant. Her cold face tingled my chest. We walked into my bedroom. I flicked on a tiny night light.

I said, "What happened?"

She slipped out of the bulky overcoat and threw it across the bed. She was nude. She said, "There's a cabby out front waiting for his fare and coat. Johnny, please take a five-dollar bill and his coat out to him for me."

I went to the closet and put on an overcoat. She passed me going to the bathroom. I smelled whiskey and the sharp, raw perfume of her crotch. I went out the back door to the shivering cabby.

He said, "Man, thanks for the tip and coat. Let me tell you it was one bitch of a sight seeing a naked broad running down South Parkway in zero weather. Is she your old lady?"

As I turned away, I said, "No, she's my crazy sister."

I rushed back to my bedroom. The night light was out. I went through the bathroom to Midge's room. She wasn't there. I wondered if she'd lost her mind and become a pneumonia buff. Maybe she was naked out in the backyard having an orgy with Jack Frost.

I was looking out my bedroom window when Midge's muffled voice said behind me, "Peek-a-boo. I see you."

I spun around. I saw a vague lump in my bed.

She said, "Stop wandering around, square. Get in bed and warm me up. I'm chilled to the bone."

I said, "Are you nuts? What if Blue catches you in my bed? Go to your own bed, Midge, before you get me thrown out into the cold."

She laughed and said, "Don't be a square. Angel, aren't you hip that Blue hates lesbians so much he'd weep for joy to find me in just any man's bed? If you don't come and hold me, I'll go back into the street just like I am.

"Then your conscience will haunt you for the rest of your days. 'Poor Midge froze to death because I was too square to grant her one last, humble request.' Come on, Johnny. Hold me and I'll tell you what happened."

I hung my coat in the closet. I took off my pajamas and got into bed beside her. She threw her thigh across my middle. She had her head on my chest. I had my arm around her back.

She said, "I almost got murdered tonight. Oh, Johnny, I did the dumbest thing. I got crocked and went home with a cute little waitress at Cocktails For Two. Her boyfriend was supposed to be in jail under high bond.

"Two weeks ago he almost stabbed to death a girl that he thought was going with Francine. We were making mad love in the bedroom. We heard a key in the front door.

"Somebody had gone her boyfriend's bail. Lucky for me her apartment was made like our house here. I ran naked through the connecting bathroom into a vacant bedroom. I hid under the bed.

"I didn't know what to do. My dress and coat were in the closet. My panties, bra and slip were on a chair in the bedroom. My shoes were somewhere in there.

"I could hear him talking to her. I was terrified that he'd notice the strange clothes and start searching for me. He came into the bathroom. I heard him taking a leak. I saw his legs and big feet through the half open door.

"I almost fainted when he said. 'What the fuck is that strange stink I smell? Bitch, did you have money to buy perfume while I was rotting in jail?'

"He went back into the bedroom. I heard the tinkle of perfume bottles being knocked about on the dresser. Then I heard him open the closet door. I crawled from beneath the bed. I tried to raise a window. It was stuck.

"I heard him shout. 'This ain't your coat and dress. Them ain't your underwear in that chair. One of your freak bitches is hiding in my house. I'm gonna cut her pussy out, and your throat, bitch.'

"Johnny, Blue doesn't believe in God, but I'm like Mama was. I do. God let that window finally slide up. It made a loud noise. I went out the window to a gangway. Lucky for me the apartment was on the ground floor.

"I was so cold I could hardly breathe. I heard him cursing me through the open window. I ran down South

Parkway. I looked back. He was running toward me.

"I hailed the jitney cabbie that brought me home. I wonder if that maniac killed Francine? I'll have to stay off Forty-seventh Street. He'll kill me. I know he will. Johnny, please don't tell Blue what happened."

I said, "Midge, I won't tell him. But everything that happened was your own fault. Why don't you stop that freakish stuff with girls?

"Some guy is going to kill you one of these days. Any normal guy or dame despises lesbians. Straighten up and get yourself a fellow before it's too late."

She mounted me and lay there on top of me. I put my hands on her back at the waist. I strolled my fingertips over the soft satin.

She combed her fingers through my hair. I felt the prickly knives of her fingernails slashing tenderly across my tingling scalp.

She feathered her tongue tip through my eyebrows and across my eyelashes. I felt an almost unbearably delicious thrill tickle my face nerves and race down the side of my throat.

Our open hot mouths locked together. Our tongues fought a sugary duel. She slid her mouth away and whispered, "I want to tell you a secret. But I want to look into those blue pieces of sky when I do."

She flicked on the night light. It ignited midnight-blue skyrockets in her jet hair. We gazed into each other eyes for a long moment. I felt myself throbbing and swelling, aching against the rim of her secret core.

She sighed and whispered, "Most girls are afraid of beautiful boys like you. But I'm not. I know you can make me never want another girl to touch me.

"You can make me forget Robert Taylor and Charles Boyer or anybody else. Make love to me, blue eyes. Thrill me out of my senses. Save me. Take me. Hurt me. But make me love you. Make me your slave."

I kissed her hard. Then I nursed like a starved baby at her heaving breasts. She moved forward on me. I felt her gentle hand tenderly aim me. She sat down and slowly impaled the core.

She cried out. Her face was twisted. I saw her belly muscles jerking. Then she started to dry swallow. Young fool that I was, I thought she was in ecstasy.

She whimpered and moaned, "Oh dear God! Please don't let it happen now."

I really believed that I was so good to her that she was pleading with God to stall her orgasm. I braced my feet against the footboard of the bed and rammed myself into the very bottom of the hot pulsating core.

She shuddered. I heard the throaty bellow of her retch. The stinking flame of her vomit seared my face. My burning eyes were blinded by the acid slime. I was dead, limp inside the core. I scooted out from beneath her. I groped my way to the bathroom. I cleared my eyes with a washcloth.

I looked into the mirror over the washbowl. My face and hair looked like I had dunked my head into a bucket of green snot.

I puked into the bowl until my aching guts dry locked. I stood there weakly, trembling, fighting for breath. Midge streaked by me weeping in hysterical gasps. She slammed the door to her bedroom. I heard her put a chair under the doorknob on the other side.

I brushed my teeth and gargled. I got into the tub and scrubbed myself from head to toe with my soapy hairbrush until I was red raw.

I put on my pajamas. I snatched the sheets off the bed. I threw the sour pillow to the floor. I lay on the mattress and hoped that Midge's wild sobbing wouldn't awaken Blue. I got up and knocked gently on her door.

She wailed, "Please leave me alone. Please, please."

I went back to bed. Finally all was quiet. I lay there thinking about Midge. Now I knew what had happened when Midge tried to have sex with Tommy. No wonder she hadn't wanted to tell me about it. I wondered how she could get kicks with freakish lesbians and get sick with boys.

I was still trying to solve the riddle when dawn's bleak blade slit night's miserable throat. I heard Blue moving around in his room down the hall. I got up and put fresh linen on my bed.

I guessed he was getting ready for the trip with Memphis Kid. Then I heard Midge drawing water into the bathtub.

She shouted above the roar, "Yes, Blue, I'm home. I'll pay the gas bill today. Just put the bill and the money on my dresser."

I heard Blue's footsteps coming toward my room. He knocked.

I said, "Come in."

He opened the door and stepped in. He was wearing a camelhair overcoat and a beige hat. He looked like a rich sportsman on his way to a football game.

He smiled and said, "Good morning. How long has Midge been in?"

I said, "Hi, Blue. She came in shortly after you went to bed. You're sure leaving early."

He said, "It's a long way to Decatur, Illinois. Say listen, remind Midge to pay the gas bill. I don't lag my bills like a sucker.

"All right, Folks. I'll see you in a couple of days. Keep those lessons working in your head."

I said, "Goodbye, Blue, and good luck. Don't worry, I'm going to be a crackerjack at the con next spring."

He grinned and walked away. I dressed and knocked on Midge's door.

She said, "Come in."

I stuck my head in and asked her if she wanted breakfast.

She kept her eyes down and said, "No thanks, I'm not hungry. Will you pay the gas bill for me? I'm not going out."

I said, "Sure, darling."

She went to the dresser and gave me the bill and

money. She said, "Forget that darling jive, huh? We both know it can't be like that. I'm sorry for what I put you through last night. I was a square to even try it. I knew what would happen. I'm nothing, Johnny. I'm just a nasty, lowlife freak."

I said, "Midge, we can't give up. I'm game to try it again sometime. Honest, honey, before you got sick, it was the best pussy I ever had. You just couldn't help it. That's all. Next time, it will be so good to us, we'll blow our tops."

She smiled sadly and gently pushed the door shut in my face.

I went to the kitchen and fried an egg. I couldn't get it down. I stared out the kitchen window and thought about Phala, Dirty Red and Midge.

Snowflakes floated from the sleazy sky like frozen confetti. A sudden gust of angry wind twisted the dots into a funnel of frothy madness.

"Yes," I thought, "Life and people are like that wind and the snowflakes."

Midge didn't leave the house for almost a month. Blue was happy as hell. He didn't know that she was afraid to go out. He probably thought she'd reformed.

Midge and I still talked to each other and we were friendly. But it was somehow different than it was before that night in my bed. She told me to answer the phone and tell all callers for her that she was out of town. There were a lot of callers. All broads.

On the afternoon of Saint Valentine's Day, a dozen orchids came for Midge. Lucky thing for the orchids that I accepted them from the messenger at the door. Blue and Memphis were hunting deer in Wisconsin.

The card read, "From your love mate, Celeste."

Blue would have dumped the bouquet in the garbage can. Midge was excited. Midge called her. I listened to Midge's chatter on the phone. Celeste had been one of her most ardent admirers and now she was back in town.

I heard her make a date for that night at the Royal Box

Bar on Fifty-first Street. Gee, she was pretty when she left that night. I told her I'd stay at home so if she got into a jam she could call me.

I got the works of Voltaire from Blue's bookcase. I read the heavy stuff until midnight. I figured I'd better get well read. I might run into some educated marks in the spring.

I ate a cheese sandwich and drank a glass of milk. I took a bath and went to bed. I was reading an adventure story in *Liberty* magazine when I fell asleep.

I woke up and looked at the Bulova. It was three A.M. I heard the toilet flush. I finished my adventure story and went to the bathroom to take a leak.

I heard a hissing sound in Midge's room. I wondered if she was letting a snake take a turn. I flushed the toilet, turned out the light and walked over and banged the door shut on my side of the bathroom.

I kneeled down at Midge's keyhole and peeped inside. Her night light was on. She was lying flat on her back, wide legged. She had her eyes closed and she was flopping her head from side to side on the pillow. She was sucking air through her teeth making the snake noises.

Midge's hands were plastered to the top of a vague bulk wedged between her legs, making grunting, suckling pig noises. In the dimness I couldn't tell whether it was a man or a woman, or even a large real pig.

Then a dark brown hand and arm bigger than my own reached up and started to stroke across the nipples and yellow belly. It sure turned Midge on. Her hissing sounded like a snake pit. Finally a woman's big head and wide shoulders loomed up from between the pyramid.

Midge opened her eyes. She spoke to the bulk. It was a burly broad. Except for her lighter skin-color and no pecker, she was the burly, big-tit broad in my half-nightmares come to life.

The broad got on top of Midge. She rubbed her crotch across Midge's for awhile. She pressed Midge's breasts together so the nipples touched. She licked and sucked them hard.

Then they took a position I'll never forget. And that's the guaranteed truth. Midge smiled up at the giant freak. She jackknifed her legs. She held them back with her hands. Her knees and thighs were flat against her chest. Her core was gaped open.

The broad got on her knees facing me. Then she scooted backwards and up. She pressed the bottom of her crotch flush on the top of the core. She leaned forward with her huge hands outstretched on the foot of the bed for support.

She hunched her crotch forward and backward across the core. I couldn't see Midge at all.

She was hissing and shouting, "Oh! Daddy! Daddy, it's good! It's your pussy, sweet Daddy. Please don't ever leave me again. I'll kill myself if you do."

The jockey's moon-face was shiny with sweat as she rubbed her crotch faster and faster across the core. Finally they stopped and Midge lay in the brawny arms of her lover like a tiny child.

They lay there and chatted like a straight couple would do after making love. Their voices were too low for me to catch much of the chatter. I did hear Midge call the broad Celeste.

I just couldn't take my eyes off them. The sight of two lovers like that hypnotized me.

Finally Celeste started kissing Midge at the crown of her head. Then she did the eyebrow and eyelash bit that Midge had thrilled me with.

The broad kissed Midge all the way to her tiny feet. Celeste's big paw grabbed around Midge's trim ankle. The other paw was busy as hell caressing the belly, the core, the inside of the thighs.

She flicked the tip of her unbelievably long tongue across the tips of Midge's toes. Midge was shuddery and giggly in joy.

I started to get the glimmer of a message. I was absolutely bush-league as a lover. Maybe Midge had vomited on me in pure disgust.

Then the cannibal swallowed the foot up to the instep into her cavernous mouth. She sucked that foot like a little kid sucking a popsicle.

Midge was hissing and grinding her fists into her cheekbones. That busy other paw never stopped stroking across the velvet yellow.

That faint message was crystal clear to me now.

Finally Midge was silent and limp. She lay there in a kind of coma with her eyes closed and breathing through her open mouth.

Celeste got out of bed and stood looking down at Midge. Midge fluttered open her dreamy eyes, and gazed up at her burly lover. She closed them. Celeste turned away and strode toward the keyhole.

I got off my cramped knees and scrambled into my bedroom. I had just eased my door shut when I heard the door on the other side of the bathroom open.

I lay down on the bed. I felt hot and horny. I heard Celeste washing up. I thought, "So that's why lesbians don't really need a jock to run a broad crazy with joy. The freakish bastards use a devilish technique."

I heard Celeste shut the door on the other side. I got up and went into the bathroom. I sponged off in cold water to bring my fever down. The cold water did nothing for me.

My watch had six A.M. I started dressing. I had to go out and find a broad somewhere. Red, black, purple, old, young, ugly or pretty, it didn't matter. I had to have a broad.

I was putting on my overcoat when I heard the front door slam. I wondered if Blue was back from the hunting trip. I raced down the hallway to the front of the house.

All was quiet. I heard a car engine start. I looked out the front window. It was Celeste pulling away from the curb in a new black Cadillac.

I went out into the fresh January chill. I went to the corner of Sixty-third Street and Cottage Grove Ave. It was bare except for the working stiffs waiting for streetcars. There wasn't a whore to be seen. I passed a curvy light brown-skinned girl waiting for a streetcar.

She smiled. I remembered Blue's rundown on the con approach. I went back to her and tested it.

I said, "Good morning. I know it's very impolite to approach a stranger on the street, especially a young lady, without a proper introduction. But I'm seeking information. Will you be kind enough to help me?"

She smiled at me and said, "Why yes, if I can."

I said, "I'm a stranger in town and I want to know where I can find a nice clean hotel in the neighborhood."

She said, "Are you really a stranger? Where's your luggage?"

I said, "It's in a locker at Union Station. I'm not jiving you, beautiful."

She blushed and said, "I don't know too much about hotels. But I suppose all of them are pretty clean up in this neighborhood. Why not try that one across the street?"

I said, "Thanks. I will. Say, what's your name? No, let me guess. I'll bet it's a beautiful one like Dawn, or Diane, or maybe Angel. Did I hit it?"

She giggled and said, "You're way off. It's Jackie. Disappointed?"

I said, "No. Jackie was on the tip of my tongue. I like it. It's cute and jazzy. It fits you like a glove. My name is Johnny. Where are you going?"

She said, "I'm going to work. Where else?"

I said, "Are you married?"

She said, "Yes, I am. Why?"

I said, "If I had a pretty wife like you, I'd work two jobs so you could stay pretty at home."

She said, "I haven't been working long. My husband got hurt on his job. He hasn't worked in a couple of months. We have two babies. I have to work."

I raised my eyebrows in disbelief. I said, "You look like a little girl of fourteen. I just can't believe you're married and a mama, too. Excuse me for asking, but what do you make a day on your job?"

She sighed and said, "Oh, about seven dollars. Why?"

I said, "How would you like to work for me this morning for twice that ?"

She said, "Doing what?"

I said, "Just keeping me company for a couple of hours in one of those hotel rooms across the street. How about it? I'm in the mood, Jackie, to be the best company you ever had."

She frowned and said, "I'm respectable. I'm no whore."

I said, "Any fool can see that. Jackie, I'm so lonely in this big city. It would never cross my mind that I was paying a whore. Besides, I know some ways to make love to you that could make you fall in love with me."

She bit her bottom lip and looked at her streetcar rattling toward us a block away.

She said, "I can't do it. My boss might call my husband at home if I didn't show up for work. I'm a fry cook in a hotel grill. The morning is very busy. I just can't do it. You're very handsome and nice. You won't have any trouble finding a girl. I'm sorry, Johnny."

I said rapidly, "Jackie, you've got to. I'm about ready to pop off in my pants. I know I can't find a girl as cute as you. Go to the hotel with me and call your boss. Tell him you'll be late a couple of hours."

The streetcar came to stop in front of us. People started climbing aboard it. She walked two steps away toward it. She came back. She said, "Will you give me the money before we—?"

I said, "Sure, Jackie. I'm on the level."

I gave her the money and the wildest thrills she said she ever had. I followed Celeste's routine almost to the letter. I didn't have the equipment for the crotch scrape. And I just couldn't cut the cannibal bit with the foot. But, believe me, I got my money's worth after I lit her up.

My fever was gone when I got home. I took a bath and went to bed. I turned on the radio. An announcer said it was eleven A.M. I felt sorry for Jackie's husband. He was going to be a bore in bed. Jackie had really been a pig for the lesbian technique.

I dozed off just as a soap opera came on the radio. It was Stella Dallas, One Man's Family or something. Anyway, I got sucked into the plot in my sleep. In my dream I was getting a piece of the action.

Suddenly the action stopped. I opened my eyes. I looked up at Blue dressed in hunting clothes. The radio was off.

He said, "Sorry, Folks, I didn't intend to wake you up. I peeped in to see if you were all right. You must have had a helluva night to be sleeping this time of day. Midge was asleep, too. You two must have cabareted last night."

I said, "We didn't cabaret. Blue, I laid a fine doll this morning. I cut into her with that approach for the drag you taught me. It worked like a charm. I got back from the hotel a short while ago. Did you bag any deer?"

He said, "Hell, no. I shouldn't have taken Memphis with me. The clumsy sonuvabitch got drunk. He stumbled around in the woods and spooked the game before we could get in range.

"Folks, I stuck my head into Midge's room a moment ago. It stank like a two-buck whorehouse. There's been some fucking going on in there. Has one of those slimy broads been in there with Midge? I give you my word of honor I won't tip Midge that you told me."

I thought fast and looked him squarely in the eyes. I said, "No, Blue, I haven't seen a broad in there."

He said, "Goddamn it, Folks, don't get cute with me. You wouldn't have to see a broad to know. Did you *hear* a broad in there?"

I said, "No, I didn't hear one either."

He had a sly look on his face. He said, "Now, Folks, let's get an understanding. I believe you. You know I'm not so old I can't remember how hot young asses can get. You and Midge are alone a lot.

"She's not your blood kin. She's your play sister. Look, Folks, I got a big heart and a broader mind. You were conning me about that doll in the hotel, weren't you? You ripped off a piece with Midge in her bedroom, didn't you?"

I didn't answer. I couldn't figure what road to take. He pounded me against the shoulder with the heel of his hand. He was grinning.

He said, "Why so shy? Tell me the truth. Say you did it. Can't you see I'm not mad? You shot her down, didn't you, Folks?"

I mumbled, "Yes, Blue. Like you said. That's what happened all right. I couldn't help myself. She was naked in the bathroom. I didn't know she was in there. We lost our heads. I'm sorry. It won't happen again. I deserve to be thrown out of the house."

He laughed and said, "Thrown out? You deserve a medal. It was just what she needs most. Go on and finish out your nap. I'm going to let some fresh air into Midge's room."

He went through the bathroom. Blue was a strange father all right. But I was glad he wasn't like Minnie's old man.

Blue came back into my bedroom. He had a woman's plastic makeup pouch in his hand. His eyes were flashing. His black face was gray with anger. He held the pouch before my eyes.

He said slowly, "What is this?"

I said, "It's a makeup kit. I think."

He loudmouthed, "I know what the hell it is. Since you told me there was no broad in there, I'd like you to tell me how I could pick this up on the floor in there?"

I said, "It probably belongs to Midge. She wears make-up when she goes out."

He said, "This powder and lipstick is too dark for Midge. Folks, what's been going on?"

I said, "Blue, I told you the truth the first time."

He snatched off his heavy leather belt. It whistled through the loops. He went back to Midge's room. In a moment I heard him wake up Midge.

He roared, "What is this damn thing doing in your room? If you lie to me I'll cut the blood out of you. I've got a bellyful of your freakish shit."

Midge screamed, "Get away from me, Blue. I'll put your big black ass in jail if you hit me. I borrowed that makeup from a friend and forgot to return it. Get the hell out of my room, Blue."

He shouted, "You little funky freak. You think you can play the con for Blue Howard? I'm gonna do that I should have done a long time ago. I'm going to s lit your fast yellow ass wide open and tell the rollers why I did it. How about that?"

I heard the loud smash of the leather. Then another scream and a scuffling sound. Then again and again. At least a dozen times I heard the belt blasting flesh.

I went into Midge's room. Midge was on the floor face down. Blue had his knee in the middle of her shoulders. He was leaning all of his two hundred pounds down on her, pinning her to the floor.

Her legs were flailing as he lashed her butt and back.

I grabbed his wrist and said, "Please don't hit her anymore."

His wide eyes looked up at me. He got to his feet. Midge rolled over and lay there on her back and stared up at him dry-eyed.

She gritted her teeth and almost sang in a whisper, "I hate you, Blue Howard. I've always hated you. Do you understand, Blue Howard, how much I hate you? I wish you were rotting in your grave. I hate you. I hate you."

Blue's shoulders slumped. He heaved a deep sigh and pressed his palms against his head. He extended his open hand down toward her. She rolled away from it.

He tried to speak. All that came out was a garbled cackle. I put my arm around his shoulder and guided hm down the hall to his bedroom.

He just kept shaking his head as I helped him undress and get into bed. I went back to Midge. She was in the bathroom throwing cold water on her face. Ugly red welts striped her back.

I said, "Midge, I tried to alibi for you. Your back is in bad shape. Let me put something on it."

She turned and looked at me. She smiled sadly. She said, "No thanks, Johnny, it doesn't hurt. You know something? I've really enjoyed being your play sister. Too bad that we couldn't have grown up together with Pauline our mother and Blue not our father. But some kind, clean-cut guy for our father.

"Then I could have been happy for all those years and all the ones to come. I know I wouldn't be all fouled up like I am. Johnny, I'm leaving this house and never coming back." Tears sprang to her eyes.

I put my arms around her. I said, "How will you live? You're just a girl. You'd be in trouble out there."

She said, "That's what Blue thinks. But I have an out. There's a woman named Celeste that I can count on. She was here last night.

"Johnny, we are madly in love. Nobody can make love the way she does. I can't live without it. She's got a fabulous apartment. She's begged me to live with her. She makes as much money as Blue does. Maybe more. When Blue goes to sleep, I'm going to have her come to get me."

I said, "What does she do for a living? Peddle dope? You better stay here, Midge. Blue won't beat you again. You should have seen him in his bedroom. He's falling apart. He's so sorry that he did that."

She said, "Celeste is no dope peddler. She's smarter than that. She's not forty years old for nothing. She's got three girls shoplifting for her.

"I'm going to keep the apartment and make love to Celeste like a good little wife while those boosters steal our living.

"So, don't worry about me. I'll be happier than I've ever been in my life. If you were smart, you'd get away from Blue as fast as you can. He just wants to use you. He has no real friends. Get away before it's too late."

I said, "You're angry. Blue has his faults. But he's not that bad. He's got at least one real friend. Me. I heard you say once that you wouldn't let Blue wake up if he ever beat you. Please Midge, don't sneak in there and do anything to him. He's your father, and he loves you."

She laughed bitterly and said, "You poor chump. He's really got you conned, hasn't he? Don't worry. I don't feel enough for him to kill your precious Blue Howard."

That afternoon around three, Celeste sent a cab for Midge. I went to the front window and watched the cabbie put Midge's last bag into the cab. Midge blew me a kiss as it pulled away. It disappeared into the January gloom.

Blue was snoring when I went down the hall to my room. I lay on the bed and stared at the ceiling. The moan of the wind tricked me into jagged sleep.

That long ago train from Kansas City to Chicago was hurtling through an inky night. A little boy's shoulder bounced against the ceiling of the coach as the train flew from the track and fell down, down into blackness.

I woke up in the grayish-purple fog of sunset. Blue was sitting on the side of my bed. He was shaking my shoulder. He said, "Well, Folks, Midge is gone. She's taken all of her clothes."

I said, "Are you going to find her and bring her back?"

He said, "Hell, no. She'll come back crawling on her own. I know Chicago. She can't survive in those streets. She'll have to come back.

"She'll wake up that those freaks are not her friends in need. Folks, she has to come back. I know she'll realize we are all she's got."

I said, "I'm sure going to miss her. I hope you're right. I hope nothing bad happens to her before she sees the light. She's a stubborn little girl. Yes, I hope you're right."

He got to his feet. He looked like an ebony statue of an old man standing there in the purple haze.

He said, "I'm going to the barber shop for a shave and a good massage. Want to come along?"

I said, "No, not this time. I think I'll take a bath and go to bed early."

He went down the hall. I heard the front door shut. I went to the beige leather chair near the window. I sat there and watched the wild wind bend the groaning trees.

I thought about Grandma Annie. Maybe she was lucky to be dead. I felt so sad for Blue, for Phala, Lester Gray, Midge and the trees.

CHAPTER ELEVEN

Conning in the Spring Tra La Tra La

Golden Spring burst forth with its perennial promises of beauty and love to suckers. But it brought the exciting promise of the con to me.

I went to visit Phala on the third of April. Her eyes were still vacant and she was thinner. On the way back I sent my old pal, Lester Gray, another money order.

The sharp pain of losing Midge had dulled somewhat for Blue and me. We seldom talked about her. We tried to forget. But her room and her memory were there to remind us.

After Midge left, Blue didn't take any more trips with Memphis Kid. Memphis got a new partner called St. Louis Shorty.

Blue spent all of his time teaching me the smack game. We practiced the dialogue for the game until I was hoarse.

On April twenty-third, Nineteen Forty, Blue was satisfied that I was ready for my con debut.

The night before the morning that I played for my first sucker, he said, "Now, Folks, our play together is going to be ragged as hell for a while. But don't let it give you the jitters.

"We're like a new dance team that has to learn each other's mannerisms and style. The con is our music. Each day that passes will make us dance better together. We are starting out jigging for the suckers. It won't be long before the bastards will be dazzled by our tricky ballet.

"Now the con signals I taught you are just basic ones. As we go along, I'll teach you the rest of them. I want you to memorize every quirk and reaction of the suckers we play. Every sucker is different. The bigger sucker frame of reference you have, the better and the faster you will learn to play good con.

"We're lucky to play together. Your white skin gives us a slick edge on white and black marks. I'll catch the Nigger marks and you catch the white ones.

"To the Niggers, I say, 'Let's take that goddamn peckerwood's money.' You tell the white marks. 'Let's break that bastard nigger.'

"Never mumble, Folks. Speak clearly like an actor on the stage or in the movies, so the mark can hear every word of the con.

"Don't catch any crippled or cross-eyed marks. They're jinky. And run from a mark that stutters. It's the quickest way to the pen to play for one. And for God's sake, don't catch a mark dressed all in black.

"Don't waste your sympathy on our marks. Those sons-uvbitches are thieves at heart. They'd play the con themselves if they knew how. It's the mark who's too honest to go for the con that's really on the square.

"That's all for now, Folks. There will be lots more as we go along. Any questions?"

I said, "No, everything fits like a glove so far."

He said, "Good night, partner."

He went to bed. I tipped in and got a belt of rum and coke. I played the smack in my sleep until daybreak.

By eight A.M. we were in the Caddie cruising down Cottage Grove Ave. The radio crackled with the news of a big dance hall fire in Natchez, Mississippi.

Blue said, "I'm glad that Jim Crow joint burned down. It's a little too early to work our stockyards plan for a score. We'll go to the Dearborn Station shed to test your wings.

"Stop shaking, Folks. The first mark is always the hardest. The amount of a grifter's first score isn't the least bit important to him. The first sucker money you take off, even if it's only a lousy sawbuck, will be like a million-buck score. You'll get that wonderful feeling when you break the ice with your first sucker."

Blue parked on Taylor Street near Dearborn Street. We walked down Taylor to the corner of Dearborn. We were at the point of splitting up when Blue went rigid.

He whispered, "There's no point in splitting up. We can't get down here."

I saw a tall, very skinny white guy standing on the sidewalk in front of the Dearborn train station. A dark brown-skinned redcap was standing beside him. The redcap was saying something to stringbean, who was sweeping our faces with tiny, hard blue eyes.

We turned away and went back to the Caddie.

As we pulled away, Blue said, "That redcap is a stool pigeon. He put the finger on me when he worked at Union Station. That skinny peckerwood has to be Sweeney the Snake.

"Grifters have described him and warned me about him many times. It's Sweeney all right. He's a bunco roller. That old gray-haired bastard will remember us twenty years from now. They say he never forgets a face."

I said, "He sure looks like a snake, with that chinless face and tiny eyes."

Blue said, "Those are not the only reasons for his tag. Back in the early Twenties he wiggled from a narrow ventilator to nail a team of white grifters playing a mark in a fake office in the Loop. He's clever all right."

I said, "Are we going to try at another train station?"

Blue said, "Not this morning. The Snake is probably making a tour of the stations. And he's one of those rare goddamn rollers. He's so honest, he'd probably beat hell out of the grifter who offered to grease his mitt.

"By the time we get to the stockyards, that Dutchman's joint I told you about will be jumping with stockyard suckers. The Dutchman will be cashing their paychecks."

I said, "What if he serves you? How does the game go then for the mark I've caught."

Blue chuckled and said, "Folks, there isn't one chance in ten million that he'll serve me. He hates Niggers so much that he might get a stroke when I walk in and start bulldozing him and your mark with that boodle I'm going to flash."

When we got to the Westside it was nine-thirty A.M. Blue parked on Ashland Avenue. I got out and walked around the corner to the Dutchman's saloon on West Pershing Road, a stone's throw from the stockyards.

Just before I went in, I glanced at the saloon down the street from the Dutchman's. If I caught a mark I'd have to lug him there for the smack play.

The joint was reeking of old sweat, brass spittoons and stale sawdust. It was all stag and loud with the profane horseplay of Dutchmen, Germans and Poles.

I sat between two Germans. One of them was drunk. I threw him out of my mind as a prospect. Blue had told me drunks were bad marks.

I watched the huge ruddy-faced Dutchman come down the long redwood bar toward me. He batted a wayward lock of straw-colored hair off his broad forehead with a beet-red, beefy paw.

He mopped the bar in front of me with a grease-streaked rag. He skinned his thin red lips back from a set of thousand-dollar choppers. His merry, bright blue eyes twinkled down at me. He had the kindest, friendliest face I'd seen since Grandma Annie.

He said, "You look thirsty, young friend. I bet you want Artel should get you a peppermint schnapps."

I said, "Gee, Artel, you're a mind reader. That's just what I wanted."

I sat there sipping the drink. I watched Artel serve the bar with a happy smile for everybody. I was beginning to think Blue was wrong about him. A nice happy guy like Artel just couldn't hate anybody.

The German beside me ordered a glass of draught. I saw him pay for it from a well-filled poke.

I remembered what Blue had said about cutting into a sucker. "Strike up a conversation about current events. Then confide some bullshit, intimate and personal to artificially age the acquaintance. Turn on the charm so the mark likes you. Make him think he's known you for years."

I smiled and said to the well-heeled mark, "Boy that was some fire yesterday at that dance hall down in Mississippi."

He said, "Ya, but you should have seen de one over dere at de stockyards several years ago. Now dat vas a fire."

I said, "A fire burned my folks to death and made an orphan of me when I was two. The sight of fire makes me sad."

We sat there for about fifteen minutes getting acquainted. His name was Otto. He offered to buy me a drink. I told him I'd flip coins with him. We flipped. I let him win. We flipped the next one. I won.

I glanced at the door. Blue was peering through the glass. I pulled at my nose. Blue came in and stood at the bar beside me. He was rocking from side to side like a drunk. There wasn't a sound in the joint.

The Dutchman leaped toward Blue. He was purple with rage and indignation.

He shouted, "Get out! Get out! No blacks allowed in here."

Blue grinned at him and waved a wad of bills beneath the Dutchman's nose.

Blue said, "You mean a rich, clean-cut Nigger like me can't buy a drink in this funk box? Hell, I'll give you odds that this is more money than you ever had in Holland. Shit man, wake up. You're not in the old country. This is the wonderful land of the free and the brave."

Everybody laughed except the Dutchman. Blue waved his bankroll under my nose and the mark's.

He said, "I'm going to buy this building and turn this into a Nigger bar. I'm going to bar all you laughing hunkies."

The Dutchman reached under the bar and brought out a baseball bat. Blue backed through the door. The jabber resumed. The Dutchman was his sweet, happy self again.

I said to the mark, "That Nigger had a lot of money, didn't he?"

The mark said, "Artel is an old fool. Dot money vas green not black. I vish dis vas my place. I vould have gotten all dot drunk nigger's money right across de bar."

We sat there talking about stupid niggers we had met, for about ten minutes.

Finally I said, "Otto, isn't there some bar around here that has a dame or two?"

He said, "Dere's one down de street. But dey let niggers come in. Most of de vimen down dere are black."

I said, "What the hell, Otto, there's nothing hotter than a nigger woman. I like you, Otto. Come on and show me the spot. We see something nice, I'll buy us a piece of black ass. How about it?"

It was pitch verbatim that Blue had taught me. It worked like black magic. The mark's eyes lit up like a lucky guy about to shove it into a virgin.

We went down the street. Blue was standing on the sidewalk in front of the other bar. He stepped in front of us.

He said, "Oh, whatta you know? It's two of the white hecklers from down the street. I bet that now all you've got left are loud mouths and empty pockets. I know how it is for poor white people. Come on and have a drink on a rich Nigger, unless you think you're too good to drink with me."

Blue turned his head away to cough.

I whispered to the mark, "Let's teach that smart aleck nigger a lesson he'll never forget. We'll split what we take from him."

Then I said to Blue, "We're not broke, and we have nothing against your color. Tell you what, we'll match to see who buys for the lucky one. The odd man wins. Fair enough?"

We stepped into a gangway next to the bar. We all flipped coins and smacked them to the backs of our hands. The mark's coin was odd on tails. Blue and I held heads.

I said, "Otto wins. We buy the drinks for him. Let's go inside the bar and keep our bargain."

Blue said, "Pikers are always lucky for peanuts. Come on, I'll pay for a measly drink."

I winked at the mark and said, "What makes you think we're pikers? We're not afraid to bet even as much as ten dollars or more. Just make it light on yourself, boy."

Blue said, "I take that bet. Let's match for ten and see who's lucky when it really counts."

Blue coughed again.

I whispered into the mark's ear, "Hold tails, he can't win."

We flipped again. Blue held tails. I won. I had heads. Blue and the mark gave me a sawbuck. Blue coughed. I slipped the mark's sawbuck back to him. The mark grinned.

Blue said, "Goddamnit, I'm going to chill your shit now. Let's flip for twenty."

I said, "You can't scare us. Can he, Otto?"

Blue turned his head.

I said to the mark, "Hold tails, he can't win."

I won again. They paid me. I slipped the mark's twenty back to him. Blue snatched out his roll of bills.

He shouted, "All right, my nose is open. Let's flip to a tap out. Can you white boys cover this money in my hand if you lose?"

Otto had two hundred and thirty dollars. I came up with two hundred. Blue counted out two hundred and stuffed it into his shirt pocket.

Blue turned. I told the mark to hold tails. We flipped again. I won. They each gave me two hundred.

Blue cursed and walked away from us. I stepped deeper in the gangway. The mark followed.

I was just starting to count down into the mark's palm when Blue came back and shouted, "Police! Police! You crooked sonuvabitches are splitting up my money. Police! Police!"

I said, "You're wrong, boy. I won fair and square, and

I'm keeping all of this for myself."

I walked away from the mark to the sidewalk. I stuffed all the money into my pocket.

I said to Blue, "If I go East and this guy goes West. Will that prove we're not partners?"

Blue said, " 'Course it would. Any fool would know that if you go East and he goes West, you couldn't be partners."

Blue turned away to cough. I grabbed the mark's shirt front and pulled him close.

I whispered, "I'll go around the block and meet you at the Dutchman's."

Blue stood in the middle of the sidewalk watching us go our separate way. I went straight to the Caddie. Blue came shortly. We pulled away for the Southside.

Blue said, "Folks, you're going to be a sweetheart of a grifter. You did everything right. How do you feel?"

I mumbled, "Like a guy that's layed the most beautiful broad in the world. I feel just wonderful. And that's the guaranteed truth."

I took the wad of bills from my pocket and put them on the seat beside Blue. He fanned them apart.

He said, "You must be excited. Folks, you had a C-note of your money. A hundred of your flash was mine. The mark went for two bills. Keep two bills and you've got your fifty-fifty split of the score."

I said, "You taught me every word, Blue. I'm still an amateur. You know, like an apprentice. I'm not demanding fifty percent."

He said, "Folks, you're my full partner. We'll split a million bucks before we're through. I'm going to teach you the rocks con and the drag before the year is out. Now, let's go to Powers and have some lunch."

I said, "Blue, how did the dolls look in that joint down the street from the Dutchman's?"

He chuckled and said, "They were a bunch of old dogs."

I said, "How old?"

He said, "Twenty-two, twenty-five."

We left the car at a filling station on Forty-seve: t.. Street and Michigan Avenue. Blue wanted an oil c' ange and minor tune-up for the Caddie.

We walked down Forty-seventh Street. We were .. block from the restaurant when I stopped in front of a pawnshop window. A big beautiful drum was in the window. Its chrome glittered in the sunlight.

I was gazing at it. I felt Blue tugging at my sleeve. I turned slowly and looked at him.

He said, "Can you drum?"

I said, "No, but I'd like to have that one. It's beautiful. I think I'll buy it."

He said, "Folks, it takes a long time to become a musician and most of them are starving. I thought you were going to be a grifter."

I said, "I wouldn't want to play the drum. I'd just like to keep it. But I guess you're right. What would I do with a drum? I don't even paint anymore."

We went into Powers and had lunch. Blue was quiet. It worried me. I wished that I hadn't acted like a stupid kid about that drum in the window. I didn't want Blue to get the idea I was just a young punk not really ready to play the con with him.

I said, "Blue, I wasn't serious about buying that silly drum. I was just clowning around."

He said, "Sure, Folks, I understand. Forget it."

We had stepped from the restaurant to the sidewalk when a breathless little guy rushed up to Blue. There was a bloody patch of kinky hair glistening in the top of his head. He was excitedly waving his scrawny black arms. Sweat glued his white shirt to his skinny chest.

He blurted, "Oh, Blue! He tried to waste us. He ain't human. Shorty's gotta get outta Chicago. He showed while we was blowing the mark off at Sixty-third and Stony.

"He just grinned like a crazy hyena. Poor Memphis' head is busted wide-open by the butt of his pistol. He even crushed the mark's beak. He's looking for me, Blue. I know it. Please lay a double saw on me so I can go back to

Saint Louis. Please Blue. I'll wire it back to you. I gotta get away from that crazy roller."

Blue said, "Sure, Shorty, I'll spring for the double saw. But who the hell is the roller?"

Shorty shouted, "I don't know. He's a brown-skin, speckled sonuvabitch—real lanky, with a funny walk like a broad. I know one thing, he's the screwiest roller these eyes have saw."

Blue gave him a twenty-dollar bill.

Blue said, "Shorty, you and the Memphis Kid had the worst kind of luck. That was Dot Murray. He'd swim across Lake Michigan in January to nail a grifter. That gash in your noggin looks bad. Here's another saw buck. See a croaker, Shorty."

Shorty was already on his way back to Saint Louis.

He shouted over his shoulder, "Blue, thanks for the dough and advice. But Shorty's going to give this sawbuck to a Saint Louis croaker."

We watched Shorty turn into the el station.

Blue said, "Folks, I'll have to point out Dot to you as soon as possible."

I said, "Why is he called Dot?"

Blue said, "He's got a disorder in the pigment of his skin. Ten years ago he was smooth brownskin. Now he's dotted with dirty yellow spots. We don't worry about him. We'll never let him catch us playing for a mark. Let's go pick up the car."

I said, "Blue, if we're not going to work any more today I think I'll get a haircut across the street and walk around a little."

He shrugged his wide shoulders and said, "No, we won't work any more today. If we hadn't run into Sweeney the Snake, we'd play the stations this evening.

"We'll start in the morning, early. Be careful, Folks. Don't get foxed out of your bankroll. The con is made for everybody, you know."

I went across the street to the barber shop. It was crowded with old guys arguing about the war in Europe and how soon before America would be in it.

One old guy cracked up the shop.

He said, "If Turkey were attacked in the rear, don't you think Greece would help?"

I finally got a haircut. Forty-seventh Street was lousy with young, big-butt broads. But I was too wrapped up in thoughts of the past to chase any of them.

I walked east on Forty-seventh Street. I saw the Regal Theater at South Parkway and remembered the curvy little doll that caused me to miss waiting for Phala outside the cabaret that night.

I walked to Cottage Grove Avenue. I walked down Cottage Grove all the way to my old neighborhood at Thirty-ninth Street.

I stood and looked up at the shabby apartment building where Phala and I onced lived. I thought about the pretty pink house I was living in. I felt like a millionaire as I watched slouched, familiar figures passing me on the sidewalk.

As I walked away toward South Parkway I glanced up at the window of our old apartment. I saw the lonely face of a little black kid staring down at me. He was about the age I was when I first lived there.

Perhaps he had no father. His mama probably worked in River Forest. I thought how wonderful it would be if he could go with me to the pink house.

He'd sure be happy like I was to get away from the piss stink in the kitchen sink, the roaches, and the hunchback rats that stood on their hind legs and snarled like rabid wolves.

I was glad for him that at least his face was black. He'd be able to play games in the bloodstained hallways and on the puke-streaked stoops. His savage young buddies would never bar him from their games and call him a trick baby.

I caught a jitney cab on South Parkway Boulevard. I got off at Fifty-first Street. I crossed the street and walked into Washington Park.

I found a cool, green, shadowy spot where Phala and I

used to lounge together to escape the hot summer sun. I
remembered how she used to croon me to sleep on her
bosom.

I felt so sad to think that Phala was probably in the sun
on that bench near the weeping willow tree. I could
almost see her pitiful vacant eyes and smell the sharp odor
of the lye soap in the faded blue smock.

I lay there until the orange sun floated off the rim of the
earth, and the night sky was ablaze with stars.

I got home at nine P. M. Blue wasn't home. I read Keats
and Shelley until I fell asleep. I went to the bathroom
around three in the morning.

I was sitting on the stool when I heard Blue laughing
loudly in his bedroom. I washed my hands, and I was
getting back into bed when I heard a young girl giggling
in Blue's room. It was the first time he'd had a broad for
company.

I turned on the radio. The sweet music of Guy Lombar-
do lulled me back to sleep.

I awakened to the savory scent of the frying bacon. I
was hungry. But I felt wonderful looking out the open
window at the tulips and roses, dewy and sparkling in the
bright morning sun. I was anxious for my second day of
the con.

I was getting out of the bathtub when I heard Blue
calling my name. I stuck my head into the bedroom.

Blue was standing in the bedroom doorway. He was
wearing lavender pajamas. A small, big-eyed doll about
eighteen was snuggled against him.

She was wearing white panties and one of Blue's tee
shirts. She had nice, big legs. I couldn't tell how she was
built upstairs because of the bulky tee shirt.

Blue winked and chortled, "Folks, meet Linda. I'm
going to make a Billie Holliday out of her. I heard her
singing along with a record last night in Square's Bar on
Thirty-first Street.

"She's great. I already told her about our plans to open
a swank night club in a few weeks. You were wondering

who would be our star. Well, stop wondering. It's Linda.

"Breakfast is ready. So hurry, we've got a busy day ahead of us."

The three of us had breakfast together. She was a dizzy, stagestruck little broad. And, how she was built upstairs!

I had one hell of a time coming off the top of my head with the answers to her excited questions about the night club, its color scheme and so on.

Blue sat there getting his kicks. Finally we all got in the Caddie, heading north. We let Linda off at Thirty-first, Street and Indiana Avenue—in a very bad slum section.

She had stars in her eyes when she got out. Blue promised to take her to dinner that night to discuss her wardrobe and the whole plan for her stardom in the mythical night club.

I was really puzzled. I couldn't figure why Blue would play all that con for young snatch. A sawbuck could lay broads all over the Southside who were younger and finer than Linda.

Blue said, "Folks, we're going to work the Illinois Central Station this morning, right in the Loop near the Prudential Building. Socking it into that young pussy all night makes me feel lucky and daring. Whoopee!"

I said, "That was sure a lot of con for nothing. She is really going to be disappointed tonight when you don't show to take her out."

He threw his head back and laughed.

He said, "Christ! I've got to hurry and get you out of kindergarten. That con wasn't for nothing. The thrill I got in conning that young slut was greater than banging her.

"That stupid whore has sold more pussy than Ford has cars. But when I cut into her last night, she got indignant and slick. I offered her a double saw.

"She was looking out of the bar window when I drove up. She saw my clothes. She figured I was a rich sucker that she could play a clean-cut, square role for.

"She'd lay that hot, young pussy on me and I'd go for thousands instead of the double saw. Any broad who dreams she can con Blue Howard is doomed to disappointment."

We were lucky right after we got to the station. A black business man between trains went for four bills on the smack. We beat a young white guy at the Greyhound Terminal for a bill and a half. We were safely out of the Loop by noon.

We listened to a news broadcast on the car's radio as we drove back to the Southside. It was all about the war in Europe. The fabulous cripple in the White House was quoted several times.

Blue shut off the radio. He had a serious look on his face.

He said, "White Folks, America has to go to war. There's going to be a white man's world war to retain white wealth and power.

"You'll be eighteen years old your next birthday. America, the model of democracy and equality, has two armies. A black one and a white one.

"Folks, there isn't anything more precious than your life. I'm your friend. If I let them, they're going to draft you into their nigger army.

"I'm not going to let you die a sucker in a Jim Crow army. The black soldiers from the South would hate your guts. Folks, I'm taking you right now to a croaker.

"You're going to start treatment for a chronic heart condition. If and when they call you in for a physical, you'll have a history of heart trouble. The croaker we're going to can give you drugs that will make your ticker correspond to the proper disease picture whenever they call you. Don't worry. Leave everything to Blue."

Time flew swiftly by on the smooth slick wings of the con. Blue had been right about our play together becoming a tricky ballet. We could almost read each other's mind. We'd take our cues with split-second precision.

By August, Nineteen Forty, I had lost count of the marks we had rooked at the bus and train stations in the Loop.

I spent most of my take on expensive clothes from Marshall Field's. Blue and I went fifty-fifty on food and house expenses. I blew a lot in cabarets on weekends. I had a lot of fun with the dolls I picked up in them.

Toward the end of August, Sweeney the Snake gave us a scare. We were playing the smack on a young white mark about twenty-five years old.

The coins had been flipped for the last time in the foyer of a building about a block from the La Salle Street Station. Blue and the mark had lost the tap-out flip to me.

Blue had walked away to the street. I started to split with the mark. Blue came back and interrupted for the blowoff. The three of us stepped to the sidewalk. Blue was telling us to go in opposite directions to prove we weren't crooks splitting his losses.

I looked right into the steely-blue eyes of Sweeney passing in an unmarked black sedan. The mark was already on his way down Harrison Street to meet me around the block for the split.

The black sedan stopped about thirty yards away. Sweeney got out and rushed to the sidewalk. He ignored the curses and honkings of the drivers in the cars behind the stopped sedan.

He didn't take his eyes off Blue and me as he grabbed the mark's arm going past him on the sidewalk. They struggled weakly until Sweeney took a wallet from his hip pocket and passed the inner side of it across the mark's eyes.

They started toward us down the crowded sidewalk. Blue and I melted into the crowd. We made it to State Street. We were lucky. A streetcar was just pulling out going South.

We swung aboard. We looked at each other and shook our heads when the streetcar passed Central Police head-quarters at Eleventh and State Streets.

Blue said, "I got a hunch. Let's get off at Eighteenth and State. We'll get some of Mexican Joe's chili. A little later we have to go back and get the car off Polk Street anyway. No use going any farther South."

The Mexican was just setting steaming bowls of chili mac in front of us, when Blue's hunch reared by. It was Sweeney and the mark in the black sedan racing in hot pursuit of the southbound streetcar.

Sweeney was a sharp roller all right. But Blue's con-educated intuition had out smarted him. I took a cab home. Blue took a cab back to get his car.

I was worried about Blue. I almost leaped from my skin when the phone rang. It was Blue.

He said, "Folks, everything is lovey-dovey. I'm at the Du Sable Hotel. I'm in the bed with the finest young fox in Chicago.

"Christ, you should see the tits on her. They've got to be size forty at least. Yummy. Think of it, Folks, equipment like that on a seventeen-year-old doll. Stay cool. I'll be home one of these days. Whoopee."

I heard the musical laugh of the young broad. Blue hung up. I took a bath and went to the bookcase. I dozed off with Aristotle in my hands.

A month after our narrow escape from Sweeney, Blue decided that we'd pay a visit to Felix the Fixer. It was a good idea because that winter we planned to play the drag throughout Illinois.

The drag was a felony con game. Blue told me that Felix had high police and political contacts across the State. He also did business for burglars, heist men, whorehouses and gamblers.

He also used his influence to help a handful of Chicago defense lawyers in their murder cases. But he was practically powerless in those cases unless both the victim and the murderer were black. He was extremely effective when a white murderer had killed a black victim.

September dusk covered Garfield Boulevard like a gray shroud. The heavy odors of barbecue and deep fried jack salmon rode greasily on the crisp air. Dull neon eyes blinked in the acrid gloom.

We parked in front of the Garfield Hotel on the corner

of Prairie Avenue.

Blue said, "Let's walk down to the saloon under the el. The Fixer is probably there."

I looked up at my Aunt Pearl's white building gleaming in the murk across the boulevard. I wondered if her blubber had strangled her heartbeat since that day I went to her for help.

The Fixer was at the bar. Blue stroked his hand across his cheek as we passed him. We went to the rear of the bar and sat in a booth.

The Fixer came and sat down with us. He was as shiny and black as new boots. A toothpick waggled in the corner of his wide mouth.

He said, "Well I'll be a white whore's bastard baby, if it isn't hot-prick Blue Howard. I haven't seen you since you knocked up that preacher's teenage daughter back in Thirty-three.

"What's your story, morning glory? It costs three grand to fix cradle rape. It's higher if the pussy is less than fifteen years old. If she's white, I can't help you at all. Give me the three grand and the name of the lip that's got your case."

Blue laughed and said, "Stop the bullshit, Fixer. You'll give my partner, White Folks, here a bad impression of me.

"I'm going to play the drag with him this winter around the state. We want you to handle our beefs."

Fixer said, "Always keep this horny sonuvabitch in front of you laddie, you're mighty pretty. And never bend over when he's behind you.

"Blue, seriously, I'll handle things for you. I want twenty percent of your clean scores inside Chicago. Twenty-five percent outside Chicago. On partial kickbacks to the mark, I want half of what's left.

"I'll need fifty percent of all the dirty ones. That's when the mark's beef by-passes the police and you get an indictment. Judges and prosecutors want real dough to go along with the fix.

"Stay out of Evanston and Springfield. The goddamn chiefs of police and judges in those towns are square johns. Ten grand couldn't fix a parking ticket.

"Blue, I can guarantee that you'll never go to the joint when I'm handling things for you. But if you take off scores and I don't get my end, I'll find out about it.

"I won't tip you that I'm wise. But whenever you get a solid beef, I'll whisper in your trial judge's ear, and a Clarence Darrow couldn't keep you out of the penitentiary. Now give me a C-note so I'll remember you.

Blue gave him a C-note. Fixer gave Blue his home phone number and address. The Fixer went out ahead of us.

When Blue and I stepped out on Garfield, we saw the Fixer's bald head glistening under the street lamps as he walked toward South Parkway.

As the Caddie pulled away from the curb, I put fifty stones in Blue's lap. He gave me a puzzled look.

"I said, "You said it's fifty-fifty right down the line, partner."

On South Parkway near Sixty-first Street, Blue slowed the car quickly.

He said, "There, Folks, there! That's Dot Murray."

I turned and looked at the front of the Southway Hotel. A lean guy was on the sidewalk. His brown face was splotched with dime-sized yellow patches.

He was almost as skinny as Sweeney. As we passed him he moved toward Sixty-first Street. He had an odd walk. He had a kind of totter like a Chinese broad with bound feet.

Blue said, softly, "We have to keep our eyes peeled for that maniac this winter. Pocket told me the Memphis Kid is in county jail doing a yard. He'll never play the smack again or anything else.

"The butt of Dot's thirty-eight smashed some vital nerve centers in the Kid's skull. He's lying in the jail hospital, paralyzed."

I said, "When are you going to visit your old road

buddy?"

He said, "I'm not. I'll send him some dough. But I'm not about to go inside jails and hospitals. They're jinky as hell. Oh! I just remembered. Saint Louis Shorty hasn't sent me that dough I loaned him to get out of town."

I said, "Maybe he's getting a bad break."

He said, "Folks, there's nothing worse than a chicken shit grifter who borrows dough from another grifter with the stupid idea that the loan is really a score for him.

"The little sucker will never amount to a goddamn thing. Hell, if I had been him, I would have pawned my clothes as soon as I got back to Saint Louis. I would have rushed to Western Union to send the lousy thirty bucks back to him.

"The dumb sonuvabitch doesn't realize that one day he might need thirty hundred to keep his petty ass out of the penitentiary.

"Folks, never forget that a grifter's word has to be like a gold bond to his associates. I'm going to spread the word on him. The little tear-off bastard won't be able to borrow a nickel to make a phone call to a doctor."

On December fifteenth we played for my first drag mark. He was a small, wiry black guy about forty years old. He operated a soul food joint in Sterling, Illinois. He was in Chicago to cabaret and to sniff after big city broads for a couple of days.

Blue caught him around eleven A. M. on Forty-third Street near Michigan Avenue. I was blue with cold when I got the signal to pick up the poke for the mark.

I followed the script and gave the pitch about my boss and his office at Forty-third and State Streets. The mark was creepy. He giggled and jumped around all during the first stage of the play. Blue told me later that his name was Percy Ridgeway.

I was tied up with the mark when Blue went to my boss's office to make the arrangements for both of them to share in my good fortune.

The mark said, "I don't like that big stud. To be a white

boy, you seem to be a fairly nice sfud. I've been thinking. Why do we have to split with him? I got the equalizer stuck in my belt for those big muscles he's got.

"When he gets his share I could walk him up that alley and plug him through both hips. Then you and me could split his share between us.

"Don't worry. I know what to do with a heater. When I was young, I made a living with one."

I said, "Maybe, but where is your black brotherhood?"

He said, "Fuck black brotherhood. Greenback brotherhood is where it's at. How about it, white boy?"

I was glad the weather was bitterly cold. He couldn't know the real reason for my trembles and chattering teeth. I thought fast.

I said, "Friend, isn't it strange that I don't like him either. I'll give your idea some thought. Our big problem now is to get my boss to agree to changing those big bills for us so we can get our share."

Blue came back with the lyrical account of my boss's virtues and love for me. I left for the office to bring back Blue's share for the convincer.

I got back to Blue and Percy. I thought sure that Percy was going to heist us for the fake fortune in stage money, sandwiched between a few real bills. Blue naturally refused his share until the mark got his.

We were all in the hallway of a building at this stage of the game. The mark ripped a fat money belt from his middle. Sure enough he had a big black forty-five automatic stuck in his waistband.

I guess Percy figured he'd wait until I got back from the office with all our shares and take it all. He gave me two grand from the money belt as evidence for my boss that he was a solid citizen used to money. And he wouldn't get my boss into political hot water by attracting police attention with wild spending of his share.

I heard Percy in a fit of giggling as I walked away to the office.

I went to a greasy spoon at Forty-third and State Streets

and stalled off fifteen minutes with a cup of coffee. I walked back to Forty-third and Wabash Avenue a block and a half from Blue and the mark.

I stood there on the corner waiting for them to see me so we could work the blowoff on Percy. With an ordinary mark, I would have come a half a block closer. But I didn't know the range of that forty-five.

Finally Blue pointed me out. I waved. Blue poked a finger into his own chest. I waggled my head, no. Blue jerked a thumb toward the mark. I waggled, yes.

Percy started out for me. I started easing off the corner for the fadeaway. I saw Blue fading fast behind the mark toward Indiana Avenue. Just as I scooted from the mark's sight down Wabash Avenue, I heard the flat popping snarl of the forty-five echo in the wintry air.

I ran to the Caddie parked at Forty-first, and State Streets. Blue was just getting out of a cab. We got in the Caddie. Blue drove north down State toward the Loop.

He said, "I hope I never again in my lifetime play for a mark like that. Let's take in a movie to relax our nerves. We'll drop off Fixer's end of the score on our way home.

"Say, Folks, that crooked sonuvabitching mark wanted to follow you and put the heist on you when you walked away with the poke for your boss's office right after I caught him. He's a dishonest motherfucker all right."

That Christmas in Nineteen Forty we didn't set up a tree. It just didn't seem like Christmas with Midge gone.

Blue's birthday was December twenty-ninth, so we celebrated Christmas and his birthday at the Grand Terrace cabaret at Thirty-fifth Street and South Parkway. We were both looped when we got home in the early morning.

I gave Blue a Knox Forty hat and some shirts for Christmas. He gave me cuff links that were miniature drums with a chip diamond in the center of each. I guess he remembered that day when I acted like a little kid about that big shiny drum in the pawnshop window.

Maybe he was ribbing me about it with the cuff links. Anyway, I fell in love with those tiny drums. I'd polish the silver trim on their sides. I slept with them in my pajama pocket. He also gave me a cashmere overcoat.

I sent Lester Gray a sawbuck and paid Phala a visit. Phala's condition broke my heart. Her hair was white and she was almost bald.

In January of the new year, Nineteen Forty-one, I ran into Midge. It was a week before my eighteenth birthday on January fifteenth.

I had just paid my monthly visit to the croaker that was treating my fake heart condition. Each time he would give me a prescription so that the records would show I actually had taken medication.

He was building ironclad protection for me to get a 4-F draft rating, if and when America entered the War. I never took any of the tiny white pills. I always threw them away.

I came out of the drug store at Sixty-third and Cottage Grove Avenue with my pills. I was about to fling them in the sewer when an automobile horn blasted in front of me. I looked up. It was Midge driving Celeste's big, black Cadillac.

I walked across the street and got in. She pulled away and gunned the Caddie down Sixty-third toward South Parkway.

She said, "Hi, Johnny. I see you're still pretty as ever. And you're as dapper as a pimp. You must be doing all right. How many girls you got working for you?"

Midge looked a lot older wearing mascara and blue eye shadow.

I said, "Midge, I wouldn't be a stupid pimp. I don't kick broads around. I tell beautiful lies for my dough. Why haven't we heard from you? You could at least give your father and play brother a jingle some time."

She said, "I've thought about you a lot. But I wouldn't call the house. Blue might have answered. I never want to hear his voice again. Say, I forgot to ask if you minded riding with me for awhile. I've got a trunk load of stuff to deliver."

I said, "I'm so glad to see you, Honey. I don't mind the ride. I'm free all day. Blue and I have stopped working Chicago for a while.

"We're going to work in Southern Illinois tomorrow. I'll be back for my birthday on the fifteenth of January. Blue is throwing a party for me at home. Drop by for a while, will you?"

She said, "I can't promise that. But I'll try. I'm going to give you your birthday present before you split. What's your suit size?"

I said, "Forty-four, extra long."

She stopped at a dozen hotels and rooming houses delivering hot suits and dresses. I waited in the car for her.

I hadn't heard Felix the Fixer say anything about Blue and I having a clause in our fix insurance that covered a bust for helping some friend to lug hot goods to market.

Finally she drove me home. She saw Blue's car in the driveway. She drove fifty yards past the house. I kissed her on the cheek and started to get out.

She fumbled in her bosom and brought out a wrinkled ball of cellophane. She pulled it open and shook a tiny white capsule into her palm. She pushed the palm toward me.

I said, "What the hell is that?"

She smiled and said, "It's girl, square. You snort it up your nose and really find out how beautiful and exciting life can be.

"Celeste said nothing is too good for a queen. Cocaine, my dear hayseed, is the most expensive high there is. Go on, take it. I'll get your other present out of the trunk."

I took the capsule and dropped it into my overcoat pocket. We got out and went to the rear of the car. She opened the trunk and gave me a fine blue suit.

I could tell from the luxurious feel of the fabric that it had been at least a two-bill item in the store that lost it.

I looked down at Midge for a long moment. She was like a tiny dissipated child masquerading in a woman's clothes.

I said, "Thanks, Midge, for the suit. Are you sure that Celeste won't miss it and raise hell with you?"

She threw her head back and laughed bitterly.

She said, "It's so funny, Johnny, a queen can do no wrong. I'm a queen all right. I'm a queen bitch. Got it? A queen bitch, Johnny."

I walked away down the ice-glazed sidewalk. I threw the bottle of ticker pills and the pure white capsule into a dirty snowbank.

CHAPTER TWELVE

Livin' Swell Fats

Blue was right. The Japanese turned Pearl Harbor into a tropical cinder on December seventh, Nineteen Forty-one.

Blue and I were having a late breakfast when the charming cripple in the White House came on national radio with America's declaration to fight her second World War.

Blue said, "You see, Folks? I told you America would be in the bloodbath. But that croaker has built you a cinch pass. I'm glad you're not one of those young chumps that rush to volunteer when they hear the con of the soldier music and see Old Glory waving in the breeze."

Later that night in bed I listened to the news and music of war.

I thought, "After all America is my country. Maybe I should have a talk with Blue. Everybody doesn't get killed in a war.

"I am young. Maybe I can convince Blue that I should beat the draft board to the punch and enlist. I hear that volunteers get breaks draftees never get.

"I could go in and do my bit and be out of the army before I knew it. I'm no coward. Besides, with my fast brain, the army would probably make me an officer right away. I can play the con for some hot shot brass and be his stateside buddy."

Then I remembered what Blue had told me about the nigger army I'd be in because I had a black mother. No, I'd better stay out. Those black soldiers, many of them from the deep South, would give me perpetual hell because of my white skin. I'd be more lonesome than ever before. Blue had the right slant.

About six months after Pearl Harbor, Blue and I were at the breakfast table. Blue shoved an open newspaper toward me. My eyes followed his index finger. I read the two paragraphs of the item.

Blue said, "Can you believe our luck? Horace J. Sweeney has retired from the Chicago Police Department to take a position in private industry.

"We can go back into the Loop now and rip off suckers to our hearts' content. If I knew where he lived, I'd send him a case of champagne to honor his resignation."

I said, "I wonder where an old guy like that could fit into a business?"

Blue said, "His brain is still sharp. He'd be a valuable man for any company to have around to keep its employees honest. After all Sweeney was a bunco cop for almost thirty years. He knows all the angles. Nailing crooked working stiffs would be a lead-pipe cinch for him."

The draft board called me in for a pre-induction physical in the spring of Nineteen Forty-two. An hour before the examination I had taken a pill my croaker gave me.

The army croaker put his stethoscope to my chest. He checked my blood pressure and sadly shook his head. He advised me to strictly follow my family physician's directions. I had beaten the draft!

Blue and I played the drag and the smack throughout the State of Illinois. Sweeney had retired, so we ripped off smack marks in Chicago's Loop like we had a license.

Blue taught me the flue and the rocks con games. By the spring of Nineteen Forty-three, we were playing four alternate con games. I was going great for a twenty-year-old grifter.

Blue's nose was wide open for a young, shapely shake dancer. She was billed as Princess Tanja. She didn't give him any headaches at first. She did her act with a capuchin monkey named Albert. She danced right around the Chicago area. She was crazy about Albert. Blue told me Albert even slept with the princess.

Then she signed with an eastern agency, Moe Gale's, I think. Anyway, she started getting a lot of distant bookings on the East and West Coasts.

She had been gone a week. We were having breakfast coffee in the kitchen. Blue's brow was ridged in thought. Suddenly he pounded a fist to the table.

He said, "Folks, I have to do something about that goddamn Albert."

I said, "What do you mean?"

He said, "I mean that little ugly bastard drives me nuts when I make love to Tanja. He stares at me. He hops around on the bed. He jabbers and plays with himself. He's getting worse all the time.

"I was getting a goodbye piece just before Tanja left for San Francisco when I felt what I thought was a blow torch on my rear end. I yelped and almost jumped to the ceiling. Grinning Albert had struck a match and dropped it on me. Tanja laughed till she cried. She thinks the horny little sonuvabitch is the cutest thing."

I said, "Why not get him a monkey dame to occupy his mind?"

Blue said, "Tanja doesn't need him in the act. I'm going to poison that silly bastard the first chance I get."

Blue stayed cool through ten days of her touring. Finally he took a plane to San Francisco to chaperone her. He offered me the use of his car. I told him I was going to buy one. He parked it in the driveway and put a canvas cover over it.

I guess he couldn't stand the thought that some sweet-talking guy would hijack some of Tanja's tang. I tried, but I just couldn't picture Blue giving the princess proper bed attention with Albert's jealous eyes glaring at him and jumping around.

I missed Blue a lot. But I wasn't exactly sitting around the house in the dark devouring my fingernails in loneliness.

Our old housekeeper died. I put an ad in the *Tribune*. I hired a young broad from Sweden. She came in twice a week. Her English was clumsy. But she was agile like

Astaire on the bed, kitchen table, sofa, floor. The fifty a
week I gave her was a pittance for her all-over services.

At night I practically lived in the Club Delisa, a
Southside cabaret. It was always packed with black and
white hustlers and wealthy white socialites on nigger-
watching expeditions.

Blue would come back in town every two weeks or so
with the princess. We'd play the smack and the drag
together for several days. Then it would be back to the
road for Blue and his princess.

She was a tall, beautiful girl with patrician features and
the longest legs I'd ever seen. But the thought of Albert
killed any envy of Blue I might have had.

In the middle of August, I bought a white Forty-one
Buick. I paid almost three grand for it. Clean cars cost a
lot because the manufacture of cars stopped in Forty-two.

I pulled into the curb in front of home. I got out and
locked the car door. I walked across the sidewalk toward
the front door.

I wondered who the two guys were who were sitting on
the porch steps in the dark summer dusk. I walked closer.
They stood up. I came closer. It was one guy.

It was Lester Gray! He bolted to the walk and bear
hugged me. I threw my arms around his shoulders.

I said, "Les, it's good to see you. I hardly knew you at
first. In fact, I thought you were two guys. When did you
get out?"

He stepped back and said, "This morning. I been sitting
on these steps since four o'clock. I oughta kiss you, old
buddy. Goddamn, you're tall. Ain't we something? You
grew up and I grew out.

"If it hadn't been for that bread you sent me every
month, the inmates up at Saint Charles would have called
me 'The Thin Man' instead of 'Livin' Swell Fats.' The
chow up there would turn the guts of a starving dog. I
traded commissary stuff for steak and whole milk from an
inmate who worked in the screw's kitchen."

I said, "I wrote you a letter long time ago when I first

started sending you dough. But the joint sent the letter back to me."

He said, "I tried to get you on my mailing list. But that dirty mail-screw wouldn't go for it. I got your address from the envelopes that you sent the bread in. How is your mama?"

I said, "Not too well. She's on a funny farm. A gang of niggers ran a train on her down on Thirty-ninth Street."

He said, "Jeez, I'm sorry, Johnny."

I took him inside to the living room. We sat on the sofa.

I said, "I've got some roast beef and macaroni and cheese in the box. How about a snack?"

He yawned and said, "Yeah, I go for that. Geez, Johnny, you must have got to be a bitch of a cannon since we hustled the el trains together. This looks like some rich paddy's crib.

"I gotta find a crib. I went to Thirty-seventh Street to find my foster folks, but they've moved. Johnny, I'm glad you've got a short, maybe you can help me find a crib and a clean two-buck broad."

I said, "I haven't picked a pocket since you took your fall. I stay here with a nice guy that I hustle with. I dropped that square tag, Johnny. I'm known as White Folks now.

"Blue's going to call me tonight around nine. He's heard me talk about you. I'm pretty sure it will be okay with him for you to stay here until you get on your feet.

"A broad is easy. I'll take you to Forty-seventh Street after I get the call. Come on, Livin' Swell, I'll show you where you can wash up. I'll have supper warmed up in five minutes."

Blue called from Seattle, Washington, about an hour after we'd eaten. I knew he wouldn't let me down. He was glad that I'd have Livin' around for company until he could persuade Tanja to give up show business and Albert.

I told him to give Albert my best wishes. He shouted that I should do something that was very difficult to do to myself. Then he hung up.

I took Livin' into Midge's bedroom. He just stood there with his mouth open. He was a happy jailbird. Like me, he had never lived in anything but a roach and rat nest.

He looked like a king-sized eight ball wrapped with burlap in the dress-out prison suit. I tried to find something in my closet that he could put on for the trip to Forty-seventh Street. I had nothing that could fit a guy with a forty-eight inch waist.

We got into the Buick and went to Forty-seventh Street. I parked in front of the poolroom on Calumet Avenue. We got out and walked toward the corner at Forty-seventh Street.

Two mangy junkie whores passed us. Livin's bullet head swiveled around on his almost neckless shoulders like Grable and Harlow had paraded by in the nude.

His strange tawny eyes were flaming in their deep sockets. He vised my arm in an iron paw.

He said, "Geez, that tall one is got a groovy butt on her. And her pussy is so fat it pokes out the front of her skirt. White Folks, give me the price and let me go and talk to her."

I took his wrist and steered him toward the corner.

I said, "Livin', I understand that you've done a long, hard bit. But that broad is a junkie and old enough to be your mother.

"Be patient. We'll find some young cute broad on Forty-seventh. You know, one that's got enough life left in her to bullshit you that it's good to her too."

We turned the corner. Livin' rammed into something. It was old man One Pocket, the flat-joint outside man for Blue.

Pocket was gasping for breath from the collision. Then he saw me behind Livin'.

He grinned and said, "White Folks, is this tank with you?"

I said, "Pocket, meet a hustler pal of mine, Livin' Swell."

Pocket said, "I didn't know his name. But I knew damn well he was a hustler when we bumped. He put his arm to the elbow in my pocket."

Livin' said, "I wouldn't have shot on you if I had been hip you knew White Folks. I'm rusty. That's why you felt me in your raise. I just got out of the joint."

Pocket said, "I knew that from the vine you're wearing."

I said, "Pocket, Livin's looking for a nice, hot, young broad. He's got a six-year-old cherry to bust."

Pocket sucked his front choppers. He shook his head.

He said, "There are a flock of hot broads around this corner. But they're so hot a sucker's Jim Dandy might rot off after he's layed one. Why don't you take your buddy to a cathouse? The broads there are certified clean."

I said, "I don't know where to find one."

Pocket laughed and said, "You've got to be ribbing me. You're Blue's road buddy and you don't know where to find a cathouse?"

I said. "Pocket, I'm serious."

He said, "You got Blue's car?"

I said, "I've got my own."

He said, "All right, give me your pen and that card in your shirt pocket. I'll give you an address in Indiana Harbor. It's only a dozen miles or so from Chicago.

"The joint is run by an old broad I used to sweetheart around with when I was a young buck. She's got some young fancy pussy over there. They call her Aunt Lula. Tell her Pocket sent you and everything will be all right."

Livin' and I pulled up in front of Aunt Lula's at ten-thirty. I gave Livin' a double saw. We got out of the car and went up the walk to the front door of the red frame house.

We could hear the muted madness of a Jimmy Lunceford record. All the shades were down and there wasn't a glimmer of light from the inside. I pushed the doorbell. I heard faint chimes. In a moment I heard the peephole open in the door.

A broad's gravelly voice said, "Who are you? What do you want?"

I lowered my mouth toward the peephole.

I answered, "We're friends of Pocket's, White Folks and Livin' Swell. He sent us to see Aunt Lula."

The door swung open. It was like stepping into a perfumed cave. The only light came from a red glow behind a massive white sofa.

We looked down at Aunt Lula. If she'd had a set of horns growing out through her mass of krinkly white hair, she would have been a midget stereo of Satan wearing a wig.

Her light gray eyes gleamed in the red glow like cat orbs in the glare of headlights. She put a pale yellow hand, glittery with diamonds, in my arm.

She said, "Pocket called me and told me you were on your way. Now boys, we'll all have to be very quiet and stay in the back of the house. A bunch of goddamn nosey housewives went past my vice-squad arrangement and got me busted last week. Follow me and choose a girl. It's ten for a short time, and twenty for longer. A party with two girls is fifty."

The swish of her red silk kimono floated a heavy wake of lilac perfume behind her as we followed to a large, well-lighted kitchen.

Four broads in baby-doll pajama bottoms were posing in a line. One of them was a white, bleached blonde. Two were sexy light yellow boots. I stared at the fourth.

She was the blackest broad I'd ever seen. Her skin was like luminous velvet. She flashed her brown saucer eyes at me. Then she started licking her lips and lapping her long red tongue across the top of her chin.

She raised her arm to her thick red lips. She sucked and licked her wrist and forearm. She lifted one of her big tits to her wide mouth. She pretended to gnaw at it with white teeth.

She never took her eyes off mine as she moaned in phony passion for a sale. She was ugly compared to the other broads. But I forgot they existed.

Livin' chose the white broad. Lula opened a trapdoor in the kitchen floor. The four of us went through it down into clean, nice-looking bedrooms.

I gave the black broad a double-saw note. We stripped.
She sat on the side of the bed. She took my hand and
pulled me toward her. I stood between her beautiful hairy
legs. I looked down at her upturned face and noticed she
had a patch of silky hair across her top lip.

She shifted her eyes and gazed at Jim Dandy. She
tickled him through her shiny mop of hair. She rubbed
him across her cheek and the tip of her flat nose. She baby-
talked him.

She crooned, "Black Kate is just so happy that this
precious pink baby came to visit her. You're glorious. I
love you. You naughty, naughty little boy. Why did you
wait so long to come to your mama?"

She smothered him with kisses. My knees quivered as I
watched him disappear and appear again and again and
again. Finally she was on her feet beside me. In one swift
graceful motion, she swung her right leg to my shoulder
and stood on one long leg with the back of her calf resting
on the ridge of my shoulder. My supporting hands were
slippery around her back. Jim Dandy rushed to disappear
again, up, up.

Livin' and I started the drive back to Chicago. I don't
remember any of Livin's chatter about the white broad. I
was thinking about Black Kate and how she had petted
Jim Dandy after it was all over and begged him to hurry
back to his sweet mama.

The way he tingled at the thought of her, I knew there
wasn't a chance that he wouldn't. After all, no other broad
had ever flattered him so, and treated him like a precious
baby.

The next day, I took Livin' Swell to Bert's Haberdashery
on Forty-seventh Street near the el. We went down the
street to Power's Restaurant for a sandwich while Bert was
getting Livin's garments altered at a tailor shop across the
street.

When we came out of Bert's, Livin' had two suits, a hat,

shoes, sport shirts and a topcoat. I spent close to five bills to give him a respectable appearance. He looked as good in his clothes as a five-nine tank can look.

He was so happy he almost cried. We went to the poolroom and shot the breeze with Pocket and Precious Jimmy.

Jimmy had become quite a dude. He wasn't belly-sticking any more. He had a stable of whores kicking mud for him.

Old Man Mule was hustling slum on the Westside. We knocked around the poolroom until seven that night. We left and stopped at Sport's Lounge on South Parkway Boulevard near Fiftieth Street.

At eight-thirty, I remembered that Blue was going to call me at home. We were just walking into the house when the phone rang.

It was Blue. We talked fifteen minutes or so. He was coming home in a couple of days with Tanja and Albert. Then in a week, it would be Vancouver for Tanja's six-weeks booking up there.

Blue asked me how Livin' was getting along. It was the cue I needed to ask him a very important question.

I said, "Blue, Livin' is all right. But he's anxious to go into the streets to hustle. He wants me to hustle with him. But I'm not a cannon. I was wondering if it would be a violation of that con code you told me about to wise Livin' up to the smack. Nothing else?"

Blue said, "Hell, no. I was talking about rank suckers, squares. Your pal is already a grifter. The only difference between you two is that he grifts with his mitts instead of his mouth. Go on, pull his coat. I hope you can turn him out."

It took hours to convince Livin' that con was better than the cannon hustle. I guess it was because Livin' was a physical type. He wasn't a dumb guy. We started rehearsing the cues and the lines of the smack. I found out later Livin's awful flaw. He was lazy.

Blue, Tanja and Albert came home on August nine-

teenth. Blue liked Livin'. He made him officially welcome
to stay with me for as long as he wanted.

Blue glowered at Albert for a week. Always when Tanja
wasn't looking, of course. Then they were gone again. I
was beginning to think Blue might stay on the road with
the princess until one of them died.

She sure must have been a sweet customer in the bed.
But I'd bet a grand against a nickel that she wasn't
qualified to hold Black Kate's red baby-doll pajama bottoms.

By the end of August, Livin' and I were playing a fair
smack game together. It was more like we were dancing
the Charleston for the marks, instead of like the ballet
with Blue.

Livin' was just split seconds tardy with his con backup.
It can be a sweaty situation when you're playing for a
keyed-up mark. Another handicap was that we were open
only on one end.

Livin' just couldn't catch marks smoothly. He couldn't
make them like him instantly. His cold distant personality
was all wrong for the catch. I guess that long bit in the
joint murdered all his charm.

I did all the catching. He did all the capping. The
result was, we had to dig like hell for marks. It was
discouraging for both of us. Then, like I said, he was lazy.
After we made a score, he'd have to be persuaded to finish
the day's work. He didn't want to try for the second and
third scores. He complained constantly that his feet hurt.

In the middle of September, Nineteen Forty-three, the
same year that Livin' got out of jail, Livin' started cracking
about some guy called Butcher Knife Brown.

Livin' had heard in jail that Brown could make a young
guy rich overnight. Livin's cellmate had been a dealer for
Brown, who had connections for dope.

I could mention taking a trip to Aunt Lula's and he'd
run and jump into the Buick before I finished the sentence. He was all fun and no work. He should have been a
pimp.

Around the last of September, Livin' and I were on the way home from the Loop. He insisted that we stop in Square's Bar on Thirty-first Street on the corner of Indiana Avenue. We hadn't played for a mark all day.

We stood at the bar near the door guzzling suds. A tiny, dapper guy came through the door and stood at the bar next to Livin'. I wouldn't have noticed the dwarf if he hadn't had such a strange face. He looked like a pure-blooded Chinese that had been painted black. He was a weird-looking bird with his Chinese face and kinky hair.

Ten minutes later the phone rang at the other end of the bar. The bar broad hollered down the log.

"Knife, it's for you. Catch it in the booth."

The little guy waved a tiny, manicured hand through the air and went into the phone booth across the aisle.

Livin' grabbed my elbow and whispered, "Folks, that little stud is Butcher Knife Brown. I know he is. This is his corner and he fits the description I got in the joint to a tee. I gotta cut into him. Folks, that stud can make us both rich."

I said, "Deal me out, Livin'. I'm going home. I just know I couldn't get ready for a double dime in the pen. I'll see you later."

I got into the Buick and drove South on Indiana Avenue. I was really worried about Livin'. So I went to the poolroom to see Pocket.

He was trimming some middle-aged mark on the front table. I stood by the cigar case. It was almost the same spot where I had stood when the stool pigeon, Double-crossing Sammy, goaded me into that crazy rage. It was the same day I met Blue for the first time and belly-sticked for his flat-joint.

Finally Pocket picked the sucker clean. He racked his cue stick and came over and stood next to me.

I said, "Pocket, can you give me a rundown on a little black guy that looks like a Chinaman? They call him Butcher Knife Brown."

Pocket gave me a level look and said, "Folks, you've lost

your mind since Blue has been bird dogging that young bitch all over the country. Now you're fooling around with the most treacherous nigger that God gave breath. What's the matter, Folks, you're tired of living, huh?"

I put my hand on his shoulder.

I said, "Pocket, you've got it all wrong. Livin' Swell is cutting into Brown right now on Thirty-first Street. Livin' thinks Brown can make him a millionaire. I'm worried about Livin'. Brown gives me the creeps."

Pocket said, "Do you remember the skinny dago, Nino, that checked out the flat-joint boxes on the carnival?"

I said, "Yes. Mule told us about Nino and Nino's old man, the big wheel in the syndicate. But I understand that Brown is a dope connection. Nino is a flat-joint collector."

Pocket said, "That's stale history, Folks. All the dealers around here know that Nino is now boss of all the dope traffic on the south and west sides of Chicago.

"Brown is Nino's trouble shooter on the Southside. He also distributes wholesale and to retail peddlers. Last month a wholesale H-dealer called Slew Foot Frank was found gutted from hipbone to hipbone in an alley on Thirty-fifth Street.

"He had three sales and one possession beef coming up in court against him. I heard a reliable wire say that Frank begged Brown after the second bust to let him stop dealing for awhile.

"Frank figured that with just two sales against him, he'd maybe have a chance to get a fine and a suspended sentence. And maybe, at worse, he'd get a two- or three-year bit in the joint. Brown made him keep dealing under that awful pressure.

"Frank lost a big supply of H when he got the last bust for possession. Brown forced more H on him to deal. Frank got slick. He staged a phony holdup of that stock of H he'd got on credit. Two days later he turned up croaked in the alley.

"Brown got the syndicate's message across to all the dope dealers. Don't try to back up from the operation.

And don't fuck with the outfit's dope and dough."

I said, "But Frank was in a trap. I just don't understand how Brown could expect Frank to keep dealing like that. Frank was a cinch to wind up with forty or fifty years in the joint. How can Brown get away with cold-blooded murder?"

Pocket aimed his mouth at the ceiling and laughed loudly.

He said, "Folks, you're in a trap when you start whole-saling syndicate H. You've joined a club you can't quit.

"For twenty years I've seen big-shot peddlers riding in new Cadillacs and draped in the finest vines and rocks. But I'm not stupid enough to want into their club. Old One Pocket wants to die a natural death with a cue stick in his mitt.

"There are only two ways that a big dope dealer can cut loose from the Dagos. He croaks or he catches a bit in the joint. He's like a whore in a killer-pimp's stable. I'd rather drink muddy water and sleep in a hollow log than be like a whore for the outfit.

"You like that tub-of-lard pal of yours a lot. But if he cuts into Brown, you'd better cut Livin' Swell loose in a hurry. You'd have to wind up in a world of trouble. It would be like sucking a broad's tongue that's got T. B.

"Doing business with Brown is like drinking a gutful of slow poison. There ain't no doubt something fatal bad is going to happen to you down the line. The awful god-damn thing is, you just don't know when and how.

"Folks, if you read the *Chicago Defender* for a few months, you'll read about a lot of Nigger murders on the week end that ain't important enough to make the white papers. Some of those stiffs are chicken-shit dope peddlers and stickup men.

"They got croaked for putting the hustle on outfit dough or merchandise. Now the outfit is too clever to use their knock-off trademarks on Nigger small fry. They'd finger themselves to the scared citizens and the blast of the white newspapers. Too many of the trademarks hit the papers as is.

"Say some poor bastard gets his head jellied by a shotgun blast from a speeding car. Or maybe a stiff is found stuffed in the trunk of his car measled with icepick stabs, and his Jim Dandy and balls rammed down his throat.

"Those slick, big-shot politicians and rollers on the outfit payroll shit in their pants when the newspapers blat about those trademarks. So, the outfit uses Nigger gorillas like Butcher Knife Brown for the petty knockoffs in Nigger-town.

"The white, square people that could raise a stink and stop it don't even know it's going on. And if they did, their graft-rotten white leaders would con them that the stupid, drunken niggers are just croaking one another like always —celebrating Saturday night, Nigger Christmas.

"I hope you can pull your pal Livin' Swell's coat before Brown slices some of that lard off his gut. Good luck, Folks. Say, look at that! One of my prize suckers is taking a cue stick from the rack to make the trip to trim city."

I walked to the Buick and got in. I wondered if I should race back to Thirty-first Street and use muscle to yank Livin' out of the joint.

No, it was too late for that. By this time he'd cut himself into Brown or he hadn't made it. I drove home and sat in the beige leather chair.

I left the front door unlocked for Livin'. I sat there for an hour trying to figure a way to turn Livin 'away from his sucker idea to peddle dope.

I really liked the guy. And I was getting mad at him for making me worry. That's one drawback to having a pal. Their troubles sneak in and gnaw at your insides.

I was in the bathroom stuffing a wad of cotton and oil of cloves into a small cavity in a rear tooth, when I heard Livin' come in the front door. I heard him stomping down the hallway.

I looked at him through the cabinet mirror when he barged excitedly into the bathroom. His tawny, strange eyes were blazing in triumph. He bounced a paw off my shoulder blade.

He said, "Folks, I'm in! Knife quizzed me ragged about the stud in Saint Charles who gave me the rundown on him. Then he opened the door. Folks, he's the hippest stud on drugs you ever saw.

"He ran it down to me. I invest a half a grand in cocaine and H. It's good enough so I can cut it twice with milk sugar and still have the best stuff on Thirty-fifth Street. That measly five bills will get me five grand right outta the box.

"Folks, the stud really likes me. For instance, he's gonna show me how to cut the stuff, how to cap it up and where to sell it. He said there's a junkie bar at Thirty-fifth and State where I can deal out of the shithouse and make a mint.

"Ain't I a bitch, Folks? I'm outta the joint a few weeks and a ton of bread is laying in these streets for Livin' Swell Fats. You're my boon coon, Folks. Let's do this thing together."

The pitiful slob had let Brown con him. And that mere thought shot new jolts of pain through the nerve core of the cavity. The joy and stupid triumph I saw on his face cancelled out my self-control.

I pivoted and glared at him.

I shouted, "Sucker, are you for real? You should see yourself. You look like a stupid, black baboon that's been conned with a stalk of rubber bananas.

"Brown is going to use you like a whore. One thing for sure, you'll be the dumbest whore in his dope stable."

I saw the muscles lumping and rolling at the back of his jawbone. I heard the grinding scrape of his gritting teeth. I moved my hand toward his shoulder. He hunched his shoulders and moved away.

I said softly, "Livin', when I left you, I went to an old hustler and got a rundown on Brown. He's poison. He butchers niggers for the syndicate. If you do business with him, you'll wind up dead or pulling a forty- or fifty-year bit in the penitentiary.

"Livin', we've been pals since we were little kids. Wake up. Don't be a sucker. Livin', you're nutty from that long bit you did. Let your buddy pull your coat.

"Be patient. Stay with con. I'll tell you what. I'll teach you the drag. We can get rich together. It will just take a little longer. Come on now, pal. Tell me you're going to throw Brown and the dope racket out of your mind, and make smart dough. Please, Livin'. I'm worried about you, pal. I hate to say it. But if you're going to deal dope, I'll have to cut you loose."

He stared at me with his mouth open. I stepped back from the tawny brutes raging in their sockets. He doubled up his powerful hands into black bludgeons and boomed them against his chest. He narrowed his fat lips against his clenched teeth.

He roared, "You jive, half-peckerwood sonuvabitch! If I didn't like you, I'd put my fist through you and stomp you to death. Say I won't! Say I won't!

"Don't call me a sucker and a baboon. You think it makes you great because your nigger mammy let a peckerwood pop you off in her ass. What the hell were you when I taught you to pick a pocket?

"I'm not a pussy. Why the hell should I be afraid of Brown? I can take my hands and crush him like eggshells. Cut me loose—ain't that a bitch?

"What's great about the con racket? I ain't no freak for walking and sweating my ass off to take two, three bills from some funky mark. I want big bread fast. White Folks, I'm cutting you loose. 'Livin', I'll have to cut you loose.' You think that's new? Everybody has always cut Livin' loose.

"I'm going to make more bread than you'll ever see in your life. You think your peckerwood blood makes you smarter than me? I'm going to show you like I did when I first met you that I'm slicker than you."

I couldn't say a word back to him. I realized that I had lost my temper and mismanaged the whole thing. That baboon crack was very stupid.

He stormed past me to his bedroom. I just stood and looked into the mirror and tried to clear my thoughts. I went and lay across my bed. I heard him dialing the phone in the living room.

I heard dresser drawers banging. Then for a moment there was quiet. I heard his feet scrape on the tile floor of the bathroom. He came through to my bedroom. He kept his eyes on the carpet as he stood at the side of the bed. He looked like a coy gorilla.

He raised his eyes and said, "Folks, get up and kick my ass for making that crack about your mama. You know I'm hip that you've been the only real friend I ever had. You can tell from my stupid cracks that I ain't got the sense to play drag con.

"I called a cab. I'm gonna' pad down on Thirty-fifth Street. Folks, I know that you gave me that advice about Brown because you're my friend. But I can handle myself. If things get funky, I'll cut loose from Brown.

"I ain't gonna' peddle no dope after I get rich. I'll open a big legit business and jump smack dab into Nigger society. I hope you ain't salty with me."

I said, "Livin', I'll always be your friend. I'll be seeing you around the joints. And we can hoist a few together. Be careful, pal. And if you ever really need me, I'll always do what I can.

"Livin', I'm sorry for my cracks to you in the bathroom. Put my name and address on a slip of paper and keep it on you all the time. Say, do you need dough to make up that five bills for your merchandise?"

He said, "Folks, I'm a coupla' bills short. But, you've did enough for me already. Besides, I can take off a pocket or two and make up the slack. You ain't forgot how good I can pick a pocket have you?

"Well, Folks, I hear the cabby blowing. Don't get up. I ain't got that much to move. Shake, pal? Don't think I ain't gonna' miss you."

I got up and got a fifth of rum from the liquor cabinet. I went to the kitchen table and sat there drinking away my sorrow and loneliness. Finally my misery became wildly hilarious. I laughed until my belly cramped.

I turned on the radio in the living room. A Jolson record was wailing *Swanee*. It gave me a brilliant idea. I went to the fireplace and put my hand up the flue. I looked into the mirror over the fireplace and patted soot on my face until I was coal black.

I started conning a mythical black father for the hand of his daughter.

I pleaded, "But sir, I'm the Nigger that can make her happy. I love her."

I answered in a heavy Southern drawl, "Iffen you a Nigger for real, why your hair so yellow and straight?"

"Oh, that. It's dyed with peroxide and straightened with lye and lard. Honest, sir, I'm a bona-fide Nigger."

"Mabbe, but Ise smell a white rat in de woodpile. I ain't lakin dat long keen nos uv yourn. Whar you git dat? You mus be one uv dem Watusi Niggers, huh?"

"No sir, I wish I had gotten it like that. The truth is my great-great-grandmother had big tits and a nice round ass. She was a pet house nigger for a horny white master of a slavery plantation. He socked a squealer into her and passed down this nose through her to me. Sir, just don't let it worry you. First chance I get, I'll have it flattened. Am I in, father-in-law?"

"Jes a minit, hold on dar. I warn't near 'bout worried 'bout dat nos lak I is 'bout dem funny blue eyes. Black as you is, Ise know you ain't gwine try and mak a star natal fool uv me. Ah ain't gwin heah a wurd you sayin' iffen you claimin' dat white boss-man done passed dem white folks' eyes to you frum way back in dem slavery days."

"Sir, I'll be proud to have a smart father-in-law like you. I'm glad you raised your question. The guaranteed truth is, a hoodoo woman down in New Orleans put a curse on me. Overnight that evil witch changed my Nigger brown eyes into—"

The weird black face in the mirror wobbled and faded behind the swift dark curtain of oblivion.

I woke up huddled on the carpet in front of the fireplace. The empty rum bottle glittered on the fireplace mantle in a radiant shaft of morning sun. I felt a thudding inside my ballooning head. Then I heard a faraway pounding at the front door.

I rose dizzily from the floor and walked to the door on legs of shuddery putty. I looked down through the door glass at Helga, our Swedish housekeeper.

Her blue eyes were wide with alarm staring up at me. I remembered the drunken, blackface playlet I'd performd. Helga turned and scurried away across the porch.

I opened the door and said, "Baby, it's Johnny." She came back. I took her hand and led her to the bedroom. She looked up at my black face with a puzzled look. Then she burst out laughing.

I said, "I had a wild party last night. I'm so glad to see you. Don't touch the house today. For some strange reason I need your company this morning in the worst way. Just take off your clothes and get into bed. I'm going to take a bath. When I come back I want to lie in your arms with my head on your bosom and hear you croon your sweetest Swedish lullabies."

CHAPTER THIRTEEN

The Goddess

I was twenty-two years old in the spring of Nineteen Forty-five. It was the year that Blue's princess bubble burst. It shook him up. But I was glad he lost her. It was better for both of us.

It had been pretty lonesome for me while he was on the road with Tanja. I made a lot of barroom buddies at Club Delisa and other night spots. But always when closing time came and the one for the road had been hoisted, I'd walk out alone into the dismal early morning.

Many times I wouldn't go straight home. I'd ride down the outer drive to Lake Michigan. I'd get out of the Buick and walk to the very edge of the crashing water. I'd sit there until daybreak listening to the roar of the furious waves reaching out for me with frothy claws.

I often saw Livin' racing on the boulevards in a flashy white Forty-two Cadillac. We'd honk our horns, wave and go our separate ways.

I told Blue about Livin' and Brown. He shrugged and told me I was smart to cut loose from Livin' because Pocket had given me the right rundown on Brown.

Phala had given me several bad scares. Her kidneys got infected over and over again. I wasn't surprised. She had floated them in Old Crow Whiskey for a long time.

I ran into Midge in the Brass Rail Bar on Forty-seventh Street a week before Blue came home to stay. Her eyes were black-rimmed with the fast life. Her face was a puffed, mottled caricature of the smooth, clear yellow perfection that I remembered.

Blue came home from Tanja's kiss-off on May tenth. He looked drawn and tired. He had several scabby gashes on his head. I asked him how he got them. He gave me an ugly look and retreated to his bedroom.

He stayed in his room a lot for a week getting himself together, as he put it. I was really curious to find out what had happened between him and Tanja. I figured that Blue had finally murdered Albert and left clues that woke up Tanja that Blue was the killer.

The day before Blue told me about how he was cuckolded, Helga the Swede called and said she wasn't coming to work anymore. She was going back to Sweden to become the bride of a childhood flame.

Blue was sipping coffee at the breakfast table when he told me about Tanja.

He grinned sheepishly and said, "Folks, is there an honest, faithful bitch on the face of the earth? I trusted Tanja. I went through hell with that goddamn Albert, just for her. I got my skull split because of her. I almost tapped out buying expensive presents, dining her, wining her in the finest places.

"For the first time since Pauline died, I conned myself I'd found a second wife. Now get it straight, Folks. She didn't make a sucker out of me. I did it to myself. Not once did she play any con on me. You know that's impossible even if she had been slick enough to try.

"She was in the third week of a six-weeks stint in a Miami Beach, Florida, hotel night spot. It was a Jim Crow spot, so I couldn't even come in while she performed. I'd always get there in a rented car when the club closed to drive her back to our hotel.

"That last night when I caught her wrong, I had pulled up near the hotel where she was dancing. I waited and waited until I saw the cabaret's neon go out.

"A nigger flunkey that had seen me with Tanja walked up to me with a sly grin on his face. I asked him if he'd seen Tanja. He said maybe. I gave him a double saw and he pointed toward the beach.

I walked through the sand and wondered why the hell she'd stroll the beach while I waited out front for her.

There was a bright full moon lighting the beach. I didn't see her anywhere.

Then I heard a faint jabbering. It seemed to be coming from a cluster of beach cabanas a couple hundred yards away. As I walked closer, I knew it was Albert. I followed his jabber to the front of a cabana. The canvas screen at the door was pushed back.

I stuck my head in the door. Tanja was naked and moaning. She was on her hands and knees on a bench. A tall, naked white guy with long blond hair was standing behind her with his hands locked on her shoulders. He was pushing it into her, hard and fast.

"Albert was dancing a wild jig around them. I walked around the outside of the cabana looking for a club. I found a quart beer bottle. I tipped into the hut. The peckerwood was still banging it into her. Albert saw me and screamed.

"I brought the bottle down on the peckerwood's noggin. Blood spurted like I'd cut his throat. He ran past me, across the beach toward the hotel. I chased him all the way into a rear entrance of the hotel with that jagged broken bottle in my hand.

"He ran screaming down a corridor into the arms of a gang of hotel security police. They beat me senseless with their sticks. I came to in a cell. I thought sure I'd make the Florida pen.

"I couldn't believe it when they released me at noon the next day. I was lucky. The bastard I slugged was one of Miami Beach's most respected married socialites.

"When I got back to my hotel, Tanja and Albert were gone out of my life. Good riddance, I say. Listen, Folks, we're getting back on the con track full steam this Monday coming.

"I think I'll dress up and go to Forty-seventh Street for a haircut and a good massage. If you're out later stop in the Du Sable Hotel lounge. I'm going to be there conning some fine young broad's pants off."

The Second World War was over. And Blue and I were

back in the con groove as smoothly as ever by the end of
May. We beat an elderly white man at State and Lake
Streets on the drag for thirty-five hundred.

A week later, a bunco roller from Eleventh Street
busted us on G. P. He put us on a show-up, and we caught
the elderly white mark's finger. Fixer put us back into the
street the next day.

We had to kick back half of the score to the mark. I
guess Fixer squared the right people with his half of the
seventeen-fifty that was left. That bust cut the score to
pieces. But without the fix we'd have been in the State pen
playing the con for screw's chow and a soft job. The Fixer
sure knew the proper pockets to stuff that fix dough into.

We eased up on the drag for a while. We laid the flue
and played the smack. We took off some juicy ones using the
Dutchman's bar angle. There were a lot of hate spots like
that in Chicago where I could always pull a mark out to
Blue for the kill. We never missed a mark with that angle.
Squeezing a white mark between a black man and what he
thought was a white man was foolproof con.

The last of June I slipped over to Indiana Harbor to
Aunt Lula's cathouse. It was a wasted trip. Black Kate was
gone. A fast young New York pimp had stolen her from
her Chicago pimp.

Aunt Lula didn't have a black broad in the house. And I
was in a helluva heat for black and nothing else that night.
So, I drove back to Chicago and settled for a jet-black,
young twenty-six dice-game broad that I had been banging for a year.

I almost missed her. She had closed down her table and
was just getting into a cab when I pulled up in front of the
Music Box Bar at Sixty-third Street and South Park Boulevard.

She was a wild lay. But I'd always have a helluva time
fending off her frantic proposals of marriage after the
excitement was over. She'd plead that she'd whore for me,
do anything for me if I'd marry her. She had it bad and
that wasn't good, to paraphrase the Duke Ellington hit

record.

On the night of the Fourth of July, I was at a ringside table in the Club Delisa. I had a pretty, young, white school teacher from Philly with me. I had lugged her from the Four Eleven Club on Sixty-third Street across from the Music Box.

The joint was crowded with black hustlers and squares. And there were quite a few whites from Chicago's gold coast soaking up the rich nigger atmosphere.

There was a vacant table right next to ours with a reserved sign on it. If I had known who was going to sit at that table, I'd have run from the joint before she got there.

In fact the rest of Nineteen Forty-five was going to be even worse for me than that horrible year Nineteen Thirty-nine when they took Phala away from me.

It was too bad I didn't get a year in prison for that thirty-five hundred score from the elderly white mark that Felix fixed. I would have had a better break in the joint than I was going to get in the street. And that's the guaranteed truth.

My disaster came to the vacant table during the show's intermission. I had been half turned in my chair for half an hour sweet-talking my sexy school teacher. Then we went to the packed dance floor and stood in one spot and scratched our bellies together to the itchy music of the club's band.

I had my eyes half closed enjoying the warm, racy glow of rum and coke and the hot softness of the school marm. A delicious whiff of Chanel Number Five opened my eyes. I looked down at my side.

A tall white man was holding a Goddess in his arms. His eyes were bleary. And his face had the flaming ruddiness of an alcoholic. Her angelic face had the gleam of rose-tinted porcelain.

She gazed up at me. Emerald stars glinted in her huge, grey eyes. Her hair was a platinum crown that coruscated in the pastel light.

The music outside me stopped. Her pouty scarlet mouth

smiled and dimpled the porcelain cheeks. My enslaved eyes were chained to her as she glided away and sat down at the table next to mine.

I was in an enchanted fog when the school teacher and I took our seats. The emcee came on stage and announced the second show. Billy Eckstein and Moms Mabley were the headliners, I think.

I turned my chair to face the stage. The Goddess was just ahead and to the side of me when she turned her chair toward the stage.

Her black-haired escort was on the other side of her table, turned toward the stage away from us. He swayed drunkenly to the music for the first act.

She sipped from a tall, frosty glass. Her exquisite hands moved like beautiful creatures performing a ballet to secret wondrous music. Her face, her limbs, her body could have been created by the composite genius of all the wizard sculptors of the ages.

Her escort turned his head from the stage and hollered something to her. She answered, and her contralto voice was like the caressing lilt of a gypsy violin.

I was thundering inside with a new mad excitement that I had never known before. The strange thing about it was, it raged in my chest and thrashed inside my head. It was all above the crotch line, if you get what I mean.

I sat there and played a mirror game with her through the first half of the show. A half-dozen times she gazed at me through the mirror of her jeweled compact. Each time I'd gaze adoringly into the grey depths of the emerald-flecked magnets.

The school teacher went to the john, and gave me the break I needed. When I stood up for her leaving, I pulled my chair closer to the Goddess.

A sly smile dimpled her cheek when I sat down. I wrote a note on a paper napkin. I put my phone number at the bottom of it. I folded it and flicked it into her lap.

It said, "Seeing you for the first time makes me so sad and blue. Oh! How Johnny O'Brien regrets those worthless, empty years before we met.

"I sit here adoring you and despising the memories of the dull mortal women I have known. But then how could I have known that a Goddess would bless my path?

"May I know the Goddess's name? Is it naive to believe that a Goddess has a telephone number? Or must I climb to a mountain top and beg the stars to bring her forth for love? Shouldn't we ditch our chains and flee together into the passionate midnight?"

The large vein at the side of her long white throat was pulsing wildly as she read it. She palmed the note and stood up facing me.

I glanced across her table at her escort. His head was turned toward the stage. I looked up at her. For a long moment she stood there sweeping her smoky gray eyes across my face. When she went by me toward the powder room, I noticed the lime silk of her skintight dress fluttering over her heart.

The school marm came back with a new coat of paint and a bedroom smile. She was cute, like a carrot-topped pixie.

I was getting lots of hot, heavy action all right. I heard the swish of silk behind me. A tiny paper square fell into my lap as the Goddess floated to her chair. Her escort hadn't known she had gone and come.

I took the note to the john and read it.

It said, "Johnny O'Brien, you beautiful, dear, mischievous boy. Shame on you for exciting an old married woman with that pretty blarney.

"Apollo should not be required to climb a dusty old mountain to bring forth Camille Costain and her telephone number. Unfortunately my tipsy chain is my husband. If it were otherwise, I should be delighted to flee with you into your passionate midnight. Call me soon, any time, day or night."

Her phone number was at the bottom of the note. A P.S. was below it.

It said, "Don't be alarmed when you undress and retire

tonight, if you should hear the wild anxious wings of my curiosity beating desperately against your windowpane."

Her note was thrilling. But how could she be old enough to call me a boy? She was beautiful and tender looking. I thought maybe I had been blinded to the creeping signs of age in the first explosion of her platinum and rose dazzle.

I stared at her elbow and the back of her neck. Her skin was smooth and taut like on a young girl. After the second show the Goddess and her looped husband got up from their table to leave. She narrowed her eyes and wickedly parted her lips as she passed me.

Shortly after they left, I took the school marm to a creole gumbo joint on Sixty-first Street. I was crazy about the rich stew of lobster, shrimp, chicken and okra, when I had drunk heavily.

I liked it almost as much as roast beef or macaroni and cheese. But I liked nothing better than a filet steak with a crisp tossed salad and heavily buttered crescent rolls.

It was four A. M. when I led the school marm down the hall to my bedroom. I heard Blue's bedsprings creaking rhythmically. I wondered if he were riding a penitentiary filly that would need a Felix fix down the stretch.

The school teacher, whose name was Denise, I think, gave me the usual bewhiskered con that this was her first time to lay a guy on such short notice.

She had the agility of an arthritic elephant and a dull dogma for routine position and movement. To rescue the situation I tried to imagine that she was the Goddess. But it was no use. I had squandered an evening on a pretty dud.

I fell asleep on her ample bosom as she was expounding her theory of education for the exceptional child.

I woke up with a scorching sun searing my leaden eyeballs. Denise was spanking my cheek like she'd caught me in her classroom with a slimy finger.

It was eight A. M. and she had a date with a train going back to Philly at ten. I struggled up and went to the bathroom. I toothbrushed the stale rum stink from my mouth and stared at myself in the cabinet mirror.

I looked like a slender Santa Claus with my red nose and the pink splotches on my cheek bones. My face was puffy like Phala's used to be. I felt lousy. I'd have to stop drinking so much.

I went to the phone and called a cab for Denise. I just wasn't up to the trip to her Loop hotel for her bags and then to the train station.

I gave her a double sawbuck when her cab came. She gave me her address and phone number in Philly. She made me promise I'd keep in touch. I walked her to the front door and kissed her goodbye on the forehead.

I got the Sunday *Tribune* off the porch and went to the bathroom and sat on the stool. I read half the paper.

I was washing my hands when I remembered the slip of paper in my pajama pocket with Denise's address and phone number on it. I threw it into the toilet bowl and watched it swirl into the sewer.

I decided I wouldn't call the Goddess right away like an overeager sucker. It was a long wait for Monday to come.

The Goddess's phone number had a River Forest exchange. I wondered if she'd ever seen Phala going to her domestic job out there.

At eleven o'clock I went to a Sixty-first Street dentist and got my cavity filled. I got home about noon. It was one P.M. when I put the call through to Camille.

Her throaty voice answered, "Hello."

I said, "Mrs. Costain, this is Johnny O'Brien. Can you talk?"

She laughed and said, "Johnny, I can always talk. I have a private phone in my private bedroom. And please Johnny, don't call me Mrs. Costain. I don't want to be reminded more than is necessary. I'm sure you can find something more romantic to call me. Has stark daylight robbed you of your sweet touch?"

I said, "Camille, angel, I wish I was in that bedroom with you. I'd shower your pretty ears with sweet-talk and then devour you."

She moaned, "Oh! You precious boy. Cannibals have always made me delirious with joy. Beautiful young white cannibals, that is."

I said, "Camille, I'm not a boy, I'm a man. Can't you look at me and tell? There isn't a lot of difference in our ages. But you talk like you've been around a thousand years. I'll make a deal with you. Don't call me a boy, and I won't call you Mrs. Costain."

She said, "Agreed, Johnny. Now tell me something about yourself. Where do you live? What do you do for a living?"

I said, "I live in the Sixties on the Southside of Chicago. I'm a skip tracer for a discount firm that buys delinquent accounts from commercial businesses.

"I'm a twenty-two-year-old orphan with no wife, no family. Does my address and background disqualify me, Darling? Now tell me about yourself."

She said, "Of course not. My family lived in Cicero before Daddy founded a bearing manufacturing firm in Chicago and moved Mother and me to River Forest.

"My husband and I share this house with Daddy who is still active as president of his company. Mother died shortly after we moved from Cicero. My husband is an executive in the firm.

"Johnny, it must be terribly dismal to live in your neighborhood. I understand that almost all of the respectable whites have moved out. And all of those once fine neighborhoods have given way to coon rot.

"Oh, Johnny, if we're going to be friends, why not get a small apartment elsewhere? Say the near Northside of Chicago. I just get cold chills thinking about you living in the midst of those savage niggers.

"Johnny, you don't go about that Southside making love to those disease-ridden coon girls do you? I couldn't stand for you to touch me if I thought you did."

I loosened my tie and mopped my brow.

I said, "Camille, I'm afraid those things you said about

black people are not true. I know for a fact that most of the rundown houses on the Southside were like that when the whites moved out.

"The black girls don't have a monopoly on disease. There are people all over Chicago with disease. All blacks aren't bad. Just like all whites aren't good. My best friend is black. I didn't know you hated black people. I could be black, then you'd hate me. Maybe it was a mistake to call you."

There was a long pause.

Then she bubbled, "Oh you emotional Irish bunny. I don't hate coo— I mean black people. I don't really hate anybody. But in my circle it's always been so unfashionable to accept them as associates. They seem so stupid and unsanitary looking. I guess it's not that I hate them. Perhaps I'm terrified at the prospect of loving them. So, forgive me, and I promise not to malign your precious blacks again.

"Oh, my heavens! It's almost two. I'm going to be late for my appointment with the hairdresser. You were wonderful to call me. You can't know how much I need you. But let me miss you until I'm bursting inside. I'll try very hard not to call you.

"Johnny, wait and call me when there's a rainstorm. Wherever I am, I'll race home to get your call, day or night. And I'll rush to you wherever you are. Bye, bye, my gorgeous Irish dream."

I hung up and sat there on the living room couch and wondered how soon it would rain. She had strange ideas. But then a Goddess had to be different from ordinary broads.

I wasn't too upset and angry about her nasty attitude toward my race. I'd sex her exquisite ears off the tender lesbian way and be so sweet to her she'd fall hard for me. Then I'd change her and make her realize how wrong she had been about us.

I couldn't tell Blue about her or expose him to her until she was hooked and had taken the racial cure.

For almost two weeks I watched the sky and the weather reports. No rain.

On the nineteenth of July, Blue and I were coming from the Loop. It was close to six P.M. We'd ripped off two fat smack marks. We pulled up at Morris's Eat Shop on Forty-seventh Street for a steak.

We had gotten out of Blue's Caddie and were on the sidewalk in front of the restaurant. I felt strong sudden rain pelt my face.

I lost my appetite and ordered soup. I went to the phone and called the Goddess. There was no answer. I looked out the window and hoped that the driving sheets of rain wouldn't stop falling until I got my mouth on her.

CHAPTER FOURTEEN

The Torturer

Blue and I left Morris's Eat Shop at six-thirty P. M. It had been the hottest day in ten years. We headed south down Cottage Grove Avenue toward home.

I felt the Caddie lurch through the battering gantlet of rain and thunder. I gazed at the raindrops bombarding the windshield like platinum bullets. I thought about Camille's hair. At Fifty-fifth Street a florist's neon sign glittered feebly through the wet murk.

I said, "Blue, stop at the florist shop."

He turned his head quickly toward me and gave me an odd look as he pulled to the curb. I walked unbowed through the lightning and whipping rain into the shop. I selected three dozen light pink roses, the color of Camille's skin. I walked back to the Caddie and got in.

Blue pulled away from the curb and said, "Love must come to us all, I guess. You must have run into one of those grabby, suction pussies."

I laughed and said, "Believe it or not, I've never touched her. Blue, she's so beautiful. It's like she's from another world. You'll meet her in due time. Drop me off at the Pershing Hotel. I'll take a cab home after my date."

He was silent until we got to the curb in front of the Pershing at the corner of Sixty-fourth Street and Cottage Grove Avenue. I moved across the seat to get out.

Then he said, "Folks, don't get carried away too fast. Your eyes have a funny glassy look. Remember no matter how beautiful a broad is, she's got to take a crap like any other broad. And she's got to douche her cat, or she'll stink like a bag of dead skunks. There's no basic difference in any broad. Ugly broads are like garter snakes. Beautiful broads are like rattlers. I found that out."

I rushed into the hotel lobby. I went to the phone booth and called Camille. Still, I got no answer. I sat in a chair and thumbed through an old issue of *Ebony Magazine.*

I sat there in my soggy blue tropical suit for fifteen long minutes. I went back to the phone. No answer. I was getting worried. Had she decided to dump me even before we started?

I called home to find out if she'd called there. Blue said she hadn't. I gave him the booth phone number so she could reach me. I started pacing the lobby with the roses in my hand.

I was really upset. I loosened my tie and called her again. I went into the hotel cocktail lounge and drank two double shots of rum. I called her again and listened to her phone ring a dozen times.

I wanted to walk out of there and throw the roses in the gutter and forget Camille. But I just couldn't slough off a Goddess like that.

I was sweaty and disgusted when I dialed her number the sixth time. She picked up on the fourth ring. The sound of her lilting contralto voice soothed and cooled me.

She said, "Oh! Darling, we've suffered through the first five times you called, haven't we? Please tell me where you are. I need you so much."

I said, "I'm at the Pershing Hotel at Sixty-fourth and Cottage Grove Avenue on the Southside. I'll register as Mr. and Mrs. Jack Flanagan. Camille, tell me why you cliff-hanged us this way?"

She said, "Oh, you unsophisticated bunny. Pristine desire is forged in the crucible of torture. Aren't you aware that the purest joy is in great anxiety relieved? Only peasants seek security in the passions of the heart. Camille's going to take you in hand, so to speak, and teach her Irish dream to find exquisite joy in the evanescent maiming of the soul. I'll be there as fast as my white Jaguar can run."

She hung up. I went to the desk and got the best room

in the house for overnight. I took the elevator to the third floor. I walked down the corridor to room three-fifteen, I think. It was freshly decorated in sparkling beige and green.

I took off my soggy clothes and hung them on a chair. I put the roses in the bathroom wash basin. I flicked on a huge fan. I sat at the window and looked down through the curtain of rain at the intersection of Sixty-fourth Street and Cottage Grove Avenue.

Camille's white Jaguar would eventually flash across it. I wondered how long it would take her to drive from River Forest.

Then I remembered her screwy ideas about desire and mental suffering. I thought that perhaps I should have rented the room for a week. Right after I gave her the racial cure, I'd start chipping away her goofy ideas about romantic torture.

At eight-thirty, I realized I couldn't greet Camille in my shorts like an unrefined, eager sucker. I called the desk and had a bellhop take my suit for a pressing. I took a shower and lay across the bed waiting for my suit and the Goddess.

At nine P.M., the bellhop brought my suit. I dressed, and sat by the window tingling for her. At ten-fifteen, I saw a white Jaguar dart across the intersection. Five minutes later the phone rang. It was the desk clerk. Mrs. Flanagan was at the desk.

I mumbled, "Have her come up."

I took the latch off the door and sat on the green velvet sofa in phony composure. I looked at the door through the dresser mirror and listened to the frantic boom inside my chest. It was like hours before I heard her gentle knock on the door.

"Come in." I said and got to my feet.

I saw the door opening. Then she exploded in the mirror like a pastel bomb. For a long moment she stood there. Her magnificent grey eyes gazed into mine.

I stood mutely in the radiance. She was wearing an

iridescent, flame-red, satin-sheened raincoat that clung to
her voluptuous curves like an extra skin. Her shining hair
framed her angel face like a platinum halo.

I rushed to her and lifted her into my arms. She moaned
and trembled as I kissed and sucked and nibbled at her
lips, her face, her ears and her throat.

She purred, "Oh! You are a cannibal, aren't you? But
please, if mommy's beautiful cannibal eats her clothes,
he'll get the worst tummyache there ever was. Yes, him
will."

I lowered her feet to the carpet. I took her hand and led
her to the side of the bed. I peeled off the raincoat. She
was wearing a red brassiere and matching lace panties.

She looked like confection standing there in her calf-
high white leather boots and scarlet, pouty mouth half
open. She sat down on the side of the bed. I knelt and
took her boots off. She lay back on the bed and wiggled a
toe inside my ear.

I caressed her tiny feet against my lips. I remembered
Celeste, the lesbian, and Midge. I feather stroked my
tongue across the pink toetips.

I looked up into her slumberous eyes, almost closed. I
kissed and gnawed at her feet, her ankles, her legs, her
knees. I gazed at the thick platinum forest glinting
through the sheer red panties.

She squealed joyously and rolled away. She flicked off
the nightstand light. She glowed in the dim light from the
street lamp. I went to the phone and ordered a jeroboam
of Mumms.

She went to the window while I was calling. She raised
the window. She stood there wide legged, arms folded,
staring out at the storm-lashed night. I walked over and
stood behind her. I kissed her shoulders. She moved close
to the window. Then something stupid escaped my mouth.

I said, "It's a nasty night isn't it? Let's lie down and
make love."

She whirled around and glared at me. Her tiny hands
were tight balls pressed against her bosom.

She almost whispered, "You dreadful insensitive savage. Can you be so stupidly blind and deaf to the ineffable beauty and mystique of the lightning, the thunder and the rain. And then in that same aura of peasant oblivion aspire to be the lover of Camille Costain?"

I was wounded too deeply for anger. My head roared with anguish. I barely heard the knocking at the door. I loosened my tie and staggered to it. I opened the door and took the icebucket, champagne and long-stemmed glasses.

I gave him money. I don't know how much. I put the tray on the nightstand and sat on the sofa. I heard Camille in the bathroom. I glanced at the bed.

I couldn't believe my eyes. Her red panties and brassiere were on the bed. But I wasn't too elated. I had to be careful to avoid her cruel angles. In fact I wasn't sure any more that I could change her.

The panties and brassiere could be a cruel tease. And she'd probably come out of the bathroom and put them on. Then she'd put the boots and coat on and leave me thrilled, holding Jim Dandy in my hands.

I got to my feet and looked at the door. If I left her now, she'd really get one of her screwy bangs to find me gone after she'd made the pantie and brassiere play. But for some reason, my feet just wouldn't take me through that door to give her that big painful thrill.

I guess Jim Dandy couldn't forget she was a Goddess. I was standing there having a hot debate with him, when she came out of the bathroom. Her face was sweet and beautiful again.

She walked to me on tiptoe and smiled up at me. I went over Jim Dandy's head and took the offensive. I moved away. I went to the nightstand and popped the cork on the champagne.

I filled two glasses and walked back to her. I remembered a jazzy line I'd heard in a movie. A cruel guy had kissed off a lovesick broad. I gave her the glass of bubbly and touched the rim of my glass against hers.

I said, "We smiled at the first hello. Let's laugh now at

the last goodbye."

She looked at me with wide, stricken eyes.

She said softly, "I've been horrid to you. You can't forgive me, and I don't blame you. I felt like a champion ass when I saw those lovely pink roses. Yes, you're so right. This poor fool has lost her dream."

She took a dainty sip and averted her eyes. She was so beautiful, so innocently childlike standing there.

I said, "You're wonderful when you're sweet like this. Why must you be an in-again, out-again Finnegan? What's wrong with you, Darling?"

She sighed and said, "I've known adorable men all over the world. But with you, I'm afraid. I'm certain that I'm falling madly in love with you. I suppose that, deep inside, I'm fighting desperately against it. So please forgive me. Be patient, and try to understand. Don't leave me. Make love to me. Please give me another chance."

Tears welled in her sad eyes. What could I do? I forgot that Blue had told me the con was made for everybody. How could a dazzled twenty-two-year-old hustler from Thirty-ninth Street suspect that a Goddess could play the con for him?

I took her hand and led her to the side of the bed. I squeezed her close to me and kissed her tears away.

I whispered into her ear. "You're forgiven. I'm beginning to understand. Now I'm going to show you what the savage was going to do with the roses."

I got the roses and pulled the bedcovers back to the foot of the bed. She watched silently as I tore the petals from the roses and covered the sheet with them.

She said, "It's a perfectly charming idea. But why?"

I said, "Sweetheart, this first time I want to get your ineffably beautiful pussy on no less than a bed of roses."

She giggled and plunged onto the rose petals. I stood watching them plaster to the glorious rear-end and to the gleaming platinum forest atop the pink-lipped valley as she rolled and tumbled like an ecstatic baby in its crib.

I undressed and got a brilliant idea. I rolled the bed

flush against the open window. She turned her head and gazed raptly at the misty vapors of rain curling from the steamy window sill. Her ethereal face was lit for an instant in a blue bolt of lightning. She was the most beautiful woman I'd ever seen.

I moved the nightstand to the bed and slid in beside her. We lay there sipping champagne and caressing each other on the moist tender petals.

Finally the giant bottle was empty.

She said, "You and the thunder and the rain are all so delightfully magical. At this moment and henceforth, I am yours. Now, devour your kitty, beautiful cannibal. Make me scream."

I kissed my way to the spicy forest. I seized the tender dwarf boatman lurking there, I pummelled his rigid top with gentle ferocity. She screamed. Then I heard her breathless voice.

She moaned, "Oh, goddamnit, I'll die if you stop. I'll go crazy if you stay right there. Please visit down the block, just anywhere in the neighborhood for awhile, and then please come back. Murder me that way, lover."

And then later, I felt the cool tattoo of the rain splashing off the window sill against my back as I entered the platinum-topped core.

No other core had ever been so excitingly tumultuous and so abundantly blessed with caressful ridges and salubrious climate.

My rhythm within it was the quick violent tempo of the blasting thunder and the jagged shivs of blue-white lightning that stabbed into the wet womb of the midnight sky.

Then at the instant of the leaping explosion, the beautiful fiend twisted and scooted from beneath it. I grabbed at her as she scrambled off the bed. I lay there panting, sweating with frustration. A flash of lightning lit her up. She stood beside the bed looking down at me with a joyful smirk on her face.

She said, "What a pity that Camille had to spank. You hurt me terribly when you threatened to leave me. I had to trample my pride so to speak and beg you to forgive me. I know you won't ever do that again. I can tell."

She went to the bathroom and shut the door. I lay there loving her and hating her. I wondered if I shouldn't get up and chastize her with my belt.

Then I remembered how Blue had driven Midge away with a belt beating. I didn't want to drive the Goddess away. I wanted to make her love me. Then I would change her the con-smooth, sweet way.

Sucker that I was, I didn't know the smartest thing I could have done was cut her loose that very night.

She came out of the bathroom. She flipped a switch on the wall. The ceiling light burst on. She walked over to the bed and sat on the side of it. I flinched as she dabbed gently at my stained crotch and thighs with a hot damp towel.

She said, "Sugarkins, don't look so unhappy. You're breaking my heart. I'm a complicated woman. As time goes on, you'll learn to appreciate me. We'll have the most divine relationship.

"Now, please, don't be hurt by my next remarks. This hotel, this room, this section of town, the whole setting was all wrong for our first adventure. I won't ever meet you again in Coon Town. It sets me on edge and depresses me horribly.

"Perhaps, that's precisely why I've been less than angelic tonight. There are lots of cheerful Loop hotels for our meetings. Promise me, Sugarkins, you will never request me to come to a Southside bed again.

"And I'm going to tell Daddy how attractive and charming you are. I'm sure he'll make a position for you. You're very important to me. I want you to work and live in the best possible of atmospheres. It's just so ridiculous to chase deadbeat paupers for a living. It has no future, Sugarkins. It's selfish of me I know. Because I realize that the happier you are, the happier you will make me."

I said, "Camille, I appreciate your concern for me. But I'm not leaving this side of town. And I'm not changing jobs. I'm crazy about what I'm doing now.

"I'll go along with the change of scene for our meetings. Tell me, is it wise for me to call you at your bedroom phone at night? By the law of averages, your husband is a cinch to make it an awkward situation one night."

She threw her head back and guffawed cutely.

She said, "You can't apply the law of averages to Allan and my bedroom. I shut him out more than ten years ago.

"Darling, during the first ten years of our marriage I suffered through his abominably crude sex act. Our marriage was not really made in heaven. But rather in a bank, his bank. He was in fresh and naive possession of a quarter of a million dollars from the sale of a Montana sheep ranch left him by his father.

"Daddy was dreaming of the bearing manfacturing company. So a month after I met the sheepherder's son at a bash, given incidentally by my best friend, Cordelia Concannon, I married him.

"Needless to say, I took immediate and complete charge of the money. Some crooked wretch would have bilked him for sure. I turned it over to Daddy, and we civilized him, polished him, and stenciled vice president on the door of his office in the firm.

"It was a traumatically inequitable transaction I had made. But then there were new elegant friends, the chic clothes, holidays abroad. And of course there was the physical escape from Cicero to further cushion my dilemma.

"I approached my sexual problem with him in a practical way. I bought Doctor Van de Velde's book, *Ideal Marriage.* I gave it to Allan and suggested that he study the section dealing with the genital kiss. Three nights later I lay optimistically in bed beside him as he began his customary mauling.

I said, "Well, Allan, what did you think of the good doctor's book?"

"He snatched his hand away and pressed the back of it to his forehead in confused agony. Then he gingerly patted my thighs and kitty. He had a disgusting Mortimer Snerd tone to his voice when he said,

" 'Ha, ha. That damn book said I ought to kiss all around here and here. But if you're going to kiss all around there, you just might as well kiss right there. That doctor is tricking the public into debauchery with that hokum. I'm not violating my principles as a man on his wild quackery.'

"Then I realized that he was hopeless. So, I opened myself to fortunate men like you, who have discovered how ineffably delicious and fragrant an immaculate kitty can be.

"As I said before, I shut him out completely ten years ago when I could no longer endure his drunken, brute pile driving. He was very difficult at first. But now he's as innocuous as the carpets. He's made whiskey his mistress, and I'm ecstatic about that. So, my Irish dream, I hope it's patently clear to you how desperately I need you to love me."

She leaned over and tenderly kissed my navel. She got to her feet and put on her brassiere and panties. I got up and helped her with her boots and coat. I put on my shorts.

She stood silently at the side of the bed looking down at the crushed rose petals and their pink stains on the sheet. She pulled the coat's hood up over the platinum cloud.

As we walked to the door I said, "Should I wait for another rainstorm to call you?"

She smiled and said, "Of course not. I just wanted it that way the first time. Call me any time and at least once a day."

I opened the door and kissed her hard.

I said, "Shouldn't I slip my clothes on and take you to your car?"

She said, "No, that won't be necessary. My protection is the storm."

I stood in the open door and watched her go down the hall. Several yards away, she stopped and turned toward me.

She said, "Sugarkins, it was thrilling wasn't it to see how cruelly our bodies crushed the blood from those rose petals?"

I nodded my head. She turned and walked to the elevator. I put the light out and lay on the bed in the darkness. I had seen her go down the hallway. She was a Goddess all right, and I was bewitched. I reached for her. Her body was gone.

But she was still there in the sweet meld of the raw odor of our lovemaking. She was there in the delicious scent of the platinum cloud on the pillow.

Perhaps she was half-Goddess and half-witch. How else could it be that she had been married for twenty long years, and yet have the face and body of a young beautiful girl.

I shuddered when I remembered her awful tongue-lashing at my remark about her precious rainstorm. And I remembered her standing at the side of the bed with evil glee as I lay with my crucified joy spewing from my spastic guts. I probably felt like a chump who had taken his first jolt of H.

I knew she was dangerous. And my first taste of her was powerful pleasure riddled with pain. But I knew I had to try her again.

I lay there sleepless until nine A.M. I sponged off and started to dress. I put on my aqua shirt with French cuffs. One of the miniature drum cuff links that Blue had given me for a Christmas present was missing.

I searched the tops of the tables and dresser. I got down on my hands and knees and frantically searched the carpet. I couldn't find it. I loosened my sweaty collar and searched the bathroom. It wasn't there.

I was in a panic. I went out into the hallway and covered every square inch of carpet to the elevator. I came back to the room and stood in the middle of the floor with my temples pounding. I called the desk. It hadn't been turned in.

I had to find it. I glanced down. The corner of my eye snared a faint glitter. I became dizzy with relief. I hadn't lost the tiny drum. It had fallen into my trouser cuff.

I started out the door, then I came back to the bed. I picked up one of the crushed petals. I put it into my wallet and went to the street.

The storm was over and the valiant sun was struggling to escape through a steel gray mesh of clouds. I decided to walk the several blocks home.

I smelled the limey odor of the damp concrete. I stuffed my lungs with the new morning air. There was still the faint scent of the valley of the Goddess clinging to my nostrils.

Then suddenly the sun shot through its gray prison like a golden cannonball. I discovered I was happy. My joyous feet flailed the sunny sidewalk.

I felt the blood rioting inside me. I had walked a hundred yards past home before I realized it.

CHAPTER FIFTEEN

Buster Bang Bang

I unlocked the front door and walked into the house. I smelled coffee and Blue's cigar. I wondered why he was up so early. It was Sunday, our day off from the con. I went to the kitchen. Blue was sitting at the table sipping coffee with a grin on his face.

He said, "Good morning, stranger. That must have been a helluva pussy you laid. Your eyes are sparkling like a sucker's who is on the send. Has she got a twin sister?"

"No, I'm afraid not," I said. "She's not just pussy, Blue. Like I told you before, she has almost nothing in common with other broads. Why are you up so early? Don't tell me, you were worried about me. You know I can take care of myself out there."

He said, "Hell no, I wasn't worried. I always know you'll call me if you get into a jam. You know old pappy will rush to your rescue.

"Folks, I've got good news. I got a call from Pocket a few minutes before you walked in. He gave me a rundown on a Spook mark for the rocks con. He's a muscle man for a Harlem numbers-racket operator. He's stopping at the Grand Hotel at Fifty-first Street and South Parkway.

"The bird is no idiot. He'll have to be given a velvet play. Pocket got the line on him from Old Man Mule. Mule tried to take him off with cheap white stones mounted in sterling. He took one quick gander, kicked Mule in the ass and laughed him out of his face.

"But he's got a solid yen for the quill if he can get it. He must have a source in New York where he can turn over hot mounted stuff at a big profit.

"Pocket says he must be carrying at least eight grand

and a magnum pistol. We're not going on the heist for the eight grand so the pistol doesn't excite us. Pocket said that Buster Bang Bang, that's the mark's name, is not afraid of anything. He puts great trust in his magnum."

I cut in and said, "Buster sounds dangerous. You haven't forgotten that drag mark, Percy Ridgeway, have you?"

Blue shoved his palms through the air and said, "That's a silly question. How in the hell can I forget a mark like Percy? Believe me, Folks, I wouldn't play the drag for Buster. But with the rocks, it's different.

"Buster's not going to be blown off empty-handed like in the drag. He'll have merchandise in his mitt. Fake, but still tangible.

"We'll have to play him with high-class flash. I figure we should go to the old Jew's shop at Wabash Avenue and Congress Street to get our stock. We'll need ten to a dozen blue-white zircons ranging from five to eight carats.

"Our mark is foxy, so to cinch him we should get the zircs mounted in gold. A seven-fifty outlay should do it. What do you think now?"

I said, "It still sounds less than wonderful. Buster's monicker makes me uneasy. He didn't get it with a permanent lock on the safety of that magnum. That mark must be leery and jumpy as hell after Mule tried to sting him.

"It's going to be hard to take him off just on the authentic appearance of our stuff. He's New York underworld. Will he go for the same version of the rocks that we've been playing on hay-shakers?

"I'm not yellow, Blue. But let me remind you that a magnum pistol ain't no BB gun. Explain how the blowoff for him goes. And relieve my mind as to how you convince him our stuff is real. Do that, and I'm ready for Buster Bang Bang.

"Oh, yes, I forgot, how do you cut into him after Mule's blunder? Walk up to him and tell him we've got hot rocks for sale?"

Blue twisted his face in outraged mental pain. He rolled

his eyes to the top of his head like the movie comedian, Oliver Hardy, did when his partner, Stan Laurel, did something stupid.

I thought sure he'd whack me on the top of my head and say, "Now! Folks!"

Instead Blue said, "When is the best Nigger con man in the country going to get some respect from his partner? I had those petty particulars figured out five minutes after I talked to Pocket.

"Of course, we can't blow off a street-wise mark like Buster in the usual way. Neither can the partnership gimmick be used with him.

"Say we bought your hot rocks in partnership in the usual way, I'd either have to slip away from him here in Chicago or later when we went to New York to get my end from the sale of the fake stuff.

"Maybe something would make him suspicious right after we gave you our dough. Then he wouldn't let me shake him until he got the stuff appraised. Wouldn't that be a bitch, tied to a dynamite mark that woke up? He'd wake up even faster if I told him I'd trust him with my half of the rocks until he sold them, and I'd get in touch with him later to get my end.

"His street experience would tell him I wouldn't trust him unless something was mighty rotten about the deal. In fact, Buster can't be blown off with the partnership angle.

"The key to the proper blowoff is in the way I'm going to cut into him. I'm going into him as a dope dealer just out of the joint with no bankroll, but with a million buck contact for H. Then, I'll ease in a rocks crack that he can latch onto. H won't open his nose, but rocks will.

"Tomorrow morning we'll go to Madison Street and rent a room for you. Just as always, you're the hot white heist man with even hotter rocks. But for Buster, we'll have a slight refinement.

"Now this is the tale I'll tell him after I cut into him. You're blind. You got that way from a brain operation that failed. A sliver of a Detroit cop's bullet ricocheted into your skull as you and two of your hoodlum brothers were escaping a jewelry store heist. Your oldest brother drove—"

I cut him off.

I said, "Blue, it's no good. There's a big hole in it. Any hood with a gunshot wound would have rollers for company as soon as he got to a hospital. I couldn't turn up in a Madison Street fleabag until after I had served a bit for the heist, especially after a big heist.

"Also, it may be true that there are underworld croakers with the know-how and the equipment to handle brain surgery. But I doubt it. Buster won't go for it. It's too way-out."

Blue roared, "Folks, you silly pussy drunk, young sucker. Have the courtesy to hear me out. You might learn something.

"As I was trying to say, your oldest brother drove the stolen heap to an unattended parking lot. They hauled you from the black Ford into a red Dodge. They jumped the ignition wires, and your younger brother tailed the getaway Ford to a dump spot.

Then your brother drove you to Hamtramck, a Polish suburb of Detroit, where you lived and were well known. They turned your pockets inside out. Then on a residential side street one of your brothers fired two shots. One into your leg inside the car, and the other into the air just as they dumped you from the Dodge into the street.

"Alarmed residents called a police ambulance to the scene within minutes. You had no prior record and you were masked inside the jewelry store. So, the rollers couldn't rap a robbery victim like you with the jewelry heist.

"A week after you got out of the hospital, your two brothers got busted while sticking up a food market. The jewelry was still cooling off in a stash that you know about. Your brothers were under high bond. Your Detroit fence wanted the rocks for peanuts. Maybe you could find a fence in Chicago. But you were blind.

"You and your brothers had a real problem all right. But

then you remembered a dear old Nigger friend of the family who used to help your old man cook mash for his bootleg still.

"He would drive you to Chicago and be your eyes and protection until you found someone to buy the hot rocks. He has known you since the day you were born. He's really trustworthy. In fact he's living in a house that your father gave him thirty years ago. He's perfect. He's old man One Pocket. Got it, Folks?"

I said, "I apologize for doubting you. Blue, it's beautiful. After a sweet tale like that, Buster is going to be at least ninety percent convinced that our stuff is real. Now get your kicks and rundown to me the angle that convinces the sucker a hundred percent and puts him into our pockets."

Blue said, "Folks, you could be pussy drunk like I said. But you couldn't be a sucker to figure that old Blue was a black genius with an airtight plug for that ten percent gap.

"When I lug that sucker to you, I'm going to wink at the mark and palm a core sample of those phony rocks as you and Pocket show them to us. This eight carat blue-white wesselton rock on my pinkie is going to be in my pocket. It cost me nine grand.

"Bang Bang and I are going to leave. I'll let the mark pick a jewelry shop or pawn shop at random for the appraisal. Then his asshole is going to twitch and his feet itch to race back for the rest of those rocks at seven grand.

"He'll make the deal, and hand me a lousy half a grand as agent fee for steering him to the rocks. No blowoff problem at all. He goes East and I go West and never, I hope, the twain shall meet again.

"Now Folks, hold it! I see another foolish question lighting up your eyes. What about the differences in the phony from my own real rock? When we get our stock from the old Jew on Congress Street tomorrow, I'll have him mount one of the zircons in a yellow gold gypsy mounting just like the one on my finger.

"I switch in the phony and give it to the mark, right

after we walk away from the appraisal.

"Give me that phone. I'll brief and hire Pocket. Then I'm going to call that croaker at home that beat the draft for you. He should be able to tell me how a two-month-old surgical scar over the frontal lobe should look."

I took a good hot tub bath, brushed my teeth, and went to bed. I fell asleep and had freakish erotic dreams about the Goddess until six P. M.

I got up and warmed up swiss steak with macaroni and cheese. Blue was out. I went to the phone to call the Goddess. I walked away from it. It was a sucker play to call her so soon.

I sponged off and went to the closet for a suit. They all looked alike in the dim light from the nightstand. I flicked on the ceiling light.

I was really partial to blue suits. Hanging there were blue shadow stripe, blue plaid, blue pin stripe, robin egg blue and fancy patterned slate blues. Twelve blue suits in all. I dressed in a shadow stripe suit and a white on white shirt with a blue silk tie. I drove to the poolroom to shoot the breeze with Pocket.

Pocket was at the back of the poolroom with an old Jewish peddler of French ticklers, Spanish fly, and jock collars. I walked back to them and watched the peddler demonstrate and pitch the collar to Pocket.

Pocket was excited. He was hanging on to every word. The sure-shot sex merchant put a rubber ring, studded all around the outside with soft rubber nodules, on his middle finger.

He was patting Pocket reassuringly on the back and saying, "To make the top of the nookie love it, you must shove the collar back to your balls on your putz. To drive the nookie crazy with joy inside, you must put the collar near the end of your putz.

"I guarantee that for life, a girl will love you that you made her feel so good. A gag you should take to bed for them. No sleep for the neighbors from the yelling otherwise.

"So many girls will chase you, by appointment only, you'll be jazzing. It's the latest thing, Mr. Pocket. It's greater than Spanish fly and the tickler, which I'm fresh out of today. Two for a buck, and for that price I should call a cop to stop the robbery. For my own brother, I wouldn't give them cheaper."

Pocket looked at me sheepishly and shoved a buck at the love salesman. He put the sex machines into his shirt pocket and led me to the benches against the wall. We sat down.

Pocket said, "Folks, I sure hope these goddamn things work. To make sure, I'll put on both of them, one at the back, and one on the end of my Jim Dandy. Tonight, I got a date to lay a cute hashslinger that works in the greasy spoon around the corner.

"She's fresh in town from Mississippi. She ain't had a chance to get her coat pulled by these stinking, slick Chicago bitches. She's tender as gnat liver. I'm sixty years old and tired of sleeping with my old sour broad. I'd try anything to hook a fine young bitch like that.

"I'm healthy and full of ginger. I'd set up housekeeping for her, if I can make her love me. Who knows, I might plant a squealer in her belly. Think of it, Folks, old, ugly-ass Pocket with a pretty young wife and a crumb crusher to brighten his last days."

I said, "I wish you luck, Pocket. Well, you get a payday with Blue and me tomorrow. How do you feel about it?"

He crossed and uncrossed his legs.

He sucked his bottom lip and said, "Blue promised me a grand for my end. I was overjoyed about that, until a coupla hours ago when Trapeze Willie, a second-story man from New York, gave me a deep rundown on Buster Bang Bang.

"I didn't tip Trapeze to the play for Buster tomorrow. I cracked about the bad luck that Mule had with Buster to prime Willie for the rundown. Folks, you got to chill Blue for the Buster play.

"Willie told me the man is one of the most feared

gorillas in New York. Even the rollers in Harlem are scared shitless of him. He's crazy suspicious, and he hates white people. He's been to bat for murder one, three times. He let Mule off with a kick in the ass because Mule is old and comical looking and he was soloing.

"You're going to be conning him that you're white. If he latches on to anything shitty in the play, he'll waste you first, and then blow Blue and me to pieces with the magnum. I just know he will. If you can't chill Blue, count me out. You tell Blue to get old man Spider or somebody to take my spot.

"Jesus Christ Almighty, look at that clock! Five after seven. My big butt hashslinger got off at seven. See you later, Folks. And don't forget to tell Blue I'm off the Buster thing."

I watched him rush through the doorway. I went out to the sidewalk and walked to the corner of Forty-seventh Street and Calumet Avenue. I went into the liquor store for a fifth of rum.

Pocket and a young brown-skinned broad with cow eyes and an astounding rear-end were coming away from the candy counter. Pocket winked at me as the girl stuffed a square of bubble gum into her mouth. She smelled like a rancid frying pan when I passed her.

I drove home and sat in the living room. I sipped rum and waited to give Blue the bad news about the Buster play.

I wouldn't shed a tear if Blue couldn't get someone to replace Pocket, and the whole plan for Bang Bang fell through.

At ten P. M. the phone rang.

I picked up the receiver and said, "Hello."

There was only the muted sound of a band and some broad singing Cole Porter's *Night and Day*.

"And this torment won't be through until you let me spend my life making love to you, night and day. Day and night deep in the heart of me there's Oh, such a hungry yearning burning—"

Again I said, "Hello."

Then the line closed. It was probably some drunk chump who dialed the wrong number.

I paced and tore down the Buster play for fatal flaws until I got a headache. I went to the bathroom medicine cabinet for an aspirin.

As I raised the glass of water to wash it down, I saw and old jar of Midge's cold cream in the cabinet. I saw the words "petal soft" on the label. I walked back to the living room phone and wondered if that screwy call had been romantic horseplay by the Goddess.

I called the Du Sable Hotel's cocktail lounge for Blue. He hadn't been there since seven P.M. At midnight I got into pajamas and went to the kitchen. I broiled a steak and tossed a salad.

I raised the first forkful to my mouth. A terrible thought murdered my appetite. What if Buster really knew diamonds and brought along a jeweler's glass to examine our stuff?

I shoved the plate away and called the Brass Rail for Blue. He hadn't been there at all. I sipped the fifth of rum half empty and lay down on the living room sofa.

At four-thirty A. M. Blue shook me awake. I looked up into his grinning face.

He said, "Folks, why the hell are you bedded down on the sofa? You got spikes in your bed?"

I rubbed my eyelids and sat up.

I muttered, "I'm going to get a big kick when I puncture your big cheerful balloon. Bang Bang is a killer. He hates white people and Pocket won't play. Now, I'll bet you can't grin. Go on try it."

He fell into a chair and laughed tears down his cheeks. I just sat there for a moment and watched him fall apart. Then I started to laugh with him.

It was funny to me because I figured he was overplaying my bet. And he was covering up his disappointment over the souring of the Buster play with his charade of hilarity, but I was wrong.

He caught some breath and said, "Folks, you should stop abusing your pump with groundless worry. At three P. M. last afternoon, the world's slickest and most charming nigger grifter cut into the ugliest mark in the world. It happened in the lobby of the Grand Hotel. We laughed, drank, ate and laid white whores together until two A. M. He may hate white people, but he's crazy about young white pussy.

"I told him the tale around midnight. He wanted to go to Madison Street right then to look the stuff over. At two P.M. tomorrow he's going to tail me in his Chrysler to your hotel.

"I left him at the Greek's greasy spoon at Thirty-first and Indiana Avenue. I drove down South Parkway. Who did I spy coming out of a fast sheet joint at Forty-sixth Street? One Pocket with a young broad from big foot country.

"I picked them up and dropped her off at home. He was scared stiff of the Buster play. But when I ran down the tight beauty of it all he started getting weak for a piece of the action.

"It took close to two hours and an extra five bills from the score tomorrow to bring the leery old bastard back into the play. So now you can stop worrying and get a few hours of solid sleep. You'll need it, because we'll have to be very sharp today when we separate that gorilla from his seven grand. We could tap him out for the almost-eight grand he's got. But we don't want him stranded in Chicago.

CHAPTER SIXTEEN

Rocks for a Gorilla

I got up from the sofa and went to my bed. But I didn't sleep. I lay there mentally practicing my role as a blind hoodlum. Then I'd get up and go to the bathroom mirror and practice the vacant unfocused stare of the sightless.

At eight-thirty A. M., Blue and I had dressed and had coffee. I was edgy when I tailed Blue to Forty-seventh Street to pick up Pocket. We parked our cars in front of the poolroom.

It was nine A. M. and he wasn't in the poolroom. I was wondering if he had chickened out again, when he came down the sidewalk and got in the Buick beside me. We took Michigan Avenue to the slum dealer's shop on Wabash Avenue in the Loop.

Pocket was silent the whole way. Blue and I went in and got our stock. It was beautiful slum for only five bills. The price for the ten rings was so low because the mountings were gold-filled instead of solid gold.

The old Jew stamped fourteen carat on the inner side of each band. He assured us that only an acid test could foul us up. We drove through the Loop.

The three of us got out on the sidewalk in front of a skid-row hotel on Madison Street. We followed Blue into a drug store beneath the hotel. Blue bought a two-hundred watt light bulb, a box of children's crayons, glue, and a small box of colored birthday-cake candles.

Blue went to the side of his car. Pocket and I went up the stairs and rented a third-floor room facing Madison Street.

The wino desk clerk gave us a rheumy wink when he handed me the key. He probably thought I was a white queer about to receive a groovy transport to fairy heaven from One Pocket.

We walked into the dingy, smelly room. It stank worse than the old apartment back on Thirty-ninth Street. I raised the window and showed Blue three fingers and then ten. I went over and unlatched the door for Blue.

We waited fifteen minutes for him. I went to the window a half-dozen times. His Caddie was still parked at the curb. I started to worry when Blue came through the door with a large, stinking paper sack in his hand.

I said, "What the hell is that?"

He chuckled and said, "I went to the alley and got some atmosphere for the mark. I'm not planning to miss that seven grand. You hoodlum Detroit bastards have been doing a lot of sweating, farting, drinking and smoking in this funky sewer for more than a week.

"You know there is more to good con than what is dumped into a mark's ears. His eyes and nose should also take the con treatment."

I watched as Blue opened the dirty bag of garbage. He filled the ashtrays about the room with crushed out cigarette butts. He put whiskey and wine bottles on the rickety dresser and at the sides of the bed.

He shoved a stack of greasy paper plates and crumpled paper napkins into the wastebasket near the door. He washed his hands in the face bowl across the room.

Pocket said, "Blue, did you bring a rod just in case the crazy mark wakes up?"

Blue pushed his palms toward Pocket and said softly, "Pocket, I swear on my sainted mama's grave that the gorilla can't wake up. Our merchandise is top quality, and the best nigger con man in the country has told him the tale.

"Now you and Folks take off your clothes, down to your shorts, and hang them in the closet. Folks, then you lie down on the bed. I'm going to put that surgical scar on your noggin."

I came back from the closet in my shorts and lay on the

bed. Blue was at the dresser with his back to me. Finally he came and sat on the side of the bed.

He closed his pocketknife and dropped it into his shirt pocket. He had a ragged two-inch sliver of a deep pink candle in his palm. It was shades darker than my skin. He had pocked the top side of it so that it looked like a slice of mangled skin.

I saw the underside glistening with glue as he pasted it on my forehead. He screwed the point of a dark purple crayon into my forehead and up and down both sides of the wax scar for the healed stitches.

He went back to the dresser and brought a dime-sized uneven blob of pink wax and glued it to the side of my right calf. He dotted in deep purple stitch marks. He stood back and looked at his fake surgery.

He said, "It will look real to him. You're not going to stand up at all. So he'll never get close enough to see they're phonies.

"Make sure you turn that bullet wound so he ganders it. It will make him remember the part of the tale when your brother shot you in the leg to con the rollers that you were a stick-up victim.

"Now Pocket, you and Folks get upset when the mark cracks that the stuff *looks* real, but can't you go with us and get a jeweler's glass put on it. That will give us a chance to blow for the appraisal of the ring I palmed.

"At the instant that I palm the ring from your display, Pocket, you scoop up the stuff and put it back in this canvas bag. You're mad and irritated that the mark and I are too stupid to know real rocks when we see them.

"This makes it logical to the mark that you didn't miss the rock that I filched. Folks, you have the bag under your pillow when I bring the mark in. Pocket, display on the dresser beneath that two-hundred watt bulb in the dresser lamp.

"I'm picking the mark up at two this afternoon. No later than three P. M., I'll be rapping three times on that door.

"Pocket, when you open the door look suspiciously up

and down the hall before you let us in. Let's give the gorilla a tight play right down the line. All right, that's it. Any intelligent questions?"

Pocket said, "Yeah, I got a good one. Ain't it going to be kinda bullshitty all around when the mark comes back to buy the stuff, and everybody is wise that a piece of the stuff is missing? Ain't I suppose to miss it even when we make the deal? It could pull his coat that we're in cahoots to trim him."

Blue opened the door and said, "That's a stupid sucker's question, Pocket. I'll play the intelligent answer out for you when I lug the mark in. Just give a natural response when I play it to you."

Blue shut the door. I got up and looked in the dresser mirror. The bogus scar really looked like a croaker had been fiddling around inside my dome. I went to the open window and watched Blue pull the Caddie away from the curb.

I looked at my watch. It was noon. Two tattered Mutt and Jeff winos with scarlet faces were tussling feebly in the gutter across the street.

A tilted winebottle glittered like rare crystal in the fierce stare of August sun. Jeff stiff-armed Mutt away and sucked the amber treasure down his gullet.

I glanced down at my Buick parked in front of the hotel. A withered Madison Street siren in a vomit-stained white satin ball gown teetered her bony bottom on a front fender.

I heard a faint melody of *Stairway to the Stars* through the screech and hum of traffic. I banged the window shut and pulled the shade down. I turned away. It was Phala's favorite tune. I sat on the side of the bed and watched Pocket nervously picking his nose.

I said, "Pocket, the guy you're rolling those pills for died yesterday. Stop worrying. Like Blue told us, the mark won't wake up."

He jerked his finger out of his nostril and said, "I'm not worried about the mark. I was thinking about Clara Sue, my young broad. She's kinda' salty with me. Her thing was too tender for them goddamn collars. They rubbed her sweet pussy raw.

"I got 'em soaking in castor oil to soften 'em up. I was sitting here trying to work out the con to play on her so I can use 'em again on her. Folks, I'm thirsty. I'm gonna' slip on my clothes and go get a pint of Gordon's Gin. You want some rum?"

I said, "No, Pocket, I don't want any hard stuff. And neither do you until this play is over. Tell you what, I'll spring for a couple of quarts of Pabst Blue Ribbon if you'll make the trip."

He said, "You're right about the hooch. I'll get the suds. I want to go to the drug store too. I'm gonna buy one of those switchblades I saw. Old Pocket ain't going to play for a crazy mark like Buster without some protection.

"A wise old Chinaman once said, 'Even the shade of a toothpick is a blessing to a chump croaking in the desert sun.'"

We guzzled beer and rehearsed our lines until a quarter of three. I was propped up in bed and Pocket was in a chair beside me. We stared silently at the door.

At five after three my heart leaped at the three raps on the door. When Pocket went to the door I saw his legs trembling. He opened it and stuck his head into the hallway before stepping aside.

Blue came in followed by the brutish mark. I cocked my head sideways in the bird-like awareness of the blind. I hooked my eyes to wallpaper two feet away from the muscular black monster, as he stooped his six feet, seven inch bulk past the door frame. His slitted maroon eyes were burning through me.

Blue said, "Buster, this is Zambroski and his pal Hastings Street Harvey."

The gorilla bared gold fangs and snarled in a Hell's Kitchen accent, "Ah'm inna hurrih. Whah's de spahklahs?"

I stared at the wallpaper and fumbled beneath the pillow for the canvas bag. It was hard not to focus my eyes on his evil black face, crisscrossed with puckered razor slashes.

From the corner of my eye I saw the nostrils of his smashed, bridgeless nose quivering. I held out the bag toward Pocket. I watched as Pocket switched on the two-hundred watt dresser lamp and dumped the fancy fakes to the top of the dresser beneath the flattering spotlight.

Buster and Blue held each ring up close to the light and examined them. I saw a tiny wad fall into the waste basket at the door when Buster turned from the dresser and walked several paces toward me.

He glared down at the fake leg wound and said, "Polack, dis stuff looks kosha. But I ain't inna mood fuh no fuckin' pig inna pok. I want ya boids should go wid us and lat a jooler peep at de rocks. Polack, gimme de line on de stuff."

Blue stiffened. Pocket shuddered and his Adam's apple fluttered. I didn't get it. I thought the mark wanted a recap of the tale Blue had told him so he could cross check Blue. Deadly silence hammered my eardrums.

I was about to deliver the tale when Pocket cut in and blurted, "It's a twenty-grand line. And we're not dealing with people who look at real stuff and don't know it. We don't have to stick out our necks to get lopped off by some fink jeweler.

"We know the stuff is real. We're sorry you don't. Besides, at six tomorrow night we show the stuff to a buyer who knows what we got and won't hassle. Forget it. We don't want to sell."

Pocket angrily scooped up the nine rings and hurled them into the bag. He walked to the bed and stuck the bag under my pillow. Buster looked at Blue.

Blue said, "The man has a right to be careful. We know the stuff is real. But what the hell is wrong about a jeweler backing up our opinion? That's a lot of bullshit about having a buyer for those rocks. You hot bastards haven't stuck your asses out of that door since I talked to you

Saturday morning.

"The man hasn't got ten grand. Maybe he can raise seven grand in an hour or so. We'll be back for the stuff at seven grand. You're fucking with the cemetery if we don't get that stuff at our price. We got some muscle nailing down this hotel. So, don't try to take a powder while we're gone."

Pocket followed them to the door and blubbered, "This poor white boy is blind. His rocks got a eighty-grand legit value. Why you gonna' rob him with a measly seven grand? It ain't right and I—"

The door slammed in his face. The ancient floor boards in the hallway squeaked as Blue and Bang Bang stomped away. Pocket mopped his brow with the back of his hand and sat in the chair beside the bed.

He shook his head and said, "Folks, my ticker almost stopped when Buster cracked on you for the line on the stuff. Line means the actual price doubled. It's inside code that jewelers, pawnbrokers and fences use.

"A big time heist man with eighty grand in real rocks would know that. We're lucky your stalling didn't pull his coat that you were a phony. Let's see the rocks. We want to make sure that Blue palmed the right fake that matches his real one for the appraisal."

I dumped the bag of glass on the bed. The right one was missing. I noticed that all the ring bands were sticky. Pocket started feeling them. He reached for a corner of sheet to wipe them off.

I slapped his hand away. I got up and went to the waste basket. I remembered that I had seen something fall into it from Buster's hand. I looked down at a blob of half-chewed gum. Then it struck me.

I said, "Pocket, that suspicious Buster bastard marked every piece of our slum with sticky juice from a wad of gum. He's half conned already that our stuff is real. The slick chump sonuvabitch took out insurance against a switch in rocks.

"Pocket! I just thought of something terrible. The genuine rock that Blue is going to switch in for the appraisal has no goo on it. What if Buster gets that ring in his mitt right after a jeweler has certified it, and before Blue has a chance to switch it out after the appraisal?"

Pocket sat for a long moment frowning in deep thought.

Finally he grinned and said, "Shit, I ain't gonna' worry no more. Blue can handle that gorilla. I was leery at first. But after I heard Blue play that beautiful turn-around con for that mark, I ain't got no doubt that Blue will let him wake up.

"What did Blue say, 'Don't try to take a powder. We got muscle nailing down the hotel'?

"Ain't Blue playing some sweet con on that sucker? Blue took charge and out-gorilla'd the gorilla."

I got up and checked out my noggin scar in the dresser mirror.

I said, "Pocket, you're right. I guess Blue is just too fast and clever for a mark like Buster."

A half hour later we heard three raps on the door. Pocket opened the door. Blue and Buster stepped in. Blue had a stern look on his face. The mark was poker faced. I rolled my eyes up to my favorite patch of wallpaper and cocked my head sideways.

Blue gritted, "All right, all right; the stuff, the stuff. Come up with it. The man has his seven grand."

I didn't move a muscle.

Pocket mumbled, "It ain't right. It just ain't right."

Blue thundered, "You ugly, shit-colored uncle-tomming motherfucker. Do I have to pistol whip your nappy head to make you understand that we want those rocks now— for seven grand?"

I trembled all over and pulled the bag from beneath the pillow.

I held it out and said, "Here, Harvey, all the rocks in the world aren't worth a hair on your head."

Pocket took it to the dresser and dumped the rings out. Blue and Buster examined them again. Buster ran a finger over each band for the goo test.

Blue winked at the mark. Then he turned and exploded, "There's a piece missing. We looked at ten. Look in that bed for the missing one."

Pocket came to the bed and fumbled around the pillow. He looked under the bed.

He shrugged his shoulders helplessly and pleaded, "I swear we ain't holding out that piece. I don't know where it is."

Suddenly Blue and Buster burst out laughing. Out of the corner of my eye I saw Buster shove his hand in front of Pocket's eyes. The glass duplicate to Blue's ring was on his pinkie.

Blue said, "You're a piss-poor seeing-eye dog for the Polack. I took that sample of the rocks with us to make sure that my client was really buying the quill. Polack, you're a damn fool to let the blind lead the blind."

Buster counted a fat sheaf of bills to the dresser top. Pocket picked them up and counted them slowly.

He clucked his tongue against the roof of his mouth and said softly, "It ain't right. It just ain't right that eighty grand in rocks should go for a measly seven grand. It just ain't—"

Blue and Buster had gone through the door. We had made the score! I sprang from the bed and danced wildly to the window with Pocket in my arms.

I raised the shade and watched Blue and Buster shake hands and split up on the sidewalk. Just like Blue said, Buster went east on Madison Street toward the Loop. Blue U-turned and went west on Madison.

Pocket gave me the roll of C-notes. I counted fifteen of them into his palm. I pulled my scars off and scrubbed the stitches away with a wet thumb.

We dressed, and in less than ten minutes we were in the Buick. I U-turned and went up Madison to Kedsie, so that accidentally the mark wouldn't be confused by the miracle of a blind Polack driving a car. I took a left turn at Kedsie Avenue and headed south.

At Forty-seventh and State Streets, Pocket said, "Don't

drop me at the poolroom. Take me home with you. I want
to see Blue."

Blue's car was in the driveway and the front door was
open, when I pulled up to the front of the house. We went
into the living room. Blue was sitting on the sofa. There
were bottles of bourbon, rum, gin and scotch on the coffee
table in front of him. We sat down beside him. I gave Blue
a fifty-dollar bill and twenty-seven C-notes.

Blue said, "That mark is going to be in town until next
week. Then he's got to go back to New York to his muscle
job for his numbers racket boss. He only had a two weeks
vacation.

"Folks and I are going to lie low here in the house until
he blows. Pocket, I would advise you to do the same
somewhere."

Pocket said, "Blue, I wanted to talk to you about laying
around here with you and Folks. That is, if you got room
for me."

Blue patted his shoulder and said, "Sure I got room for
you, Pocket. Stay as long as you like. Now I'm going to get
on the phone and have three fine young pussies to come
out here and stay overnight with us. It's all on me. What
do you want? White, yellow, brown or black?"

Pocket said, "I ain't choicy, just so it's young and tender
and got a sweet taste."

I poured four fingers of rum and said, "I pass, Blue. I'm
not interested. I'm going to make a short call before you
call the broads."

I took my glass and went to the phone in the kitchen
and called the Goddess.

CHAPTER SEVENTEEN

Mr. Trick Bag

Blue, Pocket and I stayed off the streets until August. Pocket went back to his pool hustle. Blue and I went back to the smack, the drag, the flue and the rocks.

Two days after we had done our volunteer sentence at home, we were finishing our steaks in the Brass Rail Bar. We had just blown off a rocks mark. He paid a grand for the three hoops that cost us sixty dollars.

I said, "Blue, I was really tense playing for that mark. I thought he would crack something about rocks I wasn't wise to. I can't forget Buster's crack about line on the rocks.

"Blue, I don't understand why I never heard you or the old Jew that we get our slum from crack anything about line. It's a bad feeling to have a mark crack something that I'm not wise to."

Blue said, "Frankly, I didn't pull your coat to it when I taught you the rocks, because I didn't think of it. The old Jew never cracked it when we went to buy stock because you were obviously my partner.

"I got wise to it years ago when I first came to Chicago. Everytime I'd go to pawn something, the pawnbrokers would look at my goods and quibble among themselves about the line to let me have.

"I'd for instance, ask for ten dollars on a suit. Finally, they'd agree with each other on a ten line loan. I'd walk out the door with five dollars. I woke up to their price code that way.

"Folks, I wouldn't worry if I were you. Crack-wise marks like Bang Bang are few and far between. Besides, I'll lay you odds that the line was the only thing I forgot to

tell you about in any of the con games that we play. I
wouldn't put you in a trick bag. Say, Folks, why don't you
make Joe Hughes's joint with me tonight? It crawls with
fine young broads."

I said, "Maybe next time. I'd doing my playing in the
Loop tonight."

I went to the phone and made a date with the Goddess
for nine P. M. that night at the Palmer House. It was a
plush hotel in the Loop that housed the famous Pump
Room bistro. It was a favorite watering spot for top
theatrical celebrities and business executives.

I was leading a hectic double life. The Goddess and I
did our eating and drinking and sleeping together in the
Loop's finest restaurants and hotels.

She was wealthy, beautiful and lived in River Forest.
But she wasn't part of Chicago's top social crust. Her
Cicero beginnings were too humble to qualify her. Or
perhaps she didn't have enough dough to buy a member-
ship. However, this was an advantage for us. We flitted
tipsily like carefree butterflies through the neon and
chrome gardens. We didn't hide our affair.

We were together at least twice a week, and many
weeks, more often than that. We were really getting to
each other. The few nights that we didn't meet were spent
on the telephone. I had my own phone put in my bedroom
so we could spend hours lying on our beds, sweet-talking to
each other.

She had changed so much. Only rarely did she have the
cruel, mean moods that I suffered through when we first
met. I'd be in a dreamy fog while playing the con with
Blue in the street.

I never got her out of my mind for a moment. Her
emerald-flecked eyes radiated love for me.

When we met, we'd squeeze ourselves together like
we'd been separated for years. At last I knew the racy,
mad sorcery of love. Whenever I entered her, I felt the
insane excitement that perhaps a gold prospector feels
when he discovers a glory hole. We'd lie in fragrant

shadows. She'd tell me in her gypsy-violin voice how much she loved me and that one day, she knew, I'd be her husband.

My paralyzed throat would ache to speak the truth that I really was the son of a black woman. I wasn't sure enough of her yet to risk the confession. I couldn't forget the hateful flare-up of disdain in her eyes whenever she talked about coons.

When October came, we had crushed countless dozens of roses. We'd often look wonderingly at each other and remark how strange it was that our few short months together seemed like always.

We drank a lot of champagne and Cutty Sark Scotch. I went to Peacock Jeweler's and bought a beautiful platinum and ruby necklace for her. I was blowing a lot of dough. But what is dough when you've caught a Goddess in your lucky arms?

The first week in November I was alone at the breakfast table. Blue was still asleep. It was about five-thirty A. M. I hadn't slept well for weeks.

I laced my coffee with Scotch. I had been doing it for a couple of weeks. I never ate breakfast anymore. I raised the coffee cup for a sip. I glanced at an open magazine on the table.

A big type caption posed a silly question to me. "Are you an alcoholic?"

I started to read the first paragraph. I snickered at the phrases, "morning imbibing, defective sleep patterns, physical dependence and oral compulsion to drink."

I wasn't hooked on the juice. I didn't have to drink. In fact, I could stop at any time, and never miss it. I read the rest of the article. It wiped the amused grin off my face. The damn piece fitted the alcoholic symptoms to me like a glove.

I got up and dumped the heavily-laced coffee into the sink. I went to the bathroom and looked at myself critically in the mirror. Was I imagining that the whites of my eyes had an almost invisible pale aqua tint, overcast by a network of tiny red veins?

The slight puffiness of my face made my nose look shorter and smaller. I thrust my face closer to the mirror. Phantom lavender encircled my eye sockets. My palms got gluey with sweat when I remembered the scabby drunks festering on Madison Street's skid row.

I went and sat on the side of the bed in deep thought. I'd prove to myself that I wasn't a sucker for alcohol. I was certain I wasn't an alcoholic. I was too young. I would just turn twenty-three on the fifteenth of January coming.

Only old guys and broads could be alcoholics. But, yes, I was drinking too much. That's why I didn't sleep well and my face had a funny look.

Well, I was a grifter, not a weak square john. I'd stop drinking hard stuff from this moment on. Maybe I'd still sip just a little sociable champagne with the Goddess on our dates. Everybody knew champagne was harmless, probably even therapeutic.

I took the fifth of Cutty Sark Scotch off the nightstand and dumped it into the toilet bowl. I put on my robe and went to the Buick. I got three unopened fifths from the trunk.

I dumped them into the toilet and said, "Mr. Trick Bag, you bastard. I'm through with you. Don't think it's been a pleasure. It hasn't."

I'd show the cocky author of that article that his rundown on chump drunks didn't really fit me after all. For the next two days I didn't take a drop. I slept worse and I had no pep in the street with Blue.

On the third day I got a tonic for pep from the drug store, I finished the bottle that same day. It boosted me from the washed-out feeling. That night I drank half a jeroboam of champagne with the Goddess.

The fourth day after I had taken the pledge, Blue and I had just blown off a smack mark near the Greyhound Bus Station in the loop. I had a bottle of the tonic in my topcoat pocket. Blue was on the sidewalk watching me walk east and the mark west, to prove that we weren't partners, that had cheated Blue out of his money.

Suddenly, I and the milling crowd and the cars were sucked into a black, booming, nauseous whirlpool. My tongue staggered across my desert-dry lips. I tasted the brine streaming down my inflamed face.

My rubbery legs started telescoping down toward the pavement. I stumbled to a light pole, and turned and looked back at Blue. A pair of wide eyes starkly white, bobbed in a choppy sea of people.

He was staring at me with his mouth open. He glanced back over his shoulder. The mark wasn't out of sight. As sick as I was, I realized how sticky the blowoff would be if the mark saw me leaning weakly against the pole.

He'd know I wasn't on my way to meet him around the block to get his money back, and half of what we'd taken from Blue. He'd come back and loiter around to protect his dough. A bunco cop could make the scene and get wise.

Then I thought of the tonic in my top coat pocket. I struggled the bottle to my mouth and drained it in front of the curious stares of passers-by. It was like a small transfusion of pure energy.

Within a minute and a half, I felt strong enough to release my grip on the light pole. It was a long, long two blocks to the Caddie.

Blue had been following me. He helped me into the car. He pulled the Caddie away from the curb and said, "Folks, you're sick. I'm taking you to a croaker."

I closed my eyes and leaned back in the seat.

I said, "Forget the croaker. Let's go to the Brass Rail. I need a stiff jolt of Scotch."

That night at home I lay in bed and framed a slick drinking plan. No drinking at all until noon. Then I'd take no more than a pint by shots or bottle before bedtime.

After a week or so I'd made it no more than a half pint. Then after that less and less, until I didn't take any. I knew it would work. Perhaps I'd even stop drinking harmless champagne with the Goddess in time.

Too bad I'd switched from rum to the Goddess's Scotch.
Perhaps rum wouldn't have poisoned my system completely. Mr. Trick Bag had won a mere skirmish. I was sure I
could win the war.

I fell into jagged sleep. The next morning I awoke to
the whirr of a vacuum cleaner. Our old cleaning woman
was hard at work in the hall.

Blue came to the side of the bed and said, "How are
you doing?"

I said, "I don't feel like I could touch the sky. But I'm
not sick."

Blue said, "Maybe you ought to see a croaker and get
checked. You looked awful yesterday hugging that lamp
post. Anyway, we'll take the day off. Should I have the old
lady bring you some breakfast?"

I shook my head and said, "No, I'm not hungry. I'll get
up later and eat some cereal."

I dozed off. The clinking of cologne bottles on the
dresser opened my eyes.

Sister Franklin was dusting and softly humming an old
black people's spiritual, "Give Me That Old Time Religion." Her tiny hunched body and white hair reminded me
of Grandma Annie.

I propped myself up in the bed. The mattress springs
creaked. Sister's dull brown eyes met mine in the dresser
mirror. A toothless smile cheerfully creased her black face.

She turned and said, "Good mawnin', Mistah Johnny."

I said, "Good morning, Sister Franklin."

She said, "Ah warn't aimin' tu break yuh res'. Mistah
Blue perticulah tole me not tu du no cleanin' en heah atall.
But ah caint stan no devlish filt'. Ah jes hed tu dus' en
heah.

"Mistah Johnny, yuh ain' got thet spry roostah look. Yuh
'pear porely. Ain' nuthun' tu beat thet gud book en truble
time. Ah ain' nevah seed thet book en dis hous. Is yuh
evah redd it en yurh born days?"

I said, "No, I haven't, Sister Franklin. I've been too
busy for most of my life trying to keep from starving. I've

heard it's a good book. One of these days, I'll look into it."

Her mouth popped open in shocked awe. The dust cloth fluttered to the carpet. With perhaps divine agility she flung herself on her knees beside the bed.

She shut her eyes and started to pray. Her moaning plea to God to show me the holy light and to save my soul gave me an uncomfortable, trapped feeling. The pitiful old lady was so sincerely caught up in the nonsense, I had to go along.

I noticed Blue standing in the doorway shaking his head with an amused smile on his face. Finally she started pressing her fingertips against my head and then across my chest and sides. She was trying mighty hard to heal me back to that spry rooster stance. But my head still felt like I had thousand-pound dumbbells strapped to it, and her gnarled fingers tickled me silly.

Blue pressed the palm of his hand across his inflated cheeks to keep from bursting out laughing at my silly bind. She got to her feet. Blue faded down the hall.

Sister Franklin's face had a joyful, hostess type radiance. It was like perhaps she had just seated a famished Christ at His second coming to a banquet for her best corn bread and hog guts.

Breathlessly she said, "Did yuh feel Him a runnin' down mah fingertips? Ah'm gonna pray fuh yuh, Mistah Johnny. Yuh ain' nuthin' but a shell widout duh Lawd."

She picked up the dust cloth and went through the bathroom into Midge's old room.

Blue came and sat on the side of the bed.

He said, "Is you been converted by the Holy Ghost and the fire? Speak up. Is you gwine repent your sinful grifter ways and flunkey for some peckerwood for fifty a week?

"Seriously, Folks, we've never talked about it, but you know that my only religion is that lucky seven-day candle burning in my bedroom. How do you feel about religion and God?"

I didn't answer right away.

Finally I said, "Blue, you'll never lose your partner that

way. I was raised on Thirty-ninth Street in an apartment that would make a hobo puke.

"I use to look at the slick magazines that Phala brought home from River Forest. I'd see the pictures of just ordinary, middle-class, happy whites in settings that looked like palaces to me.

"It was really confusing because all the black people around me lived in pigsties and never got enough of the cheap garbage they could afford to buy.

"It was even more confusing to watch the shabby black religious buffs trudging to church every Sunday morning. I was eight years old, I think, when I asked Phala why she never talked to God or went to church. Her answer summed up the way I feel now about the whole God thing.

"She said, 'Johnny, the white people have all the nice things of life and all the money. Niggers have all the misery and poverty and their religion. White people love to see Niggers blinded by religion. It makes it easy to keep them shut out from their rights and the nicer things of life.

"'Those poor ragged Niggers you see on the way to church don't know that if there is a God, he's deaf to Nigger prayers. It's a white world and God is white. So, why waste my time when I won't be heard anyway.'

"Blue, everything I've seen since that day proves the truth of what Phala said. Now, if I didn't have Nigger blood in my veins, perhaps I would have tried to catch His ear when I was coming up. But this way I know where I stand. He doesn't want me, and I'm not interested in Him. And that's the guaranteed truth."

Blue said, "Folks, that's a smart attitude to have. But my conviction is that God never existed. I believe the Bible was written by the slickest bunch of peckerwood grifters that ever crapped between two sandals."

Blue turned and went down the hall. I lay there for a long time thinking. Maybe God didn't even exist.

By the last week of October, I knew that the pint limit I had set for myself wasn't reasonable. Twice I had attacks like that first one in the Loop. It took at least two pints a day to spark me for the con and the Goddess.

Her best friend, the widowed Cordelia, had a plush apartment on Chicago's Near Northside. Several times we used a bedroom in Cordelia's apartment for our sex fun.

We met at Cordelia's the last day of October. We had made furious love, and we were just lying in the darkness holding each other close.

Camille whispered, "Darling, I missed my period last month. Maybe there's a wee Irish dream inside me. I'm going to see my doctor next week and take the Belgian rabbit test for pregnancy. Married or not, I'm going to have—"

I cut her off.

I said, "You can't have a baby when your husband hasn't touched you in ten years. How would—?"

Her index finger across my lips silenced my protest.

She kissed me and said, "Don't worry about a thing. I might open my bedroom to my husband if I am pregnant. I'll plan and take care of all the angles."

Cordelia and I liked each other. She had been one of the original Minsky Strippers. She was tall and buxom, with Coca Cola bottle curves. And her florid face was gullied with spidery wrinkles. But even so, a faint trace of dollish beauty was still there.

She was plain spoken, and she and her ornate apartment had a kind of bawdy elegance. Her thin hair had been dyed so much it looked like old straw. But she was a fancy dresser and huge rocks twinkled brightly on her long expressive fingers.

Her husband had been a wealthy sportsman who drowned ten years before while deep sea fishing.

I was glad to meet the Goddess at Cordelia's place for two reasons. As I said, I liked her. And I was able to escape the temptation to drink past my two-pint daily limit in the Chez Paree, the cellar Blue Note and in all the other spots I usually made with the Goddess before we nested in a Loop bed.

I had been able to avoid meeting Camille's father. Just from the few tidbits of information that Camille dropped about him, I knew it wouldn't be a moment filled with bliss.

In his early twenties, he had been a slave-driving official in a South African prison.

On the twentieth of November, the Goddess and I went to a movie at the State Lake Theatre. She was gorgeous in a formfitting, sable-trimmed white woolen suit. The movie was *The Bells of St. Mary's.* The Goddess was wild about Bing Crosby even when he didn't sing.

We sat in the rear of the balcony. Just after a Lowell Thomas Travelogue, a huge burly black guy and a cute young white broad sat in front of us. Almost right away they started torrid petting and sucking of each other's tongue.

The Goddess was squirming in her seat like she was the one with the black guy's mitt rammed between her thighs.

She pinched me hard in the side and whispered, "Can't we do something? That coon beast is desecrating that poor white infant. She can't be more than fifteen. I'm going to be ill. Please do something. Get a policeman and have him arrested."

I couldn't answer right away.

Finally I got myself together and whispered, "Now, stop that. It's none of our business. And besides, you don't see a razor at her throat, do you? She looks like she's having fun. She might even be in love with him. Let's move before you make me ill."

We got up and sat on the far side of the balcony. But it was no use. The Goddess was so upset, she couldn't watch the screen. She kept darting agonized glances at the passionate couple and whispering her outrage to me.

I didn't grasp the plot of the feature at all. I vaguely remember Bing Crosby and some old guy with a sweet voice decked out in priestly robes.

When we walked to the sidewalk she was still rubbing my tender nerves raw with her bleats about the bestial black coon and his white love slave.

I had already had my two-pint limit that day in the street while playing the con with Blue. I got behind the wheel of her Jaguar and drove us to one of our cozy little hangouts on Clark street.

By eleven P. M. the affair of the white infant and the bleating and all the rest of it was almost humorous. I was feeling better than I had in weeks. I'd had a bad cold for several days. But the dozen double-shots I'd drunk seemed to wipe away the congestion and tightness in my chest. Mr. Trick Bag had won another minor skirmish all right.

I looked at the grinning row of whiskey bottles on the back bar and silently said, "Goddamnit, tomorrow's another day. You poisonous bastard. I won't touch you tomorrow, to make up for tonight. You'll see. What do you think about that, Mr. Trick Bag sonuvabitch?"

CHAPTER EIGHTEEN

The Haters

I remember sailing in the Jaguar through a sea of glittery neon to a massive port. It was the Palmer House. And the Goddess was leading me into the swank Pump Room.

A tall guy in an impeccable tuxedo and flawless smile approached us and crooned, "Ah, what a delight it is to see you, Mrs. Costain. Your father is expecting you."

I thought, "Well, she's tricked me into meeting the old bastard."

We followed him through the dulcet light and muted hum of polite conversation to a large, plush booth. A tall aristocratic guy in a blue cashmere suit was rising from his seat with lanquid feline grace.

His platinum hair was a sleek tailored cap with steel-gray emblems embossed at the temples. His glacial grey eyes held mine as he greeted us with a Madison Avenue smile. His voice was low and velvety, as he held out a pale manicured hand to her and said, "Whisty, you sweet girl.

She tiptoed and kissed his long straight nose.

"You kept your promise. This must be the wonderful Johnny O'Brien I've heard you extol. It's a real pleasure to meet you, Johnny. I'm Bradford Wherry."

His speech had a trace of arch-British crispness.

I shook his hand and said, "Thank you, Mr. Wherry. I've looked forward to meeting you."

He wrinkled his handsome face in mock pain as we all sat down.

He said, "I would rather that you called me Brad. I envision a warm relationship between us. Whisty has already laid the foundation. I've told her a thousand times what a great P. R. talent was going to waste."

A waiter came with chilled glasses on a silver tray. He tilted champagne into them from a gigantic bottle nestled in a gleaming icebucket on a stand beside the booth table. I noticed him fill an extra glass.

I was wondering why, when the Goddess said, "Daddy, have we barged into some secret rendezvous of yours? Are you expecting some enchanting glamourous woman of the world to join you?"

His voluptuous face crinkled into a vast amused smile.

He said, "Unfortunately, nothing so romantic as that. Pete Packer, that outstanding western captain of police left just a moment before you came. He went to his suite upstairs. He'll be back momentarily. You remember Pete. He was our weekend guest last year."

She said, "Of course I do. A sourpuss, but really a thoroughly nice fellow."

I raised the fragile crystal to my mouth and sipped the amber bubbly. A shadow fell across the snowy table cloth. I looked up. A slender, hawk-faced guy with a phantom smile on his thin cruel mouth was sliding into the booth beside Camille's father.

Mr. Wherry said, "Pete Packer, Johnny O'Brien, a friend of the family. I don't have to run a make for you on that exquisite female beside Johnny."

The captain nodded at me and said in a nasal voice, "Mr. O'Brien, it's a pleasure."

I nodded and said, "I'm very pleased to meet you, Mr. Packer."

His wintry blue eyes twinkled warmly as he switched them to the Goddess.

He said, "I couldn't forget one of the most beautiful women in Chicago. How have you been, Camille?"

She poked out her bottom lip petulantly and said, "Just splendid, Pete. But my evening was ruined earlier. Johnny and I witnessed the most distressing thing at the theater.

"An adult coon was doing the most horribly despicable things to an underaged white baby girl. It's nothing short of social castastrophe when coons can publicly violate the flower of white womanhood.

"Oh! How I wished for a policeman to take that black brute to the bastille. The coons have gotten completely out of hand in the North. Pete, where can one place the awful blame for this odious social condition?"

The captain looked slyly at Mr. Wherry and said, "Camille, I am proud and happy to report that my conscience is clear of guilt relative to the nigra problem. My political views are steel-hard conservative. It is the maudlin, liberal whites like Brad who must be blamed for the worsening overall nigra problem.

"Thank God, my police department in California is blessed with a realistic and practical philosophy. We strive for the high recruitment of good white policemen with Southern backgrounds who know what the nigra's place is. Their minds are not cluttered with the nonsense of equality and civil rights.

"They know that the nigras are really sub-human animals. We've discovered that ruthless containment and stern treatment are the answers to the nigra problem.

"I have known since my rookie policeman days that the nigras steal, rape, whore, pimp and murder because they are basically criminally inclined. They're derived from inferior loins. That's all. Brad, can you refute any of my contentions?"

Mr. Wherry had a canary-devoured expression on his face.

He said, "Pete, you're a fine policeman. I admire you greatly as such. But, your political ideas are all wet. I'm going to give you a few political facts of life. But first, I must preface a bit.

"I, and at least ninety percent of the whites in this country with so-called liberal leanings privately wouldn't care a whit if all the niggers in America were herded into one of your larger canyons out West and then bombed into oblivion. However, we realize that the niggers are with us and lamentably will always be with us. You conservatives can't resist your childish displays of hostility. You are—"

The captain almost stuck his ugly, beet-red face into the handsome face of Mr. Wherry and said loudly, "I'm too honest to despise the black apes in secret and kiss their backsides in public like you liberals do.

"In California, we will always club their kinky heads bloody and let them know our true feelings. I'm a police scientist. What the hell am I supposed to do, live with them in their filthy ghettos?

"Must I love them, get down on my hands and knees and beg them not to break the law? It's you liberals who are all wet, Brad. It's you liberals who have given them the freedom to threaten the white race."

I felt my sweaty collar choking me as I sat there and fought to keep my hate for the two racists from my face. The Goddess was beaming with pleasure in the excitement of the bout between them.

The captain leaned back in the booth and looked triumphantly at me and the Goddess. Then I realized that we were the audience he had to impress. For him it was something more than a hot racial discussion.

Deep inside of him, he probably hated the handsome face and polish of Mr. Wherry. My guess was that he was an ugly duckling, desperate to prove at least superiority of intellect over his attractive opponent. The captain stared at Mr. Wherry's sympathetic face smiling urbanely at him.

Mr. Wherry said, "Pete, let's not get overly emotional. This is a discussion, not an argument. Now, I was going to say that you are not aware of the master plan now in effect in these United States for the containment and control of the niggers.

"That master plan is in the competent hands of the liberal white leaders. They are the indispensable agents of the white race. It is they with their mastery of base emotion, their sophisticated analysis of nigger psychology that permits them to project a merciful sympathetic image.

"This is vital so that harassed, beleagured nigger ministers and other black leaders can have such a source to which they can appeal. Pete, a four letter word is the key to the white master plan.

"That word is hope. It means that what is desired is obtainable. The human organism when deprived of it, can become unpredictable, destructive, deadly. Pete, the liberals are aware that the great masses of niggers hope for escape from the ghettos.

"They want to spill over into the mainstream of American life and pollute it with their criminality and lust for our women. They want to rub elbows with us all. They want to lose the consciousness of their blackness at the expense of our culture and privacy. They want to contaminate our Anglo-Saxon bloodline.

"Pete, the fatal failing of the conservative is that he bluntly and stupidly strangles hope in the niggers. His rigid emotional structure won't let him practice the subtle arts of deception and guile. These are essential adjuncts in our strategy to lull, to keep alive hope in the nigger without making his wild dreams of freedom realities. Do you buy what I've said so far, Pete?"

I sat there thinking what a thrill it would be to cut their hearts out. The Goddess gushed happily. I wondered if Mr. Wherry would blow a pump artery if he suspected that he might have a nigger grandchild in Camille's belly.

The captain's slitted stare had not left the smooth, charming face as he absorbed the grand lesson in hate.

He licked his lips and blurted out, "No Brad, I can't buy it! What about the countless nigras that you liberals have helped to escape from the ghettos through appointive positions in government and industry? You liberals put those white collars around their black necks, not the conservatives. You betrayed the white race and let the nigras invade our white society."

Mr. Wherry sighed and said, "Pete, you're tragically misinformed. There are really two ghettos. One is physical, the other psychological. Now it is true that we have selected certain niggers to wear white collars.

"Almost all of them do make physical escapes from the

ghetto, with our assistance, of course. Our motives are first to give dramatic well publicized reinforcement to our liberal image.

"Secondly, those niggers whom we seem to liberate are precisely those types of niggers who possess rare intellect and academic polish. We have to remove them from the seething black masses.

"If we didn't they could conceivably give the mindless masses effective leadership against the white race. Now Pete, am I being too complex? Are you following me?"

The captain probably at last realized that all of his own bombs were duds. Sweat had popped out on his freckled forehead. He stupidly waggled his head, yes.

The Goddess quivered in joy beside me. I knew I couldn't stand much more of it. Mr. Wherry sipped delicately at his champagne. He smiled impishly at me and his Whisty.

I struggled against a wild impulse to punch Mr. Wherry in his girlish mouth. Then I gave Mr. Wherry a meager smile when I thought how lucky I was that my white face was letting me get secret, inside dope right from the haters' mouths.

He flicked a graceful hand through the Pump Room's sacred air and said, "Pete, I'm gratified to be understood. Now, the diametric differences between the nigger world and the white world afford us the devices by which we neutralize and defang the white collar escapees from the ghettos.

"The technique is roughly this. The freed nigger, elective and appointive as well, will face his entry into the white world with no little trepidation. His fears, his insecurity is born of the unfamiliar, unknown facets of the strange new world.

"Underlying all of this, of course, is his well hidden, but nonetheless strong sense of inferiority. His is an urgent, practical need, perhaps unconscious, to conform to the mores, the protocol of the new world. He has a deathly dread of conspicuous violation of these codes.

"His terror is that the whites who have sponsored him will take notice and hurl him back into the ghetto. He's compelled to emulate white emotional control and polished, patient conduct.

"We flatter him as he becomes more like us. His identity, his fiery racial resolutions, if he has any, fade and are eventually lost. If he fights the mold, we poke derisive fun at him, and make him appear ludicrous.

"One can't act like a nigger in suave white surroundings. We listen with compassion to his now guilt-ripened pleas for help for his black brothers back in the ghetto.

"We throw him a few crumbs of appeasement. But soon he becomes an alien to his black brothers and they grow to hate him. They realize that he has sold them out. He becomes worthless to them and priceless to us.

"He has lost his power to lead them, to hurt us. In his thinking and love for the creature comforts, except for his blackness, he becomes one of our troops. He helps us unknowingly to fight a brutal war against his own kind. You must forgive me, Pete, if I have been pedantic in my explanation. But I do have a deep personal involvement in affairs racial."

The Goddess said, "Daddy, you've never been more brilliant. I've got goose pimples. But what about girls like the one abused by that coon at the movie tonight? Shouldn't we save them?"

Mr. Wherry smiled sweetly. He scrutinized his polished nails for a moment.

He looked blandly at her and said, "Whisty, precious, those girls are fecal matter, dregs, sediment settled at the bottom of the social barrel.

"Historically and appropriately, the sexual peccadillos of the dregs are the petty province of conservatives, red necks, white trash and other hysterical slobs.

"You typify the inviolate flower of white womanhood that by training and breeding would rather be dead than have sexual congress with a nigger. The niggers and the dregs will always be with us at the bottom of the barrel.

So why court a coronary about it?"

The Goddess bit her bottom lip and said, "You gentlemen must excuse me. I want to freshen up a bit."

We got to our feet as she rose from her seat and went toward the powder room. We sat down.

The captain said, "Brad, that supression plan for the nigras is incredible, if in practice. Are you sure that the whole concept is not merely a fanciful child of your fertile imagination?"

Mr. Wherry smirked and replied, "Pete, you should change your politics and spend some time and money as I do with this country's liberal politicians in mysterious smoke-filled rooms. Then perhaps you could become privy to some of the progressive political plums."

Then he beamed at me and said, "Well Johnny, the future defense of white America is going to be in the hands of young Anglo-Saxon troops like you. What is your reaction to our discussion?"

I stood up and twisted as much contempt and disgust into my face as I could manage. I sucked up a gout of phlegm into my mouth. I leaned down quickly toward Mr. Wherry's startled, immaculate face.

I inhaled so deeply that bullets of pain shot through my gut muscles. I spat the filthy blob into his upturned face.

He sat there stricken, paralyzed with shock, openmouthed, staring up at me. The yellow-striped missile coasted down the bridge of his aristocratic nose.

I glared down at him and pounded my fists against my thighs. I wanted him to rise up against me, so I could shred and pulp his face.

The captain's purple face was revolving from me to Mr. Wherry like perhaps a tennis buff's at the Davis Cup playoffs.

I turned and walked toward the door. The hook in the corner of my eye snared the Goddess returning from the powder room. She was coming quickly toward me. I stepped out to the sidewalk and took a big dose of crisp November air. For a moment I thought I'd checked my topcoat inside. Then I remembered that it was locked in the Jaguar.

The Goddess rushed to the sidewalk.

She seized my arm and said, "Johnny O'Brien, are you drunk? What wrong's with you? You're deathly white. What happened? Why were you leaving without me?"

I mumbled, "I needed fresh air. Let's go to the car. And please don't talk to me right now."

We walked silently to the parking lot and got into the Jaguar.

I said, "Camille, take the outer drive to the lake front. I want to get myself together before I talk to you."

CHAPTER NINETEEN

The Confession

The Goddess was tight-faced when she parked near blustery Lake Michigan. We sat there for ten minutes and silently watched the foamy waves shatter against the dark shore. I was cold sober. But I couldn't think of one sensible thing to say.

Then I remembered that because of the movie hassle and all, I hadn't asked her about her test for pregnancy.

I said, "Did the test rabbit die?"

She stared straight ahead and said, "I'll answer your question after you answer my questions. Why were you leaving without me? And what happened when I went to the powder room?"

I said, "I wish I hadn't met your father. I'm sorry I found out how you got racial poisoning."

She said grimly, "Are you out of your alleged mind? You are the one who has been poisoned. You're an unbelievably wretched coon-lover. Did you quarrel with Daddy? Answer me."

I felt my Irish-African blood boiling up inside me again.

I said sharply, "I've got a mind all right. You can't imagine how sharp I am upstairs. So has dear Daddy got a mind. But he's got maggots for brains to believe that black people are going to grin and stay conned forever in their pig sties. I hope the day comes when your father crawls on his belly and begs to kiss a nigger's black ass for his worthless life."

The lovely rose-tinted face stripped itself barren of color, beauty and its fictitious youth. The twisted, stark-white face of a stranger, a popeyed thing gritted its fangs and hurled itself toward me in the half darkness. It stared into my eyes evilly and silently.

Then it chanted in a throaty whisper, "Mr. O'Brien, don't you ever, ever, *ever* let any, any, *any* insult to Bradford Wherry reach my ears. I could kill you. You miserable coon-loving tramp, white trash. I was insane to let you touch me. I'm going to abort this little bastard inside me. My advice to you is to see a psychiatrist and get treatment, and the reason why your stupid mania for coons. coons.

"Never come in my direction again. Find a putrid coon girl and live unhappily ever after. Now, bum, I'll take you to your car."

She ripped the ruby and platinum necklace I had given her from her throat and rammed it into my shirt pocket.

She savagely twisted the key in the ignition. She thundered the engine and shot the Jaguar into screaming reverse.

My head was in a spinning roar of anger and humiliation. I was silent until she stopped beside my Buick on Lake Street. I got out and slammed the door. I reached in and took my topcoat off the back seat.

The Goddess was grim faced, staring through the windshield. I stooped down and stuck my head into the sedan.

I said slowly, "Mrs. Costain, I really shouldn't hurt an elderly broad, but I'm going to deliver unto you one of your ineffably wonderful maims of the soul. You want to bet it won't thrill you?"

"I don't have to go to a headshrinker to find out why I love Niggers. I got the sanest reason there ever was. Mrs. Costain, a Nigger has been fucking you in your ineffably white, Anglo-Saxon pussy for months now.

"You've licked the coon like a lollipop. And you've loved every minute of it, haven't you, Mrs. Costain? Mrs. Costain, you have a bona-fide bastard nigger baby in your sacrosanct guts.

"My father is white. My mother is a coon. I can furnish proof if you think I'm a liar. I was born in Kansas City, Missouri on January fifteenth, Nineteen-hundred and

Twenty-three in a nigger pigsty just a stone's throw from Fourteenth and Vine Streets.

"Check the records if you doubt it. I don't want you to miss the full bang of the maim. But then, you don't look thrilled at all, Mrs. Costain. What's wrong? Have you lost your taste for screwy thrills?

"You look like you just heard that dear old Daddy had croaked. Which reminds me. You might tell him that nigger Johnny O'Brien spat in his face in the Pump Room. Goodbye Mrs.—"

I didn't finish. I had seen her knuckles glowing whitely on the steering wheel. Her head had been shaking on her trembling shoulders like a broad with Parkinson's disease.

It should have warned me. She stomped on the accellerator. The Jaguar had hurtled forward and flung me to the street like a rag doll. I bounced and tumbled for fifteen feet.

I was lucky Lake Street had no traffic at the late hour. I lay with the breath knocked out of me, and watched the Jaguar careen and weave at suicidal speed down Lake Street.

I dragged myself to the Buick. My pain-stabbed body throbbed like one big awful toothache. I made it to the car seat. I sat there and patted and probed myself all over for broken bones.

I looked in the mirror. My hair was matted with blood and the gritty soot and filth of Lake Street. I raised my head closer to the mirror to check the wound. It was just a half-inch gash in my scalp at the right side of my head.

I drove down State Street, south to Forty-seventh Street. I drove into a filling station on Michigan Avenue and Forty-seventh. I got some gas and cleaned up as best I could.

I pulled up in front of the Brass Rail Bar on Forty-seventh Street. Mr. Trick Bag was in there waiting to kick my ass. The sneaky bastard was going to win the war. But I didn't give damn.

I got out of the car and hobbled across the sidewalk to

the door. I stepped inside and sat in the booth near the front window. I told the waitress to bring me a fifth of Cutty Sark and a glass.

Somehow I drove home after the bar closed. I woke up at dawn the next morning lying beside my bed with my clothes on.

I stared at the rotating ceiling. I tried to move inside a straitjacket of pain. Clammy sweat spewed out of me. I sucked my cracked lips and with a grunt flipped over on my belly and raised myself on my elbows.

I groped a hand out for the top of the nightstand for support to get to my feet. The uncertain hand raked a lamp off that crashed against the bottom of the bed's headboard.

I was panting on my hands and knees when I saw Blue's bare feet on the carpet beside me. He helped me to the bed. I sat on the side of it. He leaned down close to me and frowned.

He said, "Don't tell me. I know what happened. That fabulous and mysterious broad you've been laying had a husband who caught you banging her and beat the crap out of you. Right?"

I winced as he stooped and pulled off my shoe from my right foot. It felt like it was smashed.

I said, "No, Blue, it wasn't like that. I had an accident. The whole thing seems like a nightmare. But I guess it really happened."

He took off the other shoe and said, "Don't waste your time in silly debate with yourself. It wasn't a nightmare. Your right foot looks like a balloon. Did you wreck the Buick?"

I groaned and said, "It wasn't that kind of accident. I mean I wasn't in the Buick when it happened."

He said, "Folks, you're like a son to me. I've been worried about you lately. You're fidgety and you drag ass like a steel mill chump with—"

I said crossly, "Blue, please save the lecture for some other time. I lost my woman last night. I blew her like a sucker."

He stood up and pulled my battered suit coat from my aching shoulders. He took it to the closet and hung it up. I lay back on the pillow and put my arm across my burning eyes to fend off the sharp fingers of morning light pointing into the bedroom.

He sat on the side of the bed and said, "So, you get another broad even finer. You got looks, youth and a gift of gab. For you, broads are like streetcars. You miss one, it's a cinch another will come along. You want to tell pappy what the hell happened?"

I ran the whole Goddess thing down to him from the Club Delisa, where we met, to the tumbling I did on Lake Street. I also told him why I never let him meet her.

To that he said, "I've never met a peckerwood that could resist the Blue Howard charm when I turned it on. I don't care how much that broad thought she hated niggers. She would have been crazy about me.

"She and her father are pure poison for you now, since you blew your top like a mark. You should have stayed cool and figured some con with me to separate that Wherry sonuvabitch from a few grand. The worse hurt you can give an ego-crazy bastard like that is in the pocketbook.

"You should have known that a screwy, top drawer white broad's legs wouldn't open forever for you. She had to wake up down the line that you were a nigger grifter. A broad like her who has flashed her pussy all over the world is fatal to a young fellow like you.

"One of those glorious international pussies could even con you that you'd die without it. You're lucky you blew her before you got the stupid idea that you were in love.

"Stick to young dumb broads that you can bang with no risk to the heart. Take it easy and rest for a few days. Hell, we won't starve if we miss playing the con for a while. Let's get those clothes off. I'll give you a good liniment rubdown and fix you a nice hot toddy. I'll lay you odds that in a week you won't remember what that broad looked like."

Blue left the house at noon. My body felt better after the rubdown and hot bath. The hot lemonade heavily spiked with scotch made me drowsy. But I couldn't go to sleep.

I couldn't get the Goddess off my mind. I kept hitting the fifth of Scotch that Blue had left on the nightstand. One thought kept pumping tension into my chest until I felt like I'd explode.

Why had I let the dialogue between Brad and Pete trick me, upset me, and set me up to expose myself to the Goddess like a chump? Why did I have to confess to her that I was a nigger? Why had I spat in Mr. Wherry's face? Why did I let those cruel words escape my sucker mouth on Lake Street?

I could have changed her mind in time about black people, because I knew she had been in love with me. I remembered how happy she had been when she thought she had my baby inside of her. I remembered my content-ment with my head resting on her warm satin bosom. She'd croon and baby talk to me.

Blue was all wrong. I had to have her back. I couldn't do without the torture of her, the glory of her, the thrill of her.

She was the beautiful thing that had made my life glamorous, and classy. I was just a Nigger hustler from a sewer on Thirty-ninth Street without her.

I pulled the phone into bed. I rang her for five minutes. There was no answer. I rang Cordelia. No answer.

I finished the bottle of Scotch and lay there twisting in half-sleep, half-delirium on the fiery bed. And all the while that ruthless, awful question hammered my fevered brain. Why did you let them trick you into exposing yourself as a nigger?

CHAPTER TWENTY

The Fractured Nude

The phone rang. Dreamily, I picked up the receiver. It was the contralto voice of the Goddess. My heart tried to leap up my throat. All was forgiven. She was at Cordelia's apartment. There was a most unusual party in session.

"Bodies beautiful unadorned is the theme," she said. Would I rush right over? Or was I too shy for that kind of thing? If so, then perhaps some other time I could come to a more commonplace party."

"Oh, no," I said. "I'll be right over. I wanted to see you anyway about last night."

I dressed and floated to the Buick. Then quick as a wink, almost, I was ringing Cordelia's doorbell. I thought as I stood there, Cordelia's bell doesn't sound like it used to.

A new maid opened the door. She led me to a walk-in closet. I took my clothes off. I stepped from the closet naked. I followed the maid to the living room's double doors.

The maid smiled oddly, and swung them open to pitch blackness. I stepped inside. Then suddenly the brightest light I had ever seen burst on. I cringed, and held my palms against my eyes.

An explosion of laughter rocked my eardrums. I peeped around the palms. The room was crowded with elegantly dressed white people in tuxedos and glittering evening gowns.

All of their mouths were wide with wild glee. Then the Goddess stepped forward and clapped her hands for silence. I stood there trembling. All became quiet.

She looked up at me with a sneer and said, "Ladies and gentlemen, it is with ineffable pleasure that I give you Coon O'Brien, who will give you his inimitable live imitation of Marcel Duchamp's famous painting, 'Nude Descending a Staircase.'

"Unfortunately, his performance is sans the staircase. But I can assure you that he will be as fractured as the nude in the canvas version."

The crowd's blasting laughter seemed to blow me to pieces as I stood there. I saw and felt sections of myself falling away. The crowd brayed and hee-hawed.

I screamed from the pile of tortured rubble on the carpet that had once been me, "You rotten dirty jackass bastards! You rotten dirty jackass bastards!"

I felt something jerking me, shaking me violently. I grabbed at it. My eyes strained to see it through a dark shimmery mist.

A friendly fat-lipped, flat-nosed face poked through it. It was Blue. I was sitting up stiffly on the bed in a welter of sweat.

I hugged Blue and blubbered, "Oh, Blue, I'm so glad to see you. I'm so glad it was just a nightmare. I'm so glad it wasn't real. If it had been for real, I would have lost my mind. I'm so glad to see you, Blue."

He said, "Folks, I don't give a damn whether you want to or not, but a croaker is going to see you tomorrow. You need something for your nerves and that hard lushing you've been doing.

"You should have seen yourself coming out of that nightmare. You looked like some poor chump frying in the hot seat. You're not going to con me any more that you don't need help. I'm really worried about you now. Don't get out of that goddamn bed until we go to the croaker tomorrow. I'm going to broil you a steak."

He turned to go.

I said, "Blue, I can't eat. Bring me a good stiff drink instead."

He looked down at the empty bottle on the nightstand.

He shook his head sadly and walked down the hall.

I thought, "I've got to straighten myself out. I can't stand that look of pity in Blue's eyes. I don't want to be a bum like the chumps on Madison Street. After I get the Goddess back, I'll go back on the two-pint a day plan for a starter. Goddamn, it's funny about that crack the Goddess made in the nightmare."

She made me remember seeing the Duchamp's painting in the art book that was inside the leatherette case that I left in the chili joint on Forty-third Street a long time ago. If I hadn't lost the case, I'd probably still be painting. Duchamp's picture had never made sense to me. It was a chaotic pattern of disjointed lines and angles.

Blue came back with a tall glass filled to the brim with whiskey. He put it on the nightstand and said, "Folks, this is it for tonight. I've locked the juice cabinet. I can't let you kill yourself. Call me if you want anything except more juice."

He walked away. I reached over and picked up the glass. The Scotch in my trembling hand sloshed over the rim of the glass onto the bed. I gulped down what was left.

Finally, I heard my heartbeat gentle down. I drifted into a strange, terrible kind of sleep. Raw, razor-edged consciousness sliced out a piece from my brain.

I could clearly see the bedroom furniture about me, the bathroom door. But I knew I was asleep and dreaming, because how could there be a trio of floor-to-ceiling mirrors at the window where the drapes had been?

But how could I be asleep when there I was standing before them naked, looking at myself? And that woman with the insane eyes and the platinum hair looming up behind me.

She hurled something. I couldn't move away. I screamed at the crash of it. I was no more. My image died in the three full-length mirrors. I was on the carpet in a million bloody bits of glass and the room exploded with jackass hee-haws.

Blue came and shook me back to my senses again. For the rest of the night he sat on the side of my bed. He drove me to the old white-haired croaker's office at ten A.M.

He examined me from head to toe and said, "I saw you through your draft troubles, so I hope you will take me seriously now. You must rest and eat lots of wholesome food and abstain completely from alcohol in any form.

"I'm going to give you a diet chart. I am also giving you prescription aids toward these necessary goals. Fortunately, you have youth and physical resiliency. Follow my instructions, and my prognosis is that within a matter of weeks, you will be back in the pink."

Blue and I stopped on the way home and got the prescriptions filled. There were six kinds of pills and liquid medicine.

I forced down some broccoli and carrot juice when we got home. I took two sleeping pills and fell into unmarred sleep. I woke up at seven P. M. I struggled from the bed and staggered to the liquor cabinet to see if it was really locked.

It was. And I was desperate for a drink. I peeped into Blue's room. He was gone. Then I thought about the Goddess. I went to my phone and rang her number. No answer. Dizzily, I tried Cordelia.

Her brassy voice said, "Hello." on the third ring.

I said, "Hello, Cordelia, it's Johnny O'Brien. Is Camille there?"

She didn't answer for a long moment.

Then she said, "No, she isn't here. Why did you have to tell her, Johnny? Why the horrid thing to Brad?"

I said, "Too many things happened that night. I just couldn't help it. Do you know where she is? I want to talk to her."

She said, "Johnny, the poor girl is devastated. She's gone away. I like you, Johnny, and my friendly advice to you is to forget her. She'll never see you again. I'm her best friend and I know her so well. You don't have the remotest chance with her now."

I pleaded, "Cordelia, you've got to tell me where I can find her. I know she still loves me. Please tell me."

I heard her sigh and say softly, "I can't do that. She would never speak to me again."

I said, heatedly, "You won't tell me because I'm a Nigger, isn't that right? You'd tell a white man, I bet. I guess you're just like your friend. I was a fine guy until you found out the truth about me. I guess all of you are like that."

She said angrily, "You inexperienced young fool. No members of any group are just alike. What the hell do you know about life, love, women or heartbreak?"

There was a long pause.

Then she said, bitterly, "You think I hate all black people? You think I hate you? You silly jerk. The only man I ever loved on this earth was as black as a patent leather pump. And, oh yes, Camille drove to friends in Cleveland. You can't find her without an address. And that's all I'm telling you, really nothing. Happy wild goose chase, simple Nigger."

She hung up. Yes, she was right. She hadn't told me anything. I'd never find the Goddess in a big city like Cleveland without an address.

I had to have a drink. I went to Blue's room and searched it. I couldn't find a drop. I tore the rest of the house apart. I'd have to go out to score for a drink. I finally got into a suit and overcoat.

I went out to the Buick and remembered I had no money. I went back and raised the rug beneath the nightstand. I stuffed the roll of bills into my overcoat pocket.

I drove the Buick to the Brass Rail. I sat in a booth until nine P. M. guzzling Scotch. Then I got a brilliant idea. Hadn't Cordelia said that the Goddess drove to Cleveland? Wouldn't the Goddess have classy friends? Of course she would.

Cleveland was like any other big city. All the classy

whites lived together in colonies distant from niggers and poor white trash. Goddamnit, I'd go to Cleveland and do a Dick Tracy in whatever exclusive section of Cleveland she was in.

I had to find the Goddess and win her back. It shouldn't be hard to spot that white Jaguar. Yes, I'd find her. She'd melt and rush into my arms at the sight of me.

She couldn't have forgotten how close we'd been. I knew she couldn't forget how I had kissed and thrilled her from the top of her heavenly head to the tips of her sugary toes. She had to be aching for more of my all-out lesbian-type lovemaking. We couldn't do without each other.

I got up from the booth and went to the liquor store on the corner of Calumet Avenue and Forty-seventh Street. I got two-fifths of Cutty Sark Scotch and drove to a filling station. I got a tankful of gas, oil and a road map. I drove frantically toward Cleveland and the ineffably precious Goddess.

CHAPTER TWENTY-ONE

The Search

I jabbed the whining Buick through blurry time and space and screeching near collisions. At two A. M. I found myself registering at the desk of the Majestic Hotel on Fifty-fifth Street in the heart of Cleveland's black belt.

I went to a clean, neat third-floor room overlooking the main drag. I had a fifth of cheap Scotch in a paper bag. I didn't remember why I'd bought an off brand.

I had forgotten to bring the sleeping pills. I'd fall apart without them. I wouldn't be up to the search for the Goddess unless I got some rest. I had to make a connection for sleeping pills. Now!

I looked in the dresser mirror at the haggard red-eyed stranger. I shrugged and turned toward the bed. I collapsed across it and picked up the phone from a table beside the bed. Five minutes later, I went to the door. A fat, big-eyed, black bellboy, bulging a drab monkey suit stood in the hall.

I said, "Are you familiar with Cleveland?" For a moment he looked puzzled.

Then he said, "Yeah, Jack, I'm hip to the scene. You want one for all night, or just a quickie?"

I said, "I don't want a broad. I want to know where I can find the most exclusive white section in town."

He said, "Shaker Heights is where most of the rich cocksuckers crib. For a paddy, you sound like a down stud. So I'm going to yank your coat. Don't try no hustle out there, unless you're a freak to making the joint scene. The Heights is lousy with heat. They'll bust a strange paddy as fast as they will a boot."

He took the deuce I held out and started to walk away.

I said, "I'll sweeten that deuce with a sawbuck if you could score for a few yellow jackets."

He whirled around like a pygmy ox doing a pirouette.

He looked up at me slyly and said, "Uh-huh, Jack, I cop the yellows for you. Right? Then later I cop some reefer. Right? Then you bring a pal on scene. He's got to have H. Right? I catch a double dime in the joint, with no broads, no nothing. Then you make a joy-scene with some fine, hot-ass bitch and a case of sauce to celebrate that you crossed me into the joint. Right? I ain't no dealer of nothing. Thanks for the deuce."

I stood there in the open door watching him walk away down the hall. I thought, "I really screwed that up. What can I do now? I've got to have some pills. I've got to get a night's rest."

I was just at the point of calling him back to hike his fee to a C-note when he turned and shambled back to me.

He snapped his fingers and said, "Jack, you're lucky. I just remembered, my sick old man is got some red devils from a script at his pad. But the pad is way out on a Hundred-and-six Street and Massie Avenue.

"A cab out there and back would run at least a double sawbuck. I'd miss a fin or so in tips here in the hotel while I was on a long trip like that. Aw, forget about it. You don't want them that bad, do you, Jack?"

I said, "If your sick father can part with at least two dozen devils, I'll part with half a C-note. But I want you to hurry. I have to get some sleep. I've got important business in the morning."

He said, "Righteous, Jack, righteous."

I shut the door and sat in a mustard-colored easy chair at the window. I saw a big, black guy decked out in sharp clothes go into a barbecue joint across the street. He reminded me of Blue.

I thought, "It was lousy of me not to leave a note for him. But it shouldn't take more than a day or so to find the Goddess. I'll be back in Chicago, happy and on the mend before he really gets worried about me. I won't call him.

I'm too shaky to hold still for a lecture."

I sat there and drank the cheap bottle of Scotch three-quarters empty. I was afraid to lie down. I didn't want to risk that fractured nude scene with the Goddess.

I wasn't a bit surprised to see the fatso bellboy lumbering out of the barbecue joint, toward the hotel with a stack of orders in his hands. I could only hope that he wouldn't stretch his phony con trip for the seconal until daybreak.

I looked at a calendar on the wall across the room. It was the fourth of December, Nineteen Forty-five. It seemed like only weeks ago that the war had ended, and the fabulous cripple in the White House had croaked and made the haberdasher from Independence, Missouri, a member of the most exclusive club there ever was.

I heard a rap on the door. I looked at my watch. It was two-thirty A. M. The slick bellboy was probably back from his mythical trip.

I opened the door. He was huffing and puffing and wiping his brow with his sleeve. I gave him the half a C-note and took the tiny glassine-wrapped wad.

He bared his gold teeth and chortled, "Righteous, Jack, righteous."

I undressed and showered. I stuck the back of a chair under the doorknob. The fat boy might get a yen to visit my bankroll with a pass key.

I raised the blue carpet and shoved the nearly a grand roll of bills underneath it. I took two red devils and lay down. I was trying to remember the license plate number of the Goddess's Jaguar, when the red devils' sneaky forks of oblivion plunged into my thrashing brain.

A banging at the door opened my leaden eyes. It seemed ages before my dopey brain tipped me off that I was in Cleveland.

I hollered hoarsely, "Who is it?"

A muffled broad's voice said, "The maid, sir."

I looked at my watch. It was eleven A. M.

I shouted, "Come back in an hour. I'm going out."

I lurched to the bottle at the window. I drained it dry

and fell into the chair. Thuggish winds were slamming lacy snowflakes against the windowpane. The stark whiteness of the tenement rooftops teared my inflamed eyeballs.

Finally the whiskey brushed away enough of the fog and weakness so I could get to the bathroom to wash up. I looked at my watery eyes in the cabinet mirror. My face was puffy and gray pallored. My hair was shaggy at the nape of my neck, and I had a five-day dirty yellow shadow of bristly beard.

I still ached from the bouncing I had done on Lake Street. I sponged off and dressed. I got my bankroll from under the carpet, picked up my key, and walked out to the hall.

I heard loud phonograph music as I went by the open door of the room next to mine. I glanced inside. I paused. A chubby middle-aged guy was in his doorway with a friendly smile on his ebony face.

He said cheerfully, "Good morning, neighbor. I'm George Washington Jackson."

He stuck out his hand. I smiled and shook his hand.

I said, "I'm Bill Flanagan."

He said, "Bill, how about a little taste of gin?"

I said, "No thanks. Maybe some other time."

I moved down the hall to the elevator. I dropped my key at the desk and paid two-days rent. I went through the lobby to the street. I walked uneasily on the skiddy snow-clogged sidewalk.

I went into a bar on the other side of Fifty-fifth Street. I had a fast three double shots of Cutty Sark. Then I went five or six doors down from the bar and got a haircut, shave and massage. Then I went to a restaurant in the same block. I forced down beef stew and a glass of milk.

I only felt half bad when I went to the Buick parked at the rear of the hotel. I drove to a filling station for gas and directions to Shaker Heights.

I cruised through a winter wonderland of stately trees, sparkled with puffs of ermine snow and jeweled with glittery icicles.

Marshmallow shrubbery swayed around the palatial mansions that lined the wide streets. My eyes searched every street, every driveway for a glimpse of the Goddess or her Jaguar.

At five P. M. I stopped my search. I drove back to the rear of my hotel and parked. I went to a liquor store and got two fifths of Scotch. I went to my room to drink and think.

At ten P. M., I heard someone knock. I went to the door and opened it. It was George Washington with a big smile on his face.

He said, "Bill, I hope I'm not disturbing you. I got lonesome, so I thought I'd drop over for a chat."

I stepped aside and said, "No, you're not disturbing me. Come in and have a drink with me. That is, if you can drink Scotch."

He went to the easy chair at the window. I washed a glass and put a bottle on the window sill beside him. He poured three fingers and leaned back in the chair.

He said, "I don't know what I'm going to do with myself until my next run. I'm a cook on the railroad. The only time life means anything is when I'm working. It's not much of a life with no relatives, no love in your life, nobody to care whether you live or die."

He bent my ears until midnight with his troubles. He was a likeable old, bald-headed, square john. And I felt sorry for him.

But I had tuned him out at ten P. M. so I could worry about my own problems. He was talking, but I wasn't really listening. I went to the bathroom and took a seconal to start letting down. I'd take the second one after I got rid of crying George. I took off my shoes and undressed down to my shorts. But old George didn't take the hint. He poured himself a drink and jabbered on.

I yawned and lay across the bed in deep thought. Wouldn't it be wonderful to have x-ray eyes? Then I'd be able to see through the walls of all the mansions I cruised by in Shaker Heights.

What a thrill to spot the Goddess. And then I'd run like
hell to ring the doorbell. A flunkey would open the door
And before I could speak a word, the Goddess would see
me. She'd knock the flunkey flat on his ass as she rushed
into my arms. I would—

The crippled train of thought limped into a black
tunnel. Then slowly came a rising awareness, a caressing
sensation of hot, moist erotic pull at the rigid root of me. I
giggled.

Through a smudgy veil, I saw a comical black shiny ball
doing a funny bobbing dance between my thighs. It
reminded me of the frisky dot that pranced above the
words to old songs on the screen at the Tivoli Theater long
ago when Midge and I went to all the Charles Boyer and
Robert Taylor movies.

The veil drifted away. And the black ball wasn't funny
any more. I blackjacked the gleaming bald head with my
fist and rolled away.

The naked old guy looked at me piteously and pleaded,
"Billy, sweetheart, please don't mistreat Mother Jackson
like this. I got you ready, darling. Please! Please! Put it in
and thrill this old girl's soul. You won't ever need to work.
I'll take care of you, beautiful sweetheart."

The filthy freak was lucky I picked up my shoe instead
of something heavier. I pounded his head and shoulders all
the way to the hall. I snatched up his clothes and flung
them after him.

I stood sweating and panting in my doorway as he fled
into his room and slammed the door. I shut my door and
fell into the easy chair at the window. I sucked dry the
half bottle of Scotch on the window sill.

I looked out at the whores and drunks parading in and
out of the joints across the street. I thought, "There are
two things I have to do fast. Find the Goddess and stop
this stupid drinking."

What if that horny bastard had been a sex fiend like
Leopold and Loeb? I had been helpless. He could have

butchered me like Bobby Franks. I've got to stop this sucker drinking.

Well, anyway my bankroll had been fairly safe. At least I'd had enough sense to punch a hole in the pocket of my overcoat so I could drop the roll through to the hem of the lining at the bottom of the coat.

I got up and took the second red devil. I stretched out on the bed and found that black tunnel again.

For the next two days I followed a set routine. I'd wake up in a dopey fog from the red devils I had taken the night before. Then I'd drink the cobwebs away.

I'd go to the greasy spoon across the street and at least force down a bowl of soup. Then I'd go to Shaker Heights and search for the Goddess.

I couldn't let dusk catch me out there, because I remembered the warning from Fatso, the bellboy. In my shape, all I'd need to really fall apart was a Cleveland jail cell.

I'd get a bottle after each search and come back to my room. I'd sit at the window and drink as I tried to figure angles to straighten out my problems.

On the third day after the Mother Jackson thing, I was cruising Shaker Heights in late afternoon. I was passing a white stone mansion when I saw the Goddess get out of a chauffeured Cadillac limousine in the driveway!

I made a frantic U-turn and speeded back. It was the Goddess all right, going up the steps to the front door. I'd know that platinum hairdo and torso-slinging walk anywhere.

I gunned up the driveway to a stop behind the limousine. I pulled my emergency brake and leaped out of the Buick. I raced across the snow-covered lawn toward the Goddess.

A frightened face turned and stared at me with freezing blue eyes. I froze in my tracks. It wasn't the Goddess! It was a wrinkled horse-faced broad with a large mole on her chin.

I managed a garbled apology. I could see roller stenciled on her angry face as she bee-lined for her front door. I brushed by the open-mouthed chauffeur in the driveway and jumped in the Buick.

I got back to black town in record time. Fifty-fifth Street was thick with early Saturday hell raisers. I parked in front of the bar across from my hotel. I went inside and drank myself into alternating joy and deep depression.

Around ten P. M. I got one of my bright ideas. I knew that horse-faced broad had phoned the rollers a rundown on me and the Buick. I couldn't go to Shaker Heights any more. But hadn't I met the Goddess on a Saturday night slumming for kicks in Chicago's Nigger Town?

But I was too drunk to realize that the Goddess, in her probable state of mind wouldn't be itching to seek reminders of her recent nigger headache.

I got a run-down on the cabarets from the bartender. At eleven P. M. I struck out to make a tour of them. I ducked in and out of joints on Central Avenue, Euclid Avenue and a Hundred-and-fifth Street.

I had at least one drink in each of them. But I didn't even see a broad, black or white, with platinum hair.

After midnight I found myself at the shabby corner of Thirty-ninth Street and Scoville Avenue. It was central headquarters for dope peddlers and whores.

I'll never know why I was stupid enough to park and stumble into a funky bar on the corner. It was crowded with profane whores and drunken tricks. I took a stool and a double shot in a corner near the back door.

The heat in the crowded room was terrific. I couldn't take off my overcoat because of the roll of dough stashed in the lining. I was afraid the coat might get away from me.

I stood up and was bending my elbow to drain my glass when a toothless old black whore reeled into me. Runny sores covered her face.

I staggered back and said, "Goddamn, watch it, grandmaw."

She grinned up at me vacantly.

She wiped the snotty sleeve of her mangy rabbit fur coat across her drippy flat nose and simpered, "Whitey, I got the hottest pussy on this corner. C'mon and have some fun. You can go three-way for a tray. C'mon, Whitey, and spend something with Louise."

I backed up to the wall from her stinking breath and the clouds of crotch rot.

She clutched the front of my shirt and shouted, "Why don't you spend a chicken-shit tray with Louise?"

I knocked her hand away with my elbow. She grabbed and twisted her fingers into my shirt front again. I was angry and dizzy. I had to escape the bedlam of the spinning room.

I blurted, "Louise, you're a joke. You're old and funky and ugly. You should have retired fifty years ago. Get your scabby black hand off me."

She jerked her hand away and glared up at me. I stumbled out the back door. The snowy ground was revolving like a giant record on a wobbly turntable. I threw my hands out as the frightful whiteness catapulted up toward me.

I stirred. I felt something crawling, patting and moving across and into my clothes. I opened my dazed eyes.

A dark crouching shape was silhouetted against the star-infested sky. I tried to move away from the busy shadow with the familiar rotten stink. But my muscles were paralyzed. Then the shape moved out of sight behind me.

Suddenly the sky was blotted out, and I seemed to be trapped in a pitch black tent. And the familiar stink was overpowering.

I heard a cackling giggle and a hot pungent rain splattered my face and scalded my eyes. I lay there groaning and twisting my head from side to side in the stinking blackness.

I felt a feathery sweep of the tent across my face, as it slid away to bare the cold blue stars again. I lay there gasping, and sucking in the wonderful wintry air. I felt my muscles quivering back to life.

I was rising on my elbows when a horde of shadows came through the back door and stood in a silent circle around me. They fumbled at their flies. I jerked up and sat there screaming at them, as I had screamed at the toughs who chased me with knives on Chicago's Forty-third Street long years ago.

"I'm a Nigger! I'm a Nigger!"

The cruel bastards just laughed and started kicking me. I wrapped my arms around my face against the crushing barrage of feet ripping into me from head to ankles.

I crashed on my side and faintly heard the steady patter of terrible rain against my numbness. Then the laughter, the numbness and the patter of the reeky rain was lost in a yawning black pit of nothingness.

A frigid mask on my face opened my eyes. A white face looked down at me. It belonged to a guy stooping down beside me. He was pressing a handful of snow against my face and shaking his head.

He said, "You got a home, buddy?"

I said, "Yes. Are you a cop? What happened?"

He said, "I own the bar. When I came to check the register and close up, my manager told me you were out here. He said you shot your jaw off in the bar. You have to be the dumbest Caucasian in Cleveland.

"You walk in a nigger bucket-of-blood-bar on the wooliest corner in the state and spout stupid insults. You're lucky you're alive. What happened? Those Goddamn dirty niggers beat you, robbed you, and pissed all over you. You stink so bad. I feel like passing out. Here take my hand. But don't let your clothes touch me."

I took his hand. He pulled me to my feet. I stood there trembling. I felt like I was encased in ice. My clothes were frozen stiff.

He said, "How the hell can you get home? All your pockets are inside out."

I mumbled, "I'm driving. Please give me a drink."

I followed him through the back door. He locked it behind me and went behind the bar. He poured me a big slug of Early Times whiskey into a glass.

I gulped it down and looked at my wrist. The Bulova watch that Midge had given me that Christmas was gone. I glanced at the clock on the wall. It was two-thirty A. M. I staggered to the locked front door. The pink-faced owner came from behind the bar and unlocked the door. He looked at me for a long moment.

He said, "You better get to a doctor. You're not going to beef to the police are you? This joint has enough squeals already to fold it. Mister, I did you a favor. You could have frozen into a corpse out there."

I said, "Don't worry. I'm not the beefing kind. Thanks for the drink."

I lurched to the sidewalk past a tittering crowd on the corner. I got in the Buick and searched myself for the ignition key. I rummaged through my rifled pockets.

Finally, I found it in my overcoat pocket. Then I remembered my stash at the bottom of the lining. I was almost afraid to feel for it.

I ran my fingers around the coat hem. The roll of dough was still there! I turned over the engine and pulled away from the curb.

I was one big pounding icy ache. I was suffocating with the stink on me. Somehow I parked in back of the hotel and got to my room.

I undressed to my black and purple skin. I threw the soggy pile of clothes into a corner. I got in the bathtub and dumped a can of the maid's cleansing powder into the steaming water.

I finally scrubbed all the filth off my throbbing body. I dry-swallowed two red devils and flopped across the bed.

I lay there, waiting for the merciful trip to oblivion. But my aching body tore up my ticket. I took two more red devils and rocketed into plush blackness.

My brain staggered awake. The noon sun was high in the sky hurling blinding daggers of light through the window. I ground my fists into my burning eyes. I ran my fingertips across the lumpy bruises on my body. My tongue and throat felt like they were coated with flaming gravel.

I heard it first! Then I saw it! A fat brown rat with Phala's sister Pearl's face was scampering merrily about on the carpet beside the bed. It stood on its hind legs and stared up at me.

It grinned crookedly and squeaked, "Damn, you look like a peckerwood. That dizzy bitch, Phala just had to fuck your tramp peckerwood father, huh? She'd open her legs for any bum, wouldn't she?"

I stood up in the bed and clawed the wall. Another, black rat scampered before my terrified eyes. It had the face of Double-Crossing Sammy, the fink I punched the puke out of in the poolroom.

It half closed its eyes and squeaked. "Like I told Pocket, I ain't hip to a white trick baby like you so dumb you're passing for a nigger. I just ain't never heard of it."

I shrieked! More of the squeaking monsters with human heads were frolicking on the carpet.

A lean white rat with the arrogant face of Mr. Wherry stood on its haunches and chattered shrilly, "But my Whisty would rather be dead than have sexual congress with a nigger."

A small black one leaped to the foot of the bed. It had the face of the little boy leader of the gang in the apartment building on Thirty-ninth Street.

It squeaked in a tiny voice, "I cain't play wid you. You is a nasty trick baby. My papa whup mah ass."

Then a yellow hairless one streaked blue with pulsing cable veins and the face of the old whore across the hall on Thirty-ninth Street piped up.

She simpered, "Johnny, you're the one to blame for those street niggers raping Phala. You should have been there at the cabaret to pick her up. You're to blame, Johnny."

Then they chanted Phala's awful plea on the hospital grounds that sunny September day, "Lemme feel it, huh? Lemme snatch it off, huh? Lemme mash it, huh? Lemme, huh? Lemme, huh?"

Then all together, in an insane chorus, they filled the room with their squeaking and the thudding of their scampering feet.

I turned away and banged my face into the wall. My teeth punctured my lip bloody. I squeezed my palms against my ears and jumped off the bed.

I ran to the window and raised it. I hung out of it to the waist in the icy air, until the squeaking behind me had stopped. I pulled myself back and looked down at the carpet. They were gone.

My legs shuddered. I bombed face forward to the floor. Finally, I crawled to the phone and ordered two fifths of Cutty Sark.

Time after that was murky passage through a madman's hell. It was shot through with the brain-crushing reliving of the Scoville Avenue filth and the fractured-nude horror. And the rats with human faces visited again and again and again.

The terror, the bottles, the red devils were endless. And then, in the panic-riddled darkness, I heard the Christmas carol, *Silent Night* blasting from Mother Jackson's room.

Was it Christmas? Why hadn't Blue or Midge told me? And where was the spicy pine tree banked with our gaily wrapped presents? Where was the scent of the holiday feast? Why hadn't Midge cooked?

My leaden eyes searched the gloom. I went to the frosted window and peered out. Green plastic rings of holly and cutout Santa Claus faces with red cheeks and cheerful smiles hung in the neoned windows of the deserted stores across the snow-mantled street.

It was Christmas! But that lonely street down there was in Cleveland, Ohio. What was I doing here so far from home at Christmas?

I sank into the chair and pondered the gnawing puzzle for a long time. Then the jagged bits and pieces fell into place. I called the desk. I had to be certain about Christmas. I thought the clerk would never answer my question.

Finally he said, "Mr. Flanagan, the date is December

twenty-first, Nineteen-hundred and Forty-five."

I said, "Oh, thank you so much. I'm glad it isn't Christmas. I'll be checking out right away. I'm going home."

I hung up and took a bottle to the chair at the window. I sat there in the darkness and prodded my chaotic mind to chart my way. My filthy clothes in the corner! Dough! How much did I have left, if any?

I flicked on the light. I looked into every corner. I went to the bathroom. I had no clothes! Dough, was it gone too?

I ripped up the carpet all around the room. I looked under the mattress. I looked everywhere. I was trapped. My legs gave way. I fell to the floor. I lay there wondering if I had enough red devils left to take a forever trip into plush blackness.

Then it struck me! The closet! The closet! I crawled to it. I twisted the doorknob. The door opened. My light blue suit, my navy overcoat, my gray woolen sport shirt were hanging there, dazzling and crispy pressed.

Perhaps I had stashed my dough somewhere in my clothes after they got back from the cleaners. I pulled myself to my feet. Frantically, I searched every pocket.

I ran my fingers around the hem of the overcoat. I felt a thin roll of bills. I was strangling with joy. I reached down through the lining and pulled it out. I counted it. It was only sixty dollars.

I wondered how much rent I owed. What if I didn't have enough left for gas to drive home? I went to the bathroom to sponge off. I flinched away from the gray-faced, bearded, hollow-cheeked apparition in the mirror.

I was dressing when a sharp piercing pain shot through my chest, and knocked me to my knees. I couldn't breathe. I thought I was dying. I kneeled there until my wheezing chest caught air.

I finished dressing and got the Buick's ignition key from the dresser top. Somehow I made it to the desk with the key. I stood there weakly with my luggage in my hand, a fifth of Scotch in a paper sack.

The clerk checked his ledger and said, "Mr. Flanagan, your rental is paid up until tomorrow afternoon. Have a pleasant trip and a Merry Christmas. Come back to see us soon."

I went through a rear door to the Buick. It was shapeless and almost buried under a fleecy shroud of snow. I used the flat side of the paper sack to scrape clear the front and back windows.

I got in and tried to turn over the engine. There was only a dull clicking sound. I was so tired and sick. Shouldn't I lie down out there and rest beneath the friendly winking stars?

A car with inferno headlamps groaned into a parking space beside me. I walked away to Fifty-fifth street and flagged down a cab.

On the way to the train station I lay down on the back seat and closed my eyes. I was going home. I was glad. And that's the guaranteed truth.

CHAPTER TWENTY-TWO

Sister Franklin Snares the Elusive Ear of God

I stood shaking on the sidewalk as the Chicago cab revved its motor and pulled away. The pink house glimmered through a haze of tears. I moved my ponderous feet up the walk.

I saw Blue open the front door. He ran through the gray dawn light toward me. Whirling inky clods zoomed at me. The bottom of the earth dropped away beneath my feet.

I plunged down, down, down. I had died. That was it. And the undertaker was beside me pumping embalming fluid into my arm with a rubber tube attached to a bottle above me. He was smiling down at me. Blue must have bought one of the more expensive funerals for me.

He said, "We've been worried about you. Congratulations, I think you're going to make it."

What corkscrew undertaking con was this? What was the slick bastard's angle?

I said, "Where am I? I want out of here. Don't worry, you won't have to refund the dough."

He said, "You're very weak. I couldn't hear you. Don't try to speak any more."

I tried to shout the same words.

He replied, "Oh, you're in St. Luke's Hospital. I'm Doctor Winston. You're still very ill. You need considerable rehabilitation.

"You can thank your amazing constitution that you're alive. You've survived an almost hopeless bout with pulmonary pneumonia, among other lesser complications. But you're going to be all right. Rest and let me do all the worrying."

I lay there flat on my back. Blue flew to Cleveland and

drove the Buick back. Blue and Sister Franklin visited me twice a day, every day. Sister Franklin prayed away most of the visiting hours.

Old man Pocket came with them several times. Each time before he left, he said, "Why don't you stop playing the con and get out of that bed?"

I'd laugh feebly and thumb my nose at him. Blue took me home on the Twenty-ninth of January, Nineteen Forty-six.

Blue had a small Christmas tree in my bedroom with a dozen gifts for Christmas and my birthday, which had passed on January fifteenth.

I had a Longines watch, new robe, and several sets of silk pastel pajamas.

Doctor Winston had mentioned other lesser complications. I had one of them still with me. My need for alcohol. I had been given paregoric and other drugs in the hospital.

I was dried out. But a puffy, peculiar tension inflated my chest when my mind played around with the poisonous recent past. I was certain that a drink would ease it. I was very weak. I felt like all the blood had been drained out of me.

Sister Franklin was staying in Midge's room. She was going to be my nurse and a kind of spiritual adviser until I got well.

Doctor Winston had given Blue quite a briefing on me. Two hours after I got home Blue sat on the side of my bed.

I said, "Blue, I've been lying here thinking about Phala. Is she really all right? You had a funny look when I asked you about her in the hospital. I can't remember when I've been out to visit her. I know her kidneys were in bad shape. Is she all right?"

He looked straight into my eyes and said, "You are imagining things, Folks. Sure she s all right. They're taking fine care of her out there. Don't pressure your mind. Forget about Phala. Forget that white broad. Forget

Cleveland. Forget everything but getting well.

"We're concerned with now, and the future, and you. Your croaker has given me a complete rundown on your condition. I know what you need and what you don't need.

"The worst thing that you don't need is juice in any form. The croaker wanted to send you away for a cure. But I figured that no place is better for you than right here at home with me. The croaker pulled my coat to all the angles of treatment.

"I'm going to be your doctor and Sister Franklin is going to be your nurse. She talks about being your spiritual guide, too. But if her praying makes you jumpy, tell me, and I'll put the damper on it.

"Between the two of us and you, you're going to get well and strong again. We can't do it without you. It's going to be a sonuvabitching rocky road ahead. You've got to want to get well. You've got to want us to help you get well.

"You've got to con yourself that you're through with the juice even when your asshole is twitching for a slug of juice. Let's shake hands on the proposition and kick the damn thing off."

I grinned and shook his hand. I lay there feeling spent and nervous.

I thought, "I wonder if the Goddess is still in Cleveland. There is no reason to think about her, sucker. She could climb into this bed with you, and you'd only be able to gaze at her.

"I wonder how Mother Jackson's love life is going? I wish I had just a little Scotch stashed here in the house so I could taper off right along with Blue's treatment."

I answered myself:

"Now you poor silly bastard. You've got to stay away from the sauce altogether. Do all the Niggers in the world have to piss on you and kick your stupid ass to convince you?

"Goddamn, the sauce made you a cruddy sonuvabitch.

You didn't bathe your lousy ass or even brush your teeth for weeks in Cleveland. Two things you can't ever touch again, you brainless idiot. Guess what they are?"

I came back with:

"Well, what the fuck are you hesitating for, boy? Shout it loud and clear."

"All right, I will. Number one is old demon whiskey. Number two is that mother-fucking old Goddess bitch and her ineffably hot, sweet international pussy. Right?"

"Right! You got to find yourself a safe broad to bang. You know, something you deserve, like the ugliest, blackest broad in Chicago. You're a bum, Johnny O'Brien. You're lucky if you can score for even a broad like that. Maybe you ought to send for Mother Jackson. He's half had you anyway. A bum has to settle for what he can get."

I had the last word:

"So, Sister Franklin is going to try to catch the ear of God to bring me around. That will be a miracle. She doesn't know the snobbish, cold-hearted jerk won't even listen. But I'll play the percentages. I won't tip her off that it's hopeless.

"Maybe just accidentally he'll slip up and let her through. I need help, and I'll go along with even a long shot like that. What have I got to lose?"

I heard a rattling sound in the hall. Blue came in with Sister Franklin. She put a tray on the nightstand and propped me up in bed. She set the tray in my lap. There was a small portion of finely grated swiss steak with macaroni and cheese on a small plate.

A tall glass filled with a pale cloudy liquid was on the tray. After I had eaten most of my favorite food, Blue put the glass to my mouth. I tasted the briny liquid. I shoved Blue's hand away.

I said, "What is that awful stuff?"

He pressed the glass back to my mouth and said, "Drink all of it. It's part of the treatment. It's just plain salt and water."

Somehow I got all of it down. But it was trying to

bubble up from my sick churning stomach. Supper and another glass of the foul-tasting stuff came in on the tray. It made me even sicker than the first dose.

At nine that first night every nerve end was raw. Sister Franklin came in and got on her knees and prayed for me. I twisted and turned and rolled on the bed in agony. I pleaded with Sister Franklin to get me something to drink. She just kept praying until Blue got in at midnight. He rushed to my room.

I wailed, "Blue, please get me a drink. Please, just a small one to push me past this thing I'm going through."

He turned and went down the hall. A moment later I heard the lid of his car trunk bang shut in the driveway. He came into the bedroom with a fifth of Scotch and a water glass in his hand. He filled the glass with Scotch and put it in my shaky hand.

I looked up at him and said, "Blue, you're a real pal to do this for me."

He smiled when I raised the glass to my mouth. Just the odor of it almost jerked my guts up my throat. I swallowed a mouthful. I became deathly sick.

Nauseous spasms tore through me. Blue took the glass from me. I was shaking and retching. I wanted to die. Then Blue was putting a pill in my mouth. I felt the cool rim of a glass on my cracked parched lips.

The last thing I remembered is the top of Sister Franklin's head bowed deeply in prayer at the side of my bed. The following weeks were grim battlefields of time. My racked mind and body fought harder with each passing week against a slick and cruel enemy.

New strength seeped into my whole being. Living color washed away the dead gray pallor in my face right after my appetite returned. Many times I had the urge to slip away to Sixty-third Street for a drink. Each time I'd remember the nightmare in Cleveland. And my legs wouldn't obey the urge.

Spring slipped her bright warm throat from winter's bleak noose on April third. I put on my clothes and went to the backyard. I sat there in the warm noon sun.

The new grass and flowers were so much greener and more vivid than I remembered them. I felt wonderful. I thought, "I'm strong enough now to visit Phala. I could go today when Blue gets back this afternoon from playing the smack with Pocket. I think I'll call out there.

I went to the phone and called the sanitarium.

"How is Phala O'Brien?" I asked.

I heard the faint rustle of paper.

Then the soft voice of the broad on the other end said, "How long has the patient been here?"

I said, "For years."

She said, "Please hold on."

I heard muffled conversation and more rustling of paper. Then she came back on the line.

She said, "I'm awfully sorry, but Mrs. O'Brien passed away the fifth of December last. Are you a relative?"

The receiver fell from my hand. I threw myself to the floor and sobbed in great aching gasps like a dying animal. I jackknifed my legs and rolled about the room. I banged my head against the furniture and tore my shirt to shreds.

I cursed, "God, You heartless, sneaky, dirty Sonuvabitch. I hate You! You hear! You hear! You hear me, You deaf peckerwood Bastard! God, I hate You! You hear!"

Sister Franklin came running from her room weeping. She threw herself on top of me and locked her arms around me. I cursed Blue for lying to me. Sister Franklin didn't stop praying until I stopped cursing.

Finally, I got to my feet. I went to the bathroom and doused my bruised head with cold water. I came back and sat on the side of my bed in a trance with my eyes closed.

I swayed from side to side with one brutal question tearing through my mind. "Where were you, bum, when Phala died? Where were you, bum, when Phala died?"

I was still sitting there when Blue came home. I heard Sister Franklin whispering to him in the hall. He came and stood before me. I glared up at him. I started to open my mouth.

He pushed his palms through the air toward me and said, "Now, Folks, before you say a word, I've got a fair question I want you to answer in your own mind. Then call me and we'll talk.

"Folks, if I had been the one who was cracked up and almost dead, would you have been thoughtless or cruel enough to tell me that Midge was dead? Would you have pushed me off the brink that way? Think about it, Folks. You can have only one answer."

He turned and walked away. I realized almost immediately that it was right not to tell me. I was glad I hadn't said the things I started to say. I followed him to his bedroom.

I said, "Blue, you're right. It wasn't your fault that I wasn't in town when she died. Where is she?"

He said, "I had her cremated. I remembered that you told me after your first visit to the sanitarium, she wanted it that way. I spent close to a grand and a half with a private investigator to locate you. But you had vanished without a trace that he could hook onto.

"Now, take a sleeping pill and get yourself together. You can't stop living because Phala s gone. What the hell, you're about in shape for the spring con."

I took the sleeping pill and fell asleep with the same brutal question raging in my head. *Where were you when Phala died?*

It was June twentieth, Nineteen Forty-six, and Sister Franklin was busy packing her things. I looked and felt better than I had in two years. My appetite was fine. And I never touched a drop of alcohol. I met the acid test of Blue's unlocked liquor cabinet.

Sister Franklin praised and thanked the Lord for my recovery. She was certain that all the credit was His. I just didn't know about that. I gave her the platinum and ruby necklace that I had bought for the Goddess. She gave me a final prayer and she was gone.

Blue drove her home. When he got back, I was eating a steak in the kitchen. He sat down and drummed his knuckles against the table.

He said, "Sister Franklin babbled all the way home about how God answered her prayers and made you whole. How about it? Are you a believer now?"

I gave him a level look and said, "Blue, I'm not going into the streets and preach the Gospel. But I believe that if there is a God, then that little black old lady got His ear with pure faith. Maybe she's the only black person He's ever listened to.

"Maybe He saved me to reward her blind faith. It's a nelluva mystery. I just don't know. I'll tell you one thing. From now on I'm going with the odds that He does exist. I'm never going to curse Him again. Want to hear a secret? I can't be sure He heard me, but I copped out to Him and asked Him to forgive me for cursing Him."

CHAPTER TWENTY-THREE

The Fleeting Years

For the rest of the year Blue and I never ran out of fat cream puff marks. We both got new Cadillacs. I stayed away from the sauce. My favorite drink was Seven Up.

Twice a week I'd go to Aunt Lula's whorehouse in Indiana Harbor. I was smart now. I had found out it was better to rent a broad's machinery for awhile than to romance her.

By November I had given Blue the fifteen hundred he spent to cremate Phala. Plus the fifteen hundred he spent on the search for me when I was going through the Cleveland nightmare.

Christmas, I was lounging on my bed listening to the radio. The phone rang. I picked up and said, "Hello."

Nobody answered. But in the background I heard the sexy voice of a broad torching Cole Porter's *Night and Day.* "And this torment won't be through until you let me spend my life making love to you, night and day. Day and night deep in the heart of me there's oh, such a hungry yearning burning—"

I thought I heard someone breathing on the other end just before the line closed. I spun my radio dial quickly to find out if the broad I'd heard was on radio. She wasn't.

It was a record. I remembered hearing the same song sung by the same voice when I was waiting the year before to give Blue the bad news about the Buster Bang Bang play. That call was screwy like this one.

Then I had thought it was the Goddess horsing around. Was it the Goddess who had just called? I reached for the phone. My hand froze on it. I remembered she was one of the poisons I had to leave alone.

I lay there with my heart pounding. I didn't know what I'd do if she called and I heard her contralto voice. I knocked the receiver off the cradle and fell into fitful sleep.

The years galloped by. Our luck held up in the street. Felix the Fixer fixed only two beefs for us. One in the Spring of Nineteen Forty-nine and the other in Nineteen Fifty-four.

Livin' Swell was a big dope wholesaler. Bigger even than his former boss, Butcher Knife Brown. Midge was a destroyed hag with an H habit. A Spanish whore stabbed Precious Jimmy through the heart. Sister Franklin died of old age.

Old man Mule got fifty years in Joliet prison for sodomy against an eight-year-old girl. Dot Murray the cop was naturally still around scaring grifters shitless.

The Vicksburg Kid, who turned Blue out on the grift in Mississippi, came through Chicago in Nineteen Fifty-seven and looked Blue up. He was a tiny, charming old guy with the most alert blue eyes I'd ever seen.

He stayed in Midge's room for several days. He and Blue drank and talked together until the wee hours about the con and the good old days.

We talked about the Kid for days after he left for his con operation in Montreal. I missed his yarns about the humorous marks he had played for.

In Nineteen Fifty-eight, Blue and I went to old man Pocket's funeral. We both cried. He had been a lovable old man. He'd died in a hotel room punching into a young girl from big foot country. He just hadn't been up to the job.

His pump couldn't stand the gaff. But I'm sure he died happy. Too bad he got that old. But then, we were all getting older and wiser, I thought. Blue's hair was completely white in the Spring of Nineteen Fifty-nine.

My sorrow about Phala had dulled. But I still got a twinge when I thought about her.

My own yellow hair was generously sprinkled with gray. I was thirty-five years old. Blue was sixty-seven. We were both twenty-five to thirty pounds heavier than we'd been in the mid-Forties.

Aunt Lula had a wild new girl. Her name was Roxie. She was the biggest freak I'd laid since Black Kate. She was a pretty, yellow girl who was glamorous with green eye shadow and glitter dust in her hair. Many times I got home from dates with her and found some of the sparkling dots in my navel. She swore she loved me. Couldn't we shack up? But I remembered the Goddess.

My favorite food was still steak with macaroni and cheese. I had a slight paunch to prove it. All things considered, we were a pair of fairly well-preserved grifters for our ages.

CHAPTER TWENTY-FOUR

Wedding Bells for a Slick Sucker

In April of Nineteen Fifty-nine, Blue started hanging around Thirty-first Street and Indiana Avenue at night. He was sniffing around the mob of young tramp broads that twisted their butts in and out of Square's Bar on the corner and the Harmonia Hotel at Thirtieth Street and Indiana Avenue.

Everybody down there got to know him. Including Butcher Knife Brown. In the month of April he brought home no less than ten of the half-hungry little urchins.

Next morning the house would be stinking with ripe body odor and dime-store perfume. He had always been weak for young, classy pussy. But now he was digging at the bottom of the barrel.

The first week in May, he brought home a curvy, yellow girl from Thirty-first Street. She was cute all right, with a doll face and long shiny black hair. She was a striking combination of Filipino and Negro.

She was eighteen, from a broken home. Her name was Cleo and she had found a home. She didn't have to move her clothes. She was wearing them.

She had stayed three days when Blue came into my bedroom early in the morning. His eyes were flashing and he jumped excitedly around on the side of the bed.

He almost whispered, "Folks, Cleo and I are getting married. I'm having this dingy house freshened up with new carpets and new paint. Say something. I'll bet you're surprised."

I mumbled, "Congratulations. When is the wedding?"

I heard her syrupy voice calling him, "Blue, babee, I'm lonesome."

He jumped to his feet, and on the way out he said, over his shoulder, "We're getting married up in Michigan tomorrow. We'll honeymoon at a resort in Idlewilde. Whoopee!"

I listened to a hysterical pillow fight between them for twenty minutes. Then I heard the bed springs creaking. I wondered if Blue would die a glorious death like Pocket. At ten A. M. I heard them laughing like grammar-school sweethearts on their way out the front door.

I got up and made coffee. I sat at the kitchen table. I thought, that little tramp has that slick sucker's nose wide open. She's a cinch to bump his head. But who am I to criticize? She can't do him as bad as the Goddess did me.

At one P. M. I was eating lunch when they came back. It took Blue six trips to his car to get the bride's trousseau into the house. While Blue was on his last trip, Cleo wiggled into the kitchen and leaned a big tit against my cheek as she plucked a napkin from the holder on the table. She stepped back and blotted her lipstick. She gave me a wicked smile and wiggled away.

They left for Michigan that evening. At nine P. M. I got in my Caddie and went to Lula's cat house to bang Roxie. I got back home at two A. M.

There was a note stuck in the door. I went to my bedroom and read it. There was a phone number at the bottom.

It said, "Please call this number. L. S."

I rang the number. Livin' Swell picked up on the first ring.

He blurted, "Folks, is that you?"

I said, "Yes, how are you doing, Livin'?"

His heavy breathing was rasping through the line.

He said, "I ain't doing no good. Ain't you heard?"

I said, "No, what happened?"

He shouted, "It's the dagos! The outfit! Butcher Knife Brown has bullshitted Nino that I'm stooling to a secret grand jury on narcotics. Sure I got a wholesaling beef pending, but I swear, Folks, I'd do fifty years before I'd rat on the syndicate.

"I hid in your backyard until that old white bitch next door to you kept running out to the back peeping at me. I was afraid she'd call the rollers."

I said, "Where are you?"

He said, "At Bam's poolroom on Sixty-third Street. But it's closing."

I said, "Drive over here. Maybe I can put an angle together for you. At least you won't be in the street."

He wailed, "Folks, can't you understand? The dagos are looking for me to kill me. I can't drive my wheels. It's on the street down on Lake Park where I crib."

I said, "Stay in front of the poolroom. I'll be right down to pick you up."

He shouted, "I can't stand around in the street. They're after me! I got to keep moving. Let me think."

There was a long silence.

Finally he said, "I used to live at the Pershing Hotel. The fire door to the roof is always open. I'll be there looking out for you. You park across the street on Cottage Grove Avenue so I can't miss you."

He hung up. In less than five minutes after he hung up, I had driven the several blocks to Sixty-fourth Street and Cottage Grove Avenue.

I got out of the car and looked up toward the roof. I crossed the street and went into the lobby. I went to the elevator and rode to the top floor. I went through a fire door to the roof.

Nobody was up there except two sissies smoking reefer. I thought they'd jump off the roof when they saw me. I went back to the car.

I went up and down Sixty-third and all the streets around. Then I went up and down all the alleys. Livin' was not to be found. It was dawn before I stopped trying. I went home and stayed awake until noon expecting Livin' to turn up. I fell asleep with my clothes on.

Blue and Cleo got back from their honeymoon on the fifteenth of May. The bride was radiant in a silk shantung suit from Marshall Fields.

On the eighteenth of May a crew of painters and carpetlayers freshened up the house. I checked every source I knew to get a line on Livin' Swell. It was like he never was. He had disappeared from the face of the earth.

There was a strong possibility that he was at the bottom of Lake Michigan or the Chicago River. Maybe he was weighted with his belly split open so his corpse wouldn't float to the surface. Many nights I lay in the darkness and thought about him and remembered the old days when we were kids together down on Thirty-ninth street.

In November of Nineteen Fifty-nine, Blue and I bought new Cadillacs with the exaggerated rear fins. Blue also bought Cleo a new purple Thunderbird. He was hooked and happy. So, I never cracked to him that I had seen Cleo riding around with several different young punks in her Thunderbird.

Eight days before Christmas, Blue got a call from a small-time con man on the Westside of Chicago. He drove over there. When he got back he was excited.

He said, "Folks, have I got a sweetheart of a rocks mark. He's even sweeter than Buster Bang Bang. He's an old dago fence with a used-clothing shop front.

"He doesn't know a diamond from a seashell. I've already cut into him and told him the tale. We use the standard rocks play. For this bird we don't need anything fancy.

"You turn your head and cough when we're looking at the stuff so I can palm the rock for the appraisal. I'll switch in my own rock as usual. He and I will be partners. There's no blowoff problem. I'll let him hold the stuff until it cools.

"He'll pay ten grand. We play for him tomorrow afternoon. I've already rented a room at Kedsie Avenue and West Thirty-first Street to play him in. Well, how does it sound?"

I said, "The dough sounds wonderful. But we're sure to get a beef from a hometown mark for a score that big."

Blue laughed and said, "What the hell you think we got Felix for? He can fix a rocks beef easier than a drag beef. What are you backing up for? You stop liking dough?"

I said, "So we take him off tomorrow."

He said, "Oh, I almost forgot. We'll go to the Cadillac people tomorrow and drop my car off. The transmission is slipping. I'll take a cab to the mark for the lug back to you."

Blue and I got out of the house the next morning around eleven-thirty A. M. We went to our slum connection on Wabash Avenue in the Loop. We picked up twenty choice zircons mounted in gold plate.

Blue left his Caddie at the dealers for the transmission adjustment. We ate lunch downtown and chatted and killed time over coffee until two P. M.

I drove Blue to the corner of Kedsie Avenue and Roosevelt Road. I saw him get in a cab as I drove away to the room.

Blue had been right about Frascati. He was a real cream puff. He didn't give us an anxious moment all during the play. He gave me ten grand. I gave them the glass-filled bag when Blue gave me a boodle that looked like ten grand.

They walked away grinning at the way they had rooked the hot, white hoodlum out of a hundred and fifty thousand dollars in rocks for a measly twenty grand.

At five P.M., Blue was getting out of a Yellow Cab at Forty-seventh and Halsted Streets as I pulled up to pick him up.

He got in and said, "I feel like a good steak, Folks. How about you?"

I gave him his boodle and five grand of the score.

I pulled the Caddie into traffic and said, "It's a great idea. Let's go to the Brass Rail."

Moments later, I pulled to the curb on Forty-seventh Street in front of the Rail. We got out and went through the door to the front booth. We ordered our steaks and sat there looking out the panoramic front window at the poor chumps buffeted by the violent December winds.

How could we know that Dot Murray, the roller, would bring us the bad news about Nino? And we would begin a run for our lives. . . .

CHAPTER TWENTY-FIVE

State Street Murder Cross

I had dozed off when Blue shook me awake. For a moment I wasn't sure where I was. Then I heard Reverend Josephus' Bertha Mae's snoring, I realized that we were in Jewtown, and we were waiting for that messenger of death. . . .

Blue said, "I called the house again. Cleo still isn't home. I called the Fixer. He said he saw her Thunderbird parked in front of Square's Bar on Thirty-first at one-thirty this morning. It's after three now. We'd better get out of here. It'll be daylight in a couple of hours."

I jumped from the bunk and pulled the light string.

I said, "But Blue, the Southside is a big place. "We can't find Cleo before daybreak."

He said sharply, "Folks, she's not just anywhere on the Southside. She's at one of those after-hours joints around Thirty-first Street. I know them all.

"She's down there slumming, flashing her fine clothes and letting her old pals see how she's come up in the world. I'll be able to find her before four A. M. You don't have to go. I'm going to get Joe's key to the truck."

He walked down the hall. I put on my shoes and suit coat. He came back with the key. We put on our overcoats and went to the old truck packed in front of the house. Blue got behind the wheel.

It wouldn't start. Blue hit the starter every minute or so for ten minutes. Finally, the starter made only a faint growl. Blue turned his sweat-shiny face and looked at me helplessly.

I pushed the door open and said, "Well, Blue, it looks like we'll have to make the trip in the Caddie."

We went to the shed in the backyard. I backed the Caddie out and headed for the Southside.

I stopped for a stoplight at Thirty-first and Halsted Streets. I was thinking what a sucker play it was to stick our necks out for a tramp like Cleo when Blue said, "Folks, I'll never forget the way you're going along with things. You're a real pal.

"Don't worry. When we get to the Thirty-first Street neighborhood, we'll only have to cruise a couple of streets. It will be a cinch to spot Cleo's purple Thunderbird parked near one of the after-hours joints. Like I told you, I know them all down there.

"I know it's Butcher Knife Brown's stomping grounds. But we're not going to be around long. Besides, I've given out a lot of handouts down there. The broke Niggers I passed out that dough to like me.

"Butcher Knife isn't sucker enough to make a murder play in front of witnesses. He's a sneaky little bastard who grins in your face and tricks you into a dark lonely place, like an alley or hallway, for his butchering.

"Hell, the cunning sonuvabitch will never get that near us. Say that he or one of his young punk runners spotted us and wired Nino. We'd be back on the Westside before Nino could get down there to knock us off. Go to Thirty-second Street and Prairie Avenue for a starter."

I drove down almost deserted Thirty-first Street, past Indiana Avenue to the corner of Prairie Avenue and Thirty-second Street. . We didn't see Cleo's car.

Blue bit his bottom lip and said, "Folks, try the block on Michigan Avenue between Thirty-third and Thirty-fourth Streets. She's probably at Leona's joint. Most of her old pals hang out there."

I drove south on Michigan Avenue.

Blue pounded my thigh and shouted, "Folks, I told you! There's the bird!"

I pulled up behind it near the corner of Thirty-fourth Street on Michigan.

Blue opened the door and said, "Keep your motor

running. I'll be right back with her."

I saw a tall, thin, black guy in a white overcoat with hat to match standing on the sidewalk sucking on a reefer. He threw an arm around Blue's shoulder. I watched them go through the dim foyer of a dingy brownstone apartment building.

They turned to the left on the first floor. I heard loud laughter and the blare of gut-bucket blues from the apartment. He came out in less than two minutes without Cleo.

He got in the car and said, "Folks, Cleo left twenty minutes ago with Bootsie in her car. Leona doesn't know where they went. But Jabbo, that chump in the white overcoat that you saw, thinks he knows where Bootsie and Cleo are. He's making a call now.

"Folks, before I married Cleo, Bootsie was Cleo's best friend. I don't want Cleo running around with her. The last time I saw Bootsie, she looked like she was hooked on H.

"Folks, I've got to keep Cleo away from down here. It's a dirty shame the poor little thing had to grow up down here. Folks, why don't you park the Caddie around the corner and we'll wait in Leona's joint for Cleo?"

I thought about it for a long moment.

Then I said, "I've got a better idea. It's four-ten. Dawn is only a couple of hours away. There's no point in both of us waiting for Cleo. Besides, I'm not in the mood for a lot of drunken chumps.

"I'm going to slip out to the house and get some of our clothes and personal things. Then after you take care of your affairs, Monday morning we can all drive directly to New York."

Blue got out and I pulled away. I parked the Caddie at Sixty-third and Cottage Grove Avenue and took a cab. I had the cabbie cruise up and down the block past the pink house.

I had to be sure that it wasn't staked out. The cab took me back to my car. Within a half hour I had filled the spacious trunk and rear seat of the car with Cleo's, Blue's and my things. I was feeling pretty good as I drove toward Leona's place. I had seventy-five hundred dollars in my pocket with the twenty-five hundred I got from under the rug in my bedroom.

I pulled up behind the Thunderbird. Twenty minutes passed. I got out and locked the car. I went to the door on the left ground floor. I rang the bell. An eye glistened at a peephole in the door.

A muffled broad's voice said, "Whatta' you want?"

I said, "I'm a friend of Blue Howard. I've been waiting outside for him. Will you have him come to the door?"

The eye said, "Goddamn, you nosey. You a roller?" Twenty-ninth and State Street."

I said, "Is Cleo inside?"

The eye said, "Goddamn you nosey. You a roller?"

I said, "I'm a friend of theirs. I told you I've been waiting for Blue. I drove him here."

The eye blew a gust of rot-gut whiskey through the hole and said, "Jabbo took Blue down there where Cleo is at."

I said, "Where at Twenty-ninth and State? Can't you give me an address?"

The peephole banged shut. I U-turned the Caddie and went down Michigan Avenue toward Twenty-ninth Street.

At Thirty-first Street, I heard the distant wail of a police meatwagon. I turned left on Thirty-first Street and drove toward State.

I got a strange tense feeling, driving down State Street. That wail was loud as hell straight ahead. I saw a crowd on the sidewalk a couple of hundred yards from the corner of Twenty-ninth Street.

A police ambulance was sitting in the street at the same distance. My hands were trembling on the steering wheel. I double-parked fifty feet behind the meatwagon. I leaped from the car and trotted toward the crowd. I saw two uniformed coppers lifting a stretcher into the back of the wagon. Somebody tugged at my arm. I looked down. It was an old pool hustler pal of Pocket's from Forty-seventh

Street.

He shook his head and said, "Folks, it's too bad. It's too bad."

I leaned weakly against the side of a car and blurted, "What happened? Who was that?"

He lowered his eyes and said softly, "Folks, that was your pal Blue. He got crossed out of his life. A thirty-eight slug blasted through his right eye."

I grabbed his coat front and shouted, "Who did it? Did they catch the sonuvabitch?"

My chest was a boiling cauldron of grief and shock. My hoarse sobby voice was a stranger's, far away.

He jerked his thumb. I looked. The wagon was pulling away down the street. Two plainclothes white rollers were putting Cleo and a black, scrawny broad into a car. Then in the light that flashed on inside the car, I saw the thin guy with the white overcoat and hat sitting on the back seat. The police car pulled away.

I said, "That's Cleo! Who is the guy with the white coat? Who is that other broad. Did the guy in the white coat kill Blue? Are you sure that he's dead?"

He said, "The stud in the white coat is Jabbo. He's the killer, but he won't go to the joint. He's Butcher Knife Brown's ace runner and hatchet man since Brown has got elderly and half-blind. Poor Blue musta' wasn't hip to that.

"Jabbo is been fucking Cleo off and on since she was twelve years old. That skinny broad is Bootsie, a hype. She deals H for Brown. I'm cribbing across the street. I rushed out here when I heard the shot.

"Blue was lying on the sidewalk. When I got over here, Jabbo and Cleo and Bootsie were standing around Blue. Jabbo was loud-mouthing about how it was self-defense. Blue had a long open shiv in his hand.

"Bootsie was cracking that Blue tried to croak Jabbo. Cleo was stooping down relieving Blue of that big rock on his pinky and his wallet. It was a slick cross.

"Like I said, Jabbo won't do a day in the joint. How can he? Blue was only a Nigger. And Jabbo is got Blue's wife and Bootsie as witnesses for him at the coroner's inquest. Even if he didn't have witnesses, Brown would spend the scratch to fix it for Jabbo. It would be easy since Blue was found with a shiv in his hand.

"It's too bad about Blue. It's just too bad. Well, Folks, you got a pal to bury. I can't understand how a stud as slick and classy as Blue could marry a skunky tramp like Cleo and then go for the murder-cross.

"Give me a jingle at the poolroom and hip me to the funeral day. I always liked Blue. He was real nice people. It's too bad. It's just too bad."

Somehow my palsied legs took me back to the Caddie. I drove North on State Street toward central police head-quarters. I stopped on the street at Twenty-second Street. I sat there in the car for a long time thinking about my next move. Finally, I went into a greasy spoon and called Fixer.

I blurted, "Blue is dead! Butcher Knife Brown set him up for the cross. But they're not going to get away with it. I know the whole truth about Nino and Brown's H hookup. I know that Brown used Jabbo as the executioner to please his boss, Nino, because of the Frascati score.

"I'm going to Eleventh and State right now to make a statement. Blue never carried a shiv. I'm not a copper-hearted fink. But they croaked the best friend I ever had.

"I can't let Jabbo get cut loose at the inquest. My statement will make Jabbo and Brown stand trial. Fixer, I'm going to send those dirty bastards to the big-top for murder-one. Brown will be shocked shitless when he runs to you for the fix and you laugh in his face. Brown isn't wise that Blue and I for years have been greasing your mitt with thousands and thousands of dollars. Brown won't be—"

Felix cut in. He said softly, "Folks, you've been rattling off like a sucker. Sure, Blue was all right with me. I knew him since Nineteen Twenty-seven. He was a fine fellow who never welshed on a debt or a loan. But he's gone now, goddamnit! I'll miss him.

"I got a call a few minutes after Blue got shot. The caller asked me to pull strings so that Jabbo and the two chippies could hit the street right away, without bond or anything until the inquest. I couldn't turn down two grand for an easy service like that. So, I made a call and cut them loose.

"Folks, I'm a business man. I'm seventy-two years old. I got to look out for old Felix in this cold cruel world. I can't do business with Blue. He's dead. I got to do business with the living.

"It's a fine angle you've got about making a statement to the rollers. There would be a trial, and Brown and Jabbo would have to crawl to me for the fix. I get no less than ten grand to fix even a nigger murder.

"Don't lose your nerve. Come to my place as soon as you leave the station. You know Nino has you on the hit list already. After you make the statement you'll be hotter than ever. Don't worry, pal. By the time you get out here to me, I'll have figured a hideout for you until the trial. I'll split the ten grand right down the middle with you. I'll lay it in your hand right after—"

I hung up and went to the Caddie. I wept and drove aimlessly through the lonely dawn. I thought, "Blue was smart after all to make that ten grand pre-need arrangement with the funeral home. Cleo would have given him a C-note funeral, if any at all.

I was a hundred miles from Cincinnati, Ohio, when I realized the Caddie was reeking with Cleo's perfume. I looked back at Cleo's clothes piled on the back seat and floor of the car. I pulled over on the shoulder of the highway. I opened the rear door. I threw all of her stinking clothes into a ditch.

I checked into a middle class white hotel in downtown Cincinnati. I ordered a fifth of rum as soon as the last piece of clothing was brought to the room. The next day I went to a florist shop and had them wire a double C-note worth of white roses to the funeral home for Blue's funeral.

In the following eight months I drank hundreds of fifths of rum. I couldn't count the whores that I paid to drink with me and keep me company through the long lonely nights.

I just stayed in the room and tried to drink my sorrow and memories away. In September of Nineteen Sixty, I bought the *Chicago Tribune* from an out-of-town newspaper stand.

Nino Parelli had gotten too big for his britches. The story in the paper said that his corpse had been found stuffed into the trunk of his car. He had been tortured and stabbed many times with an ice pick.

It was good news. The seventy-five hundred dollars I had brought to Cincinnati with me was gone. I had pawned all of my clothes and Blue's too. I couldn't afford rum any more. I drank cheap wine by the gallons.

I had no partner to play the con with. So, the day after I read about Nino, I hit the highway for Chicago. I couldn't think of anywhere else to go.

It was midnight when I got back to Chicago. I had a fifth of sherry wine and a lousy deuce in my pocket. I couldn't blow it on a flophouse bed for the night. I'd need to buy a piece of cheap slum to hustle.

I parked the Caddie on a Westside street, and tossed on the back seat until daybreak. Later that morning, I went downtown to State Street, and bought a bridal set of slum mounted in sterling for a buck and a half.

I got a double sawbuck for it two hours later from a sucker standing at a jewelry shop window looking at bridal sets.

I got a hotel room on the far Westside. I never went on Southside Chicago. In the middle of October, Nineteen Sixty, I stepped into the mouth of an alley next to a new Sixty Cadillac to take a leak.

I was leaning against it as I sprayed the wall of a building in front of me. The crazy little bastard owner of the Cadillac rushed off the sidewalk. He cursed me and shoved me away from his car.

I pushed him. He slugged me on the side of the jaw. I knocked him down. He had lots of heart. He got up and tore into me. We were slugging it out when the rollers came. They locked me up in Maxwell Street Station.

He was a big shot who owned a string of bars on the Westside. He showed up in court the next morning with a black eye. He pressed an assault and battery complaint against me.

I was dizzy and sick as hell when the judge said, "... or ten days in the House of Correction."

I didn't hear how much the fine was. It wouldn't have made any difference anyway. I was dead broke with only a piece of slum in my pocket.

At noon I was crammed into a big police van loaded with drunks and petty thieves on the way to the House of Correction.

The van stopped at a red light. I looked down through the wire grill at a platinum blonde in a Jaguar halted beside the van. I thought about the Goddess and wondered why the hell a bum like me hadn't swallowed a handful of those red devils at the Majestic Hotel in Cleveland, Ohio, long ago.

EPILOG

I lay in darkness on the bottom bunk in the cell and listened to White Folks thrashing and groaning through a nightmare on the bunk above me. He had done nine days of his short bit, and the next morning he would be released.

I wasn't known as Iceberg Slim because I was wildly emotional. But after White Folks had told me his life story, I couldn't help feeling sorry for him. I felt like kicking my own ass for pimping all my life instead of conning.

At daybreak he jumped to the floor and sat on the john.

I said, "Well, White Folks, you'll be hitting those streets in a few hours. I'm going to miss you. What are your plans?"

He tented his long fingers beneath his chin. He smiled and said, "Iceberg, the first thing I'm going to do is sell the Cadillac. With that dough, I'm going to buy some nice clothes and a small used car. I'm going to gas it up and go to Montreal, Canada, to the Vicksburg Kid.

"I'm going to learn all the angles of the white big con. I'm going to lose myself in the white world. I'm going to break every classy white broad's heart that gives me a second gander. I'm going to eat and sleep and fuck with nothing but white people for the rest of my life.

"I'll never hear the goddamn tag, Trick Baby, again. Iceberg, I'm going to be the happiest white Nigger sonuvabitch there ever was. And that's the guaranteed truth."

THE END

GLOSSARY

BELLY STICK—shill for a flat joint

BIG FOOT COUNTRY—in the deep South United States

BIG-TOP—state prison

BLOWOFF—to get rid of a mark after he's been fleeced.

BOODLE—fake bankroll used by con men to impress a
  sucker

BOOT—Negro

BOOST—a brace of shills for a flat joint

BREAD—money

BURNED—cheated of one's share

CAP—back up con to the catch

CANNON—pickpocket

CATCH—to lure a victim into the first stage of a con game

COP A HEEL—to flee

CRIB—room, apartment, house, etc.

CRUMB CRUSHER—infant

DEEMER—a dime

EARIE—intense listening

END—share

FINAL—blowoff for a con game

FLASH—cheap flashy merchandise used to attract suckers
  to a flat joint; also fake jewelry

FLAT-JOINT—gambling concession in a carnival

FLIMFLAM—colloquial form of verb "con"

FLUFF—attractive female

FRENCH TICKLER—a thin rubber casing studded with
  various sized rubber nodules slipped over the penis to
  tickle and titillate the vaginal track during sexual intercourse

GAFF—a foot device to control a numbered carnival wheel
GANDER—to look
GIRL—cocaine
JINKY—prone to be a jinx
JISM—seminal fluid; climatic discharge material of the male during sexual intercourse
MURDER-ONE—first degree murder
PADDY—white person
PECKERWOOD—contemptuous term referring to white men
PULL COAT—to inform or to alert
PUTZ—penis
QUILL—real, authentic
RAISE—pocket
SCRATCH—money
SHED—railroad or bus station
SHILL—confederate of a con man
SLUM—fake jewelry
SMACK—short con played with coins
SPANISH FLY—powdered insect used medicinally to increase urine flow—sometimes used as an aphrodisiac to seduce a woman
SPOOK—Negro
SQUEAL—victim's complaint to police
TRAIN—mass rape
TURNOUT—to teach and train for the con
TRICK BAG—any disadvantageous situation or condition
WASTE—kill, murder
WHITE STONES—crudely simulated diamonds

THE NAKED SOUL OF ICEBERG SLIM

ROBERT BECK'S REAL STORY

By Iceberg Slim

Don't cry for his soul because he's black, though black is pain, black is death, black is despair, black is the ghetto where he was born—and lived as a pimp, dope addict, brutalizer of women…and other blacks. But he cured himself of the ghetto rot to write—as no other man ever has—about his people and his life. His name is Robert Beck, better known by his ghetto name, "Iceberg Slim." His first three

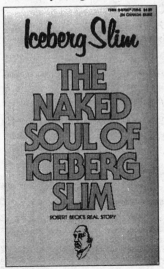

books brought him fame: *Pimp*, *Trick Baby*, and *Mama Black Widow*, a tragic bitter family portrait. They were honest books—sensitive portraits of ghetto life and people. But this book is his most disturbing, because it has hope, because it is now, because he searches the artist's soul in a collection of personal essays that are full of passion and razor-sharp perception. And when his soul is naked, you see the hurt of a man who feels too much and cares too much.

HOLLOWAY HOUSE PUBLISHING CO.
8060 Melrose Avenue, Los Angeles, CA 90046-7082

PIMP

THE STORY OF MY LIFE
By Iceberg Slim

AUTOBIOGRAPHY—Iceberg Slim is the name he used in the black ghetto. His real name is Robert Beck and he was a pimp. This is his story, told without bitterness and with no pretense at moralizing—the smells, the sounds, the fears, the petty triumphs in the world of the pimp. No other book comes anywhere near this one in its description of the

raw, brutal reality of the jungle that lurks beneath the surface of every city. Nobody but a pimp could tell his story and no one ever has...until Iceberg Slim. He was young, ambitious, and blessed with a superior IQ. He spent twenty-five years of his life in hell. Other pimps died in prison or in insane asylums, or were shot down in the street. But Iceberg Slim escaped death and the drug habit to live in the square world with the woman he loved, and to write about his people and his life.

HOLLOWAY HOUSE PUBLISHING CO.
8060 Melrose Avenue, Los Angeles, CA 90046-7082

AIRTIGHT WILLIE & ME
THE STORY OF SIX INCREDIBLE PLAYERS
By Iceberg Slim

When it comes to hos and the men who run them, when it comes to intriguing and super-paced rivalry between the ambitious pushers and dealers who sell dreams in the blizzard of white powder, when it comes to knowing the streets, it takes a real player, and that player is Robert Beck. For more than a decade, Beck, writing as "Iceberg Slim," has fascinated or horrified readers of his books and stories.

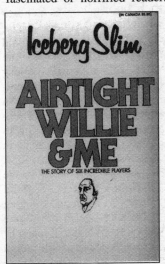

Beck doesn't create superflies and superhos, he gives the reader real live people, people with hopes and fears who breathe and bleed and who have grabbed hold of the only ticket they can find out of misery. But the ticket is often a one-way trip into hell and suffering. This anthology of stories by Beck is a monument to the courage of the people of the streets. Some of them make it; most don't. Laugh along with them; cry when they cry; hurt when life turns against them.

HOLLOWAY HOUSE PUBLISHING CO.
8060 Melrose Avenue, Los Angeles, CA 90046-7082

THE LONG WHITE CON

The Biggest Score Of His Life

By ICEBERG SLIM

Known in the "straight" world as Robert Beck, "Iceberg Slim" astounded and captivated readers with his first story of Trick Baby, that blue-eyed, light-haired, white-skinned black called "White Folks." The most incredible con man Beck ever met, Folks rides again in this spellbinding new novel, playing for the biggest scores of his life! No chump-change scores for him. He's out to prove he's a "true blue nigger." But the con-game struggle between the greedy spider and the rich honkie fly is made all the more difficult by Folk's traumatic visions of the past...the stigma of being a trick baby, having a mother who was gang-raped, and himself mercilessly violated by those who thought he was white. Beck's unique talent for brilliant characterizations do justice to a superb cast of grifters, including High Pockets Kate, the High Ass Marvel, and the Vicksburg Kid.

DOPEFIEND

By Donald Goines

For twenty-three years of his life Donald Goines lived in the dark, despair-ridden world of the junkie. It started while he was in military service in Korea and ended with his murder at the age of thirty-nine. He had worked up to a hundred-dollar-a-day habit. And out of the agonizing hell came *Dopefiend*, the shocking nightmare story of a black heroin addict. Trapped in the ghetto, a young man and his girlfriend—both talented and full of promise—are inexorably drawn into the living death of the hardcore junkie.

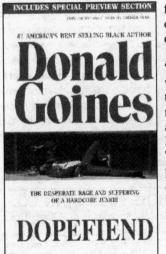

"All those [other black] writers, no matter how well they dealt with black experience, appealed largely to an educated, middle-class, largely white readership. They brought news of one place to the residents of another. Goines's novels, on the other hand, are written from ground zero. They are almost unbearable."

Michael Covino
The Village Voice

HOLLOWAY HOUSE PUBLISHING CO.
8060 Melrose Avenue, Los Angeles, CA 90046-7082

THE
NIGGER BIBLE
By Robert H. deCoy

Why is a Nigger not a Negro? Should we integrate or segregate? Is Christianity for Niggers? Islam? Judaism? Do Nigers need a God of their own?

THE NIGGER BIBLE is "written by an acknowledged Nigger about the experience of Niggers, addressed and directed exclusively to my Nigger people for whom it was purposely conceived." Thus does the late internationally acclaimed author Robert H. deCoy introduce this explosive

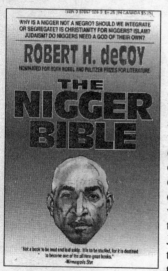

best seller. First published in 1967, THE NIGGER BIBLE is universally accepted as one of the true classics of the literature of the American Black experience. Robert H. deCoy has been praised and damned around the world for this volatile work. In his introduction to this edition, entertainer Dick Gregory calls deCoy "one of the literary giants of our time" who has "dared to discard the traditional vestiges of Judeo-Christianity in order to find and reveal the spiritual truths of being Black."

HOLLOWAY HOUSE PUBLISHING CO.
8060 Melrose Avenue, Los Angeles, CA 90046-7082